MW01286205

SHOT CLOCK

SHOT CLOCK

Andrew Bourelle

SEVERN
HOUSE

First world edition published in Great Britain and the USA in 2025
by Severn House, an imprint of Canongate Books Ltd,
14 High Street, Edinburgh EH1 1TE.

severnhouse.com

British Library Cataloguing-in-Publication Data
A CIP catalogue record for this title is available from the British Library.

ISBN-13: 978-1-4483-1530-7 (cased)
ISBN-13: 978-1-4483-1531-4 (e-book)

This is a work of fiction. Names, characters, places and incidents are either the
product of the author's imagination or are used fictitiously. Except where actual
historical events and characters are being described for the storyline of this novel,
all situations in this publication are fictitious and any resemblance to actual persons,
living or dead, business establishments, events or locales is purely coincidental.

All Severn House titles are printed on acid-free paper.

MIX
Paper | Supporting
responsible forestry
FSC
www.fsc.org   FSC® C013056

Typeset by Palimpsest Book Production Ltd., Falkirk,
Stirlingshire, Scotland.
Printed and bound in Great Britain by TJ Books,
Padstow, Cornwall.

Praise for Andrew Bourelle

Shot Clock

"A slam dunk of a thriller. Action both on the court and in the field merge into a riveting, throat-clutching climax. *Shot Clock* should be on everyone's must-read list"
James Rollins, #1 *New York Times* bestselling author of *Arkangel*

"A pulse-pounding thriller where every second counts. Readers won't be able to put it down"
Victor Methos, bestselling author of *The Silent Watcher*

"A breathtaking, full-court-sprint of a novel about professional basketball, the Vegas underworld, and the risks we'll take for the ones we love"
Michael Kardos, award-winning author of *Bluff*

48 Hours to Kill

"The best thriller I've read all year"
James Patterson, #1 *New York Times* bestselling author

"A perfect ticking-clock thriller, with depth, character and mystery – very highly recommended"
Lee Child, #1 *New York Times* bestselling author

"A breathless, twisted, ticking clock of a novel"
Christopher Golden, *New York Times* bestselling author

"Propulsive . . . Bourelle is a writer to watch"
Publishers Weekly

"A fast-moving tale . . . [and] a great way to kill, if not 48 hours, then at least three or four"
Kirkus Reviews

"Fantastically written . . . For fans of Baldacci and Coben"
Manhattan Book Review

About the author

Andrew Bourelle is the author of the novels *Shot Clock*, *48 Hours to Kill*, and *Heavy Metal*, as well as co-author with James Patterson of *Texas Ranger*, *Texas Outlaw*, and *The Texas Murders*. He teaches creative writing at the University of New Mexico.

www.andrewbourelle.com

For Ben

PRE-GAME

Caitlin dribbled the ball up the court, eying her options for passing.

Garrett was guarding her, ready to cut her off if she tried to rush around him. It was almost midnight, but the court was lit with high streetlights splashing the cracked asphalt in pools of yellow. This was Arizona in August, which meant the courts were empty during the hundred-and-ten-degree days and only started to populate when nightfall brought the temperature down into the nineties. A sheen of sweat covered Caitlin's arms and face, and her T-shirt was matted to her skin.

She scissored her legs, pistoning the ball in between them, trying to throw Garrett off before she made her move. Garrett backed over the three-point line, giving her space.

He should know better.

She brought the ball up. He saw what she was doing a fraction of a second too late, and when he jumped forward, hand raised for the block, her feet were already in the air and the ball sailed over his fingertips. The shot spun in a high arc, and the eyes of everyone on the court rose to watch it. Below the rim, Danny and Donnie Blakesly – brothers playing tonight on opposing teams – jockeyed for position, ready to snatch the rebound.

The ball soared through the basket without even glancing off the rim. The metal net snapped in its wake.

'Boom!' Caitlin's roommate Yazmina called, her braids bouncing as she skipped down the court. 'Count it!'

'Nice shot, Glass,' Garrett said.

This was just a pickup game, of course. They were in a park with no bleachers and no fans. No music pumping up spectators.

No game clock.

No shot clock.

Just a friendly contest among guys and girls from Arizona State's men's and women's teams before their seasons started. Still, Caitlin took it seriously – it was a chance to prove herself against the boys.

Garrett would normally take the ball up the court, but he

inbounded it to his brother, Jake, the only person on the court who didn't play for ASU. As Garrett approached the top of the key, Caitlin shadowed him close, hoping to cut off any pass.

'If you want to get physical,' Garrett said, 'let's go back to my place.'

Caitlin fought off a smile. They'd been dating three years and, once they were done playing tonight, they would shower together and fall into bed still wet. She could smile at him all night, but right now, this was business. She gave him a shove – hard but friendly – and pushed him out of the position he was trying to establish.

'What's the count?' Jake said, keeping his dribble.

'Seventeen–fifteen,' Danny answered.

'Play to twenty?'

'Yes,' Caitlin and Garrett said at the same time.

Yazmina was laughing.

'Y'all realize Caitlin's scored every single point on you?' Yaz said. 'She's beating you all by her damn self.'

'Is that right?' Donnie said, looking around.

'Wait,' Jake said, picking up the ball. 'Time out. Is that right?'

They paused the game to figure out if what Yaz said was true. Caitlin was playing well but couldn't believe all the points were hers. Still, Yaz and the others all claimed to have zero.

'It's been all you, girl,' Yaz said.

Caitlin grinned.

'All right,' Danny said. 'Let's get her those last points.'

'Come on, guys,' Jake said, dribbling again to signal the game was resuming. 'We've got to shut her down.'

Garrett's team had three guys, two girls, and Caitlin's had the inverse ratio. Danny and Donnie, one a senior and the other a sophomore, were the tallest on the court, six-seven and six-eight respectively, but they were guarding each other. Caitlin and Garrett were the only ones guarding someone of the opposite sex.

'Yo, Garrett,' Donnie called out. 'You gonna let your girl do you like that?'

Garrett didn't answer, but he had a determined look in his eyes. It was possible Garrett had been taking it easy on her – he usually did, even though she asked him not to. But he wasn't going to now. That was clear by his expression and body language.

Caitlin stuck close to him, legs bent, arms out, determined to stop him from getting the ball. But Donnie set a high screen for him, and as Garrett ran through it, he caught the ball at the top of the key. Caitlin couldn't get to him in time, and he rose up for a long three.

Swish!

Seventeen–eighteen.

'Nice shot, Street,' she said begrudgingly.

Yazmina inbounded the ball to Caitlin, but this time Garrett smothered her on defense before she could get to half court. She passed it away, but the whole focus of the game had shifted. Her teammates moved the ball, using quick passes, but none of them would take a shot. They wanted her to score the winning point.

She needed to rise to the moment.

'Come on,' Garrett said. 'If there was a shot clock, it would have gone off a long time ago.'

Caitlin knew he was right. They couldn't just pass all night.

She ran to a spot at the free-throw line, just as Yazmina lobbed the ball to Danny down by the basket. There was a split second where it looked like they'd just let him score if he wanted to, but then Garrett rushed him and threw a hand on the ball, popping it loose. He and Danny lunged for the ball, both sprawling on the pavement, but it rolled away into Caitlin's hands. Garrett was on the ground and no one moved to cover her yet.

A two would give them the lead.

A three would win it.

She took two dribbles while stepping back behind the three-point line. Jake rushed her, lunging awkwardly. She jumped into the air and let the ball go. She kept her arms extended, wrist bent, as she drifted back to earth. For a moment, the ball was lost in the glare of the sodium lights. Then her foot came down on something, and her ankle twisted. A lightning bolt of pain shot through her leg, and she collapsed in a heap.

She heard the quiet clink of the chain but she didn't see the ball go through the net.

'Oh, sorry,' Jake said. 'You OK?'

She'd landed on his outstretched foot.

Caitlin winced as Jake helped her stand. She'd rolled her ankle plenty of times, but this felt different. She couldn't put any weight on her foot. Each time she tried, pain shot through her leg. A wave of nausea crashed into her like a breaker on a beach. Garrett jogged up and supported her.

'Let's get some ice on that,' he said.

'Did I make the shot?' she asked.

'You didn't see?'

'No.'

'Hell yeah you made it,' he said. 'You were amazing.'

The ball had rolled out into the grass. It didn't seem like it would have gone that far if she'd made it. More likely, she'd shot an air ball that clipped the outside of the net. She caught Yazmina throwing a glance at some of the others. Caitlin couldn't tell if the expression was just worry or if it seemed to say, *Should we go along with this?*

'Don't lie to me, Street,' she said to Garrett.

'I wouldn't lie to you.'

'You beat them all by yourself, Cait,' Yazmina announced. 'Most. Dominant. *Ever!*'

Everyone applauded. The sound – nine people clapping in a dark city park with no one around – seemed hollow and empty.

Caitlin looked at Garrett, studied him. Three years together and she'd never known him to lie.

Whether he was now or not, Caitlin had a strange feeling her world had just changed. The earth, through no fault of her own, had spun off its axis. The future she'd envisioned for so long – playing basketball professionally, spending the rest of her life with Garrett – all seemed in question now. She told herself she was making too much of what happened, but as she hobbled off the court, Garrett supporting most of her weight, Jake still apologizing for what was clearly an accident, she couldn't shake the feeling she might have missed more than just the shot.

GAME ONE

2

Caitlin drove her cruiser down a backroad east of the town of Hill Haven, Ohio. The edges of the roadway were choked with weeds, and leaf-filled branches of hickory and oak provided a canopy overhead. She drove over the Miami River, swollen to its banks with all the rain they'd gotten this summer.

She took a right and headed along an empty road with a cornfield on one side and the town's water storage tanks atop a hill on the other. She found a wide gravel pullout next to a copse of poplars and eased the cruiser into the spot, positioned like she was looking for speeders. It was a good place to catch drunk-driving teenagers cruising the backroads late at night. But really what Caitlin was looking for was a quiet place where she might not be disturbed for a few hours.

She turned her police radio down so the static and voices were a dull background noise, then she scrolled through her phone, searching for the ABC app. She turned the volume to its max setting and sat back to watch. The announcers were making their introductory remarks.

From the phone, commentator Chuck Walla announced the starting players for Game One of the NBA Finals. For the Las Vegas Lightning, the roster was highlighted by Jaxon Luca, a six-seven shooting guard who was arguably the best player in the world right now. He jogged on the court, his face focused, as always, and his signature dreadlocks tied back and bouncing between his shoulder blades. He was a one-man wrecking crew able to score practically at will. This season, he'd won his second league MVP award and third scoring title.

Still, the Lightning had their work cut out for them. The home team, the Cincinnati Sabertooths, had not one but two stars. The first was Elijah Carter, a six-ten power forward who could dominate in the post and shoot well from mid-range. He was a catch-and-shoot specialist, better at scoring from passes than trying to create his own shots. Which was why he worked so well with the team's other

star, its point guard, a pass-first, shoot-second facilitator who made
his teammates better.

His name, of course, was Garrett Streeter.

3

C aitlin settled into her seat, shifting her position so the Glock
on her belt wouldn't dig into her side. She wanted to watch
from a dispassionate remove, but relaxation was impossible.
Her body was a jumble of nerves. She always felt anxiety when
she watched or listened to Garrett's games, but now she felt so
apprehensive it was as if she was the one getting ready to play.

At opening tip-off, Sabertooth center Rodrigo Sandoval lobbed
the ball into Garrett's hands, and he dribbled up the court. He didn't
look half as nervous as she felt. He passed the ball, and the team
moved it around quickly. As the shot clock wound down, the ball
came back to Garrett, who threw up a mid-range jumper that banked
off the glass and through the net.

The crowd erupted.

The bucket calmed her nerves, as it would if she was playing.
There's nothing quite like that first made basket to tell yourself,
Everything's going to be OK. The teams settled into a quick back
and forth, both playing well, neither dominating. The image on the
phone was tiny, but she could see well enough.

Her phone beeped with an incoming text.

Alex wanted me to tell you Streeter scored the first basket.

Then, a second later:

Do you want updates? Or are you able to watch/listen?

She texted back that she didn't need updates.

Love you, Owen wrote.

Her husband, Owen Reese, was at home watching the game with
their seven-year-old son. Caitlin felt guilty for not being with them.
She could have traded shifts with someone. But she didn't like the
idea of her husband watching *her* as she watched her ex on the
biggest basketball stage in the world. And she didn't want her son,
a huge Sabertooths fan, to think the level of emotional stress she
might feel was an appropriate response to any sporting event.

She liked that her son was a sports fan.

She didn't want him to be a sports fanatic.

When Alex was a baby, the NBA announced it was going to expand the league from thirty teams to thirty-two, and Caitlin couldn't believe nearby Cincinnati was going to get one. She'd thought watching games could be something she and Alex might share. Before he could talk, she would prop him up on the couch and let him watch with her. She and Owen were disciplined about limiting Alex's screen time, but watching basketball with Mommy was an exception. He was sometimes allowed to stay up past his normal bedtime for games. Caitlin loved that it was something they did together, and Owen went along with it because it seemed like a much healthier pastime than playing video games or watching weird YouTube videos, which it seemed like most of Alex's peers at school were doing.

Two years ago, when she heard the Sabertooths signed Garrett Streeter, she felt queasy. Her college boyfriend was toiling away in Sacramento as the only decent player on a perpetually bad team. She hardly ever heard about him. Suddenly he was back in her life. The whole three years they'd dated, he'd never once visited her home state, but now he would be living two hours away.

Worse, she was stuck in her fandom. She'd already established Sabertooths games were Mommy–son times. She couldn't just stop watching. She had to walk a fine line of showing interest in the team, but not too much.

When Alex found out the new guy on the team was an old friend of Mommy's – Owen told him, not her – he became a huge fan of Garrett Streeter. He asked for a Garrett Streeter jersey so he could wear it during the games, although Caitlin never gave in to the request, feeling mortified on behalf of her husband. Owen knew she'd dated Garrett. She'd never hidden that from him. But she'd never expected Garrett to be much more than a footnote in the NBA.

But now he played on *her* team.

And he *thrived* in Cincinnati.

He quickly clicked with Elijah Carter. Their games complemented each other, drawing comparisons to the partnership of Karl Malone and John Stockton of the 1980s and '90s. Elijah's scoring increased. Garrett's assists per game shot up. Suddenly, neither of them had to carry a team by themselves. And the Sabertooths, routinely failing to make the playoffs or getting bumped off in the first round, became one of the most formidable teams in the league. They made it to the Eastern Conference Semifinals last year before being eliminated in seven games. This year, they truly found their rhythm, winning sixty games, the best record in the league.

It felt unreal to her, knowing her ex-boyfriend – a man who was once as familiar to her as her husband was now – was able to live out his dreams. Most of the time, Caitlin was too jealous to be happy for him. She watched his games with conflicting emotions, a pendulum swinging back and forth between rooting for him and secretly hoping he would fail. She was self-aware enough to know her jealousy wasn't about him – it was about her never getting the same opportunities.

Tonight, alone in her police car, with no son or husband around to watch her, she let herself feel what she wanted to feel – which, she discovered, was unfiltered enthusiasm. The Sabertooths took an early lead, and every time Garrett hit a shot, she experienced a jolt of excitement. And when he got the ball to Elijah Carter for a score, she pumped her fist and made a mental note of how many assists he was racking up.

Outside the cruiser, twilight darkened the landscape. Caitlin turned off the car and rolled the windows down, and the steady thrum of insects became the background noise, like the applause of an extra audience.

After halftime, things started to fall apart for the Sabertooths. Caitlin watched with dread as Jaxon Luca went on a rampage, scoring at will, no matter who was guarding him. The Sabertooths went flat. Actually, it was Garrett who was flat. He made bad passes. He missed shots. Elijah Carter did his best to make up for Garrett's lousy play, but he wasn't nearly as good without Garrett.

At the end of the third quarter, the Sabertooths were down by fourteen.

'Come on, Garrett,' Caitlin said aloud, with no one around to hear except the cicadas singing in the fields. 'Get your shit together.'

She couldn't believe how elevated her heart rate was. She'd been in car chases where her adrenaline didn't spike this hard.

God, it sucked being a sports fan sometimes.

But then, in the fourth quarter, Garrett came out on fire and she was reminded why she loved the game of basketball. He stole an inbound pass and made a quick score. A few seconds later, he drained a three from the top of the key.

What followed was a hard-fought quarter, with the Sabertooths slowly chipping away at their deficit. They brought the Lightning's lead down to five. Then three.

Are you watching this? Owen texted her.

She ignored the message until a timeout, then replied simply, Yes.

Alex is jumping up and down on the couch, Owen wrote.

She wished she could see Alex's expression, hear him cheering on his team. How selfish she'd been for wanting to watch this game alone.

With less than thirty seconds left, the Sabertooths were down by one point. Jaxon Luca brought the ball up the court for the Lightning. Taking his time. He dribbled the ball at just past half court, letting the shot clock tick away.

Only two seconds separated the shot clock and the game clock. If the Lightning chewed up the whole twenty-four, the Sabertooths would have only two seconds left. Luca made a motion to the basket, and Garrett joined his defender for a double-team. Instead of passing, Luca backed up again. As he moved, though, Garrett and his fellow player switched on defense.

Caitlin's ex-boyfriend was guarding the best player in the world. Her fingers gripped the phone tightly. Her lips were clamped shut.

Eight seconds.

Seven.

Six.

Luca darted forward. Garrett kept his body in the way. But there was a height mismatch – Luca was a good four inches taller than Garrett. He pump-faked, but Garrett didn't fall for it. He kept his feet on the floor, pressed his body close, careful not to foul. Elijah Carter came in to help swarm Luca.

Four seconds.

Luca jumped. Garrett leaped, arm extended. Luca shot over him, but Carter – at six-ten – got the tip of his fingers on the ball.

It spun in the air.

And fell into the hands of Garrett.

'Call timeout!' Caitlin said aloud, nearly shouting, but the announcers were explaining what she hadn't realized: the Sabertooths had no timeouts left.

Elijah took off toward the other end of the court. Garrett dribbled twice to get away from Luca's reaching arms, then lobbed the ball.

Elijah caught it on the run, fifteen feet from the basket, and jumped straight up with it. The ball left his fingers a fraction of a second before the horn sounded and the red light lit up around the basket.

The ball kissed the glass and fell through the net.

Caitlin let out a scream. She jumped out of the car and bounced on the gravel outside. She thrust an arm in the air in celebration. On the screen, Elijah ran down the court and tackled Garrett in celebration. Every Sabertooth player on the bench rushed the court, pumping their fists in the air and falling over themselves to chest-bump Elijah. Garrett looked dazed.

The Sabertooths had taken the first game of the NBA Finals in one of the best games she'd ever watched.

She turned off her screen and set her phone on the hood. She leaned back and closed her eyes, then took a deep breath and tried to enjoy the aroma of the trees and the nearby cornfield. She felt a pang of sadness.

What she wouldn't give to trade places.

4

G arrett showered in a state of shock, letting the water spray his face and run down his chest. His teammates were bois-terous, talking and laughing as they relived the game. Whatever excitement Garrett felt in the moment had quickly faded to a strange sort of numbness. He dried off and walked in a towel back to his locker. He sat for a moment, not ready to get dressed for the news conference.

The locker room was expansive, with Berber carpet and individual leather chairs in front of each stall. They weren't actually lockers. More like mini-cubicles, where the players came in every night to find their uniforms washed and ironed. The Sabertooths logo was embossed on the ceiling, a huge three-dimensional snarling cat with teeth three feet long.

He pulled up his boxer shorts then stabbed his legs into his suit pants. A minute later, he was tying his tie and slipping on Oxford shoes.

'Yo, Streeter.'

Elijah approached, wearing only a pair of black boxer briefs. He was six-ten, and his muscles looked sculpted out of granite. He wore a close-cropped beard and six-inch braids that flopped over his ears and down his neck. His hands were the size of T-bone steaks, and he slapped one of them on Garrett's shoulder.

'Hold up a minute,' he said. 'I'll go with you.'

They usually sat together at the podium, sharing the spotlight after their victories. Elijah was gregarious and comfortable in front of the camera. Disarming reporters with his big smile, he would do most of the talking and take pressure off Garrett.

'Sure,' Garrett said. 'But hurry up. I want to go home and sleep for twenty-four hours.'

As Elijah walked back over to his locker, Garrett reached into his duffel bag and pulled out his phone. There was a message from his girlfriend, Summer – CONGRATULATIONS. YOU WERE AMAZING! – and a handful from other friends.

He looked over his shoulder and saw Elijah had put on pants, but he was still shirtless, distractedly talking to one of the assistant coaches. Garrett looked around to make sure no one was watching, then he reached into his duffel bag and pulled out his other phone.

Good game, the message read. Your brother thanks you.

Attached to the message was a photo of Jake, his eyes swollen, his cheeks peppered with stubble. He looked miserable in the photo, similar in many ways to a mug shot where the arrestee can't hide his mortification that he's been apprehended. But unlike a mug shot, Jake wasn't holding a placard with name, date, and booking number. Instead, Jake was holding an iPad, with a web browser opened to ESPN's home page. The lead article was about the Sabertooths winning Game One – proof, for Garrett's benefit, that the photo was taken only moments ago.

Proof his brother was still alive.

GAME TWO

5

'*Police*,' Caitlin shouted. '*Open up.*'

She balled her fist and pounded on the door, which was made of cheap fiberboard and shook in its frame. The trailer sat in a lot surrounded by forest. The only way to get here was by two tire ruts winding through a maze of trees. The yard – if you could call it that – was overgrown and filled with old appliances that rose out of the high weeds like metal islands in a sea of green. The trailer wasn't fit for human habitation. The paint was all but gone, the roof sagged like a horse's saddle, and the windows were boarded up like bandages on a boxer's face after a losing match.

Nobody lived here.

That was obvious.

A distraught mother arrived at the sheriff's office an hour ago, claiming her drug-dealing ex took her baby. She'd rattled off a list of places he might have gone, including an old meth lab down by the river. But it didn't look like anyone had been here in a while. There were no cars except for a rusted old frame on blocks, and there were no fresh wheel ruts in the grass except for those made by Caitlin's own police cruiser.

She tried the doorknob.

It was locked.

She listened carefully but couldn't make out anything except birdsong and the whirring of insects. Tall maples and oaks surrounded the clearing. The temperature was high, the humidity oppressive, but the sun was lowering, filling the trees with an eerie orange glow. There was a window air-conditioning unit sticking out of the trailer, but it wasn't running. The heat inside would be like an oven.

No way anyone was in there.

She stepped off the makeshift porch made out of stacked cinder-blocks and checked the time on her phone. She saw a message from her husband.

Alex wanted me to tell you the game is about to start. Are you going to be home in time to watch?

I'll try to be there by halftime, she typed.

Feeling guilty for not watching Game One with her family, she'd really wanted to make it home tonight for Game Two. She used her radio to call into the station to report what she'd found at the trailer. *'Sheriff's working on getting a warrant,'* she was told. *'Sit tight and keep an eye on things.'*

'Copy that,' Caitlin said into the mic strapped to the shoulder loop of her uniform.

She checked the ESPN app on her phone and saw tip-off was seconds away. She pocketed her phone and allowed her mind to drift to her college years spent with Garrett.

As much as she loved Owen and loved having a son, she tended to think of her time in Arizona as the best years of her life. It wasn't just playing basketball. Living there gave Caitlin her only real glimpse of life outside of Ohio. Hiking in the desert hills, living in a metropolitan area of more than five million people, traveling with the team to cities like Eugene, Boulder, Berkeley. Every road game a window into a new world.

Once she returned to her home state, she was never quite satisfied. She'd been given a taste of another life.

And then it was all taken away.

She huffed in annoyance – unhappy with the direction of her thoughts – and decided to wade through the long grass to have a look around the property. She made it about five feet when she heard a noise like a cat mewing, but then she realized what it was: the faint sound of a baby crying. Not wailing. Fussing, like it was coming out of a nap.

Caitlin put her hand to the gun on her hip.

She heard a voice inside the trailer, trying to shush the baby.

'Police!' Caitlin roared. *'Open this door now!'*

She heard clattering around inside, then a pounding – like someone trying to bust out one of the plywood squares nailed over a window.

'Someone's in there,' she shouted into her radio. 'I hear a baby crying. I'm going in. For its safety.'

The dispatcher responded that backup was being deployed.

'I'm two minutes away,' another voice crackled from the radio. *'Wait for me, Caitlin.'*

She recognized the voice – Deputy Pete Ryle. Caitlin snorted in frustration. Backup? More like dead weight.

Inside, the baby began crying in earnest – loud whines indicative of an oncoming frenzy.

It must be a hundred degrees inside that trailer.

'Fuck this,' Caitlin said, pulling her pistol from its holster. She charged up the steps and slammed the heel of her boot an inch from the doorknob. The door exploded inward, throwing splinters of wood from the frame. She rushed in, her gun outstretched in both hands.

The room was dark, but she could see well enough to spot syringes and other drug paraphernalia lying on the table and countertops. The room stank of mildew and body odor.

She caught sight of a shirtless man, skinny but with ropy muscles over his skeletal frame, pushing headfirst through the crack where a sheet of wood was loose over a window. The skin of his back was peppered with acne, and as he crawled through the opening, the nails protruding from the board scratched his skin. Caitlin thought about grabbing one of his feet and yanking him back inside, but her attention was taken by another sight – the baby, wailing, its legs kicking and hands grabbing the air. The child, a boy, was lying on a blanket adorned with smiling *Thomas the Tank Engine* faces. The cleanliness of the fabric was in sharp contrast to the surroundings – like a splotch of color in an otherwise black-and-white movie.

The child's face was contorted and angry, and Caitlin felt a moment of terror recognizing how hot the room was. The baby's hair, what little there was of it, should have been slick with sweat, but it was dry and coarse, suggesting dehydration.

Caitlin holstered her gun and rushed to pick up the baby. As she lifted the child, the man's legs disappeared through the crack. The baby was naked except for a diaper, which was soaked and heavy with urine. She pulled the child to her chest, and, in the same fluid motion, raised her foot to kick the board covering the window that the man had escaped through. The plywood flew outward and landed in the grass. The man, running, arrived at the edge of the tree line. He was carrying an enormous crescent wrench that looked almost too heavy for his skinny arms.

And then he was gone, disappearing into the shadows of the trees.

Caitlin ran back through the front door and found the air outside – which seemed so hot before – mercifully cool.

She held the baby close, bouncing his body slightly, while talking into her radio.

'I've got the baby,' she said. 'Suspect is fleeing. He's armed with a wrench.'

She unfastened the soaked diaper and it dropped into the grass like a weight.

Another cruiser pulled into the clearing. Pete Ryle heaved his big belly out from behind the steering wheel and stepped from the vehicle out of breath, as if he'd sprinted here instead of driven.

'Here,' she said, holding the baby out to him. 'I'm going after the suspect.'

Ryle took the baby but held it with his arms outstretched, like the child might be radioactive.

'What do I do with it?' he said.

'Take him in the air-conditioned car,' Caitlin snapped. 'Try to calm him down. You've got kids, Pete. Didn't you ever comfort them when they were crying?'

He opened his mouth to answer – or to object – but Caitlin was already running away, her gun back in her hand.

6

Caitlin bounded through the tall grass like it was deep snow. When she passed through the tree line, the air was cooler, like entering a cave. She hopped over logs and slalomed around trees, foliage slapping at her. She couldn't see where the guy had gone, but the ground sloped downward in the direction of the river, and she guessed he was headed that way.

The river came into view – glimpses of muddy water through the trees – and she heard a large splash, big enough to be caused by a human. She raced in that direction. As she got closer, she spotted a log – rotten and dead and at least six feet long – floating out from the muddy bank. She eased up her pace, figuring the guy tossed the log in as a decoy.

About ten feet from the shore, she passed a big sycamore, and as she did, the man lunged out with his wrench. She leaned backward, like doing the limbo, and the metal soared above her face. She fell onto her butt and rolled away as the wrench slammed into the tree, leaving a sizeable gash.

She scrambled to her feet, aiming the gun at the man's chest. The guy lunged at her again, his teeth clenched. She could have shot him – probably should have shot him – but she found she couldn't do it. Instead, she backpedaled toward the water's edge. Her foot caught a log, and for a brief instant, she thought she was going to fall backward into the water. But she righted herself with her other foot, squelching in the muddy bank.

The wrench came flying at her again, and she leaned back in time for it to whoosh by, close enough to hear the wind. She was still holding her gun, and she brought her arm across her body, intending to backhand him. The guy, having trouble with his unwieldy weapon, was off balance, and Caitlin slammed the butt of her pistol into his mouth. He stumbled back, blinking from the shock of the pain.

Cursing herself for leaving her pepper spray and her taser in the car, along with her baton, she jammed her gun into its holster. She'd never shot a person and didn't want to start today. Her hands free, she reached for the guy's arm and wrapped her fingers around his wrist in an iron grip. He tried to tug his hand away, still holding the wrench, and shot her a look of surprise when he wasn't strong enough to do it. She spun her body around, kneeling down, and pulled his chest against her back. In a move she'd only practiced in a gym, she yanked him forward, flipping him over her. He landed with a splash in six inches of water. The wrench dropped, still visible through the murk.

'Enough of this shit,' she spat. 'Put your hands behind your head.'

The man, his eyes wide and bloodshot, and darting around as if they were incapable of focusing on one thing, started to rise. Fighting the mud, his progress was slow, but there was no doubt he intended to go after her again.

Shit, she thought. *This guy is really going to make me shoot him.*

She moved to kick him in the chest as he rose, but her foot was suctioned into the mud and wouldn't come up. His body slammed into hers, and she fell back into the sludge. He reached to choke her, his hands like animal claws. She struggled beneath him, squirming her body and fighting off his hands. All the hand-to-hand training she'd done never accounted for wrestling someone in five inches of mud. Every move she made was impeded, and getting any leverage was impossible.

He reached for her gun.

As his fingers brushed the handgrip, she threw her knee into his groin. He grunted, spraying moisture into her face. She got ahold of his hand and twisted it sharply. He hissed in pain. She kept his wrist locked and wriggled out from underneath him. She'd intended to wrest his arm behind his back, but, with the mud, she couldn't keep her grip and his hand slipped free. She grabbed a handful of his hair and yanked him backward into the shallow water. She grabbed his arm, pinned it behind his back, and forced his face under the surface. She reached for her cuffs and clicked them around his wrist. His body thrashed as she twisted his other hand behind his back and cuffed the wrists together. Finally, she grabbed him by the hair and yanked his head up. He gasped loudly, muddy water streaming from his face and hair, pink with blood from his mouth. She dragged him to his feet and marched him through the muck until the ground became solid. She pushed him on to the ground, where he flopped onto his side in the grass, flaccid as a noodle, finally giving up the fight.

Soaked and muddy, her chest heaving for breath, Caitlin gasped hoarsely, 'You're under arrest, you son of a bitch.'

7

By the time Caitlin marched the guy up the hill to his trailer, a train of vehicles was pulling into the property: police cruisers, an ambulance, and the familiar little Volkswagen owned by a local newspaper reporter.

Two deputies ran to help her with the kidnapper, hands cuffed behind his back, mouth bleeding and full of loose teeth he kept complaining about. Caitlin's adrenaline was wearing off, and she felt tired and shaky. She let the others take him. She opened the door of her cruiser to get a bottle of Gatorade. Her uniform seemed to weigh ten pounds, wet and clumped with grunge. The mud on her face and hands was drying and felt tight on her skin.

Pete Ryle walked up, the baby naked and asleep on his chest.

'Hey, Caitlin,' he said, smiling, proud he'd figured out how to calm the boy.

The child looked adorable, using Ryle's belly as a mattress, the face cushioned against his breast next to his badge. The newspaper reporter, Shelby Slate, whom Caitlin had known for years, snapped pictures of them with a compact camera.

A network television truck from a station in Cincinnati pulled into the clearing. They must have been covering something in the area to get here so quickly. Behind the van, a cruiser pulled in with the sheriff in the passenger seat and the undersheriff driving. Caitlin thought it was disgraceful for them to be beaten here not only by the local media, but also a network from the big city.

'Nice work,' Caitlin said to Ryle, knowing that was what he wanted to hear.

'Thanks,' he said, beaming and not bothering to return any approbation to her.

Instead, he turned so the photographer would have a better angle for the shot.

She didn't think about the NBA Finals until two hours later when she and her colleagues were wrapping up their work at the scene and she climbed into her cruiser, her uniform still damp, and checked her phone. There were a half-dozen texts from her husband with updates. The last one, received only a minute ago, stated simply:
Sabertooths lost.

8

Garrett sat on the couch and reached for the remote. Summer was upstairs getting ready for bed, but he knew he wouldn't be able to sleep. He felt a numb exhaustion throughout his body, physical and mental. Often, after home games, he'd veg out on the couch and find something to watch on TV until he became sleepy. He didn't think it would work tonight, but he turned the TV on anyway.

The 11 O'clock News was coming on. The top story, of course, was the Sabertooths' loss. With the series tied one–one, the anchor presented the story as bad news, but not quite the end of the world.

'*Let's hope they do better Wednesday night in Las Vegas,*' she stated, then switched gears. '*There was a daring rescue tonight in the town of Hill Haven as police recovered a kidnapped infant.*'

The name Hill Haven got his attention. He'd lived in southwestern Ohio all of two years now – spending a lot of that time on the road – and he didn't know the difference between Middletown or Miamisburg, Trotwood or Centerville. But Hill Haven? That sounded familiar.

Wasn't that where she lived?

As the anchor gave her report, the screen showed footage of police cars clustered in front of what looked like an abandoned trailer. Footage showed a big-bellied police officer all smiles as he held a baby to his chest. There was a brief interview with the sheriff, who looked more excited to be on TV than most NBA players in their post-game interviews.

When the camera came back to the studio, a rectangular portrait was displayed in the upper corner. Garrett's breath caught in his throat. The picture was of Caitlin, an official department photo with her in uniform and looking serious. Garrett felt a peculiar emotion he couldn't quite identify rise up inside him.

'*Police identified Deputy Caitlin Glass as the officer who appre-hended the suspect,*' the anchor said. '*There was a struggle between the suspected kidnapper and Deputy Glass, and assaulting a police officer has been added to the list of charges. Deputy Glass,*' she added, her cadence suggesting the report was coming to its conclu-sion, '*was not injured in the conflict.*'

As the anchor started talking about a new effort to remove litter on Cincinnati roadways, Garrett's mind went elsewhere. He'd been aware that Caitlin had moved back to Ohio to become a police officer – he'd remained in touch with her roommate Yazmina, who filled him in now and then – but he'd always resisted the urge to look her up.

He grabbed the remote – heartbeat racing – and rewound the report, pausing on Caitlin's picture.

An idea sprung into his head, forceful though not yet fully formed, and he didn't know if he was crazy or if he was stupid for not thinking of it earlier.

9

'Did you hear me, Mom?'

'Sorry,' Caitlin said. 'My mind was wandering.'

She was staring at the front page of the *Hill Haven Gazette*, with a big article about the rescue of the infant. The picture, which was huge and took up almost a quarter of the front page, showed Pete Ryle holding the baby close to his chest. It was a good picture: the baby looked angelic – and safe – and Pete looked both official, in his uniform, and caring. Caitlin, mud-covered and barely recognizable, was visible in the background.

She'd been scanning the article while Alex was talking to her. Shelby interviewed both her and Pete, and even though Caitlin tried to downplay her fight with the assailant, her appearance – a muddy mess – prompted Shelby to keep pushing with questions. Caitlin knew Shelby fairly well, having met her numerous times at ribbon-cuttings and educational programs where Caitlin was asked to represent the sheriff's office. The article was flattering to both Caitlin and Pete, and it painted the sheriff's department as competent and capable.

'Did you think about shooting him when he attacked?' Shelby asked last night.

'*I knew I could subdue him without using my firearm,*' Caitlin was now quoted in the paper saying.

If this doesn't get the sheriff's attention, Caitlin thought, *I don't know what will.*

She was up for a promotion to detective and was expecting to hear the pronouncement any day. The only other person up for the job was Pete, whom she'd left with the babysitting last night. Surely it was obvious she was a better choice.

'Earth to Mom,' Alex said. 'Come in, Mom.'

'Tell me again,' Caitlin said, folding the paper and tossing it into the recycle bin under the sink. 'You've got my attention.'

'I said, "I can't believe they lost."'

He sat at the table, finishing off a bowl of Honey Nut Cheerios while scribbling with a marker in a Sonic the Hedgehog coloring book. He lifted the bowl and drank milk from it, spilling some down his chin and onto the table.

'Here,' Caitlin said, handing him a paper towel. 'And it happens – losing, I mean. I never thought for a minute they'd sweep the Lightning. It will probably go back and forth like this.'

Caitlin started to shove dirty dishes into the dishwasher while eying the clock, hoping to get out the door to go for a run before it got too hot.

'Do you think they'll win the whole series?' Alex said.

'I don't know, sweetie,' she said. 'As long as they play their best, I'll be happy.'

For being only seven, Alex was an astute student of the game.

When they watched together, he asked questions about fouls and rules. He'd learned quickly why most buckets were two points but others were three and free throws were one. He loved asking questions about anything – animals, history, outer space, how stuff worked, you name it – but at least with basketball, she knew the answers.

Caitlin took Alex's empty bowl and finished the orange juice he'd left in his cup. Then she closed the dishwasher, half loaded, and went to the door where her running shoes lay in a pile with Alex's and Owen's shoes. After lacing up, she kissed Alex on top of his head and wrapped her arms around him, which he didn't let disrupt his coloring.

'Mommy's going to go for a run,' she said. 'When I get back, I'll spend the day with you.'

She held him for a few seconds longer. Most days, she didn't much like her life. But she loved her husband and son – and if she was magically given the chance to have everything she ever thought she wanted: a career in professional basketball, a life where she didn't have to worry so damn much about the mortgage – she would not have traded her life now for that life if it meant she had to give up Alex and Owen. But she hated how much time she spent dwelling on the question of why she couldn't have both – the life she wanted *and* the son and husband she had.

'I love you so much,' she said to him, kissing the top of his head again.

'Love you, too, Mom.'

She poked her head into the bedroom, where Owen was stepping out of the master bathroom with a towel around his waist, his skin pebbled with moisture.

'Is it OK if I go?' she asked. 'I need to work some of this stiffness out.'

She'd woken up sore as hell after mudwrestling the kidnapper. Her body felt like the time in college when she'd played nearly every minute of a double-overtime loss to Oregon State. Her body was saying, *You asked too much of me.*

'Yeah,' he said. 'What's Alex doing? Has he eaten?'

The bedroom – small, barely enough to fit their king-sized bed – held a sliding-glass door to the backyard. Owen squeezed himself around the bed to close the curtains before dropping his towel and pulling on a pair of underwear.

Caitlin told him Alex had vacuumed up a bowl of cereal and was now coloring. She also promised to be back in an hour. Owen had a ride today with his bike club, and she needed to be home in time for him to make the meetup.

Owen took the towel and ran it through his wet hair. He had a svelte body without a stitch of fat. Clothed and with his glasses on, he had an unassuming quality, looking more studious than athletic, even though he was a serious road biker with impressive endurance. He was handsome, but not the type to necessarily turn the heads of women on the street. There was a subtlety about him she'd been drawn to. She'd spent her life around jocks and cops – two worlds dominated by men and their machismo. Most of the guys she knew were always acting tough. She assumed the airs they put on came from a place of insecurity. If you had to act tough, it was because you were worried that you weren't.

But Owen, a high-school history teacher, wasn't that way at all. He was funny and fun, without being particularly assertive or showy. She'd been in an unhealthy headspace – after Garrett, after basketball, after coming to terms with returning home to Ohio, her dreams unfulfilled. Owen turned out to be a lighthouse for her to get her bearings.

That was almost nine years ago, and the gulf between then and now was filled with the challenges of life: jobs and bills and nursing a baby and teaching a toddler to pee and ride a bike and swim and read. Sleepless nights with a child who woke her up after having a nightmare or wetting the bed, then long days where she dealt with drug dealers and wife beaters and colleagues who thought they could do the job better than her because they were born with penises.

Life had taken a toll on her – and on her relationship with her husband. She and Owen hardly had time for each other. More and more they were like roommates who shared custody of a child, rather than lovers who shared a life together.

Today, she was feeling especially guilty about cheering so hard for Garrett in Game One. Wanting to make up for it, she stepped into the room and put her arms around Owen, naked except for the pair of underwear. They stood nose to nose – both five-foot-eleven; he was slightly above average for a guy, she was definitely above average for a woman – and she gave him a firm, affectionate kiss.

'I love you,' she said and, as she spoke the words, it occurred to her how infrequently she actually said them. 'I'm lucky to have you.'

'I'm the lucky one,' Owen said, then added, 'I bet Garrett Streeter rues the day he let you slip through his fingers.'

Caitlin smirked. 'Have you seen his girlfriend?' she said. 'The next time I get a Victoria's Secret catalogue in the mail, flip through it. You can't miss her – she'll be the prettiest one.'

'The camera cut to her a few times last night,' he said, pulling on a pair of shorts and reaching for a T-shirt on the bed. 'She's got nothing on you.'

Caitlin made a *pfft* noise with her lips as she headed back to the kitchen to fill up her water bottle. As she turned on the tap, the doorbell rang. She reached to shut off the water, but Owen called from the hallway that he would get it. She assumed it was a UPS driver to drop off a package, but she heard Owen talking to whoever was there.

The other voice sounded vaguely familiar.

10

'**H**on,' Owen said, walking into the kitchen with their visitor. 'Someone here to see you.'

Caitlin blinked.

She'd heard the expression *I couldn't believe my eyes*, but she'd never actually known what that felt like. It seemed like she was hallucinating, seeing something that didn't compute inside her brain.

Garrett Streeter was standing in her house.

'Hey, Glass.' He smiled his crooked grin she'd fallen for all those years ago.

She cleared her throat. Then she said something she never thought she'd say again.

'Hey, Street.'

Caitlin didn't allow herself to smile. That's what she wanted to do. This man had always made her smile. But she was agonizingly aware of Owen standing next to him, watching her carefully. She couldn't let on that somewhere within her – against her will – her soul was vibrating with energy, like she and Garrett were two circuits placed too close together, and the electricity arcing between them would be visible to anyone paying attention.

She was relieved to see Owen didn't seem put off by Garrett's visit. His expression was more like amusement. But then, to her horror, Alex exploded out of his seat and barreled toward Garrett, throwing his arms around his waist. It was like a boy going to Disney World and hugging Mickey Mouse.

Garrett patted Alex on the back and said, 'It's nice to meet you.' Now when she looked at Owen, the bemused expression was gone, replaced by hurt he was trying to hide but couldn't quite cover up.

'OK, OK,' Caitlin said, trying to untangle Alex from Garrett.

Owen put a mask of cordiality back on and said, 'We've been watching you play.'

'You've been amazing,' Alex added.

'You know,' Garrett said to Alex, 'your mom was an amazing basketball player herself back when I knew her.'

Alex's seven-year-old eyes widened, and he looked at her with new admiration. He'd known she played, of course, but having the validation of someone he'd seen on TV seemed to elevate her to a new level.

'We used to practice together,' Garrett said. 'She helped make me better.'

Caitlin became aware of the dirty dishes she'd left in the sink, the crumbs under the chair where Alex sat, the milk stains on the table she hadn't cleaned up yet.

Caitlin's mouth felt very dry.

'I'm sorry,' she said, unable to hide the bewilderment in her voice. 'What did you say you're doing here?'

'I need some advice.' He turned toward Owen and said, 'I'm sorry to intrude on you like this. I know it must be weird. But,' he added, turning back to Caitlin, 'I'm sort of panicking. Going through a crisis of confidence, I guess you'd call it. Caitlin and I used to help each other when we were in slumps or going through something. I thought it might help if I talked to her.'

Garrett's delivery seemed sincere and open, but something didn't feel quite right. He was playing *well*. His playoff stats were higher than his regular-season numbers.

'I was wondering,' Garrett added, 'could we go for a walk?'

'Today's not really a good day,' Caitlin said. 'I wish I could help but—'

'It's OK,' Owen interrupted. 'You two go ahead and talk. I'll hang out with Alex.'

'But your ride,' she said. 'I don't want you to miss it.'

'I'm not really feeling it today, anyway.'

She knew that wasn't true. He lived for these weekend rides.

'I'll try to be back,' she said.

'It's no big deal. I promise. You two go catch up.'

If he'd dated someone who went on to become some kind of superstar model or television actress, would she have been so understanding? She doubted it.

She hugged Alex. Then, before they left, she made a point of giving Owen a firm kiss – not sure if she was trying to send a message to Garrett or Owen.

Or herself.

11

They left the house, neither speaking. There was a yellow sports car parked on the street behind Caitlin and Owen's minivan. The vehicle – obviously Garrett's – probably cost as much as most of the houses on the street. It was a Mercedes but looked like a racecar, curvaceous and sleek, squatting low to the ground on wide tires.

Caitlin almost said something about it but held her tongue.

With every step, she felt herself relaxing. She didn't know what all this was about, but at least she didn't have to put on a performance in front of her husband and child anymore.

'It's good to see you,' she said, turning her head slightly so she could look at him. 'In person, I mean. I see you on TV all the time.'

'I saw you on TV last night, too,' he said, giving her his crooked smile. 'I knew you'd look good in a police uniform.'

Now she let her own smile come out. She felt her cheeks flush. Her limbs felt numb.

They walked on, smiling, giggling. They both recognized how dreamlike the moment was.

Garrett was wearing top-of-the-line Nike sportswear: running pants, T-shirt. Even his flip-flops were Nike. Every item looked like it came fresh out of the package – and maybe they had. Garrett had an endorsement deal with Nike – more than half of the NBA players did – and his closet was probably full of brand-new athletic gear vacuum-sealed in plastic. Caitlin felt self-conscious about her faded shirt and her off-brand shoes with the tread worn down to almost nothing.

The street they were walking along ended at a small community park, which led to the river path where she always ran. There were two kids shooting hoops on the basketball court. One boy kept bouncing the ball off the back of the rim. Caitlin wanted to tell him to shoot with a higher arc – make the rim bigger – but she didn't want to draw attention to the fact she was walking with a Sabertooth.

'How did you find out where I live?' Caitlin asked.

'Yaz.'

'Of course.'

Yaz and Garrett butted heads back in college – Yaz protective of Caitlin and Garrett never wanting any competition for her time – but the two had settled into a comfortable long-distance friendship afterward. They were, after all, the only two people in their friend group who made it to the pros.

'I missed you at her wedding,' he said.

'Alex got really sick right before,' she said. 'I felt terrible about missing it. I still have the bridesmaid's dress in my closet.'

'Lots of us were there,' Garrett said. 'Most of the girls' team. Donnie and Danny, too.'

Garrett's old teammates, who'd been there the night she'd fractured her ankle. They'd stayed in Arizona and, last she heard, now owned a dance club in Scottsdale.

'How are the Twin Towers?' she asked, using their old nickname for the brothers.

He shrugged. 'They asked me for a loan a year or so ago. I guess the nightclub is struggling a little.'

'Did you give it to them?'

'Of course.'

Garrett gestured toward a picnic table under a big oak tree and asked if they could sit.

'So,' he said, as he slid onto the bench seat, 'do you bike with your husband?'

'I used to. Not so much since Alex was born.'

'Do you like it?' he asked. 'Biking. Or cycling, I guess they call it.'

'Eh,' Caitlin said. 'It's pretty boring.' She burst out laughing, surprised by her honesty. 'It's not like a basketball game.'

'That's what I thought.' He laughed along with her. 'I know you too well. I can't see you sitting on a bike for fifty miles.'

She felt guilty that they were making fun of her husband's favorite pastime, but she knew Garrett was building up to explaining why he was here. He didn't look much older than she remembered. Some lines were developing in his forehead. The first few gray strands were cropping up in his dark hair. But the aging actually made him look more handsome. He still had the square jaw, the penetrating eyes, but his boyishness was gone, replaced by a more distinguished, wiser version of himself. He was the type of guy who was only going to become more handsome as he aged.

But he looked tired, puffy around the eyes.

'So tell me why you're really here,' she said. 'And don't give me any BS about a crisis of confidence or whatever you said. I know you, too, Street.'

He reached into his pocket and pulled out a phone. He tapped the screen a few times, then slid the phone across the table to her.

Curious, she looked at the image. She didn't understand at first, but then – despite the summer heat – goosebumps rose on her skin.

The picture showed Garrett's brother, Jake, his face shiny with sweat, his hair askew and greasy. He was crying. It took a second for Caitlin to figure out why, but once she pulled her eyes away from Jake's face, she could see. A hand was coming in from out of the frame holding a gun to the side of Jake's head.

'My brother's been kidnapped,' Garrett said. 'I'm being black-mailed to fix the Finals.'

Caitlin lifted her eyes off the screen and stared at Garrett. What she'd thought was a little bit of fatigue from last night's game was something else – fear.

'I need your help, Glass.'

12

'Street,' she said. 'Listen to me. You need to call the FBI. We can do it now. I'll help you through it.'

Garrett shook his head vehemently.

'I can't do that. They said if I did, they'd kill him.'

'Of course they said that. That's what kidnappers say.'

'I'm not going to call the FBI,' he said. 'And you need to promise me you won't either. My brother's life is on the line, Glass.'

Caitlin thought of Jake, Garrett's sweet brother, a freshman when Garrett was a junior, who'd never hurt anyone in his life – on purpose anyway. He cried after she and Garrett broke up, saying, 'I thought you'd be in my life forever.'

'Promise me, Glass,' Garrett said.

'No.'

'What do you mean no?'

'This is a crime,' she said, pointing to the phone on the table. 'I'm a cop. I can't keep quiet about it.'

Now he stood up. He opened his mouth, as if to shout, then looked around to make sure no one was listening. Over at the basketball court, the two boys were leaving, but Garrett lowered his voice anyway.

'I came to you because I don't know what else to do. I need your help. *Your* help. At least listen to what I have to say.'

Garrett was highly emotional. Victims of crime needed someone calm and steady to talk to.

'OK,' she said. 'Tell me. I'll listen.'

'And you won't tell anyone?' he said, easing back into his seat.

She felt trapped. She thought her best hope was to agree to his terms, then convince him to reconsider.

'I won't report it if you don't want me to,' she said. 'But,' she added, 'I hope you know you're putting me in a tight spot. If anyone ever found out I had knowledge of this but didn't report it, I'd lose my job. I'd never wear a badge again.'

Garrett looked stricken. He hadn't thought of this.

'I'm sorry. I shouldn't have come.'

'I already know too much,' Caitlin said. 'I might as well know it all.'

Garrett supported Jake financially, he explained. In exchange, his little brother helped him out as a sort of de facto manager. One of the things Jake did, from time to time, was fly to other cities to watch teams on the Sabertooths' schedule to report his observations back to Garrett. The NBA's eighty-two game schedule is usually so intense there isn't a lot of time to prepare for what's next, and the idea was Jake could informally advise Garrett about what he would be facing. It was mostly an excuse for Jake to travel, Garrett knew.

It gave him time to explore cities he liked: New York, LA, Miami. The Sabertooths already had a coaching staff for this sort of thing, but Garrett liked making Jake feel he had a purpose and wasn't just accepting Garrett's charity.

When the Sabertooths were up three games to one against the Celtics in the Eastern Conference Finals, Jake approached him about the idea of going to Las Vegas to watch the Lightning play. The Lightning were up by the same margin against Utah, and it was clear the Sabertooths and Lightning were on a collision course for the NBA Finals.

'I figured he was going to gamble,' Garrett said. 'If the game was in Salt Lake, I doubt he would have gone. But I didn't care. I kind of didn't want him around. No distractions, you know.'

She knew from experience Garrett didn't like distractions during playoffs.

When the Lightning wrapped up their series in Vegas, Garrett didn't hear from his brother. Then when the Sabertooths won the next game, securing their place in the Finals, congratulations poured in from players and friends, and Garrett didn't look at all his texts or listen to the messages. But the next day, when he was watching ESPN analysts discuss the Finals matchup, he realized he hadn't heard from Jake.

'I figured maybe he was partying a couple extra days in Vegas,' Garrett said. 'I was focusing on getting ready anyway. I had ice baths and acupuncture. Practice. Studying game plans. Watching film. Watching more film.'

Then, the day before Game One, the game Caitlin had watched in her police cruiser, he received a package in the mail with a Las Vegas postmark. Jake's name was on the return address. Inside was a cellphone and a note that said to look at the photo inside. He opened the screen – no passcode required – and went to the camera app. There was only one image: the picture of Jake with the gun to his head. There was also a text message saying, If you go to the police or FBI, we pull the trigger. Instructions will follow.

And they did: Two hours before tip-off Thursday, he received a text instructing him to ensure the Sabertooths did not cover the spread. Sports books had the Sabertooths winning by six and a half points. The goal of a spread, based on what little Caitlin knew about sports betting, was to give the favored team a handicap. The Sabertooths, with homecourt advantage after a better regular-season record, were favored, at least for the start of the series.

'So you could win,' Caitlin asked, 'just not by seven points?'

'Exactly.'

'The problem,' Caitlin said, remembering Game One, 'is you guys were playing too well in the first half?'

'Yeah. I checked the phone in the locker room at halftime, and they'd sent me this picture.'

Garrett showed her the image. Jake sat with his back to the camera, a TV in the foreground with the game on the screen. Again a hand came from out of frame, pointing the gun at the back of Jake's head.

Garrett said he freaked out and, when the third quarter started, he made sure he was missing shots, making bad passes. His poor play rubbed off on the rest of the team. In no time, they were in a hole.

'Then what happened?'

'At that point, it would be a miracle to win at all. No way we were going to win by seven points. So it was freeing, actually. The competitor in me woke up. I couldn't go down without a fight.'

Garrett said the instructions for Game Two were the same: Don't cover the spread.

'This time, though, they outplayed us from the start. We were never within ten after the first quarter. Jaxon went off.'

Garrett went quiet, lost in thought.

'OK,' Caitlin said, 'so their initial threat spooked you. You didn't call the FBI. That's understandable. But it's not too late.'

'If I go to the FBI, they're going to dig into my past and Jake's.'

'So?'

Garrett explained that Jake had had a gambling problem for a while, specifically when it came to sports betting.

'What's that have to do with you?'

'I told him never to bet on my games,' Garrett said, 'but I'm pretty sure he did.'

'I'm sure it's against the rules for you to bet on games in your sport,' Caitlin said. 'But can you really be punished because your brother did?'

'If they think I shaved points for my brother,' he said. 'And even if I didn't blatantly help him out, it might still look like I did. Jake knows when Summer and I have a fight. He knows when I'm coming down with a cold. He knows when I don't get a good night's sleep. No one else knows that stuff.'

'And you think Jake used that information to place bets?'

'One time I got food poisoning,' he said. 'I was in the bathroom all night. Vomiting. Diarrhea. I was in terrible shape. Jake knew. But the thing about food poisoning is it runs its course. By the time I made it to the locker room the next day, I was starting to feel better. The team doctors hooked me up to an IV, gave me a B12 shot for energy, told me to chug a bunch of Gatorade. When the game started, my legs were shaky, but I found my rhythm. I ended up having one of the best games of my life. We blew out Miami by twenty.

'When I saw Jake after the game,' Garrett went on, 'he looked sick. Like he was the one with food poisoning. He snapped at me. "How the hell does someone with food poisoning go off for forty points?"'

Caitlin had watched the game he was talking about – one of the highest-scoring games of Garrett's career.

'I *knew* he bet against me,' Garrett said.

He and Jake had a huge fight, which led to Garrett intervening in his brother's gambling. Jake confessed to how bad it was – how much money he owed – and Garrett threatened to cut him out of his life. Wanting to make amends, Jake agreed to limit his gambling and never bet on Garrett's games.

'I gave him a thousand-dollar-a-week allowance for gambling. That might sound stupid, like it would make the problem worse, but I figured it was a way to keep him from going deep into debt. I gave him a line and told him not to cross it. As far as I know, he didn't.'

Doing the math in her head, she figured Jake's gambling allowance was damn near as much as her annual salary, more than her husband's. She didn't show her surprise, though. As a police officer, she'd gotten good at looking stone-faced, regardless of what a victim or suspect told her.

'So,' Caitlin asked, 'you're thinking that if someone scrutinized your history of games, and Jake's history of betting, they'd see a correlation?'

Caitlin wasn't sure how possible such an investigation would be. Of course, every game Garrett played was recorded, the stats filed away into databases. Any evidence about his past play was available if someone took the time to find it. She didn't know enough about sports betting to know if such an exploration into Jake's gambling would be feasible. But the possibility was obviously enough to worry Garrett.

'I signed a two-year contract when I came to Cincinnati. I took a gamble on myself, believing I could do well here. And I have.

Now I'm a free agent after this series is over. Win or lose, Cincinnati is going to give me a big contract. Or someone else will. Maybe a max contract.'

That meant he could make somewhere in the realm of thirty or forty million a year, depending on how long the contract was for. Caitlin was stunned. The figure seemed unfathomable.

Caitlin opened her mouth to tell Garrett to stop being so selfish – saving Jake would be worth risking his career – but, as if reading her mind, he cut her off before she could speak.

'If I had confidence they could get Jake back, I'd do it in a heartbeat. I'd throw away my whole career. But I don't have any confidence they can do it. If I call the FBI, they're just going to spin their wheels figuring out if I brought this on myself. I'll be signing Jake's death warrant.'

Caitlin didn't agree with his reasoning, but let it go – for now.

'OK, so what do you want from me?'

'Last night, I was wishing there was someone I could call to help me out. Like a private investigator or something. Someone I knew personally. Who I could trust. Then I saw you on TV. I realized I *do* know someone.'

'I still don't understand,' Caitlin said. 'What is it you want from me? Advice? Call the FBI – that's my advice.'

'No, not advice,' he said, exasperated. 'I need you to find my brother, Glass. Figure out who took him and get him back.'

13

All the breath seemed to leave Caitlin's lungs.

Was he nuts?

'Please,' he said. 'I need you.'

'Street,' she said, pausing to collect her thoughts. 'I don't know much about sports betting, but I know it's not like in the old days when you could only place bets in Vegas or at illegal betting parlors, if that's what they're called. With online gaming, whoever is responsible for this could be anywhere in the world. Not just the United States. The *world* – do you hear me?'

Garrett looked mortified by the thought, and Caitlin hated that she was probably making him feel hopeless. But she needed him to understand the situation.

'But he went missing in Vegas,' Garrett said. 'That has to mean something, right?'

He had a point. But the scope of what he was asking was unbelievable.

'The FBI would put a whole *team* on this,' she said. 'They can trace phone calls or texts. Maybe track Jake's phone. If Jake has a computer in his apartment, they can scour his search history for contacts and clues. They probably have a long list of informants that could give them leads. For all I know, they can examine sports books and look for irregularities in betting – find out who's getting big paydays on these games. They could definitely help you communicate with the kidnappers, coach you on what to say. They'd attack the case from multiple angles, with personnel trained to handle these kinds of cases.'

Dozens of agents – all of them more qualified than Caitlin – would be assigned the task he was asking her to do alone.

'They might do all that,' Garrett said, 'but they'd also waste their time investigating two people I know are innocent.'

'Who?'

'Jake,' he snapped. 'And *me.*'

There was some truth to that, she knew. They would devote manpower to looking into Jake's background, and they might scrutinize it alongside Garrett's playing career, as he feared. They wouldn't be doing a thorough job if they didn't. But if he reported the kidnapping, they wouldn't seriously think he had anything to do with it. And studying Jake's history would only be one small part of their overall investigative plan, and Caitlin was sure it wouldn't distract them from the larger issue of finding the blackmailers and, most importantly, bringing Jake home.

'If they put twenty agents on this,' she said, 'and two of them are told to look into Jake's past, that leaves eighteen investigating every other possible avenue. That's seventeen more than me and all of them will have more experience with this kind of thing than I do. Your best chance of saving your brother is calling the FBI.'

He opened his phone and pointed to the picture of Jake with the gun to his head.

'I don't think they're bluffing about killing him if I contact the authorities. My best chance of saving him isn't calling the FBI. My best chance of *killing* him is calling the FBI.'

'Then why risk telling me?' Caitlin said.

'I thought you could be inconspicuous,' he said. 'I don't know – the FBI will come in like a wrecking ball.'

'I'm sure the FBI can be discreet,' Caitlin said.

'I don't trust them not to fuck this up,' he said, throwing his hands up. 'I trust you, Glass.'

Caitlin huffed and blew a strand of hair from her face. She couldn't believe what Garrett was saying.

'I'm sorry you're in this situation,' Caitlin said. 'I really am. And thank you for thinking enough of me to ask. It means a lot. But the answer is no. Hell no.'

They walked in silence back toward Caitlin's house. When they reached the driveway, Garrett told her to hang on, and he opened the passenger door of the Mercedes. The car had a luxurious cockpit, with leather bucket seats and plenty of leg room, and the inside was immaculately clean, as if the car just came off the showroom floor. She thought of her own vehicle, the minivan, and all the filth accumulated inside: crumbs from Alex eating in his booster seat, toys left behind, sticks and rocks he seemed to pick up anywhere they went. What a completely different life Garrett must lead.

He pulled out a piece of paper from the glovebox, then quickly wrote something on it. He handed it to her. His phone number.

'If you change your mind,' he said. 'Game Three is Wednesday in Las Vegas. You have time to think about it.'

'I'm not changing my mind, Garrett. I hope you do.'

Garrett glanced at the house.

'I hope it goes without saying I would pay you. However much you want.'

It was as if the mention of money didn't occur to him until he glanced at her little suburban house. With one look and a comment, Garrett had made her feel ashamed of a home she loved.

'I don't need your charity,' she said, her voice rough with the anger she was trying to suppress. She should have stopped there, but she didn't hold back. 'I've got a good life here, and I don't need a max contract and some fancy car to be happy.'

This wasn't entirely honest. She wasn't happy with her life, although she didn't think it was just money that was missing from it.

'I'm sorry,' he said. 'I didn't mean—'

'If you want to throw money at the problem,' Caitlin said, 'why don't you offer the kidnappers cash?'

'I did,' he said. 'I offered them five million dollars. As much as I could realistically get my hands on.'

The number left her speechless.

'They said it wasn't enough.'

14

Caitlin came in as Owen was finishing loading the dishwasher. Alex passed by her on his way outside.

'I'm going to shoot baskets, Mom.'

'OK,' she said, and then to Owen, 'is it too late for you to make your ride?'

'Probably,' he said, drying his hands. 'That's OK.'

'I'm sorry if that was weird,' she said, shaking her head at the absurdity of Garrett's visit. 'I'm as shocked as you are.'

Owen, with a half-grin on his face, filled up a water glass and said, 'He was taller than I expected. On TV, he seems short and scrappy. But in real life . . .'

Caitlin laughed. 'Six-three is pretty tall among us mortals, but on the court, he's standing next to guys who are six-eight, six-nine – seven foot.'

From outside, she could hear Alex narrating his own game like he was the announcer.

'And Streeter takes the ball up the court,' he declared. 'The shot clock is counting down. What's he going to do?'

Caitlin didn't know how to feel about her son playing her ex-boyfriend in his pretend games. Part of her felt a strange pride – she knew her son's hero. Mostly she felt it was inappropriate.

'So what was that all about?' Owen said. 'For real. The truth.'

She gave him a look that said she didn't like the insinuation she would lie. But, of course, she was going to.

'He wanted to hire me,' she said, which she told herself wasn't a complete fabrication.

'Hire you? For what?'

'To, like, help him with his game.' The words sounded ludicrous once they were out of her mouth. But the truth was more unbelievable.

Lying to Owen was a betrayal. But she didn't know what else to do. Garrett wouldn't want her to share his problem. And telling Owen the truth would have opened up a can of worms she didn't know how to deal with.

Luckily, Owen believed her – only he couldn't believe she said no.

'How much did he offer you?' he asked.

'We didn't talk about money. I just said no.'

'You've been pretty unhappy lately. Do you think you might enjoy doing this?'

'I wouldn't want to leave you and Alex for that long.'

'I can take care of Alex. It's summer. I'm not teaching. Besides, I owe you.'

He'd taken a long biking trip over spring break, leaving Caitlin to juggle her job and solo parenting. But he more than picked up the slack in the summers when he wasn't teaching, so she certainly didn't feel like he *owed* her anything.

'You want me to go to work for my ex?' she asked.

'Not really. But I want you to be happy. What you love most in the world is basketball. Having some connection to it again might be good for you.'

In the past, he'd encouraged her to try coaching at the high school, using the same argument: 'some connection to basketball.' But she didn't want to coach. She wanted to *play*.

'First of all,' she said, 'what I love most in the world is you and Alex. Second, Garrett doesn't really need me. That's what I told him. He's freaking out because he's three to five games away from accomplishing his lifelong goal – or falling short of it. He needed someone to tell him to calm down.'

'So you weren't tempted?'

She shook her head.

'I'm sorry to ask this,' he said. 'But did you, you know, still feel something for him?'

She huffed.

'Look,' she said, 'I'm not saying I wasn't in love with him back in college. But basketball was the tether that held us together. When it became clear my basketball journey was ending and he got to keep going on his, I saw him in a new light. He's a good guy. We were really good friends. But without basketball, our lives together didn't make sense.'

'I just want you to be happy,' Owen said.

'I am,' Caitlin said.

He smirked. This was a lie he could easily see through.

'How did it feel, seeing him?'

Caitlin sighed. Owen was fishing for some kind of reassurance, and she could see she wasn't getting out of this conversation without it.

'It was weird,' she said. 'I once cared about him very much. I follow his career.' She gestured with her arm toward the front door, where Alex apparently made a game-tying shot in the last second to send his make-believe game into overtime. 'But Garrett feels more like a brother. Or an old friend I haven't seen in a long time. I'm not in love with him, if that's what you're worried about.'

His eyes searched her face for any sign of dishonesty.

'All right,' he said. 'I trust you.'

Now she wondered if he was the one lying.

15

Garrett parked the Mercedes in the garage between his Jeep and Summer's Lexus. He walked through the laundry room and into the kitchen, which was connected to an expansive living room probably not much smaller than Caitlin's entire house. Through floor-to-ceiling windows, Garrett could see Summer out back swimming laps in the pool. She was a graceful swimmer. Whenever he swam laps, he felt like he was flailing around. Summer made it look easy.

She climbed out of the pool and grabbed a towel. She'd been photographed in dozens of skimpy two-piece bathing suits, but when she swam at home, she wore a simple black one-piece. Nothing flashy. A rubber cap covered her head – something she wouldn't be caught dead wearing in a photo shoot – so she could protect her hair from the chlorine. She wrapped the towel around her shoulders like a cape and pulled off the cap, letting her long hair spill down her back. She dropped onto a chaise lounge and closed her eyes.

She wouldn't be in the sun long, just enough to dry off. She worked hard to protect her skin.

She was beautiful. There was no doubt about it. She had arresting eyes and a long, lithe body. She exercised like crazy, but it was all in the service to staying thin. He thought about her in contrast to seeing Caitlin today. His ex looked as healthy as ever. If anything, she'd gained muscle mass. Not like a bulky body builder, but there was undoubtedly strength in her arms and legs, and in the way she carried herself. In college, she'd been a good match for him, able to keep up with him in anything they did: climbing at a rock gym in Tempe, running the desert hills in Phoenix, hiking in the mountains outside of Flagstaff. She'd been his best friend.

He didn't know what to expect today. Last night, it seemed like such a good idea to go see her. As dawn approached, he hadn't slept and suddenly the notion seemed silly. But what other options did he have? He texted Yazmina and asked if she could give him Caitlin's address. Even though it had been very early in LA where she lived, Yaz offered it without comment. She gave him a phone number, too, but he thought showing up would be better. He didn't want any record of them talking.

It was particularly surreal to meet Caitlin's son. He could see Caitlin in the boy – similarities in the cheekbones, the same dark eyes and long lashes. Girls were going to fall in love with those eyes when the boy got older, if they weren't already. Seeing him, Garrett wondered what their child might have looked like if he and Caitlin had stayed together.

He felt guilty about the thought as he watched Summer rise out of the chaise, wrap the towel around her suit, and head in. She spotted him through the window and her face lit up. He smiled back.

He hadn't told Summer about Jake because he knew exactly how she'd react. She'd tell him to call the FBI. He didn't know why he'd expected something different from Caitlin, but he had.

'Hey,' Summer said, as she came through the door, 'how was the workout?'

She assumed he'd gone to the practice facility. He didn't correct her.

'I'm worn out,' he said. 'I couldn't sleep.'

'What are you going to do the rest of the day?' she said, opening the refrigerator and pulling out a bottle of water.

Her approach to dealing with him during the playoffs seemed to be cheering like a madwoman at his games while giving him a wide berth whenever they were around each other. They had an unspoken agreement that everything – including her – took a back seat during the Finals.

'I told Coach I'd watch some film before the team meeting this afternoon.'

'Sounds fun,' she said, taking a drink. 'I'm going to take a shower. Unless you want to go first.'

'You go ahead.'

He walked down to the basement to a room set up for watching film. The temperature was cooler down here, and he pulled on an old ASU sweatshirt he kept hanging from a hook on the door. He fired up the projector. Last night's game flickered onto the screen, and he plopped down in a recliner with his laptop to control what he was watching. Ordinarily, he would watch a play, rewind, rewatch it, think about it, what he could have done differently. But today, he let the game run. He stared in a daze until he felt his phone buzzing in his pocket. He had a moment of hope that it was Caitlin, calling to say she'd changed her mind.

But it was the burner phone the kidnappers gave him. There was a new text message.

Change of plans for next game.

Win. And cover the spread.

'Cover the spread?' Garrett said aloud. 'Are they crazy?'

GAME THREE

16

Caitlin squeezed the trigger of her Glock, and the recoil kicked against her hand. She took aim again, drew a centering breath, and squeezed another shot. She wore both earplugs and earmuffs, and the noise of the shots was reduced to a muffled bark. In the indoor range, a long concrete warehouse where the air smelled of gunshot residue, other shots were going off, making *pop! pop!* noises, like a bag of popcorn in the microwave.

The range was about half full, and everyone there was a cop. Once a week, the local gun range was reserved for the sheriff's office. Around her, some of the men were laughing, joking. This was the highlight of their week – actually getting to fire their guns, but without any of the dangers associated with needing them on the job. Caitlin came to blow off steam. She told herself – for the hundredth time since yesterday – she'd done the right thing by refusing Garrett's request.

She holstered her Glock and hit the button on the steel column next to her. The paper target she'd been shooting lurched toward her. The concrete floor in front of her was littered with spent casings, from her and from others.

The target arrived – a black human silhouette with red circles in the center of the chest and the upper third of the face, meant to indicate where the heart and the brain would be. There were concentric ovals emanating out of the two reddened areas, each with numbers printed in a point system with the higher number closer to the two bullseyes.

She was among the best shooters in the department. Maybe the best. She'd always excelled at anything that required hand–eye coordination and depth perception. Basketball was the obvious example, but throughout college she'd been good at shooting pool or playing darts or throwing a Frisbee. Anything involving getting an object from point A to point B. It turned out shooting wasn't much different. If Steph Curry had been born a hundred and fifty years earlier, he probably would have made a hell of a gunfighter in the Wild West.

Of course, like anything, getting good required practice. When she'd first been hired on the police force, she was a mediocre shot. She pulled too hard on the trigger. She flinched in anticipation of the recoil. But she set her mind to improving and practiced regularly, enjoying the routine. Her qualification scores improved year after year, until last year when she tallied the best marks in the department. Not that the sheriff or anyone else congratulated her on it.

She pulled the target down and put up a fresh one, sending it down the track. On the counter in front of her was a small gun safe, about the size of her son's school lunchbox. She'd brought it so she could practice with her personal guns, not just the department-issued Glock. She punched in the code and opened the lid, revealing two subcompact pistols lying sight-to-grip in mirrored positions.

The first was a SIG Sauer P365, with a polymer frame and stainless-steel slide. Less than six inches long and only an inch wide, the gun was small enough to fit inside a purse or tucked into a pocket, but it packed a hell of a punch. When she'd bought it, looking for a personal firearm aside from her department-issued Glock, the salesman said the gun 'fought above its weight.'

The second gun was a Walther PPK, the same gun James Bond carried in so many 007 films. Tarnished with age, it was actually Owen's gun, although he'd never shot it (or any gun, actually). It was a family heirloom inherited from his grandfather, who supposedly won it in a hand of cards when he was in the army. Owen was going to sell it, but Caitlin said he might as well hang onto it. She kept it in her safe and practiced with it occasionally. Today, she shot both the SIG Sauer and Walther PPK.

Anything to take her mind off Garrett's visit.

When her time was almost up, she ran a target out one last time, only to about five yards. She tucked the SIG Sauer into the belt at the small of her back. This was a good way to shoot yourself in the leg, she knew, but she was also aware that in a real-world situation she wouldn't have all day to take a shot.

She calmed her breathing, focused her mind – not unlike when she would take a free throw back in her basketball days. Hands at her side, she focused not on the center mass, but at the number 9 on the head of the target. The font size was so small the numeral looked like a period at the end of a sentence.

She flung her arm behind her back, snatched the gun, brought it around, and fired.

Then she pressed the button to bring the target in. The number 9 was gone, replaced by a small hole in the paper only slightly bigger than the width of a pencil.

'Swish,' she whispered.

Two deputies passed behind her, and, through the ear protection, she thought she heard the muffled voice of one of them say, 'Looks like Caitlin missed one.'

She let her mouth crack into a small smile. Go ahead and let them think that. She hadn't been aiming for the bullseye. The minuscule numeral was a much smaller target.

She put the SIG Sauer back in the safe next to the PPK, then she reloaded her Glock, holstered it, and headed toward the door, carrying the safe like a briefcase. The two young deputies were loitering next to the door, talking.

'Hey, Caitlin,' one of them said.

'Hi, guys,' she said, trying to be polite.

'You know,' the second one said as she passed, 'I've got a gun you can practice with anytime you want.'

'Sorry,' she said. 'I stay away from guns that go off prematurely.'

They cackled with laughter, and she regretted the comeback. That kind of banter would only encourage them in the future.

Outside, Caitlin opened the door to her cruiser, sat down, and took a deep breath. She stared at the field next to the range, crowded with soybean plants. She could hear the muffled discharges of the guns inside.

She thought about the path that brought her here, to this life.

Back in college, it hadn't taken long for her injured ankle to heal, but her coach suggested limiting her playing time until Caitlin was one hundred percent. But she played tentatively, never found her rhythm. A sophomore took her starting slot. She was bitter and frustrated the whole season, watching her dreams slip away while also watching Garrett get closer and closer to achieving his.

She remembered asking Garrett what he thought he would do if a career in basketball didn't pan out. He was an English major, picking it simply because he liked to read, and had no other career aspirations besides basketball. She was a criminal justice major, declaring it mostly so she and Yaz could be in the same classes and so she could tell her parents she had a backup plan if basketball didn't work out. But she'd never wanted to go to law school like Yaz did. Never wanted to be a lawyer.

Instead, the more she learned about the justice system, the more she thought about going into law enforcement – an idea that, at first, seemed more preposterous than trying to become a pro basketball player.

'I'm thinking about becoming a cop,' she said to Garrett one night after a home game where she played only four minutes. It was the first time she'd admitted the idea to anyone. 'I think I could make a difference. There are a lot of bad cops out there. I'd like to be one of the good ones.'

She'd expected him to laugh, but he said with sincerity, 'You'd be a great cop.'

'Really?'

'You're a quick thinker. A problem solver. You're tough as hell. And you're a good person. Some cops probably aren't much better than criminals, but your heart's in the right place.'

The support bolstered her confidence – suddenly the idea didn't seem so outlandish – and she began a slow transition of giving up on her old dream and focusing on a new one.

It was also, she realized now, the beginning of the end for her and Garrett.

They'd been best friends bonded by a love of basketball – not soul mates meant to be together through every up and down of their lives.

Her radio buzzed.

'*Caitlin,*' said the dispatcher, '*the sheriff's wondering if you could come in. He wants to talk to you.*'

This is it, Caitlin thought, her heartbeat accelerating as she put the cruiser in drive. Her dream of being a pro basketball player hadn't worked out, but at least her dream of becoming a police detective would. She imagined coming home and asking Owen how he liked the sound of '*Detective* Caitlin Glass.'

17

Caitlin pushed through the glass doors into the building the sheriff's office shared with the county court system. There was a queue of people going through the metal detector, but Caitlin, in her uniform, sidestepped the line.

In this part of the building, where the public was allowed, burnt-orange carpet filled the floors, and the walls were red brick decorated with scenic framed photographs. She opened a nondescript door marked EMPLOYEES ONLY; behind it, the decorous Midwestern façade disappeared. The floors were covered in antiseptic white tile, and rectangular LED lights in the ceiling lit the place like a hospital.

As she passed the intake door to the jail, Shelby Slate, the newspaper reporter who wrote the recent article, almost bumped into her. Her point-and-shoot camera hung from a strap around her neck. She held a reporter's notebook in one hand.

'Hi, Caitlin.'

'What brings you here, Shelby?' Caitlin asked, trying to sound sociable, although really what she wanted to know was what she was doing in this part of the building. A press pass didn't give you unrestricted access to the sheriff's office.

'Just finished interviewing the sheriff and the new detective,' she said. 'For what it's worth, I think it should have been you.'

Caitlin frowned. Then, as Shelby kept walking, Caitlin glimpsed movement down the hall. The break-room door opened and a deputy barreled out, laughing. With the door hanging wide, the boisterous sound of men in a celebratory mood came down the hallway. She saw someone shaking the hand of Pete Ryle. Ryle, his thick neck bulging over his collar like dough squeezed too tightly into its packaging, was beaming. He might have looked pleased with himself the other day, holding the sleeping baby, but that paled against the self-satisfaction emanating from him now.

'You've got to be kidding me,' Caitlin muttered.

She stomped down the hall toward the sheriff's office. She could feel the heat rising to her head. She pushed open the door without knocking and stepped in without invitation.

Bob and Hank, the sheriff and undersheriff, were both kicked back in chairs and having a laugh.

'You gave Pete the detective job?' she said.

Her voice trembled with anger.

'Come in, Caitlin,' the sheriff said, sitting up straighter. There was a chair across from his desk, next to the undersheriff, and even though he gestured for her to sit, Caitlin didn't.

Bob Cosby was serving his fourth term as the county sheriff. He'd run for office unopposed every time. Rumor was that he planned to retire after this term, and he was grooming his undersheriff, Hank Cox, to take over. Which meant, between the two men, she was

staring at her boss for the foreseeable future. But something in her
snapped. She'd played by the rules ever since she started working
for the department, and it had gotten her exactly nowhere.

'I can't fucking believe this,' Caitlin said.

'Now calm down,' Bob said, flustered. 'I've got some good news
for you, too.'

'It's true,' Hank added. 'We gave Pete the promotion. It was a
hard decision. Both of you are well qualified.'

'One of us is,' Caitlin said.

Bob shifted in his chair, as if he couldn't get comfortable. He
had swearing-in photos of himself hanging on the wall, one for each
term, shaking hands with a different mayor every time. His belt line
had steadily grown over the years. He was like Pete, an out-of-shape
man who spent more time at the Elks Lodge than doing any kind
of physical exercise. Hank, his undersheriff for the last two terms,
was built from a different mold – he was stick thin. He was taller
than Caitlin but probably had a twenty-eight-inch waist, and his
uniform hung off him like it was two sizes too big.

She could probably kick both their asses – and Pete Ryle's too
– at the same time.

'Please sit,' Bob said again.

'I'd rather not,' Caitlin said. 'I've got work to do.'

Hank smirked and gave a look to his sheriff, as if to say, *See?
We made the right decision.*

'We'd like to promote you,' Bob said. 'Just not to detective.'

Caitlin felt some of her anger subside. Maybe she'd jumped to
conclusions too quickly. She approached the wooden chair and sat
down next to Hank.

'Blaine Carlton is about to retire,' the sheriff said, talking about
the department's long-time public information officer. 'We think
you're the best person for the job.'

'Blaine has an old-fashioned perspective about the job,' Hank
added. 'He answers the phone whenever there's a media inquiry,
gives the minimal facts. Otherwise, he tries to fly under the radar.
We want the new person to have a more twenty-first century
approach. Be proactive. Do social media. Put a positive spin on
things. Think of the job not just as a liaison to the media, but as
our community spokesperson. You know, a real PR person.'

The sheriff leaned forward on his elbows. 'I'm going to start
taking a backseat on some things, hand off more responsibility to

Hank here. When it comes to election season, we want people to know how integral he is to this office.'

Caitlin looked back and forth between them.

In other words, she thought, *I'm supposed to help Hank get elected. Make sure the handoff from one sheriff to the next goes off without a hitch.*

She had no idea why they thought she would be good at this. Sure, she did a fair amount of community-engagement activities – talking to Girl Scout troops, visiting elementary classes, being the face of the department for career day at the high school. She did it willingly, mostly to send a message that, *Yes, girls could do this job, too.* But she wasn't a bubbly extrovert at ease in front of crowds, comfortable BS-ing with the media. She was stiff, proper, professional. Hell, Pete was the gregarious type. She should have been offered detective, him the PR position.

They only wanted her for this job because she was a woman. And maybe – probably – because she wasn't half bad looking. She'd been hit on enough times in her life to know what men thought. The sheriff and undersheriff wanted her to be the pretty face of the department. That's it. This offer wasn't based in any way on her qualifications.

'It comes with a bump in salary,' Bob said. 'Two thousand.'

Caitlin swallowed.

'With all due respect, sir,' she said, 'is this your way of saying you'll never be willing to make me a detective?'

Bob sat back in his seat and exhaled.

'Caitlin,' he said, 'you're a fine cop on paper. But you don't have the toughness being a detective takes.'

She scoffed.

'I don't think you'd be saying that if you'd seen me down at the river the other night.'

'That's precisely what I'm talking about,' the sheriff said, staring at her from behind puffy mounds of skin crowding his eye sockets. 'A guy comes at you with a weapon, you don't get into a goddamn wrestling match with him. You shoot him.'

Caitlin stared in disbelief. She thought she'd handled that situation well. She saved the baby and caught the suspect. She didn't need to kill anybody. If the sheriff was worried about PR, did he really want an officer-involved shooting on the front page instead of a cute photo of a baby cuddling a cop?

She felt like such an idiot. Here she'd been thinking she'd be commended for her actions. Instead, they were using them against her. They'd been looking for an excuse not to promote her, and she'd handed it to them on a silver platter.

'What if that guy had gotten your gun?' Hank asked.

'He didn't,' Caitlin said.

'He tried,' Hank said. 'You said so in your report.'

Caitlin didn't know how to respond. Sure, the guy was a handful, but she'd never thought of him as a major threat. She thought often in terms of basketball, and that's how she saw this. He was like a weak team with no real chance of winning, even if he made the game closer than expected.

'You don't have the killer instinct it takes to do this job at the highest level,' Bob said. 'You'll be good in PR. It's perfect for you.'

She wanted to tell him to go to hell. But the adrenaline that fueled her stepping into the office, ready to fight, was gone. She was never going to win in this department.

She was never going to be taken seriously.

'Can I think about it?' she said, hating how weak her voice sounded.

18

Caitlin came in from the kitchen with a bowl of microwave popcorn in each hand. She plopped one onto Alex's lap and handed the other to Owen, then settled down on the other end of the couch. Alex usually sat on the carpet to watch TV, but today he was nestled on the couch between his parents. On the flatscreen, the announcer Chuck Walla was asking color commentators Harding Able and Dirk Justice, one a former coach and the other a former player, what each team needed to do to win tonight.

Alex started devouring his popcorn, dropping pieces onto the couch and floor. Caitlin ordinarily would have told him to be more careful, but her mind was elsewhere.

On screen, Garrett and Elijah were on the sidelines talking to their coach, six-six Guillermo Ware, a forty-something ex-player who had a brief stint in the NBA when he was young. Back then, he'd had cornrows, a full beard, and plenty of attitude and heart. But he'd been short on talent and never played more than a few professional minutes here and there. He was a good tactician, though, and he'd worked his way up through the ranks of assistant coaches, bouncing around the league, until the Sabertooths took a chance on him the same year they signed Garrett. The cornrows and beard were long gone, replaced by close-cropped gray stubble on his scalp and a trim salt-and-pepper mustache. But he had the same heart and the same tough attitude.

Caitlin always thought Ware deserved a lot of credit for developing the chemistry between Garrett and Elijah – together the three of them comprised the trinity that made this incarnation of the Sabertooths so effective.

Ware patted them both on the backs, and Garrett and the other players stripped off their sweatshirts and athletic gear and found their positions on the court. Garrett stood in the backcourt. Rodrigo Sandoval, the seven-foot center from Spain, stood ready for the tip-off. He and the Lightning's center jockeyed for position. Then the whistle blew, and the ref tossed up the ball. Sandoval leaped into the air, swiping the ball with his fingers, and tapped it backward into the hands of Elijah Carter, who immediately passed it back to Garrett, who dribbled up the court as his teammates charged ahead.

If Caitlin was alone, she'd be on her feet, pacing in front of the TV. Game One had been bad enough. But knowing what she knew now, watching this was too much.

Garrett dribbled to the top of the three-point line, and even though his defender wasn't giving him much space, he sprang up for a shot. The ball missed the rim entirely – an air ball – and fell straight into the arms of Jaxon Luca. He put the ball on the floor and raced up court.

Two seconds later, Luca jumped into the air and slammed the ball through the rim with such ferocity that the Las Vegas crowd was on its feet, roaring their approval.

Next to her, Alex moaned, 'Oh, no.'

'Jeez,' Owen muttered. 'Maybe he does need your help.'

By halftime, the Sabertooths were down by twenty-four points.

19

In the locker room, Coach and his subordinates went into a separate room to discuss strategy while the players, dejected, collapsed into the chairs in front of the lockers. Garrett's mouth was dry, his muscles tight. The days of sleep deprivation had caught up with him. Worse, his teammates were struggling. Elijah was his usual self, but the other starters weren't shooting worth a damn. Off-nights happened – you just hoped they didn't happen in the Finals.

Garrett looked around, then discreetly reached into his duffel bag and found the burner phone. He opened it and read the words.

We told you to cover the spread not lose in a blowout.

Garrett stared. Furious. He'd told them they were crazy and begged them not to make him do this. It was one thing to ask him to shave points, but to demand he win was ludicrous. And even more outrageous to expect him to cover the spread, which was four and a half. Garrett had to somehow get the Sabertooths to win by five. Bookies might be favoring the Sabertooths in this series because they had the better record, but Garrett was in the thick of the series and knew better – the Lightning were *good*. He couldn't guarantee a victory against them.

You're asking the impossible, Garrett typed.

A second later, a new message popped up.

You did it in game 1.

That was a miracle!!! Garrett texted. We're behind by even more.

The response was swift: You did it in one quarter. Tonight you have a full half.

Garrett couldn't believe it. Did these assholes even watch basketball?

Fuck you, he typed, but stopped before sending it.

A new text popped up.

We'll make some in-game bets to try to cover our losses.

Then another.

You need to score at least twenty points this half. Your teammates can't hit water from a boat. You need to take over.

Garrett stared at the phone. He averaged twenty *per game* this season. Still, scoring twenty in the half seemed more doable than orchestrating a win, much less covering the spread.

Make it happen or we shoot your brother.

A picture came through of Jake's face with a gun barrel jammed into his mouth. Garrett's chest tightened.

His brother was two quarters away from dying.

20

Caitlin watched with nervous anticipation as Chuck Walla and his crew discussed what they expected in the second half. Both Harding Able and Dirk Justice were trying to make it sound like the twenty-four-point deficit wasn't insurmountable – especially since the Sabertooths had already mounted a herculean comeback this series – but it was clear they didn't want bored viewers turning the channel.

Caitlin was trying to look past the men to the players warming up on the court. As they transitioned toward a commercial break, the camera cut away to show Luca warming up, then Elijah Carter, and finally Garrett, who was scowling, like he was mad at the whole world – the kind of expression Jaxon Luca wore all the time – as he ran around taking shots during warmup with ten times the energy he'd exhibited during the first half.

'He looks different,' Caitlin said aloud, unable to stop herself. 'He's going to play better now.'

'He couldn't play much worse,' Owen commented, not unkindly.

As the second half began, Garrett got the ball and dribbled slowly up court, his eyes focused, his expression stone faced. He passed the ball, ran through two screens, got the ball back, and took a long two-point jumper.

Swish!

Alex jumped on the couch and gave Owen a high five.

The Sabertooths buckled down on defense, getting two stops and cutting the lead to twenty. When Jaxon Luca drove to the basket again, Elijah Carter stood like a statue in his way. Luca crashed into him, sending Carter backwards, and the ball sailed into the net.

Two points.

But there was a whistle.

It was a charge called on Luca, and the points were waived away. He threw his arms and stomped down the court. That was his fourth foul. The camera cut to a close-up of him, and it was easy to tell he was shaking his head at the coach, saying, *Don't take me out.*

The commentators talked about the risky move of keeping Luca in when he had four fouls – especially with such a big lead – but the coach was deferring the decision to his star player.

On the next possession, Garrett took the ball down the court, dribbling far out from the arc and waited for the right defensive matchup. When he saw what he wanted, he drove at Luca. He leaped, thrusting his body into a mid-air collision with Luca. The ball went flying – no chance of going in – and Garrett crashed to the floor.

Luca was called for his fifth foul.

'Luca's foul trouble might save them,' Caitlin muttered, more to herself than her family.

Garrett popped up and fist-bumped Elijah as the commentators argued about the foul, split on whether it was a bad call.

One more and Luca was out of the game.

With more than twenty minutes left, the coach had no choice but to keep Luca on the bench.

Next to Caitlin, Alex was beside himself with anxiety. He was holding a pillow, and when the Sabertooths took a shot, if the ball went in, he sprang into the air and bounced on the couch. If they missed, he covered his face and groaned.

Luca stayed warm, pedaling on a stationary bicycle in the tunnel. When there were only five minutes left, the Lightning coach finally motioned for Luca to go back in.

By then, the Sabertooths were only down by eight.

21

Coach Ware called a timeout, and Garrett jogged over to the bench. He was drenched in sweat. An assistant coach tossed him a towel, which he put over his legs, and he looked up at the scoreboard.

The problem wasn't that they were down by eight. Or not just that. The Sabertooths were favored by four and a half points. Which meant if they were going to cover the spread, they had to win by five.

To everyone else on the team, the deficit was eight.

But to Garrett, it was thirteen.

If they didn't get within striking distance soon, they would have to start fouling, stopping the clock and hoping the Lightning would miss their free throws. That wouldn't help them win by five.

'Let's get that lead and hang onto it,' Garrett said after Coach went over a play they'd practiced dozens of times. 'Let's not leave it to a last-minute shot.'

Coach nodded his approval – he'd been wanting Garrett to become more outspoken.

Garrett took another swig of Gatorade and headed back on the court to get into position. The Lightning dancers were exiting the hardwood, shuffling sideways and waving to the stands. The arena speakers blasted an ominous beat reminiscent of 'We Will Rock You' and the crowd clapped and stomped along with it. The team mascot, Electric Ernie – a guy in blue tights and a foam suit shaped like a lightning bolt – hustled along the sidelines, throwing his arms up and down to get the crowd to scream louder.

The court cleared of non-players, and Garrett positioned himself for the inbound pass. Jaxon Luca bumped against him, trying to push him off his mark. Their sweat-slicked skin slid against each other. Heat radiated from Luca like a campfire.

Elijah tossed the ball high and Garrett bolted to it, getting there a split second before Luca. As planned, Elijah darted toward the basket while Garrett tried to get into position to pass. But Billy Croft's screen failed, and Garrett didn't have a good passing lane to Elijah. Garrett backed up well past the three-point line. Jaxon kept his knees bent, his head low. Luca was six-seven but had the wingspan of someone four inches taller.

Garrett glanced at the shot clock. The smart thing to do was to take all the time he needed, move the ball, make sure they got a good shot.

But that was only if they were down by eight.

If they were down by thirteen – which *he* was – there was only one thing to do.

Garrett jumped and – even though he was a good six feet past the three-point line – launched the shot. Jaxon Luca was so startled by the long-range attempt he didn't make an effort to stop him.

The ball soared through the air.

The arena fell silent.

On the sidelines, he heard Coach Ware grumble, 'What the . . .?'

The ball snapped through the net – *swish!* – and the crowd groaned.

Instead of running back down the court to get ready on defense, Garrett darted forward into the Lightning's territory.

'Watch out!' Luca yelled.

Too late.

Garrett snatched the inbound pass out of the air, took one dribble, and laid the ball into the basket. The Sabertooths' bench jumped to their feet, hooting and holding their hands high. The Lightning called another timeout, and Garrett's teammates mobbed him with chest-bumps and attempts at high fives.

The Sabertooths were down by only three with three minutes to go.

But Garrett was down by eight.

22

C aitlin, Alex, and even Owen were all on their feet in the living room.

'That was incredible,' Owen said.

Caitlin was too nervous to speak. She wondered what Garrett's directives from the kidnappers were.

On the screen, Garrett smothered the Lightning's point guard as he came up the court. He brought the ball up to pass it, and Garrett popped it out of his hands. Both players went scrambling while Garrett's teammate Kevin Mackey darted up the court. Garrett lunged, swatting the ball forward. It rolled down the court and Mackey picked it up underneath the basket and laid it in.

Down by one.

'*If they pull this off*,' Chuck Walla said, practically out of breath, '*it will be the biggest comeback in an NBA Finals game in the last forty years.*'

Alex couldn't stop jumping.

'If all basketball games were like this,' Owen said, 'I'd watch with you guys more often.'

Caitlin was frozen in place, staring at the screen.

On the next possession, Garrett was guarding Jaxon Luca and he raced him around the court, never letting him get free. The shot clock ticked toward zero, and the Lightning panicked. Their power forward got the ball at the three-point line and threw it up, but the horn sounded before it left his hands.

Shot clock violation.

Luca yelled at his teammates as they went back down the court.

Garrett got the ball on the inbound pass and raced down the hardwood. He wasn't messing around. Without waiting for his teammates to be in position, he launched a three.

Swish!

The crowd groaned audibly through the TV. The Sabertooths' bench went crazy, jumping and waving towels.

'*Unbelievable!*' Chuck Walla announced. '*The Sabertooths are up by two with twenty-seven seconds remaining.*'

23

The Lightning used their final timeout, and Garrett – dripping sweat and out of breath – walked to the bench.

If the Lightning didn't score, the Sabertooths would win by two.

If the Lightning hit a two-pointer, the game would go to overtime.

If the Lightning hit a three-pointer, they would win.

But none of that mattered. What mattered was Garrett needed three more points to save his brother.

Coach Ware was shouting at them to lock down on defense.

'Garrett, you're on Luca,' he barked.

Garrett didn't speak.

'If they don't score, hang on to the fucking ball. Make them foul.'

Garrett headed back onto the court, positioning his body next to Luca. Because of his five fouls, Luca had spent more time than usual on the bench tonight, and he looked as fresh now as he was when the game started.

The arena was on its feet, shouting and clapping, cheering with the music. When the whistle sounded, it was hard to hear it because of the noise. Luca darted away and grabbed the inbound pass, but Garrett stayed on him. Luca dribbled between his legs, shuffled his feet, tried to get Garrett to make a misstep.

Three seconds separated the shot clock and game clock.

Both ticked down.

Elijah swung over to help. But this time, once he was double-teamed, Jaxon lasered the ball over to the open man.

The shot clock was at one second.

The Lightning player jumped, let go of the ball. The shot clock horn sounded as the ball rainbowed through the air, then clanged against the rim. Rodrigo Sandoval swatted the ball, trying to get it away from the Lightning players crashing the board. Garrett snatched it out of the air and took off running. He made it to half court before the game clock was at 00:01.

He lobbed the ball toward the basket a split second before the buzzer sounded.

24

Caitlin held her breath as the ball sailed through the air.

'*Streeter throws up one more shot,*' Chuck Walla said.

The ball bounced off the rim, rocketing back out into the court.

'*Almost,*' Walla commented. '*But it wouldn't matter anyway. The Sabertooths have done it again. Mounting a major comeback to take a two–one lead in the NBA Finals.*'

Alex ran around the room, screaming in excitement. Owen gave him a high five and said, 'Wow, bud, can you believe it!'

Caitlin stared at the screen, knowing something was wrong. The camera showed the Sabertooths celebrating, everyone except Garrett, who'd fallen onto his knees, his head down. Elijah Carter was trying to pick him up to join in the merriment, but Garrett wasn't having it. He looked physically ill, like he might throw up.

'*Garrett Streeter is utterly drained,*' Chuck Walla commented.

'*When they say leave everything on the court,*' Dirk Justice added, '*this is what they mean. Garrett Streeter doesn't even have the energy to celebrate.*'

Caitlin knew better.

Whatever Garrett was supposed to do – whatever the kidnappers demanded – he'd failed.

25

Garrett gained the strength to rise to his feet. The floor was swarmed with people: players, coaches, reporters. He stared up at the scoreboard. He'd gotten his twenty points for the half, but he'd failed to cover the spread. He hoped it was enough to save his brother's life.

Someone thrust a video camera near his face, trying to get his reaction. He turned away from the camera, heading to the tunnel and leaving his teammates to celebrate on their own. Once in the locker room – the first one there – he took out his cell phone and looked for a message.

Nothing.

He showered in silence, a sick dread turning his limbs numb. As he dried off, his teammates filed into the room, boisterous in their celebration. Coach gave a speech. He was smiling, jubilant.

'Yo, Streeter,' he said, and all eyes turned to Garrett, standing in his boxer shorts with one arm through his T-shirt. 'That was a hell of a second half.'

Garrett faked a smile as his teammates roared their approval.

'Anything you want to say?' Coach asked.

Garrett looked around. All eyes on him.

'No,' he said. 'I'm good.'

Ware looked disappointed and turned instead to Elijah, who didn't pass on the opportunity to pump up the team. Afterward, Garrett dressed and approached Elijah. One of the team's medical officers was wrapping ice around his shoulder.

'Hey, man, can you handle the media tonight?' Garrett asked.

'Dude, come on!' Elijah said. 'They're going to want to talk to you, bro.'

'I'm wiped out,' Garrett said.

The assistant finished wrapping and Elijah rose to his feet, the large cellophane blob bulging from his shoulder.

'No problem,' he said. 'I got you. You keep balling like that, I'll do any favor you want.'

Ordinarily, Garrett would have to wait on everyone before the bus could take them back to the hotel, but he couldn't imagine doing that now.

'Hey, Josh,' he said, pulling a young assistant coach aside, 'I need to get out of here. Can you make up some excuse for Coach?'

Josh was actually the one who'd introduced Garrett to Summer. He'd known her in college at the University of Washington, where he'd been a backup point guard. When Garrett had joined the Sabertooths, he and Josh had clicked right away. They were close in age – one a coach on the rise and the other a player in his prime – and Josh brought him along when visiting Summer and a bunch of her model friends one night after playing the Clippers in Los Angeles. The meetup was meant to fix Josh up with one of Summer's friends, but it was Garrett and Summer who hit it off. They did the long-distance thing for a season before, last summer, buying the house together in Cincinnati.

'Sure thing,' Josh said. 'Hang tight for a minute, and I'll get a car for you.'

'Nah,' Garrett said. 'I want to walk. Get some fresh air.'

Josh took an extra-long look at Garrett. 'You OK?'

'Just wiped out.'

'You might get mobbed out there,' Josh said, referring to the crowd exiting the arena. 'Or mugged.'

'I'll put my sweatshirt on,' he said. 'Pull my hood up.'

Garrett didn't think he'd attract much attention. It would be different if he was Elijah or Rodrigo, towering over the crowd, but he was short enough to blend in. When the bus of the 1992 Olympic Dream Team was stuck in traffic, John Stockton famously stepped off and walked through the crowd of Olympic fans, and no one noticed. The other players on the team – guys like Patrick Ewing, Larry Bird, Karl Malone – could never have gotten away with it. One perk of being the shortest guy on the team.

'OK,' Josh said. 'Get out of here.'

Garrett walked along the Strip. Music blared from casinos. Lights flashed. People jostled around him – some drunk, others bemoaning the Lightning's loss – but no one seemed to recognize him with his hood pulled up. It was a warm night, too hot for a sweatshirt, but he kept it on until he distanced himself from the arena and the crowds of basketball fans. When he was close to his hotel, he stripped it off and continued in his T-shirt. The sky was overcast and seemed to pulse with the lights of the city.

His personal phone was blowing up, but the burner was horrifically silent. Images of his brother with a bullet hole in his head filled his mind.

His hotel was a short walk. In the elevator, riding up to the penthouse, he stared at his reflection in the mirrored walls. His skin was sallow, the half-circles under his eyes surprisingly dark. He looked like a drug addict, strung out and overdue for his next fix.

He pushed through the door to his room, shuffling to the huge floor-to-ceiling window looking out over the city. Below, Las Vegas was alight with casinos and cars. While it was noisy down on the street, none of the sounds penetrated his penthouse, and the effect was like watching a movie with no sound.

He heard the *ding* of an incoming text.

There was a video on the burner with no accompanying message. He closed his eyes, swallowed, told himself he *had* to watch.

The video displayed his brother sitting in front of the TV, which showed the final summation from the commentators. Jake was watching attentively. A loyal brother. Even held prisoner, he was genuinely interested in what they were saying. The conversation turned to Garrett's play, and Jake leaned forward to listen.

Three men came onto the screen, all dressed in black from head to foot, wearing face masks and dark sunglasses to cover their eyes. Two were quite a bit taller than the other. The shorter one turned the TV off. Saying nothing, Jake looked back and forth between them. The men sprang into action. The big ones grabbed Jake and brought him to his feet.

'What are you doing?' he could hear Jake saying. 'He *won!*'

One man put Jake in a headlock and the other started throwing punches into Jake's body. He hunched over, and the man holding him, unable to keep him upright, let Jake slide to the floor.

'But he won,' Jake said. 'Why are you—?'

The shorter guy started kicking Jake while he curled in a ball and covered his head.

Garrett put his fist in his mouth and bit his hand to contain any sound – a scream, a roar, a wail – that threatened to escape.

That was his brother.

His *brother*.

The image – taken from a cell phone – was shaky as the operator moved it around to get the best view. Still, the level of brutality was apparent.

One of the big guys knelt and tried to pull Jake's arms away from his head. The other squatted down, digging his knee into Jake's chest, and punched him in the face. Blood spilled from his nose and coated his teeth. Jake, dazed but conscious, didn't speak, didn't beg them to stop, but he couldn't hold his tears in.

The assault ceased. The men stood over Jake, then stepped back out of view. The cameraman knelt down, putting the camera close to Jake's tear- and blood-streaked face. A hand came from out of the frame – presumably the camera operator's – and held a gun.

The hand pressed the barrel against Jake's face. He squirmed away, rolling over onto his stomach. But the gunman held the barrel against the back of his head. Jake made a growling, sobbing sound – a primal expression of fear unlike any sound Garrett had ever heard.

Garrett thought the gun would go off any moment. He expected a flash of fire from the end of the barrel.

The screen went black, a change so sudden Garrett recoiled in horror, thinking the gun had gone off. But the video had simply ended.

Garrett tried to control his breathing. He was hyperventilating.

The phone started ringing.

26

'**Y**ou motherfuckers!' Garrett roared into the phone. 'You—'

'*You almost killed your brother tonight!*' the voice on the other end shouted. The caller was using a voice-distortion app. The sound was like a grumbling animal.

'No,' Garrett rasped, having trouble breathing. 'You're the one holding a gun.'

'*Your brother's life is in your hands. Shut your mouth and listen.*'

The voice was calmer now, but it still sounded animalistic – like a grizzly bear learned to talk.

Garrett kept quiet, his chest heaving.

'*Because of the prop bet on you, our losses weren't as big as they could have been, but we still didn't break even. You cost us a lot of money tonight.*'

'What you asked was impossible,' Garrett said, hating how whiny and helpless his voice sounded.

But it was true. How could you fix a game by asking a player to perform *better* than he was capable?

'*We were going to let your brother go tonight,*' the voice said. '*But because you've screwed us over, we're going to have to keep him a little longer.*'

This was the first they'd said anything about letting Jake go, and Garrett felt certain the voice was lying.

'*Your instructions for the next game are simple,*' the voice said. '*Lose.*'

Garrett waited for more but there was none.

'That's it? Just lose.'

'*That's it.*'

'OK,' Garrett said, his mouth dry. 'And you'll let Jake go?'

'*No,*' the voice said. '*We need to make back our losses, and that's going to take longer than one game.*'

Garrett wanted to argue, but what leverage did he have?

'*There's someone here who wants to talk to you.*'

'Go on,' a voice said, this one not distorted.

The app had been turned off and the phone switched to speaker.

'I love you, bro.'

It was Jake's voice. Nasally and strained. But definitely his.

Tears filled Garrett's eyes. He wanted to tell his brother he loved him, but he couldn't form any words.

'You don't have to do what they tell you,' Jake blurted. 'Win, brother. Win!'

Then the noise of a scuffle burst through the phone. Voices, not disguised, were cursing Jake, and it sounded like they were kicking or hitting him again. Jake grunted in pain. Then the phone went silent. They'd hung up.

Garrett stared at the phone, then a text came through, reiterating the previous message.

Lose and your brother lives.

Win and he dies.

27

'Can I be done?' Alex called from the bathroom.

He stepped out into the hallway, his mouth dripping toothpaste foam, his hand holding his brush aloft like it was a torch used to light a dark tunnel.

'Did you get every tooth?' Caitlin asked.

'Yeah.'

'Every part of every tooth?'

'I did a good job, Mom.'

'Rinse your mouth out,' she said. 'And wipe off your face.'

Alex smiled, the foam running down his chin like he was a rabid dog.

She waited in the hall while he did this. The door was wide open, and she studied her son in his mismatched pajamas. She'd only bought the pants a few months ago, but already they were too short, even though the elastic was loose around his waist. That was the way it was with most of his clothes.

He had his mom's height, that was for sure.

She had the intrusive thought that if she'd married Garrett, their child would be even taller. She pushed the thought away.

'Can I stay up and play?' he asked.

'No way,' Caitlin said. 'It's way past your bedtime.'

'But I'm not tired.'

He said this, but she could tell the opposite was true. After he relaxed for a few minutes, he was going to crash.

He climbed into bed next to a mountain of stuffed animals, and she tucked him in. The kid was fascinated by outer space, and models of the sun and planets hung above his head. She sat on the edge of the mattress and sang her usual two songs – truncated versions of The Beatles' 'Ob-La-Di, Ob-La-Da' and Bob Marley's 'Three Little Birds.' As her mouth sang the words on autopilot, her mind reeled, a storm of thoughts she couldn't keep under control.

Garrett's visit.

Pete getting the promotion over her.

The look on Garrett's face at the end of the game.

As she kissed her son goodnight, letting her lips linger on the top of his head, she knew what she had to do. She'd been thinking about it since the sheriff broke the news that she wasn't going to be a detective. The image of Garrett at the end of the game – distraught, unable to stand – solidified her decision.

Owen came in to say goodnight to Alex, and Caitlin left him to it. In their bedroom, she went to draw the curtain over the sliding-glass door before changing. The lock wasn't latched, and she rolled her eyes in irritation. Owen was always forgetting to lock it. He thought of this as a safe small town, but she knew there were plenty of break-ins. She saw it every day. And this was the room where she kept her guns. They were all in safes – her Glock under the bed, her SIG Sauer and Owen's PPK in the closet – but she didn't like the idea of a burglar walking in and grabbing them. What happened to Jake was proof that this wasn't a safe world they were living in. She pushed her annoyance with her husband aside – now was not the time to pick a fight.

Owen came back as Caitlin finished changing into the shorts and T-shirt she slept in. He took one look at Caitlin's face and stopped before climbing into bed.

Caitlin stood before him, arms crossed, and said, 'I'm going to take Garrett up on his offer. I'm going to Las Vegas.'

'Oh,' he said hesitantly. 'OK.'

'Let me do this, let me be a part of basketball again,' she said. 'For a little while.'

She didn't say what she was actually thinking – *let me be a police detective for a little while.*

28

Garrett lay curled on his side on the couch in the penthouse. Light from the window danced across his face. His eyes were focused on nothing. His mind was frozen with fear. He'd managed to call Summer – otherwise she might show up to his room – and somehow managed to get through a conversation. But now he lay in the dark, nearly catatonic.

He didn't know what to do and felt paralyzed with helplessness.

His phone buzzed. He looked at the number. The call was coming from Ohio, but it wasn't one of his contacts.

He felt a glimmer of hope.

'Hello?' he said.

'Street?'

'Glass?'

'Yeah,' she said, 'it's me. I'm coming to Vegas. I'm going to help you.'

GAME FOUR

29

Caitlin crept down the street, looking at addresses. She was driving Owen's little four-cylinder Toyota pickup, which had been old when they'd started dating, and she felt very out of place in this neighborhood. Each home was a mansion.

'You've got to be kidding me,' Caitlin said as she turned onto a long driveway that wound up a small hill to what could hardly be described as a house – more like a compound. There were four garage bays next to a two-story house that had to be at least five thousand square feet, with large vertical windows and a high, angled ranch-style roof. There were several other buildings, all shaded under a tall canopy of trees, and she wasn't sure if they were guest houses or storage buildings or what.

God, what Garrett must have thought of her little podunk house.

When she talked to him last night, he'd asked when she was going to come to Las Vegas, and she'd told him today, but not until the afternoon. First, she wanted to look in Jake's apartment, if Garrett could get her a key.

Garrett had a spare at his house in Cinci.

'Summer will be there,' he told her. 'She could get it for you. I'll tell her Jake left some kind of scouting report there that I need.'

Caitlin was confused at first. During the comeback last night, the camera cut more than once to Summer cheering in the stands. Wasn't she in Vegas?

'She's flying back,' he said. 'She'll be back for Game Four, but she's got a meeting or something. I don't know.'

Caitlin called the sheriff first thing and, after inquiring about the status of the baby she'd saved, asked for time off to do some soul-searching.

'How does a week sound?'

Caitlin estimated how long the series could go if it went to a Game Seven.

'How about two?'

'It's your vacation time,' he said. 'When you get back, we'll have a sit-down and figure out how to best support you in the new position.'

In his mind, she'd already accepted.

She walked up the front steps of what appeared to be the main house. She stood on a porch framed by columns, like she was entering some Greek fortress instead of a house in southwestern Ohio.

She pressed the doorbell and waited.

No one answered.

She pressed it again, then pounded on the door with her fist.

A moment later, the door swung open and the beautiful woman she recognized from catalogs stood there. She wore Lululemon leggings and a tight top that left her smooth stomach exposed. Her hair was pulled back and damp with sweat and she wore no makeup, but she was, nevertheless, stunning. She was as tall as Caitlin, but with a waist that seemed impossibly thin for someone her height.

She wiped sweat off her face with a hand towel, then she flashed an apologetic yet electric smile that Caitlin was sure had the power to disarm and disorient almost anyone she leveled it at, male or female. She exuded charisma even before she opened her mouth.

'You must be Caitlin?' she said, friendly but out of breath from whatever kind of exercise she'd been doing. 'Or, I guess, as Garrett calls you, "Glass"?'

'Yes,' Caitlin said, hating herself for how nervous she felt. 'Caitlin's fine.'

'Come in,' Summer said. 'Please.'

Caitlin stepped over the threshold, apologizing for bothering her.

'No problem,' Summer said. 'I was just on the Peloton.'

She led Caitlin into a huge living room, with vaulted ceilings twenty feet high and massive windows overlooking a swimming pool in the backyard. The room was spotless, with crimson throw pillows perfectly positioned on an ivory couch. The carpet, thick and the color of cream, looked like no one ever walked on it.

She remembered Garrett's apartment in college. He slept on an air mattress that needed to be pumped up every few days. His books sat on shelves made of cinderblocks and two-by-fours. His clothes were in milk crates. She couldn't believe the same person who lived there now lived here.

'It's great to meet you,' Summer said. 'I've heard so much about you. The one who got away.'

Heat rose to Caitlin's face.

'I knew you'd be pretty,' Summer said, 'but I didn't know you'd be gorgeous.'

Caitlin didn't know how to answer. She wanted to enjoy receiving such a compliment from a woman who'd been on the cover of the *Sports Illustrated* Swimsuit Issue, but Caitlin was afraid Summer was patronizing her.

'Garrett said he's hiring you as an advisor or something?' Summer said.

This was the lie they'd come up with since it was what she'd already told her husband.

'Something like that,' Caitlin explained, feeling preposterous suggesting she could be of use to Garrett. 'Honestly, I don't know how much help I'll be – he's playing great – but I've been away from the game for a while and thought it would be a nice change of pace.'

'What do you do now?'

She was being friendly, but Caitlin wanted to get out of here and get to work.

'I'm a police officer,' she said. 'A deputy in our county's sheriff's office.'

Summer's eyes widened.

'Like a real cop? Carrying a gun and everything?'

Garrett must not have mentioned that part.

'Yep,' said Caitlin.

'That's so cool.'

Caitlin glanced at her watch. Summer noticed Caitlin's impatience and said she'd go find Jake's key.

'I should have grabbed it before you got here,' she said. 'But I flew back late last night and had an early appointment this morning.'

Caitlin was surprised – and impressed – she had the energy to be doing a workout. She must have gotten very little sleep.

Summer left the room. Out the back window, past the swimming pool, Caitlin spotted an outdoor basketball court tucked behind a row of oaks. Garrett's own court.

Garrett once told her that, through much of his childhood, he and his brother shared a pair of basketball shoes because they couldn't afford two. They'd play at the park, taking turns untying and switching their shoes between games. The other kids laughed at them, and that motivated Garrett to show them up on the court – it helped make him a better player. If not for Garrett's athletic scholarship and Jake receiving a scholarship from a statewide initiative targeting low-income students, they never would have gone to college.

Looking at where he lived now, Caitlin felt a swelling of admiration for Garrett.

You did it, Street. You really did.

'Here it is,' Summer said, walking back into the room, holding a single key in her outstretched hand.

She had a way of walking, even here in her own living room, that looked like she was gliding an inch or two above the floor.

Caitlin took the key and thanked Summer for her help.

Summer said, 'Maybe I'll see you in Vegas.'

30

Jake lived in a tall condominium complex overlooking the Ohio River. As the elevator door opened onto the top floor, Caitlin wandered down a hall with high windows on one side, which gave her a nice view of the river, wide and brown but quite beautiful in the afternoon sunlight. From here, she could see the Sabertooths arena, tucked along the river next to Paul Brown Stadium and the Great American Ball Park, where the Bengals and Reds played respectively.

Caitlin inserted the key into the lock and turned the handle. She instinctively put her hand to where the butt of her sidearm would be, but she wasn't carrying. She planned to take the SIG Sauer to Las Vegas with her, which she was allowed to do if she checked the safe as its own bag, but right now the safe was hidden in her suitcase, where she stashed it so Owen and Alex wouldn't see. She told herself she didn't need a gun now anyway – she was only taking it to Vegas as a precaution – so she pushed through the door and used her elbow to turn on the light.

A nice apartment came into view, the kitchen, dining room, and living room all visible from where she stood. In contrast to Garrett's place, Jake's was somewhat messy, Caitlin was relieved to see, with magazines and papers scattered on the dining-room table, shoes lying on the floor by the couch, and dishes in the sink.

Caitlin searched through paperwork stacked on a little desk next to the refrigerator, but it seemed mostly to be junk mail and magazines. The refrigerator was peppered with magnets from all over the country – cities with NBA teams where Jake traveled to watch Garrett's games. She found several business cards tucked under magnets: a masseuse, an acupuncturist, a physical therapist, a landscaper. She assumed most of these were for Garrett. Jake didn't have a lawn that needed to be landscaped, and most of the others seemed like the kinds of behind-the-scenes healthcare a professional athlete might use.

There were two matching tooth-shaped reminder cards for upcoming dental appointments, one for Garrett and one for Jake. She thought it was cute, but also maybe a little pathetic, that they scheduled their dentist appointments together.

Another card caught her eye. Partly hidden behind a magnet, the occupation under the name said *COUNSELING*.

She wondered if Garrett was in therapy or Jake.

In the living room was a huge television set into a massive bookcase, full of decorations and memorabilia. There weren't any actual books – Garrett had been an avid reader, but apparently Jake was not – and instead it held mementos of Garrett's career: signed basketballs, buttons, towels, newspaper and magazine cutouts. Caitlin took a close look to see if there was anything from Vegas – a casino chip, maybe, or a deck of cards – but there was nothing.

She spotted a framed picture of Garrett and Jake, back when they were kids, squinting into the camera. Garrett, maybe fourteen at the time, was grinning and shirtless, starting to look like the man Caitlin would meet in college. Jake was smaller, pre-puberty, looking scrawny in a too-big Phoenix Suns jersey. Even then, he looked like nothing made him happier than being next to Garrett.

She thought she understood the situation between the brothers. Garrett, two years older than Jake, tried so hard to lift them out of their hardscrabble roots. They'd never known their father, and their mom, an addict most of their lives, died of an overdose when Garrett was a senior in high school. Garrett always looked out for his little brother. Jake, it seemed, relied too much on his brother and never ventured out from his shadow. But seeing this shrine, she thought she understood Garrett's reluctance to do much about it. Jake worshipped him.

She walked into the bedroom and found a small IKEA-style desk. She opened one of the drawers and found hanging file folders, where she discovered paperwork for two bank accounts, one a shared account with Garrett. The other, Jake's own. Apparently Garrett's brother was like her husband, who, despite the availability of digital records, insisted on getting monthly statements in the mail.

She looked through the documents and determined the solo account was the one Jake used for gambling. Besides a handful of cash withdrawals now and then, there were virtually no other transactions, except with something called NetBookie, both withdrawals and deposits.

Caitlin told Garrett to get a burner phone – in addition to the one the kidnappers were using – and she texted him on it now, using a pay-as-you-go phone of her own. She asked if he knew about the separate account.

He texted back right away.

No idea. What's in it?

She spread the papers out on the floor and put them in order. There was a weekly $1,000 transfer to the joint account that Jake promptly withdrew and redeposited in the other account. From there, he made payments to NetBookie, presumably in the amounts he was betting, and then there were deposits, periodically, for what she assumed were his winnings.

The dollar sizes of the bets were usually in the hundreds or thousands. Nothing higher than four figures. For a period of more than a year, the account balance ranged from $50,000 to $70,000. He seemed to make more money than he lost. Then there started to be a downward trajectory – lots of bets, very few wins – and, in a matter of months, the account balance plummeted. Three months ago, the account balance was only $578. The two most recent envelopes from the bank were unopened, and when Caitlin tore into them, she saw there were no transactions whatsoever. Nothing going in, nothing coming out.

The most recent statements from the joint account were nowhere to be found. She called Garrett and asked him to check their joint account on his phone or laptop. After a few minutes of searching, Garrett deduced that, in recent months, the gambling allowance stayed in the joint account.

Conclusion: Jake was saving his gambling money rather than spending it.

'Check for recent transactions,' she told him. 'Anything right before he went missing.'

Garrett took a minute to look.

'An Uber charge,' he said. 'That's it.'

He told her the date, and she quickly checked Google to verify that was the night of the last game of the Eastern Conference Finals.

'How much?' Caitlin asked.

'A hundred and seventy-six dollars,' he said.

'That's an expensive car ride, isn't it?'

'What do you think it means?' Garrett said. 'I mean, the separate account, not the Uber thing.'

'It looks like this other account was devoted to gambling,' she said. 'Probably to keep what he was doing hidden from you. Or, like you said, to make sure he only used his allowance for it. But it looks like he was only betting with his winnings. Kind of like someone who goes to Vegas and says, "I'm only going to gamble with five hundred bucks. Once it's gone, I'm done."'

'Except there are plenty of people who can't stop when they get to that point,' Garrett said. 'I'm not confident Jake would be the kind of person who could stop.'

She had a thought.

'Wait a sec,' she said, walking back into the kitchen.

She looked through the business cards stuck behind magnets on the fridge again. From behind a magnet showing the skyline of Portland, she plucked the card for the therapist.

Ashley Hartmann
COUNSELOR, LPCC
Addiction: Alcohol, drugs, sex, porn, gambling

'You're not seeing a therapist, are you?'

'No,' Garrett said. 'Why?'

'I think your brother was trying to quit gambling.'

31

Caitlin sat at a table next to a balcony in the Cincinnati/Northern Kentucky International Airport, overlooking a spacious atrium busy with families and individuals bustling through on their way to different terminals and restaurants.

She'd checked her SIG Sauer, in its safe, and her roller bag, but she had a large purse with her laptop inside as her carryon. She had forty minutes before her flight was scheduled to board, and she felt sad. She'd never been away from Alex for more than a couple of days. He was growing so fast, and she cursed herself for not spending every moment she could with him. Life was mostly looking at the clock and knowing you were running out of time. She was in her thirties – it wasn't like she was getting old – but having a child was a dramatic way to mark the passing of time. She had only ten years left before he would be getting ready for college. If the last seven were any indication, it would be here before she knew it.

She picked up her phone off the table and opened the calendar. Today was Thursday. Game Four was tomorrow in Vegas. Game Five was Monday, back in Cinci. Game Six was a week from today, in Vegas. And Game Seven, if the series went that far, was the following Sunday.

Garrett told her he was supposed to throw tomorrow's game. Assuming that happened, the series was guaranteed to go at least six. She had a feeling the kidnappers wanted the series to go all seven games. They could maximize their profits that way. Garrett hadn't delivered Game Three the way they wanted, and he said they beat Jake up pretty badly as a result. But they hadn't killed him. Their threats of killing Jake were probably empty until the end of the series. They might hurt him, but as long as there was another game, they wouldn't kill him. But once the series was over – to use an expression that seemed particularly apt in this case – all bets were off.

At that point, she figured Garrett was correct – Jake was dead.

If she stayed in Vegas that whole time, that was well over a week away from Owen and Alex.

She often grappled with the knowledge her most important role on earth was being there for her son, yet she went to a job every day that put her in danger. She reconciled this conflict by telling herself someone had to do the job. But there was no fooling herself into thinking that taking a gun with her on a secret kidnapping investigation to Las Vegas was a reasonable risk to take.

This isn't your job, she scolded. *You're trying to prove something to yourself.*

But if she didn't find Jake, who would?

Someone had to do it.

She needed to distract herself from these thoughts, so she opened her laptop, did a quick search to find who regulated gaming in Nevada, and found the website for the Nevada Gaming Control Board. After a minute of browsing, she discovered a law enforcement branch. She searched for a number to call.

She checked the time, thought about waiting until she was in Vegas, then decided this was at least something she could do now.

'Nevada Gaming Control Board,' said the friendly female voice on the other end. 'How may I direct your call?'

Caitlin told the receptionist she was an officer in a police department in Ohio and she wanted to talk to someone specializing in sports betting.

'Oh,' the voice said, 'if you want to know about sports betting, you'll want to talk to Levi. Hang on a sec.'

While she was on hold, Caitlin searched the site and found a profile for a man named Levi Grayson, deputy chief of the Las Vegas office. There was a picture. He looked to be in his fifties, with a full head of graying brown hair and the kind of face that looked like it had a five o'clock shadow even when it was freshly shaved. He had a square jaw and a chin dimple, looking a bit like a grizzled version of Huey Lewis. She preferred music from the Seventies over the Eighties, but she remembered the singer's face from old cassettes her mom had in her car growing up.

'Grayson,' said a hoarse voice on the other end of the phone.

'I'm a police officer in Ohio,' Caitlin said, nervous even though she'd thought through what to say. 'Our department is looking into a possible illegal sports book in our county. There was the suggestion from a source that point-shaving might be going on in the NBA Finals. I thought it wouldn't hurt to call and see if you've heard anything.'

Grayson, all business, asked Caitlin her name and department, and she felt herself sweating under her shirt as she answered. This was a stupid idea, she realized, but she couldn't think of a way to get out of it now that she'd begun.

'I'm looking for background information,' she said. 'Honestly, I just don't know enough about sports betting.'

This was true. She and Owen went on a riverboat casino in Indiana last summer with his bike club, and Owen entertained himself by betting on some of the baseball games going on that night, but she hadn't been remotely interested. Any sort of gambling seemed like throwing money away.

'Well,' Grayson said, sounding like he was relaxing. She thought she could hear him easing back into his office chair. 'To start with, it's really unlikely the NBA Finals are rigged. That kind of thing just doesn't happen.'

'Really?' Caitlin said. 'I mean . . .' She tried to sound like she was speculating. '. . . what about point-shaving? Is that what it's called?'

'Not likely,' he said.

He explained that point-shaving was more common in college. For one, point spreads were often larger in college. There was more room for error. But NBA spreads were tighter, making such a thing trickier, especially if the player wanted to shave points but still win.

'Hell of a lot easier making sure the score falls within a thirteen-point range than a three-point range.'

Another reason: NBA players made a lot of money, especially the ones who had the power to control games. A broke college player might get involved in something like point-shaving, but there wasn't much motivation for a pro.

'I'm not saying it's never happened,' he said. 'There were rumors in the Eighties that the Bad Boy Pistons shaved points to pay off gambling debts, but nothing was ever proven. And there was a ref who went to jail for betting on games he was working. But that was fifteen or twenty years ago, and the league really cracked down after that. So refs are really scrutinized these days, and players have no motivation for doing it. That's not much of a recipe for rigging games.'

'What if, I don't know, someone was compelled to do it against their will?' Caitlin asked, and when there was a pause on the other end, she added, 'I'm just curious. Trying to figure out the viability of all this.'

'The thing is,' he said, 'if you had some dirt on an NBA player, you could just ask for a bribe. No need to go through the extra effort. That's a lot of risk and effort for everyone when you're talking about someone who probably already has access to a lot of wealth. A college player, maybe, but not a pro.

'Look at it like this,' he added. 'Let's say you bet ten grand on the Lightning last night to cover the spread. Or not even to cover the spread – just a money line bet.'

'What's a money line bet?'

'You just pick the winner and don't worry about the spread. But how much it pays out depends on whether the team was favored or not.'

'So if you pick the team that's favored, you make less?'

'Yeah,' Grayson said. 'And if you pick the underdog, it pays a little more. But the point I'm trying to make is that ten grand is a big bet. In a Vegas casino, that's going to draw some attention. They're going to call the manager down and get him to approve it. So you're on their radar. And if you win, you're definitely going in their book. They don't let you walk away with a big payday without taking note. Plus, they'd have to do a CTR – a currency transaction report – which means there's a paper trail, and no one rigging games is going to want that. Even if you went through all that trouble, a ten grand bet would get you only nine grand in return. Nine grand is a lot to you or me – we're cops, not high rollers – and it's probably a lot to your average college player. But not when we're talking about an NBA player's salary. If you had enough dirt on a player to get him to shave points, you could probably get him to give you nine grand.'

Caitlin remembered Garrett saying he'd offered the kidnappers five million and they'd refused.

'If you were looking to make lots of money, a million, or ten million, or more, you're going to have to place bets all over the place. In Vegas. Online. At illegal books. There are illegal Asian markets that might let you make a hundred grand bet. To make really big bucks would be a hell of a lot of work, especially when the person at the center of it all is already pretty damn well paid.'

'I see,' Caitlin said.

She had the feeling whoever was behind Jake Streeter's kidnapping might not know what they're doing. Either that, or they *really* knew what they were doing.

'It just wouldn't happen, not in today's game,' Grayson said. 'Jaxon Luca makes forty million *per year*. Not counting endorsements. Elijah Carter probably makes thirty or forty. Garrett Streeter makes a lot less, but he's still a millionaire.

'And you'd have to get a star to do the shaving,' Grayson said. 'A scrub on the bench won't have much control over the game one way or another. Even the bench warmers are not exactly poor – the league minimum is over a million dollars a year, I think.'

Caitlin felt a little sick from Grayson's talk of money. Someone who was in the league for one year would make more than she would in fifteen as a cop.

'Elijah Carter and Garrett Streeter play for the Sabertooths, right?' Caitlin said, trying to act stupid.

'Not a basketball fan, huh?'

'Not exactly,' she said, her mouth dry. 'And I know less about gambling. Which is why I called you. Sounds like there's probably nothing to this.'

She was anxious to get off the phone. She wanted Chief Deputy Levi Grayson to move onto other things and forget this phone call ever happened.

And she had a plane to catch.

'You know,' Grayson said, drawing the words out, 'come to think of it, these games have been pretty wonky. I mean, there have been two huge comebacks. Completely improbable.'

'Is that right?' Caitlin said, again trying to sound clueless. 'Like you said, it doesn't really make sense for someone to try it.'

'I'll tell you what,' Grayson said, 'there are organizations that look into this type of thing. One called Athletic Integrity here in the States, and another in Europe called SportWatch. They analyze betting at hundreds of books around the world, legal and illegal alike. They look for anomalies. Like if there's an unusual surge in betting, especially betting that ends up paying out, they pick up on it. Then the sports association, like the NBA or FIFA or NCAA, can take a look at the game to see if there were any questionable actions on the parts of the players or refs.'

'And they monitor illegal sports books as well?' she asked. 'The criminals give them that information?'

'Illegal books don't want people cheating either,' he said. 'The whole point of being a bookie is to make money, not lose it. Athletic Integrity and SportWatch aren't trying to crack down on them. They're trying to crack down on cheaters in sports. The players or refs or whoever.'

Grayson told Caitlin he'd put in a couple of calls to see if the watchdogs noticed anything.

'You don't have to do that for me,' she said, rising from her seat and heading toward the terminal with her purse over her shoulder. She wanted to get off the phone. 'I'm just looking into a small-time bookie here in Ohio.'

'Oh, I'm curious now,' he said. 'This isn't the type of thing I usually do. My job is mostly to crack down on illegal books. This is Nevada – we want to make sure gambling happens in tax-paying casinos. But if someone is fixing the NBA Finals, holy crap, that would be something.'

32

The sun was low in the sky as Caitlin steered her rented Ford Explorer down the Las Vegas Strip, dumbfounded by the sights. She'd only been to Vegas once before when she and Yaz and Jake drove up for the NCAA playoffs when Garrett's team went deep in the tournament. But it was one night only. They were college kids with no money, crashing in one of the older, less expensive casinos off Fremont Street. She and Yaz shared the bed. Jake slept on the floor. He and Yaz stayed out late and explored the city, but Caitlin hadn't been in the mood after Garrett's loss, which is why she'd ended up driving Yaz's little Subaru back to Phoenix while they slept in the car, stinking of cigarettes and beer.

Now, a decade later, she looked around the city with a strange sense of awe. Not really impressed but more stunned that a place like this existed.

A fake volcano in front of the Mirage erupted with fire and what appeared to be water illuminated with a red light to look like lava. She passed the monstrous Caesars Palace and its pools and faux marble columns. In front of the Bellagio, she spotted the fountains she'd seen in the movie *Ocean's Eleven*, spraying in a coordinated routine.

The city was an assault on the senses – noise and color coming from every direction, too much to take in at once. But it didn't look nearly as fancy or romantic as movies might lead people to believe. Everything was a simulation – a spectacle – of something else. New York-New York came into view, like a giant child's model of the city, and then the Luxor, a huge black pyramid that looked more like a space station than anything the ancient Egyptians might have built. Even more alien, the Las Vegas Sphere stood in the distance, like a giant marble dropped from another dimension.

She spotted Bolt Arena a few blocks off the Strip, where the Lightning and Sabertooths would be playing tomorrow. Among the spectacle of Vegas, the arena actually looked demure.

Garrett's hotel, the Florentine, was up ahead, looking like a cathedral from Italy, with long arches, gothic buttresses, and a massive dome tiled with brick-red shingles. She found herself circling upward in a tall parking garage, then taking an elevator that smelled like urine down to the hotel. She walked through the lobby, looking up at the arched ceiling which was painted to look like some kind of Italian fresco. Here, the hotel did come across as quite glamorous, unlike the kitschy simulacrum she'd observed driving through the city. The polished floor gleamed with reflected light. The walls were lined with statues of robed men, no women, with placards underneath identifying them with familiar names like Dante Alighieri and Leonardo da Vinci. They couldn't have been made of actual marble but looked real enough.

She waited to text Garrett until she was in her room. For all the Florentine's opulence, her room was nothing special. Small even.

What room are you in? she texted Garrett.

502, he answered.

When she got into the elevator again, she saw 50 was the top floor. Once out of the elevator, the first door she passed was 501. She heard female laughter and hip-hop music coming from inside. Garrett poked his head out of the neighboring room, ushering her to hurry. Caitlin stepped quickly past 501 and ducked inside Garrett's.

His room was ten times the size of hers, with a high ceiling and huge windows overlooking Las Vegas. As she walked past the bathroom, she spotted a bathtub nearly as big as a twin bed. There was a sunken living-room area she stepped down to, with couches facing each other.

'Nice place,' she said, as she walked to the window and looked out at the city.

'Is your room OK?' Garrett asked

'It's just like this one.'

'Really?'

'No,' she said, and let out a laugh. 'But it's fine.'

Garrett pointed out that Elijah's room was next door. They could hear the muffled sound of music through the walls.

'He likes that one because it has a stripper pole,' he said.

'I think he's making use of it right now.'

'He'll get it out of his system tonight,' Garrett said. 'Then it's all business tomorrow.'

'Whatever works,' Caitlin said, lowering down into one of the couches, which was stiff with very little cushion – more about appearance than comfort.

Garrett sat adjacent to her. He looked slightly better today. Tired and anxious, but not as strung out as the last time she'd seen him.

'Will Summer be staying with you?' Caitlin asked.

He shook his head. 'Unofficial policy,' he said. 'Family and friends in another hotel. It's not usually an issue during the season. Families don't travel that often. But wives and girlfriends want to come to the Finals, bring the kids, you know. So they stay in a different hotel.'

'So you're not distracted?'

He tilted his head side to side as if to say she was close, but not quite.

'Ah,' she said. 'I see. To make room for other guests. Like whoever's dancing on Elijah Carter's pole.'

Garrett looked embarrassed.

'Lots of guys have things on the side,' he said. 'Elijah has girlfriends in half the cities in the Eastern Conference.'

Caitlin rolled her eyes. Fucking professional athletes.

'I never do anything like that,' Garrett said. 'I'm not that kind of guy.'

'I know, Street. You didn't even have to say.'

He sat back, looking relieved she still held him in high regard.

'It's got to be rough on a relationship,' Caitlin said. 'All the travel you do.'

'Summer travels a lot, too. We're used to being apart. Now can we talk about my brother, please?'

'Sure. Do you know where Jake was staying?'

'The Galaxia,' he said. 'Same place Summer's staying.'

'What do you think happened to your brother's stuff?' she asked. 'You think the hotel cleaned it out? Took it somewhere?'

'When I got the message from the kidnappers, I called the hotel to see if he'd checked out, and he had. Right after the Eastern Conference Finals.'

Caitlin pulled out her phone – the burner – and called the hotel.

'Hi,' she said to the person who answered. 'I work for Garrett Streeter, the basketball star. His brother was checked in over there and I have a question about the reservation. The credit card is in Garrett's name, and I can give you the card number if you'd like.'

Once the person looked up the account information, she asked Caitlin what she could do for her.

'Did Jake leave anything behind in his room?' she said.

The woman said there was nothing in the file. Caitlin couldn't get her to disclose the room number, but the woman said people have been in and out of the room for more than a week. If he'd left behind anything, it would have been reported. Or thrown away.

Caitlin hung up.

'So either Jake was taken after he checked out,' Caitlin said, 'or whoever took him packed up his stuff before his reservation expired.'

'What does that mean?' Garrett said.

She explained that if the FBI or local police were involved, they could check the hotel's security footage and might see when Jake last left the room and if anyone went in or out afterward.

'But it's just me,' Caitlin added, pointedly. 'So it doesn't help much.'

'What do we do now?' Garrett asked.

'I've got some questions for you,' she said. 'Can you think of anyone who might be behind this?'

He shook his head with a look that said, *What a stupid question.*

'Most crimes,' Caitlin said, 'are committed by people the victim already knows. Whoever is doing this probably has some connection to you. I need you to think about anyone who might have seemed at all suspicious lately. Your teammates. Your coach. Your girlfriend. Your opponents.'

'We're in the NBA Finals,' Garrett said. 'Everyone's under a ton of pressure. No one is acting normal. But,' he added, 'no one seems to be acting in a way I wouldn't expect.'

'Keep your eyes open.'

'Fine,' he said. 'But Jake disappeared in Las Vegas. The gambling capital of the world. That's not a coincidence. I don't think it's someone *I* know. I think it's someone Jake knows.'

'Fair enough,' she said.

He nodded, and she was quiet. The silence sat awkwardly in the room.

'What's going through your mind?' Garrett said. 'I'm not some perp you can't open up to.'

'You're not going to like what I have to say.'

'Spill it, Glass.'

'What about Jake?' Caitlin asked.

'What about him?'

'Is there any chance he's involved in this voluntarily?' she asked.

'That he's faking it?'

'If Jake needed money, all he'd have to do is ask,' Garrett said. 'Maybe you two had a falling out you're not telling me about. Or maybe he's afraid you'd cut him off if he asked. Or maybe—'

Garrett yanked a phone out of his pocket. He pulled up a video and handed it to Caitlin. She watched, her stomach roiling, as the men assaulted Jake.

Garrett hadn't shown this to her yet.

'Now you see that's the stupidest idea in the world,' he said, pocketing the phone.

'I'm sorry,' Caitlin said. 'It was a reasonable question. No decent investigator wouldn't at least ask the question.'

'Yeah,' Garrett said, looking exhausted. 'But that's why I came to you. You know Jake. You know he wouldn't do this. You don't have to waste your time on that shit.'

'OK,' she said. 'I don't want this to be adversarial. But I need you to understand I'm running this investigation. When I've got a question, you answer it. No holding back. Otherwise, I walk, and you can deal with this on your own.'

Garrett glared at her but agreed. She wanted to ask him about Summer but knew she'd get the same answer, and the question would just piss him off more.

'Have you told me everything you can think of?' she asked. 'Anything you forgot to mention?'

He shook his head. She got the feeling he might be holding something back, but she decided not to push it.

'I need money to cover my expenses. Reimbursement for my flight. Rental car. Hotel. Spending money, too – for who knows what. Food. Gas. I don't want to need the money and not have it.'

'You want one of my credit cards?'

'Nothing can be in your name,' she said. 'I'll use my own credit cards if I can't use cash, but I'll reimburse myself with what you give me. I'll keep track of everything like I'm a private investigator.'

'No need for that,' he said. 'I trust you. How much?'

'Ten thousand,' Caitlin said. 'I'll give back whatever I don't spend.'

Garrett waved off the idea, then rose to his feet and walked into one of the bedrooms. He came back a few minutes later and fanned out ten stacks of hundred-dollar bills on the glass coffee table in front of her. It didn't look like much, actually. Ten stacks of ten bills – one hundred thin slips of paper.

'I didn't expect you to give it all to me right now,' she said. 'You always carry this much with you?'

'Usually.'

'Why?'

He shrugged.

'Seriously,' she said. 'What could you need ten grand for?'

'I'm not in college anymore, Glass. We don't eat McDonald's on road trips. We don't order pizza from Domino's. Every major city in the country has a restaurant where the entrées will run you a hundred bucks or more. Or if some of the guys want to go to a club to celebrate a win, everybody throws money around on three-hundred-dollar bottles of champagne. And we don't take an Uber to get where we're going. We take limos. We don't skimp on tips. No waiter or bellboy out there is complaining about serving the Cincinnati Sabertooths. I'm more frugal than most of the guys, I think, but I keep cash on hand just in case. It's the life.'

She couldn't believe how different his life was from hers. She and Owen didn't have ten thousand in savings. Not even close. To Garrett, it was pocket cash.

Caitlin gave her head a little shake, then thought for a moment.

'Can you get me a ticket for tomorrow's game? I want to have a look around. See if I spot anything suspicious.'

'No problem,' he said. 'What else?'

'Get a good night's sleep.' Caitlin rose to her feet. 'You've got a big day tomorrow.'

'They want us to lose.'

'But you have to *seem* like you're trying to win.'

'What about you?'

'I'm going to get started.'

'I'm coming with you,' Garrett said.

'Not a chance, Street. No one can see us together. We don't know who could be in on this.'

33

Garrett walked her to the door. She wasn't two steps into the hallway when the door to Room 501 swung open and two women tumbled out, laughing. One had long black braids – probably extensions – hanging down to her waist, the other had chocolate hair layered with purple streaks. Both were in short skirts that barely covered anything and tight blouses that showed off ample cleavage. They had long fake lashes and glitter on their skin and colored nails like velociraptor talons. When they spotted Caitlin, they stifled their giggles.

Elijah Carter stood behind them, wearing only boxer briefs and holding the door open with one hand. His face was alight with his signature smile, and when he glanced at Caitlin, then to Garrett, then back to Caitlin, the smile broadened.

'All right!' he said, clearly enjoying catching his straight-edge, one-woman-only teammate with someone besides his model girl-friend. 'Way to go, Streeter!'

Caitlin ignored him as she walked past.

'It's not what you think,' Garrett said.

'Of course not,' Elijah bellowed, laughing loudly as he closed his door.

So much for not being seen together, Caitlin thought.

She pressed the elevator button. When it arrived, the two women joined her inside, their demeanor different. They'd dropped the façade now that their customer was out of sight.

'How much does he pay?' Caitlin said. 'If you don't mind me asking.'

'A lot,' the girl with the braids said, checking her reflection in the mirror and applying lipstick. 'What about your guy?'

'We're friends,' Caitlin said.

'You're pretty,' the other said, looking closely at Caitlin. 'You've got great skin. And those lashes – they're not even fake, are they?'

Caitlin shook her head.

'Get the right clothes and put on some makeup,' the girl said. 'You could make a lot of money.'

'Is your company hiring?' Caitlin quipped, trying to keep the playful conversation going.

'Honey,' she said, '*I'm* my own company. But if you want some tips about getting started, give me a call.'

She handed Caitlin a card with the name *Amethyst* in a flowing purple script. Underneath, in more legible writing, was a 702-number. In the bottom right-hand corner was a small illustration of a red rose.

The elevator arrived at the bottom, opening to the noise of the casino.

'Thanks,' Caitlin said. 'I might be looking for a career change.'

The women headed through the lobby toward the exit, but Caitlin entered the casino. Slot machines clanged around her. Cocktail waitresses zipped past with trays of drinks. The place was a labyrinth, and she walked around confused for a few minutes, passing a zone of blackjack stations and craps tables, past a roulette wheel, until she spotted what she was looking for.

The sports book.

She came to the threshold of the large area and squinted through a haze of smoke to the huge wraparound screen on the wall, probably a hundred feet long and ten feet high, divided into rectangles showing various sporting events from around the world. Baseball was on most of the screens, but others featured soccer, golf, tennis, rugby, a horse race, an MMA fight, a game of cornhole, and a hot-dog-eating contest. She had no idea if any or all of the events were live – or if you could bet on everything on display – but the sports book had plenty of bettors nursing drinks while staring up at the screens. Everyone was watching intently, seriously. There wasn't the same bombast you'd experience in a sports bar on a game day. The atmosphere was subdued. These guys – and they were mostly men – looked more like people awaiting the results of an MRI than fans rooting for a favorite team.

She wasn't sure what she could find out here, but, with the exception of one tiny kiosk on a riverboat cruise, she'd never been in a sports book before and mostly wanted to see what it was like. The area was massive, maybe half an acre, with lots of seats positioned facing the screen. The chairs swiveled so patrons could get a look at different angles of the various games. There was a bar with at least fifty different beers on tap and a large board extending toward the ceiling listing all the available betting lines – lots of numbers written in a code she didn't understand.

She slipped her engagement ring and wedding band off, tucked them into her pocket, and approached the counter where bets were made.

'My boyfriend wanted me to place a bet,' she told the guy behind the counter. 'But I don't know what I'm doing.'

'What sport do you want to bet on?' he asked, smiling at her with teeth that looked yellow in the muted light.

'Basketball,' she said, 'but, you know, come to think of it, I can't remember if he told me he places his bets here.'

'There are twenty sports books on the Strip.'

She pulled out her phone and opened a picture of Jake that Garrett sent. In it, he was standing in front of the Cincinnati Art Museum and smiling. 'Do you recognize this guy?'

The bookie, if that's what you called these guys, shook his head. 'Sorry,' he said. 'We get lots of customers. And I wouldn't be allowed to tell you anyway.'

'Really?' she said, trying to come across as friendly, borderline flirtatious. 'You wouldn't tell me?'

'I might tell you,' he said, smiling. 'But I'm not supposed to.'

If there were twenty sports books on the Strip, not to mention off the Strip, she would be in for a long night if she showed Jake's picture around all of them. She was looking for witnesses – people who'd seen him in the days or hours preceding his disappearance – but, for all she knew, he might not have set foot in a single sports book. All evidence of past betting was online. And, she reminded herself, he might not have been gambling at all before he was taken.

Then again, why did he come to Vegas early, before the Finals started, if he wasn't planning to gamble?

She told the guy she was too nervous to place the bet and would come back after talking to her boyfriend. He moved on to a different customer.

She checked the time, considered the time difference between Nevada and Ohio, and realized she'd missed the opportunity to tell her son goodnight. There were plenty of times where she felt desperate for a break from being a mother, but now that she had it, all she could think about was how much she missed Alex.

Even if she couldn't talk to Alex, Owen would be expecting a call. She tried him but, when he didn't answer, she headed out of the sports book and back into the casino. She had an idea.

If her charm couldn't get her any answers, maybe the wad of Garrett's money in her pocket could.

34

aitlin found a cage where she could exchange money for chips. She peeled off ten one-hundred-dollar bills and handed them to the woman behind the counter. The employee took the money like it was a trivial amount and slid her a plastic dish with ten black chips. Caitlin thought the amount didn't look impressive enough, and she handed the woman two thousand more, asking for different denominations.

As the woman was assembling her tray of black, orange, and green chips, Caitlin checked her phone. Missed call from Owen.

'Shit,' she muttered.

She thought about calling back, but then she considered the noise of the casino all around her and the difficulty she might have in giving Owen her attention.

Sorry I missed you, she texted. I'll call you in the morning.

Back at the book, Caitlin waved down a cocktail waitress, who was wearing a sparkling skirt with a hem almost as short as the ones that the prostitutes coming out of Elijah Carter's room had been wearing.

'Can I get you something, hon?'

Caitlin ordered a Corona with a lime and held her tray of chips prominently, wanting the woman to make note.

'You ever see this guy before?' she asked, holding out the pic of Jake on her phone.

'Hmm,' the server said, really looking. 'Maybe. Lots of guys come in here.'

Caitlin told her he might have been here for an NBA playoff game.

'Can't be sure,' she said. 'But you know what you could do?' She gestured toward a group of guys. 'That gentleman over there in the cowboy hat is Richie. He places bets all over town. He might remember your friend.'

Caitlin watched Richie while she waited for the woman to return with her beer. He had long stringy hair coming from underneath a black cowboy hat. Despite the hat, he didn't look like a cowboy.

He had round wire-rimmed glasses, a narrow, bearded face, and a cerebral look to him, almost like John Lennon trying to go under-cover at a rodeo. The three guys around him all looked younger and kept turning to Richie to make comments, never the other way around. It was easy to see they were the sycophants while Richie was the leader.

She thought about what tack she should take with Richie. Her flimsy story about placing a bet for her boyfriend wasn't going to work. She needed a new plan.

She slipped her rings back on her finger.

When the waitress arrived with her beer, Caitlin squeezed the lime and pushed it down into the bottle. She approached the four men and stood in front of them, blocking their view.

'Hey, guys,' she said, trying to sound over-the-top friendly, which she knew she wasn't quite pulling off – another indication, if she needed one, that the PR job the sheriff was offering wasn't a natural fit.

She looked at the three lackeys, not directly at Richie, then pulled three chips out of her case and flipped them to the men one at a time.

'I saw an open blackjack table over there with your names on it. Why don't you boys go play a few hands and let me talk to your friend here?'

Richie stared at her, unsure what her game was, but he nodded and the three men sauntered off, as happy as a trio of frat guys given free beers. Now that she was in front of him, she saw Richie wore a T-shirt with the words, *WHAT HAPPENS IN VEGAS HAPPENS TO ME EVERY DAY.*

Caitlin sat down, crossed her legs – which didn't quite have the effect it would if she was wearing a skirt – and sat back. She took a sip from her beer.

Richie tipped the brim of his hat. 'What can I do you for, ma'am?'

'Call me "miss,"' she said. '"Ma'am" makes me sound like an old lady.'

'Miss,' he said. His eyes traveled up and down her body. 'You sure ain't an old lady.'

She held up her hand and showed him her rings.

'My dirt-bag husband has a gambling problem,' she said.

'Sucks for you.'

She showed him the picture of Jake.

'Ever seen this guy?' she said. 'Here or at any of the other casinos?'

He leaned forward, looked at the picture.

'No.'

'You sure?'

'I'm good with faces.'

'You'd remember him if you saw him?'

The corners of his mouth curved slightly into the hint of a smile. 'I'm going to remember yours.'

She took a black chip, placed it on the surface of the table, and slid it forward with one finger. 'No, you're not.'

His grin widened. 'You're right. You've got a forgettable face.'

'What's the highest bet you can make at a place like this?' Caitlin said, trying to sound conversational.

'A nobody walking up to the counter?' he asked. 'Someone they haven't seen before? Two or three grand, maybe. A big game, with a lot of bets down on both sides, they'd take more because now they've got insurance whatever way the coin lands. They might go as high as ten.'

Caitlin leaned forward, trying to look as serious as possible.

'Chump change,' she said. 'Where do you go in this town if you want to lay down real money? And where do you go if you want to make those bets on credit?'

What she really wanted to know was who were the major players in charge of illegal sports betting in Vegas.

'Lady,' Richie said, sitting forward, so they were both leaning toward each other, talking closely, 'can I give you some advice?'

She could smell his body odor – the smell of a man who needed to get out of the casino once in a while and take a shower.

'Go home,' he said. 'Get a divorce lawyer. File the papers. Leave your husband behind and never think about him again. You got dealt a losing hand on your wedding day. Best to go ahead and fold now before it gets worse for you.'

'I plan to,' she said. 'But first I want to know how deep he's in.'

'No, you don't.'

'Where would someone go if they were placing big bets?' she said, ignoring his suggestion. 'And if someone was in debt to someone else, who would that be?'

His eyes darted down to the stack of chips. She regretted getting so many now. How much was it going to cost her? He exhaled and leaned back in his seat, before speaking again.

'Two possibilities,' he said, holding up his fingers like a peace sign. 'There are plenty of people who will loan you a grand here or there. Loan sharks who will let you make bets on credit. With a steep vig. But if you're talking big money, tens of thousands of dollars, fifty grand and up, *on credit* – if that's the kind of thing your husband is into – then he's got to be dealing with one of two people.'

This was exactly what she wanted to know.

'I'll tell you.' He grinned. 'For a thousand dollars a name.'

35

Caitlin leaned back, showing her annoyance. She wondered about the world this guy inhabited. How did someone get to the point where they were a regular at a casino sports book? It must be addictive, she supposed, the thrill of winning. The flood of dopamine into the brain from the first time you picked a winner must be something you seek more and more. Maybe gambling was like basketball in that way – chasing the highs you once felt. In basketball, your body tells you when you're done. But in gambling, maybe you never get the message.

The money wasn't hers and Garrett had plenty to spare, but she felt like she was being taken advantage of.

Smug prick.

'I'll give you the two grand,' Caitlin said, using a firm voice. 'But if I find out you've led me astray, I'm going to come looking for you. It won't be hard. All I need to do is ask around, say I'm looking for Richie. Looks like John Lennon in a cowboy hat.'

'You're not some disgruntled housewife, are you?'

'That's exactly what I am,' she said, meaning every word, although not the way Richie understood her.

She took out two grand in chips and put it on the table in front of Richie.

'Names?'

He pulled the chips to him.

'Silas Bennett,' he said. 'You know the name?'

She shook her head.

'Kind of a minor celebrity around here. Owns a brothel out of

town. Rubs elbows with county commissioners and B-grade movie
stars. Seems like a respectable businessman, or as respectable as
you can be running prostitutes. But he's got his fingers in other
things. One is sports betting. Makes a lot of money on high-interest
loans to gamblers hoping for a payday. Steep interest.' He pointed
a finger at Caitlin for emphasis. 'He always collects. Doesn't matter
if you have to sell your house or if you have to give blowjobs in
back alleys – everybody pays.'

'Sounds like a lovely guy,' Caitlin said.

'You better hope that's who your husband is in with,' Richie said.
'Because the other guy is worse.' He looked around, lowered his
voice. 'Alexei Maxim. Russian mafia. Into everything. Prostitution,
of course – and not the legal kind out in brothels or the high-end
stuff you can get in the city. We're talking girls brought in from
other countries, hooked on heroin. Use the girls up and toss them
aside. He loves betting. Any sport, legal or illegal.'

Caitlin made a face to question what an illegal sport would be.

'Street racing,' he said. 'Cockfights. Dog fights.'

'Oh.'

'They call Vegas Sin City, but this guy really does peddle sin.
As dirty as it gets, to anyone who will pay for it.'

Caitlin fought the urge to swallow. Maybe Alexei Maxim was
the kind of guy who would kidnap an NBA star's brother.

'Only the most desperate or stupid go to him for loans,' Richie
said. 'I told you Silas Bennett always collects. Well, people who
are into Alexei Maxim for a lot of money sometimes disappear.
Rumor is he's got a doctor who will harvest your organs to sell on
the black market. If giving up a kidney is enough to pay your debts,
it will end there. But if it's not, they'll take everything. And you'll
agree to it because they'll threaten your wife and kids. Understand
what I'm saying? They keep you alive on the operating table for as
long as they can. Take your kidney, your liver, a lung. Once you
flatline, they take everything else they can get. Your heart. Your
eyes. That is how someone at the end of their rope pays their debts
to Alexei Maxim.'

Caitlin felt sick.

'If your husband up and disappears,' Richie said, 'then maybe
take that as a sign he died to protect *you*.'

Caitlin let out a breath. She looked down at her chips. She had
six hundred dollars' worth, minus the five-dollar tip to the waitress.

'One more thing.' She slid the chip case over to Richie, who raised his eyebrow in surprise. 'This is to make sure you forget about me. Don't even think about going to one of these guys and telling them I'm looking for them.'

'Lady,' he said, 'you don't have anything to worry about. I steer clear of those guys. I do everything by the book.' He gestured to the sports book around him, as if the evidence was in the fact that he was in a legal casino. 'But I'll take your tip, thank you.'

He gathered the case toward him and started placing the loose chips into the empty slots.

'Have a nice night,' he said, looking at her pointedly. 'Ma'am.'

36

'Mommy,' Alex said, 'did you know a day is longer than a year on Venus?'

'It is?' Caitlin said.

She was staring at her son on FaceTime. He was eating his breakfast while showing her a book about outer space that he and Owen checked out of the library.

'Yeah,' he said. 'It turns on its axis slower than it revolves around the sun. Can you believe that?'

'I can't,' she said, amazed for the millionth time about all the things she'd learned by having a curious kid.

She was sitting at the little table by her hotel window, a plate of rubbery fried eggs and a slice of limp toast in front of her.

'We probably should go,' Owen said, wedging his face onto the screen next to Alex. 'Tell Garrett we're rooting for him.'

Caitlin was touched by the sentiment.

If he was feeling any insecurity about her hanging out with her ex, he at least wasn't showing it.

'Love you both,' she declared before pressing the *END* tab.

Alex seemed to be doing OK without her, which hurt her heart a little. She missed her family. She longed to be in her own home, with her everyday domestic challenges, rather than here in this weird world, daunted by an investigative task far beyond her experience. Richie's talk last night of brothel owners and Russian gangsters rattled her. This was a dangerous game, and it felt like a betrayal to her family that she was here playing it.

Out her window, Vegas looked different in the bright morning light. With the garish neon turned off, you could see through the façade a lot easier. It looked like a parody of a city: a bunch of cartoonish-looking buildings thrown up in the middle of the desert with a growing suburbia spreading out around it. The sky was a brilliant blue – nothing like the faded-denim color back in Ohio – and the weather app on her phone told her it was already ninety degrees outside, with a high of one hundred expected today.

She finished her juice, ignored the remainder of her food, and pulled out her cell phone to study the images and video Garrett sent to her. She looked carefully at each photograph, then watched the video over and over.

The gun in the first message was a Glock 19, same as the one issued by her department that she carried every day. It was one of the most popular handguns in America. Hers was gray. This one looked more like a battlefield green. In the later videos, it was a revolver. A .357 or .38 – hard to tell which – with a snub nose.

There were at least four men. One who held the camera and three who committed the assault. They wore black, including face masks and gloves, and it was impossible to tell much about them, even their skin color. In the video where they beat on Jake – which was difficult to watch, an exercise in separating her emotions from her role as an investigator – she got a sense of the men's sizes. One guy seemed about Jake's height, which, if she remembered correctly, was a hair taller than her. So the guy was around six foot. The other two were quite a bit taller, probably at least six-five, maybe taller. They were big bodied, more like football linemen than long-limbed basketball players.

She noted Jake's surprise when they attacked him. Garrett had been told to cover the spread, and, even though the Sabertooths were victorious, he'd failed in that regard. Jake must not have realized what was expected of Garrett.

She put away her phone and got out her laptop. She searched for information about Alexei Maxim and found nothing. He apparently flew completely under the radar. She found a little bit about the Russian mob working in Las Vegas, but even that was just ranting on blogs. If the law enforcement world knew about him, they weren't public about it. Nevada officials probably went to great lengths not to draw attention to criminal behavior in the state's major tourist destination.

When she looked for information on Silas Bennett, she found pages and pages about the brothel owner. While prostitution was legal in some Nevada counties, it was apparently illegal to advertise. However, it seemed Silas Bennett was good at staying in the public eye and raising the profile of his brothel. There were dozens of articles about him in southern Nevada newspapers, and he'd been interviewed on Fox News and the *Howard Stern Show*. He was the president of the Nevada Brothel Association – Caitlin hadn't known such a thing existed – and was active in lobbying the state legislature and donating to the campaigns of Republican politicians.

Silàs Bennett was fifty-four years old – according to his own Wikipedia page – and there were plenty of pictures of him online. He had a trim build and a head as bald as a cue ball. He usually wore a simple outfit of black pants, black jacket, and white button-down shirt. No tie. In most of the pictures, he was posing with working girls, porn stars, or pseudo celebrities. There was a picture of him with a man she didn't recognize licking whipped cream off the cleavage of a giggling woman, her buxom breasts barely covered by a plunging tank top. The other guy had bleached hair, buzzed close to his scalp. Another quasi-famous Las Vegan, she assumed.

She concluded Silas Bennett was a complete narcissist. He liked the public eye, and it was hard to imagine him committing a major crime and not bragging about it to everyone who would listen. Still, he was obviously a sports fan. There were several pictures of him with low- to mid-tier professional athletes who visited the Red Rose Ranch, including some former basketball players she recognized. She wondered if she might find a picture of him with Elijah Carter, but no player of that caliber appeared in any of the photos. No bona fide stars.

Apparently his love of sports betting was well known, with several articles about big sporting events featuring his opinion. There were pictures of him at UNLV basketball and football games. She couldn't find anything about him running an illegal book, or letting bettors make bets on credit, but she wouldn't be surprised if he did. His X and Instagram pages, mostly full of pictures of him posing with his barely dressed employees, showed him at the occasional Lightning home game.

If he bet any money on the Finals, he hadn't posted about it.

She started to close her laptop but stopped herself. She did one more search to find the website for the Red Rose Ranch. The brothel's name was in large letters at the top of the screen, with an illustration of a red rose and the words, *Come inside the Red Rose for a little R&R.* Caitlin was surprised at the restraint in not spelling 'come' as C-U-M. But that was where the site's restraint ended. Below the words, the screen was filled with pictures of women posing seductively in lingerie that hardly covered anything. There were places where you could click and find calendars of the women's availability.

Caitlin poked around for a few minutes. In some of the photo spreads, the women abandoned their clothes altogether or were posed in various stages of undress. Most of the prostitutes – or 'courtesans,' as they were described – were pretty. There were quite a variety of ages, races, and body shapes. There were garishly made-up women with big hair and tons of makeup, but there were also plain-faced girls who couldn't have been much more than eighteen and who actually looked somewhat homely, perhaps capitalizing on men's fantasies of the girl next door. A few of the women's faces were obscured in their photo spreads – either cropped out or turned away from the camera or covered by their hair – but most of the women weren't guarded about their identities.

She pulled out the card the prostitute gave her. The rose illustration on the card matched the logo at the top of the website. She did a search for the name Amethyst and the woman who popped up was one who hid her face in the pictures. But the purple in her hair was recognizable.

Caitlin called the number on the card.

A breathy female voice answered.

'This is Amethyst. I make dreams come true. Leave a message.'

Caitlin did.

37

Several cars came and went through the pickup area, with the bellboys busy keeping on top of the valet parking. She checked her phone to see if her Uber was approaching. It was a white Honda CR-V and, as it rolled up, she climbed into the passenger seat. 'Heading to the game, huh?' the driver asked. He was a thirty-something guy in a plaid button-down shirt and thinning hair on top. 'Traffic's going to be pretty crazy over there. Is it OK if I just get you as close as possible?'

'Sure.'

Ordinarily, she would not have paid for an Uber ride for such a short distance. She could see the roof of Bolt Arena from here. Even in the Las Vegas heat, she would have walked it. But she had other motivations for taking the ride.

She pulled out a one-hundred-dollar bill – brand new, nearly as stiff as card stock – and waved it in the air.

'I've got a nice tip for you,' she said, 'if you can answer a question for me.'

He looked dubious.

'What is this?' he said, glancing around at the traffic on both sides. 'A TV game show?'

'Nope,' she said. 'I have a question I'm hoping an Uber driver can answer.'

'OK,' he said skeptically. 'What's your question?'

'Do you have any idea where you'd need to go to spend a hundred and seventy-six dollars on an Uber if you were staying somewhere in the vicinity of the Florentine or the Galaxia?'

He looked at her side-eyed.

'That's an expensive car ride, right?' she said. 'Las Vegas isn't that big. You can't charge that for zipping people from casino to casino or going to the airport.'

Caitlin had played around on the Internet, trying to find prices. A ride from the Harry Reid International Airport to the Strip ranged from twenty-five to forty-five dollars. A trip from the Strip to the Hoover Dam *and back* wasn't even a hundred and twenty.

'A one-way trip?' the guy asked.

'I'm not sure.'

'Taking an UberX or XL or what?'

'Just an ordinary car.'

They were nearly to the arena already, but the traffic was now bumper to bumper. On the sidewalk, pedestrians decked out in Lightning gear were making better time than the cars.

The driver let out a big huff, as if he knew the answer but wasn't ready to say it.

'Let me guess,' the guy said. 'You found a charge on your husband's credit card?'

'Maybe.'

'How close do you want me to get?' he said, looking out at the traffic jam and changing the subject.

'Look,' Caitlin said, 'this hundred-dollar bill is going to end up in an Uber driver's pocket. It's up to you whether that's you or not.'

'OK, OK.' Another deep breath. 'A lot depends on the time of day. Surge pricing and all that. The same trip can cost you different amounts depending on how many people want a car and how many cars are on the road, you know?'

'I understand,' Caitlin said, 'but I think you've got a location in mind.'

He frowned. 'I'm sorry to tell you this, but it sounds like your husband took a ride out to Green Lawn.'

'What's Green Lawn?'

'A little town out in the desert. Maybe ten thousand people. Over the county line. On the way to Death Valley. I don't know why it's called Green Lawn. It's smack dab in the Mojave Desert. No lawns there and nothing green.'

'So what *is* there?'

The guy looked at her sideways, then out at the traffic. She didn't understand why he seemed so damn reluctant to talk.

'Spit it out,' she said. 'Or I'm getting out of the car and taking my hundred-dollar bill with me.'

'Fine,' he said. 'There are plenty of reasons why someone would go to Green Lawn. But in my experience, all the times I've taken people out there – and it's all usually around a hundred and seventy or a hundred and eighty dollars – is for one reason.'

'Which is?'

'Brothels,' he spat, like the word tasted bad in his mouth.

'Oh,' Caitlin said, understanding the guy's reticence.

He thought her husband cheated on her with a prostitute.

'Prostitution's illegal in Las Vegas,' he said. 'You see plenty of it, but it's not legal. But there's a bunch of brothels out there in Nye County. I've run plenty of guys out there late at night, drunk, with new winnings, and wanting to . . . you know?'

'Is the Red Rose Ranch one of the brothels there?'

She realized this should have occurred to her earlier.

'Yes,' he said. 'That's the biggest. Top-tier, I'd say. By its reputation, I mean.' His cheeks reddened, mortified Caitlin might think he was a customer.

Caitlin said nothing for a moment.

'Miss,' he said, 'you OK?'

'Yes,' she said. 'This has been helpful.'

She reached over and tucked the hundred-dollar bill in the breast pocket of his shirt.

'You can let me out here.'

The car was already at a standstill in the middle of the road, so she went ahead and unfastened her seatbelt and opened the door.

'I'm really sorry if it turns out that's what your husband's been up to,' the driver said, looking at her sympathetically. 'He's clearly got shit for brains. I feel bad taking your money.'

She stopped herself, one foot on the pavement. Up ahead, cars were starting to ease forward.

'It's OK,' she said, and gave him a wink. 'It's my husband's money.'

38

Caitlin approached the arena. The entrance was made of fifty-foot-high glass walls standing over multiple entry doors. Lines of fans snaked out onto the sidewalk. She picked one that looked shorter than the others and waited. Through the glass, she could see inside the lobby of the arena, where massive screens showed highlights of the Lightning's season. Most of the clips were of Luca – slam dunks, steals, come-from-behind blocks where he pinned the ball to the backboard. A smaller screen showed the team now – live – in the hallway leading out to the floor. They were wearing their warmup tracksuits over their uniforms. While there was no sound playing, they were obviously listening to music. They danced, gave each other fist bumps and hand slaps. Luca didn't really participate. He stood alone, doing exercises to loosen up: running in place, tuck jumps, hopping side to side.

An arena employee scanned her ticket, and she walked through the metal detector with no problem – her gun was back at the hotel. She checked her seat number, then merged into a big hallway clogged with fans.

The atmosphere was electric.

A handful of people in Sabertooths gear were sprinkled into the crowd, but mostly the hallways were filled with fans wearing the Lightning's blue and black. She wore an old Sabertooths T-shirt. She'd bought it for herself when Alex was a baby and she'd purchased him a matching onesie, years before Garrett played for the team. Alex grew out of his onesie quickly, and, over the years, she replaced several of his Sabertooths shirts. But she'd kept the same one, using it as a workout shirt that was now faded and thinning.

She walked through the concrete passageways. Blue and black streamers hung from the ceiling. Jagged bolts of blue were painted over the cinderblock walls, sporadically adorned with casino advertisements and posters for local lawyers or plastic surgeons. The air thrummed with voices and music. Beer lines were long, but the lines to the women's restrooms were longer.

Caitlin found her section and was delighted to see she was descending to the lower levels. Every professional game she'd ever been to, her seats were in the nosebleeds. Now, she dropped lower and lower until she found her row, only ten up from the bottom. She was practically on top of the court. The arena rose around her like she was in a mountain valley, with two rows of suites halfway up, followed by nosebleeds sloping up to the rafters. The place was like the rest of Vegas – an assault on the senses. Music blasted, lights shone, and advertisements for gambling and liquor were everywhere. The Jumbotron above the court was sponsored by Jack Daniels.

Both teams were doing their pre-game warmups now. Garrett – close enough she could have thrown him a pass – was dribbling with two basketballs, behind his back and between his legs. He'd seen her doing that back in college, and he'd started the habit then, working it into his warmup routine. It felt weird to see some small influence she'd had on him being practiced here on the world's biggest basketball stage.

Under the Sabertooths' basket, Billy Croft, their shooting guard, spent his warmup time practicing with the backup point guard, Jamie Vaughn, slipping picks and shooting off of pocket passes. Kevin Mackey, small forward, practiced cutting to the basket while one of the backups threw passes to him. Rodrigo Sandoval spent almost the entire warmup practicing free throws. Elijah was on the floor, stretching, with a trainer pushing his back or holding a leg to increase flexibility.

On the other end, Jaxon Luca was shooting three pointers as an assistant fed him ball after ball. The shots went in one after the other. Net. Net. Net.

She let her eyes drift to the courtside seats and thought she saw a handful of Las Vegas-based celebrities scattered around the court. Was that the quarterback for the Raiders? She thought she recognized boxer Floyd Mayweather. She definitely recognized Mike Tyson. And Nicolas Cage. And she thought a couple sitting courtside below her might be Andre Agassi and Steffi Graf, but from this angle it was hard to be sure.

She felt herself geeking out, caught up in the excitement of the game, but reminded herself she wasn't actually here as a fan. She needed to watch the audience, the coaches, the sideline people. Refs and other players – everyone *but* Garrett.

She felt her phone buzz in her pocket and pulled it out to see an incoming FaceTime call from Owen. Around her the arena was noisy, with music blasting and fans talking, but Caitlin answered the call and put the phone close to her face so she could hear.

Owen and Alex appeared on the screen, and one glance at her son told her he'd been crying.

'Sorry to bother you,' Owen said. 'I've got a little boy here who's missing his mommy.'

Caitlin's heart ached, hearing those words and seeing Alex's miserable face.

'Oh, sweetie,' she said. 'I miss you, too. I miss you so much.'

Alex's mouth curved involuntarily into a frown as he tried to keep himself from crying.

'We were getting ready to watch the game,' Owen explained, 'and he got upset, saying it didn't feel right watching another game without you.'

'I only got to watch one of the Finals with you,' Alex said, beginning to cry.

Caitlin welled up – it didn't feel right being here without him either.

She asked Alex if he wanted to see where she was. She flipped the camera around and showed him the arena, which was rapidly filling. On the screen, Alex's eyes went wide with excitement.

'Look how close I am to the court,' Caitlin said.

This seemed to be cheering him up – or at least distracting him. He sat up on the couch and held the phone himself, looking closely at everything Caitlin showed him.

'There's Mr Streeter,' Caitlin said, pointing the camera at Garrett down on the court. He was shooting three-pointers now.

Alex squinted.

'It's exciting to be here,' Caitlin said, flipping the camera back, 'but it's not as much fun without my basketball buddy.'

'When are you coming home?' Alex asked.

'I don't know, baby.'

Beside Alex, Owen looked confused. He was no doubt expecting her to come home for the next game, which was in Cincinnati. Even if she had to leave again for Game Six, there was no reason she couldn't sleep in her own house while the team was in Ohio.

'I might need to stay in Vegas,' Caitlin said. 'It's complicated, but that might be the best thing for me to help Garrett.'

'How?' Owen said, unable to hide his incredulity.

This wasn't a conversation she wanted to have now, not with the game about to start and with Alex already upset.

'I'll call you tomorrow.' She turned her attention to Alex. 'I love you so much, sweetie. I wish I was with you.'

'I miss you, Mommy.'

Caitlin hung up and sat back in her seat, her knees pressed against the row in front of her. She hated lying to her family.

'Caitlin!' she heard someone say enthusiastically, and she turned to see Summer Morgan coming down the row, holding her arms out like she was going to hug Caitlin.

Then she did just that, wrapping Caitlin in a tight embrace. Caitlin threw a confused arm around her.

'Hi,' Caitlin uttered, realizing that Garrett had failed to mention her ticket was going to be right next to his girlfriend's.

39

Summer flopped down in her seat next to Caitlin and started chatting with her like they were old friends. The model was wearing a bright Sabertooths jersey, and her hair was tied in a French braid that hung over one shoulder. Whatever makeup she was wearing really brought the color out of her eyes. Her perfume smelled amazing.

'What the hell is going on with Jake?' she said. 'I can't believe he's missing the NBA Finals. He must be really sick.'

Caitlin realized what Garrett must have done – he'd given her the ticket he normally would have given to his brother. Garrett was afraid the FBI couldn't be inconspicuous – did he not realize at least once per game the camera panned to his girlfriend celebrating one of his shots? Anyone here or on TV would see Caitlin sitting with Summer. So much for going to the game incognito.

The arena lights darkened, and the fans held up their phones, creating a galaxy of stars around the court. The jumbo screen overhead lit up with cartoon lightning bolts. Sound effects of a thunderstorm filled the air, and spotlights swirled around the floor. The announcer introduced the Sabertooths in a subdued but respectful voice, and Caitlin watched with Summer as Garrett took the court. He and Elijah gave each other a simple head-nod.

Once introductions for the visiting Sabertooths were over, the stadium filled with the opening riff of AC/DC's 'Thunderstruck.' The whole arena was on its feet.

'*And now,*' the announcer declared, '*here are the starters for* your *Las Vegas Lightning.*'

Jaxon Luca was the last to run onto the court, and the crowd roared and stomped its approval so loudly the floor vibrated. People screamed and waved towels. Caitlin had never seen fervor to match it. The NCAA playoffs weren't even close.

'God, I hate that guy,' Summer said.

'Do you know him?' Caitlin asked.

'Oh, no,' Summer said, shaking her head. 'I don't hate him personally. He's so damn good. If he was Garrett's teammate, I'd love him.'

Caitlin watched as the lights came back up and people stood for the national anthem. The singer Ne-Yo, who was apparently from Las Vegas, took the court and crooned a respectful version of 'The Star-Spangled Banner' in a lovely tenor voice.

The starters prepared for the opening tip-off. The players shuffled around, shaking hands or bumping fists with opposing players, quick gestures of sportsmanship. Garrett and Jaxon Luca gave each other one of those shakes that turns into a one-armed hug, each patting the other on the back with a fist. They separated without a word.

Caitlin felt her scalp tingle. Her ex-boyfriend was out there hugging a player who could legitimately be the next LeBron James or Michael Jordan.

'I get so nervous,' Summer said to her. 'I'm glad you're here. You seem so calm. Jake's a goddamn trainwreck in these situations.'

'Is that right?' Caitlin asked, although she knew it to be true.

She sat next to him during NCAA playoff games when Jake was squirming in his seat and cussing at the refs. Caitlin wondered now if his anxiety also had to do with betting.

She looked around the arena, not sure what she was searching for. She'd come with the idea she might spot something, but that mission felt overwhelming. There must be twenty thousand people here and she was going to somehow spot the one person who looked out of place?

Impossible.

She looked at Garrett's teammates and coaches. She moved her eyes to the photographers and videographers crowded along the sidelines on each end of the court. She looked at the TV commentators courtside – Chuck Walla, Harding Able, and Dirk Justice, whom she'd only ever seen on TV. She scanned the crowd for something – anything – but everything was as she would expect. People looked nervous or excited – completely normal in this venue. Sports fandom wasn't a passive experience.

On the court, the Lightning got the ball at the tip-off, and Jaxon brought it up. The team moved the ball around. Then, with four seconds on the shot clock, Luca got the ball back, did a quick crossover that rocked Sabertooths' shooting guard Billy Croft back on his heels, and took his signature mid-range jumper.

Swish!

The Sabertooths seemed tense, nervous, trying too hard. She didn't think it was Garrett throwing the game. No need, yet anyway.

'Sabertooths look like crap, don't they?' Summer said when they called their first timeout, down fifteen to six.

'Yes, but they'll loosen up,' Caitlin said.

Dancers and cheerleaders rushed onto the court during the break. Caitlin craned her neck to look in the seats around them. As she did, she made eye contact with a man in a Lightning sweatshirt that mixed the team colors in a camouflage pattern. He had coffee-black hair, rather bushy, and a thick mustache that looked like a fat caterpillar was glued to his upper lip. He held her eyes for a moment – just the two of them staring at each other – then he averted his back to the court.

Caitlin turned around, wondering if it was a coincidence they'd made eye contact.

Or was the guy watching her?

40

As the game went on, more than once, Caitlin glanced at Summer and caught the model watching her. Caitlin felt self-conscious. This was exactly the kind of scrutiny she'd wanted to avoid from her husband when she skipped watching Game One with her family. Now she had Garrett's girlfriend studying her reactions.

When the horn sounded for halftime, the Sabertooths were down by twenty.

She glanced behind her to see the man who'd made eye contact with her. He offered her a sly smile, which she couldn't tell might be flirtatious or malicious. She turned away and asked Summer if they could get a selfie together.

'My husband won't believe I'm sitting with you.'

Summer did it willingly, although she seemed to have something on her mind she wanted to say. But once they were in the camera frame, the anxiety disappeared and her captivating glow came out. Then Caitlin asked if she could take one only of the model. Summer shrugged, and Caitlin leaned over the seats in front of them as Summer flashed a smile. Caitlin zoomed in over her shoulder on Mr Mustache, not bothering to get Summer in the shot. Once Caitlin pocketed her phone, Summer's smile disappeared.

'Sorry. I can't hold it in any longer,' Summer said. 'Why don't you tell me what's really going on with you and Garrett?'

'Excuse me,' Caitlin said. 'What did you say?'

Summer stared daggers at her. Then the lights dimmed for a halftime show with a guy and his Chihuahua performing acrobatic tricks.

'Do you really expect me to believe he's brought you in as some kind of basketball consultant?'

'Summer,' Caitlin said, 'I'm sure Garrett has no interest in me. And,' she added, 'I have no interest in him.'

Summer's tough exterior cracked and she slumped back in the seat.

'Sorry,' she said. 'I had to ask. It shocked me when he said he'd gone to see you.'

'I didn't mean to cause you any anxiety,' Caitlin said, although in truth she felt a little proud a supermodel could feel threatened by her. 'What Garrett and I had was a million years ago. I'm happily married.'

'It's just Garrett has been so weird lately,' Summer said. 'He fired Jake, brought you on board. All of this without talking anything through with me.'

'Fired Jake?'

Summer obviously suspected there was more to it than Jake being sick.

'I assume so,' Summer said. 'He used to do what you're doing – an unofficial consultant. They must have had a falling out, but of course I can't get a word out of Garrett about it.'

Below them, the dog was balancing on a basketball, rolling it forward while it walked.

'Look,' Caitlin said, 'when I was with Garrett, he was different during the season. Focused. Removed. Our relationship took a back seat. I don't think it bothered me because I was the same.'

Summer was watching her with anxious eyes.

'The thing is,' Caitlin said, 'you've only got to wait a week and it will all be over. One way or another, win or lose, this series is going to end. I think you'll find the man you love will get back to his old self.'

Caitlin felt weird having this heart-to-heart. She actually felt bad for Summer, especially knowing Garrett's behavior wasn't due to basketball. If he was difficult when he was focused on the game, he must be insufferable to live with right now.

'Are you sure there's nothing going on between you two?' Summer said.

'All of that was a long time ago,' Caitlin said. 'I've moved on. Garrett's moved on. It wasn't meant to be.'

Summer finally seemed to be satisfied, and Caitlin, sensing the conversation had run its course, said she was going to buy something to drink.

'You want anything?'

'I'm good,' Summer said.

Caitlin squeezed past her and headed up the stairs. She needed a break from Garrett's girlfriend and wanted to have a look around for anything suspicious. As she climbed, she glanced over to see what the mustached man in the blue-black camouflage was doing.

But he was gone.

41

W hen Caitlin made it to the main corridor above, she felt her phone buzz in her jeans. She stepped to the side of the hallway, away from the crowd's two-way traffic, and checked to see a text from Owen.

We saw you on TV. Alex couldn't believe it. You're sitting with Summer Morgan.

As Caitlin started to text back, another message popped up.

I was right. She doesn't hold a candle to you!

Caitlin grinned.

You're such a liar, she texted back.

Hope you're having fun, Owen wrote. Miss you.

She responded, Miss you too. Tell Alex I love him!

As she was pocketing her phone, another message came in. This one from her college roommate, Yazmina.

OMG. Are you at the game?????

Caitlin felt a surge of excitement, followed by a wish she'd never come tonight. If her family saw her and Yaz saw her, then who else saw her? Not that most people would recognize her, but still. Kidnappers watching the game might wonder who was with Garrett's girlfriend. She hoped they'd assume she was just Summer's friend.

WAIT, Yazmina texted. The game is in Vegas, not Cinci! And you're sitting with Summer Morgan!!! What is going on???

It's a long story, Caitlin responded, looking around for any sign of Mr Mustache returning to his seat.

Yaz wrote, Are you coming to Game 6? I told Brook if you're going, we're going. She's down for it. It's only a 4 hr drive. We're coming if you'll be there!!!

Yaz and her wife met when they played for the Seattle Storm. Yaz was mostly a bench warmer, but Brooklyn – a six-foot-three power forward from the University of Tennessee – was a genuine star until injuries started to take their toll. When Yaz left the pros and went to law school at Ohio State, Brooklyn went to med school. Yaz clerked for the Ohio Supreme Court after graduation, waiting for Brooklyn to finish her residency. Since they were only about ninety minutes away, Caitlin visited them from time to time, but Yaz and Brooklyn were always busy, and Caitlin's own career and motherhood limited the trips. Now they were living in Los Angeles, Brooklyn an ER doc and Yaz working for a powerhouse law firm. Caitlin hadn't seen them in at least three years. Under ordinary circumstances, Caitlin would have loved to get together with her old friend.

But these were not ordinary circumstances.

Maybe, Caitlin wrote. Then, not knowing what to say, she added, Hopefully the Tooths will wrap it up in 5.

No chance, Yaz wrote. They're playing like shit tonight.

A big TV stationed above a concession counter showed the second half was about to begin.

Caitlin started to put the phone away and another text came in. Is Garrett still in love with you?

Caitlin stared at the words.

Another message popped up: I bet he'd leave Summer Morgan in a heartbeat if you weren't married.

She couldn't get involved in this conversation. She pocketed the phone and looked around her. A good fifty feet away, she caught a glimpse of the guy who'd been watching her in the stands, whom she now thought of as Mr Mustache. He looked away, hit the push-bar on a nearby door, and disappeared from sight.

The hall was emptier now that the game had begun, and Caitlin reached the door within seconds. The door, and half a dozen like it, opened onto a large landing at the top of a high, wide set of stairs that dropped a good twenty feet then split to the sides. She ran to the rail to try to look down, but there was hardly any gap. This was one of the stairwells that led directly to the ground-floor exit. At the end of the game, the steps would be packed shoulder-to-shoulder with fans. But, right now, there wasn't a soul on them. She heard shoes squeaking below. She hurried down, taking the steps three at a time. She spun around the corner, hanging onto the railing to keep her momentum. When she approached the bottom, she heard a door opening. It latched closed before she got there.

She hesitated for a moment, only steps from the bottom. Once she left, she wouldn't be able to get back into the game. But this guy might be a lead. She questioned her own perceptions – had he really been looking at her? Or had they just happened to make eye contact?

She thought about it: No one leaves in the early third quarter of the NBA Finals – not when you're wearing the colors of the team that's winning.

Caitlin pushed through an exit door into the hot desert air. There weren't many people around the arena – give it another hour and the place would be a madhouse with fans streaming from every exit – so it took her only a second to find her guy. He was crossing a street, headed back to the heart of the Strip. His phone was to his ear, and he was clearly talking. But, as he did, his body twisted, and he glanced behind him.

From this distance, it was hard to tell if he had any reaction to seeing her. As he looked away, he said something into his phone, pulled it from his ear, and shoved it into his back pocket. Then he was across the road, and the light changed. Cars surged forward to block her way. He took off in a brisk walk.

She didn't wait for the crosswalk to give her a *WALK* sign. As soon as there was a break in the traffic, she bolted into the street after the guy.

42

She reached the other side and slowed her pace, walking quickly but not running. She kept him in sight, trying to close the gap between them without making her pursuit obvious. It was difficult. She had long legs, but she wasn't closing the distance.

She tried to judge his height compared to people who crossed his path and then hers. She figured he was around six feet or six-one, a little taller than her.

The guy cut away from the main sidewalk, ducking under a billboard advertising Cirque de Soleil, and headed toward the Odyssey hotel-casino, a big brown building with a giant replica of an old ship out front. Caitlin cut across an expanse of grass to shorten the distance, but as she did so, the guy looked back. She ducked behind the pylon holding the billboard. She waited a few seconds, then peeked out. He headed toward the casino entrance, not looking back. After he disappeared through the casino doors, she jogged forward and stepped into the chill of the air-conditioned building.

She walked into the maze, trying to look like a tourist over-whelmed by the sights. She passed blackjack tables and slot machines. In the distance, through the glare of lights, she spotted Mr Mustache's camouflage Lightning shirt leaving the casino floor down a hallway. She headed that way and when she got to the opening of the corridor, she found herself in an expansive family area, which included a ropes course suspended from the ceiling, an arcade full of video games, a bowling section, and – the most dominant feature – a surprisingly large indoor miniature golf course. There were people everywhere, kids eating ice cream and adults sipping colorful cocktails, and the air was filled with the thrum of music and raised voices trying to be heard over the noise.

Caitlin spotted Mr Mustache cutting through the miniature golf course, stepping over ropes and walking through the greens, inter-rupting players about to take their shots. She decided to curve around and see if she could flank him. She found the edge of the room to be clogged, with a long line for a laser tag room and a crowd around some kind of virtual reality game. She wedged her way through the people but lost Mr Mustache.

She spotted a lit sign for *PARKING* and had a hunch he went that way, planning to make an escape via the garage. Caitlin didn't know what she'd do if she found herself alone with the guy, but she kept going anyway. She arrived at a bank of elevators, with a family of five waiting, and she saw a nearby sign for stairs. She pushed through the door and bounded up the concrete steps, the stairwell empty and quiet in stark contrast to the madhouse she'd left behind. She came to a second-floor landing and hesitated. The door held a long rectangular window, crosshatched with wire, that let her glimpse into the parking garage. She saw nothing, but she didn't hear anyone running on the stairs above her either.

Shit, she thought. *I've lost him.*

She pushed through the door and stepped into the garage. Out of the corner of her eye, she saw a shape rush toward her, and she instinctively flinched. Mr Mustache swung something at her and she moved just in time for the golf putter to smash into the window of the door, making a loud *thwack* and spraying flakes of glass.

Caitlin stumbled away, too shocked to do anything else, and Mr Mustache advanced, holding the golf club like a sword.

'Who are you?' he snarled. 'Why are you following me?'

'I'm not,' she lied.

She tried to keep her distance by backpedaling out into the garage, which was full of cars but otherwise desolate. Behind Mr Mustache, the circular button by the elevators was lit, suggesting the elevator might arrive any moment.

She backed into the fender of a parked car, and he lunged at her, taking a swing. The club whooshed by as she leaned back, and it collided with the edge of the windshield, sending out a spiderweb of cracks. Before he could retract the weapon, Caitlin grabbed the shaft with both hands and tried to wrest it away from him.

The two of them stood for a moment, both tugging on their ends. Behind him, the elevator dinged and the doors opened. Mr Mustache let go of the club and Caitlin stumbled back in front of the parked car. The man darted into the elevator and began pressing buttons.

Caitlin rushed toward the elevator as the doors were closing. She thrust the golf club through the crack, and the doors sprang back open. Mr Mustache yanked the club out of her hands. He jammed it into her sternum, pushing her back. She lunged for him and grabbed a handful of his hair, intending to haul him through the doors, but his hair came off in her hand, and – carried by her own momentum – she staggered backward and fell down. As she looked up, the doors sealed shut.

In her hand was a brown wig.

And Mr Mustache – whoever he was – was gone.

GAME FIVE

43

Caitlin had trouble sleeping, convinced she'd messed up and blown the whole investigation. Mr Mustache would report to his fellow kidnappers that Garrett recruited her to find Jake, and they'd kill Jake as punishment. But as the sun rose, Garrett forwarded a text message from the kidnappers with a photo of Jake, alive and holding an iPad with the game results displayed. The message said, Your brother likes when you do what you're told.

Caitlin sent Garrett the picture she'd taken of Mr Mustache and asked if he recognized the guy, adding that she thought he *might* be wearing a wig. But of course Garrett had never seen him before, and Caitlin had to admit to herself that there was a reasonable chance the guy had nothing at all to do with Jake's disappearance. Maybe her police instincts had picked up on the fact that this guy was up to no good, but he just happened to be some other Las Vegas lowlife involved in something possibly criminal. In *The French Connection* – which she reminded herself was based on a true story – the narcotics detectives didn't know what the bad guys were up to when they started tailing them, only that they felt 'wrong.'

Once she'd convinced herself she hadn't gotten Jake killed, she thought about going back to sleep, but there was something else weighing on her mind – she needed to call her husband and try to explain why she wasn't coming home yet. She pulled her phone out and stared at it. She wasn't mentally ready for the conversation she was going to have to have. As she stared at the screen of her personal cell, her burner buzzed on the nightstand.

It was an unfamiliar 702 number.

'Hello,' she said.

'So you want to start making some real money, huh?' said the female voice on the other end.

'Amethyst?'

The woman laughed. 'Call me Debbie. Amethyst is for Johns.'

'How much would it cost for me to buy your time for a few hours?'

'Depends,' Amethyst – or Debbie – replied. 'What are you wanting to do?'

'Not sex,' Caitlin said quickly. 'I want to pick your brain. And, if possible, could you show me around the Red Rose Ranch? You work there, right?'

'Yeah,' the woman said. 'You ain't asking for much, so I can hook you up. But my time does have a value.'

'It's only fair you're compensated,' Caitlin said.

What Caitlin didn't say was that she wanted to ask some of the employees of the Red Rose Ranch about Jake, maybe show his picture around. She'd cross that bridge when they got there.

'OK,' Debbie said. 'How about a thousand dollars?'

Caitlin thought that was awfully steep for getting 'hooked up,' but she was OK with it. It was Garrett's money, after all.

'When can we go?' Caitlin asked.

'Later today,' Debbie said. 'I need a nap. I'm just getting done for the night.'

Squinting out the window at the sun-bleached streets of Las Vegas, Caitlin tried to picture the life of a woman now heading home after several hours of late-night sex with strangers.

'How about two o'clock?' Debbie said.

'Perfect.'

'You're at the Florentine?' Debbie asked. 'I'll swing by and pick you up. We'll chat on our way to the ranch.'

Caitlin hung up, stared at her phone. She couldn't put off the inevitable any longer.

'Nice of you to call,' Owen said when he answered. Before she could say anything, he added, 'I assume you're calling from the airport, and you'll be home this afternoon.'

He hadn't come across as insecure yesterday, but he was now – and she couldn't blame him. When she left, she said nothing to indicate she might not come home when the series returned to Ohio.

'I'm in Las Vegas,' Caitlin said.

'Why?' Owen said, making no effort to hide his irritation. 'The next game is in Cincinnati. Surely the team's on their way home, if not there already.'

'Garrett wanted me to stay and scout things for him.'

She knew the lie didn't make any sense. The Lightning's practices weren't open to the public. There was nothing to scout. Nothing for her to learn by staying here that she couldn't by coming home. He had every right to be skeptical.

'I'd like to say hi to Alex,' she said, hoping to change the subject.

'He's watching *Octonauts*,' Owen said. 'I'll get him when it's over.'

There was silence on the other end. Caitlin knew she should fill it, but what could she say?

'So,' Owen said finally, 'are you going to tell me what's going on, or what?'

'Nothing's going on.'

'I've been patient with this whole thing,' Owen said. 'I'm not ordinarily overbearing or untrusting—'

'You're not always supportive either,' she said, although she knew this was unfair. He'd encouraged her to work for Garrett in the first place.

'That's not true,' Owen said.

'You hate that I'm a cop,' she said. 'You'd love nothing more than for me to take that PR job and spend my career behind a desk.'

'I never once expressed that.'

'But you think it.'

He took a deep breath. 'I don't want you to die. I don't think that's the same as not being supportive.'

'I was already a cop when we met,' she said. 'You knew what you were getting into.'

He ignored the direction she'd taken the conversation and brought it back to his point. 'I don't think you're being forthcoming with me. Even though I put up with a lot of shit, I don't ask much of you. Well, I'm asking: What is going on?'

'Put up with a lot of shit?' Caitlin said, suddenly angry. 'What kind of shit do you put up with?'

'*You*,' he snapped, 'perpetually unhappy with *our* life.'

Caitlin felt sick. She knew he was right.

She wanted to reassure him her unhappiness had nothing to do with him. She'd plateaued in her career. Her coworkers treated her like she wasn't worthy of wearing the badge she took such pride in. Being a mother was hard. Money was tight. Life was too fucking hectic and challenging and unfair. He was one of the good things in her life.

She wanted to tell him the truth – she missed him terribly.

But their conversation had already derailed into a fight. She didn't know how to put the train back on the tracks without coming clean about the lies she'd already told him. And if she did, it would make things worse when he tried to convince her to come home and she refused.

'You don't have anything to say?' Owen said, and the fact his tone hadn't softened told her how much trouble she was in.

'I'm sorry. I've been a shit wife. But I need you to trust me.'

'Alex's show is almost over,' Owen said. 'They're doing the song now.'

'Owen,' she said. 'Please . . .'

She wanted Owen to tell her he trusted her, that he would be waiting for her with an open heart. Instead, he said simply, 'Here's Alex.'

Then her son was on the phone, and she tried to listen as he told her what he learned about the immortal jellyfish, the latest sea creature highlighted on the show. After a few minutes of this, she heard Owen in the background telling him it was time to say goodbye.

She thought Alex might put his dad back on, but instead he told her goodbye and hung up.

44

Amethyst showed up in a midsize Audi, which certainly didn't cost as much as Garrett's Mercedes, but Caitlin was pretty sure cost more than her minivan back home. The woman pulled into the drive-through pickup lane where Ubers arrived and waved to Caitlin from her open window.

Caitlin opened the passenger seat and got in. The car smelled heavily of air freshener and perfume.

'Thanks, Amethyst,' Caitlin said, pulling on her seatbelt.

'Debbie. Remember?'

'Sorry. Thanks, Debbie.'

The Audi zoomed onto the street. There was a film of Nevada dust on the dashboard, and the backseat was strewn with various articles of clothing: bras and thongs and stiletto shoes, not to mention a foot-long string of condom packages.

Debbie wore tight-fitting athleisure pants and a tank top with a sports bra visible underneath. She seemed to be in her mid- to late twenties. Her purple-highlighted hair was pulled up in a messy bun, and it didn't look like she had a lick of makeup on.

To Caitlin, she looked much prettier than she had the other night. 'You really thinking of becoming a working girl?' Debbie asked, side-eying Caitlin as she drove. She held the wheel with one hand. The fake nails were gone, and she wore a thick silver ring on one finger, the only piece of jewelry she appeared to have on.

'Not really.'

'So what's this all about?'

'Curiosity mostly. I'm interested in seeing what a working brothel looks like.'

'You're still paying me, right?'

'Of course.'

The landscape outside of the city quickly emptied. They passed billboards and the occasional rundown gas station, but otherwise there was little sign of human presence, aside from the telephone poles along the road and a handful of cars heading in the direction of Vegas. Windswept sand encroached on the blacktop, and sagebrush filled the desert to the left and right. A speed-limit sign looked like it had been punctured with buckshot.

As they talked, Caitlin found herself impressed with Debbie, how articulate she was, how intelligent. She wasn't sure why, but she'd expected the girl to be dumb, like she'd gotten into this line of work because there was nothing else available to her. But she seemed like someone who could probably be successful in a number of professions.

Debbie explained that she and the other girls had residencies at the Red Rose Ranch. Two weeks there, two weeks away. While she was on campus, she ate, slept, did everything there. Then she was off for two weeks. Most of the girls had apartments in Vegas. Some lived out of state and flew back home during their time off.

'We're independent contractors,' she explained. 'We charge whatever we want. Negotiate it on a case-by-case basis. But we have to give the house fifty percent.'

'Fifty?'

'That's why, when I'm off my residency, I do work on the side.'

Debbie explained that she meets clients through the Ranch, and if they express an interest in seeing her again, she suggests she can make house calls. She only does her on-the-side work for high rollers.

'At the Ranch, no one gets inside me for less than a grand. But if a guy's got money to burn, if it's nothing for him to drop five grand – or ten grand – then I get it from him. I make sure he has a good time. Then I hint that I make house calls.'

She told Caitlin that everything she made at the Ranch she paid taxes on. When she made house calls, she pocketed every dime.

'I give them a little discount. Eight grand in my pocket is better than ten I have to split with the house and the IRS.'

'Is that legal? Or allowed by the brothel?'

'No, and hell no. Silas would kill me if he knew I was stepping out on the Ranch.'

'Do you mean that literally?' Caitlin asked. 'Or is that a figure of speech?'

Debbie laughed. 'Not literally. He would fire me. He probably wouldn't even try to get my license revoked, though. He's really a softie. He acts like he's a surrogate father to all the girls.'

'Does he . . .' Caitlin didn't know how to delicately ask: *Does he sleep with his courtesans?* Debbie seemed to get the message anyway.

'He pays like everyone else.'

Caitlin almost asked if Debbie had ever been with him but stopped herself. Instead, she changed the subject.

'Do you have protection?' she asked.

'Everyone has to wear a rubber.'

'No, I mean, when you're out on your own, doing house calls, does anyone go with you? Like a security guard or . . .'

She didn't want to say the word 'pimp.'

'That's the good thing about the Ranch,' Debbie said. 'It's safe. You got cameras and security guards. No one's going to beat the shit out of you. When I do it on my own, I don't have that. But I try to vet the guys pretty carefully. And I've got mace in my purse. And this.'

Keeping her wrists propped on the steering wheel, she pried up a tiny curved blade about half an inch long out of her ring. Then she switched hands on the wheel and held out her hand toward Caitlin like she was showing off a wedding band.

The blade looked sharp, not much wider than a toothpick but curved like a bird talon.

'Anyone messes with me and I'm going to turn him into a geyser.'

45

The Audi rolled into the town of Green Lawn, which, like the Uber driver said, was not green and contained few actual lawns. The landscape was as brown as the desert, with a handful of fast-food restaurants, banks, and gas stations. There weren't any tall buildings and not nearly as many palm trees as in Vegas. It seemed no different than any other small Western town, maybe a little less run-down than most, thanks to its status as a bedroom community for Vegas. But then Debbie turned down a street labeled Brothel Boulevard – that was the actual name on the green road sign – and Caitlin checked out the businesses for which the street was named.

She'd expected old-looking motels with gaudy pink paint jobs or cheap manufactured homes converted into businesses, but these facilities were nothing like that. The brothels sat on expansive pieces of property and looked more like weekend retreats for honeymooners than houses of ill-repute. There were multiple bungalows, restaurants, swimming pools, and walking paths through desert-landscaped yards. They passed one called the Love Shack and another named Pussy Palace. The Red Rose Ranch, which seemed bigger and fancier than the other two, sat at the end of the street in a cul-de-sac. Debbie drove under a large archway with the name painted in big letters.

The parking lot was white gravel, but Debbie bypassed it and drove around back, where she entered a code to go into a dirt parking lot for employees. Back here, tucked out of sight, were the living quarters for the girls. A few sat on lawn chairs outside of their rooms, clearly off shift because they were dressed in baggy shorts and pajamas, their hair piled atop their heads.

Caitlin got out of the car and was assaulted by the heat. The sun had no filter here.

'What's up, ladies?' Debbie said to her coworkers as they approached.

One woman, wearing nothing but a long T-shirt with Minnie Mouse on the front, was eating a bowl of cereal. Another, in pajama pants and a tank top, was scrolling mindlessly through her phone.

The third, with the longest fake fingernails Caitlin had ever seen, smoked a cigarette.

'Hey, girl,' the smoker said to Debbie. 'I thought you didn't come back till next week.'

'Got a new recruit,' Debbie said, gesturing to Caitlin with a nod of her head. 'She's thinking about getting into the biz.'

The girls appraised Caitlin up and down. Minnie Mouse gave a head-nod as if to acknowledge Caitlin had what it took. She and Debbie left the girls, and Debbie gave Caitlin a quick tour of the grounds, pointing out what was open to customers and what was off limits, including the girls' rooms and a garage where the brothel's two limousines were housed. There was a restaurant separate from the brothel area, where tourists could come if they wanted to set foot on the property and maybe buy a T-shirt without actually interacting with courtesans. There was another similar restaurant, but this one was for paying Johns, with a stage where the girls would line up, hoping to be selected. Debbie didn't take Caitlin inside, but rather pointed the building out from a distance. Silas wouldn't want them in there if they weren't working, she explained. They might distract paying customers away from girls who were available.

Debbie took Caitlin in through a back door and down a hall of 'party rooms.' She showed Caitlin one of them. It was done up in red colors, with a massive bed and lots of pillows, with a mirror on the ceiling overhead. An open closet door revealed a rack of feather boas and lingerie. There were candles and a radio, and a large bathtub in one corner. Two pairs of furry handcuffs hung from the headboard, one on each side. A candy bowl sat on the bedside table, filled with condoms, next to what looked like an industrial-sized bottle of lubricant.

Debbie shut the door, and, further down the hall, they came to a door labeled SECURITY. Debbie knocked and they found a big-bodied guard, dressed in black, sitting in front of a bank of TV monitors, showing various angles of the property. He was stretched out on a folding chair, flipping through a comic book and barely paying attention to the screens. He was probably at least Garrett's height, maybe two or three inches taller, but looked like he would have outweighed him by a good seventy-five pounds. His black hair was buzzed close, and he had a pudgy, non-threatening face.

'Hey, Dickie,' Debbie said.

'Hey,' the guy said, sitting up straight and dropping the comic into a box of various periodicals. He looked like he'd been about to fall asleep. 'Who's this?'

Debbie introduced Caitlin as a friend interested in becoming a courtesan. She didn't give her name, and the guy didn't ask. Debbie showed Caitlin the bank of security monitors and Dickie let them look, as if humoring people on tour was a completely normal part of his job duties.

Caitlin studied the cameras. There were images of the restaurants and the swimming pool, various hallways. It appeared there were no cameras in the actual party rooms, but otherwise the place was pretty well covered. There only appeared to be one camera outside, covering the front parking lot. Back where girls lived was apparently not recorded.

'There's Silas,' Debbie said, pointing to one of the monitors.

Silas Bennett, with his recognizable bald head, sat at the bar in the tourist restaurant, chatting with a customer. The image quality wasn't bad. The guy he was talking to said something funny, and Bennett laughed with his whole body. Seeing him reinforced the impression she already had – he was gregarious and friendly in an over-the-top, off-putting sort of way. Like a car salesman who acts like your best friend the moment he meets you. Or a politician clearly trying to get your vote.

'Do you want to meet him?' Debbie asked. 'He'll take one look at you and give you his recruitment pitch.'

Caitlin considered it but said, 'No thanks.'

If Silas Bennett was behind Jake's kidnapping, she shouldn't show her face to him, although she felt more and more that kidnapping didn't seem his style. He was a narcissist who liked to be in the public eye, not a criminal mastermind able to keep his misdeeds hidden from the world.

She and Debbie walked back out toward the car, approaching the row of bungalows where the three women were chatting. Caitlin reached into her jeans and pulled out a wad of cash. She peeled off ten one-hundred-dollar bills and handed them to Debbie. She made sure the other women noticed the money that remained in her hand.

'I've got another question for you,' she said, eyeing all four women.

They looked at her with interest. Caitlin pulled out her phone and showed them the picture of Jake.

'Do any of you recognize this guy?'

46

'Oh, shit,' Debbie said. 'Are you a cop?'

Caitlin didn't answer. Instead, she looked at the other girls' faces. She thought they might be angry, but mostly they looked interested – interested in how to get the money from Caitlin's pocket into theirs.

She told them the date she thought Jake came to the brothel. They all shook their heads.

'Sorry, we was off rotation then,' Minnie Mouse said.

'I was here,' Debbie said.

'Did you see him?'

'Who are you?' Debbie asked.

'Do you remember seeing him?' Caitlin said.

'You tell me first.'

Caitlin took a deep breath. 'Better you don't know,' she said. 'Better you forget I was here at all.'

She handed all four women a hundred-dollar bill. How easy it must be to be rich – you could just pay people whenever you wanted something.

'Do you remember seeing him?' Caitlin asked Debbie again.

She held the phone up in front of her face.

'I don't,' she said. 'But the way you're throwing hundred-dollar bills around makes me wish I did.'

'What makes you think he was here that night?' asked the girl with the long nails.

She wasn't sure if she should say, but Caitlin explained that there'd been an Uber charge on his credit card. The amount equaled about what it would take to get here.

Debbie put her finger to her lips like she was thinking. Then she said, 'If there was only one charge on the credit card, that means he didn't take the Uber back to Vegas, right?'

'Makes sense,' Caitlin said.

'Red Rose gives complimentary rides in its limo to and from Vegas,' she said. 'So he might have taken an Uber out here but got a ride back after he was done.'

'So who drives the limo?' Caitlin asked.

'Dickie,' she said.

The guard who'd been monitoring the security cameras.

'Let's go ask him,' Caitlin said, shoving the remaining dollars into her pocket. 'He likes money, too, right?'

Caitlin followed Debbie back over to the security room, but they found it empty this time. Caitlin checked the monitors. Silas Bennett was still in the bar.

She couldn't see Dickie anywhere.

'Come on,' Debbie said. 'I bet I know where he is.'

They walked back outside into the heat and Debbie spotted Dickie walking toward the large garage building, accompanied by a skinny guy with short bleached hair.

'Yo, Dickie,' she called.

He parted from his friend and changed course back toward them. He was carrying a Styrofoam food container. From the smell, she guessed it was a hamburger and fries.

'My friend wants to know if her boyfriend was here a couple weeks ago.'

'You know I can't tell you.'

Now that she was standing next to him, Caitlin confirmed he was at least six-six.

'Come on,' Debbie said. 'I'll tell Tilda to give you your weekly blowjob on the house.' She leaned over to Caitlin and whispered, 'You'll have to give me money to pay Tilda.'

Dickie objected, but when Caitlin pulled out her phone and showed him the picture, she saw recognition in his eyes. He looked back and forth between the two women, unsure whether to break the rules.

'Sure. I seen him. Gave him a ride back to town.'

'Do you remember where you took him?'

'These guys all blur together. Maybe the Galaxia?'

Jake's hotel. Caitlin felt goosebumps rise on her arms.

'What was he doing here?' Caitlin asked.

'What do you think?'

'So he was a customer?'

The guy chuckled. 'I hate to break it to you, honey, but your boyfriend came here to dip his fishing pole in someone else's pond.'

'Do you know which courtesan he saw?' Caitlin asked.

He shook his head. 'Sorry. I just drive the car.'

'What about the security tapes?'

'The recordings are only on file for a week. If we don't physically go in and save something, it's gone after that. Silas doesn't really want a record of what goes on here, if you know what I mean. Police can't subpoena what doesn't exist.'

'Don't tell anybody about this,' Debbie said to Dickie.

'Don't worry,' he said. 'If Silas found out I tattled on one of our customers . . .' Instead of finishing his sentence, he whistled through his teeth.

Dickie headed back toward the garage, lumbering like a bear.

'I'll ask around for you,' Debbie said. 'See if I can find out who he was with.'

'Thanks.'

Debbie stared at Caitlin, as if waiting for something.

'Oh,' Caitlin said, and she pulled out a few more hundreds.

This had been an expensive trip.

47

The next morning, while eating breakfast in her room, Caitlin watched one of the debate shows on ESPN. Desmond Wang, a retired player who'd been a frequent all-star early in his career and later won a ring as a bench player, was the guest. Now that the series was tied at two games apiece, the hosts were split on who would win the next game. But Wang, the former player, was firmly in the Lightning camp.

'They've got Jaxon Luca,' Wang said. 'That's all you need to say. It's a miracle the Sabertooths have this thing knotted at two. Luca wins Game Five in Cinci, then closes it out back home in Vegas. Lightning in six.'

'Give us your insight as a former player,' one of the hosts asked him. 'How good is Jaxon Luca?'

Wang, decked out in a flashy suit with a championship ring on his finger, explained that as soon as Luca burst onto the scene, everyone could tell there was something special about him. He existed on another level.

'Look at it like this,' said Wang. 'Think of your average high *school varsity player at sea level. Maybe college players are playing on top of small mountains in Appalachia. We're talking three or four thousand feet. Well, your typical NBA players, they're playing from the peaks of the Rocky Mountains. Ten thousand feet for guys riding the bench. Twelve thousand for starters. Garrett Streeter and Elijah Carter – they're fourteeners. Literally miles above your average college player. Hell, maybe Elijah Carter is Mount Denali in Alaska – twenty thousand feet.'*

'*Let me guess,*' said one of the hosts. '*Jaxon Luca is Mount Everest. Thirty thousand feet – twice as good as most NBA players.*'

'*No,*' Wang said, grinning. '*Jaxon Luca is Olympus Mons.*'

The two hosts both frowned. They'd never heard of it. But Caitlin knew exactly what he was talking about. She'd learned more from having an inquisitive child than she ever did in college.

'*Olympus Mons,*' Wang said, '*is a volcano on Mars. Seventy-two thousand feet. The tallest mountain in the solar system. More than twice as tall as any mountain here on Earth. That is how good Jaxon Luca is.*'

'*Out-of-this-world good?*' said one of the hosts.

'*Exactly.*'

Caitlin turned off the TV and rose to brush her teeth when her phone rang with an unfamiliar 702 number. She thought it must be Debbie, aka Amethyst, with information about Jake's visit to the brothel.

'Hello,' Caitlin said.

'Deputy Glass?' a hoarse voice said. 'Levi Grayson, Nevada Gaming Control Board.'

The Huey Lewis lookalike. 'How are you, Detective?'

'Good,' he said. 'I've heard back from Athletic Integrity and SportWatch, and there's definitely some wonky betting going on in the NBA Finals. Any chance we can meet up?'

Caitlin's blood went cold. He said the words in a faux chipper voice she'd heard a hundred cops use before, disguised as friendly but actually condescending. The subtext was easy to read: *I've got you.*

'Meet up?'

'I'm guessing you're in Vegas right now.'

'Why would I be in Vegas?' she stutter-laughed.

'Look,' he said, his tone changing to one that was more pointed. 'Don't hang up. I'm calling you from a burner phone. If I'm ever questioned, I'll deny this conversation happened.'

'I'm not following,' Caitlin said.

'I know you dated Garrett Streeter once upon a time,' he said. 'I know that what you're doing – whatever you're doing – is not part of any official investigation.'

Caitlin wanted to hang up. The fact that he'd told her not to – that he'd anticipated it – gave her pause.

'Why would you say that?'

'Because I'm good at my job,' Grayson said. 'I called your sheriff's office and asked for you, and they said you'd taken a leave of absence.'

Caitlin's scalp tingled with anxiety.

'I checked the website, where there's a picture of you,' Grayson said. 'Then I started looking into you. I found out you played for ASU. It took a little while, but I scoured the Facebook pages of some of your old teammates and found pictures of you and Streeter from a long time ago. I can't say for sure what's going on, but *something* is going on.'

Caitlin's heart pounded. She never should have called the Nevada Gaming Control Board. If this guy knew she wasn't working on an actual case, he could get her fired. Her career could be over. And if he could connect her to Garrett and the point-shaving he was doing – especially if no one knew or believed it was under duress – they could both be in big trouble.

Forget about their jobs – prison was a real possibility.

I'm sorry, Garrett, she thought. *I really fucked up.*

'So,' Grayson said, his fake chipperness returning, 'are you in Vegas? Can you meet up?' When Caitlin didn't answer, he added, 'I've got a place in mind. A restaurant. Very public. But no cameras.'

'I don't understand,' Caitlin said honestly.

Grayson took a deep breath, as if exasperated. 'Public – so we both feel confident no one will try anything. No cameras – so there's no record of us meeting. Just like there's no record of this phone call. I'm calling you from a burner phone,' he repeated, 'not my official one.'

'I still don't understand,' Caitlin repeated.

'I want to help you,' he said. 'But I don't want anyone to know I'm helping you.'

48

Caitlin parked a block from the meetup, a restaurant called Atomic Psalm, far from the cluster of casinos around the Strip. This was Las Vegas suburbia. When you were staying on the Strip, it was easy to forget Las Vegas was more than black-jack tables and slot machines. People lived here too.

Caitlin pushed through the door – a bell rang overhead to announce her arrival – and she spotted Levi Grayson alone at a table. He'd positioned himself to see her arrive and raised a hand to acknow-ledge her. He was wearing jeans and a long-sleeved Hawaiian shirt. He looked like a cop pretending not to be a cop.

She'd spent a few minutes on her laptop, trying to find information about him. He'd clearly done his homework on her, and she tried to do the same on him. But besides a handful of articles in the *Las Vegas Review-Journal* about various gaming-related arrests and fines over the years, she couldn't find anything.

She sat across from him. The place was big and busy, with servers bustling from table to table, packed with what seemed like locals rather than tourists. The walls of the little restaurant were adorned with black-and-white pictures of nuclear explosions. In the foreground of some of the pictures were old casinos – Sahara, Sands, Riviera – with mushroom clouds in the distance.

Grayson noticed where Caitlin's eyes were drawn and said, 'Back in the Fifties, tourists used to come to see explosions at the Nevada Test Site. You could see the mushroom clouds from downtown. Hotels would jack up the prices on the rooms with the best views. Apparently back then,' he went on, oblivious to her discomfort – or perhaps because of it, 'the locals were worried gambling would fade away. Like it was a fad that might go out of style. And Vegas might dry up and blow away. Look at us now.' He raised his arms as if gesturing to the city around them. 'Vegas is one of the fastest-growing cities in the country, and gambling is everywhere – Indian reservations, riverboats, online. Gambling, nationwide, generates a hundred billion dollars a year in revenue.'

'Thanks for the history lesson,' Caitlin said, wanting to get this over as fast as possible. 'What were the betting anomalies you talked about?'

Grayson shook his head. 'That's not how this works. *I* get to ask the questions.'

'No,' Caitlin said. 'If you want to help me, this isn't an interrogation.'

He frowned – in thought more than disapproval.

'Sorry,' he said. 'Old habits die hard.'

Grayson was in his fifties, she guessed, which made him look older than her image of Huey Lewis, although probably younger than the singer actually was now. Still, the resemblance was there. It was the chin dimple that did it. But Grayson looked a little more hardened, more grizzled, than she'd ever seen the singer look in videos or interviews or *Back to the Future*. His brown hair had gray streaks and was starting to recede. He had a mole or a birthmark, shaped a little like the state of Ohio, on the upper right side of his forehead, next to his hairline. Thick lines were etched across his brow. He had the look some people got from living in the West too long, with dry, sun-damaged skin thirsty for humidity.

It was hard to judge his height sitting down, but she guessed he was somewhere around Garrett's size. He had the build of a former athlete, and Caitlin wondered if he'd once played basketball.

'You should know before we begin,' Caitlin said, 'there are some things I can't tell you.'

'Can't or won't?'

Caitlin didn't answer. There was no point. She wouldn't betray Garrett. She decided that on the drive over. Grayson could assume all he wanted, but she wouldn't verify. This guy might bring her down, but she wouldn't help him take Garrett down with her.

'OK,' he said, 'here's what I think is going on. Garrett Streeter has hired you or asked you as a favor to help him. For whatever reason, he is being asked to or is being coerced into fixing games. Am I right?'

She said nothing – neither a confirmation nor a denial.

Grayson laughed. 'You've got a good poker face, Caitlin.'

The server came and took their order. Caitlin wasn't hungry but, not wanting to raise any suspicions, she quickly scanned the options and ordered something called 'the Atomic Bagel.'

'So the anomalies?' Caitlin asked when the server left.

'An uptick in what would be expected,' he said. 'Not the number of bets exactly – more the amounts. Online betting and some illegal books in Europe and China. Several big bets that, since they ended up paying out, drew attention. Plus, some in-game bets during Game Three. Enough to raise eyebrows.'

'What's going to happen?'

'Probably nothing,' Grayson said. 'They've alerted the NBA, which will probably scrutinize the tapes for wrongdoing by the refs or the teams. Try to figure out if someone is deliberately shaving points. But,' he said, holding up a finger, 'I don't think they're going to find anything because Garrett Streeter is having a great Finals. If not for him, the Lightning might have swept this series already.'

Grayson leaned back, settling in to what he had to say.

'One of the things I love about basketball,' Grayson said, 'is, more than any other team sport, one player can really affect the outcome. A team puts only five players on the court at any time, so one guy can ensure a team's greatness for a long period of time. That's why you see dynasties in basketball more than other sports. LeBron James went to the NBA Finals nine times in ten years, playing for *three* different teams. Or Steph Curry. Five Finals in a row and, even after Kevin Durant left, he brought them back. Michael Jordan – six championships in eight years. The 1980s – Larry Bird and Magic Johnson. There wasn't a single Finals in the whole decade that didn't have at least one of them playing, if not both. Because of what *one* player can do, it's the perfect sport to try to get someone to adjust the outcome.'

'Garrett Streeter is no LeBron James or Steph Curry,' Caitlin said. 'Maybe Jaxon Luca could be one day, but we don't know that yet.'

'That's the genius of it,' Grayson said. 'Garrett Streeter is better than people realize. If Jaxon Luca was up and down in this series, that's all anyone would talk about. Same with Elijah Carter. But Streeter flies under the radar. Hell, he only made the All-Star Team once before he came to Cincinnati. NBC Sports did a top twenty players list at the beginning of the season. He didn't make it. But he's better than that. I'd put him in the top ten in the league, wouldn't you?'

Caitlin nodded. She'd been thinking this about Garrett for a long time.

'Garrett Streeter came within two missed three-pointers from being in the 50–40–90 club this season,' Grayson said. 'Did you know that?'

He was referring to players who, over the course of a season, make at least fifty percent of their field goals, forty percent of their three-pointers, and ninety percent of their free throws. It was an obscure distinction – not like the scoring champion or league MVP – but only a dozen or so players had ever accomplished it. People like Larry Bird, Reggie Miller, Steve Nash – all stars in their eras. Caitlin didn't realize Garrett was so close. Garrett might not realize it. No one did. That was Grayson's point. Everyone recognized Garrett Streeter was a good player. Most people didn't realize how good.

'You told me this type of thing is unlikely,' she said. 'Maybe in college but not the pros. Those were your words.'

'What I said earlier still stands. This can't be common.'

'But it does happen?'

'I think it *is* happening,' Grayson said, arching his eyebrows as if to say, *As you well know.*

'But why?' Caitlin said.

Grayson gave her a look that indicated now might be the time for her to divulge some information. Seeing she wouldn't, he went on.

'One reason could be Streeter,' he said. 'He can affect the outcome more than people realize. So it's him who makes this possible.'

'That can't be all,' Caitlin said.

Grayson opened his mouth to speak, but their food arrived. They sat silently as the plates were placed in front of them. Caitlin's bagel sizzled on a metal tray, smothered in some kind of gooey, tomato-chunked cheese that made it look like it was melted with radiation. Grayson placed his napkin in his lap.

'Another reason,' Grayson said, 'is it's the Finals. Books will take bigger bets than a regular season game. And I suspect whoever is doing this is not just trying to rig one game. Right? They're rigging the whole series. That's seven games if it goes all the way. If you could place a lot of bets each game, more and more as you made more money, then the math adds up. Let's say you had a million dollars, and you could spread that out over ten or twenty bets. You turn that into almost two million. Next game you turn that into four. Then into eight. Sixteen. Maybe along the way you make other bets. Like the over-under. Proposition bets. If bets. Team totals.

Player props. Money line. Futures. Maybe you bet on how many points a particular player gets in a quarter or half. Maybe you bet from the start that the series would go a certain number of games. There's a lot someone can bet on in a seven-game series.'

Caitlin tried to wrap her brain around the magnitude of what they were talking about.

'You'd need a huge network of people placing bets, right?' she said. 'To make tens of millions of dollars, you'd need dozens if not hundreds of people betting.'

'Not necessarily,' Grayson said, pausing to drink his lemonade. 'You could make fake online accounts. One person, or a few people, placing lots of bets. Someone who seriously knows the betting world – specifically the online and illegal betting worlds.'

'But it would take resources, wouldn't it?' she asked. 'You're talking about dozens, if not hundreds, of bets.'

'Yes,' he said, nodding. 'And you have to be careful where you bet. A book won't let you keep taking their money game after game. You keep winning, they'll figure something is up. So you have to move your bets around.'

Caitlin wished she knew more about sports betting and had a moment of hope this guy, Grayson, might actually be able to help her, although she was skeptical whether she could trust him.

'Why are you helping me again?' she asked.

Grayson bit into his burger and chewed a large bite. Whatever sauce was on it slopped all over his chin. He wiped his face while chewing.

Caitlin, impatient for his mastication to end, said, 'Is this some kind of shakedown?'

Grayson smiled, his teeth dirty with chunks of sandwich.

'I wouldn't call it a shakedown,' he said, then ran his tongue over his teeth to clean them. 'How about a finder's fee?'

Caitlin glared at him. 'How much?'

'Ten thousand.'

She'd been afraid it was going to be a million. But she also felt disappointed. Levi Grayson came across like a halfway likable guy.

'Must be easy to be a crooked cop in this town,' Caitlin said coldly.

Grayson narrowed his eyes. Then he sat back, looking sad rather than angry. His burger was forgotten on the plate.

'You ever get hurt when you played ball?' he asked. The question was a non sequitur, and she had no idea why he changed the subject. 'Any season-ending injuries? Career-enders? Or something that side-lined you for a while?'

'Once,' she said.

'What happened?'

'What does this have to do with anything?'

'Humor me.'

'Avulsion fracture,' she said. 'A ligament was strained to the point where it pulled off a chunk of bone.'

'Surgery?'

'No. Just RICE.'

Rest, ice, compression, and elevation.

'But I never got back to my old self. It was my last year, supposed to be the jumping-off point for a career in basketball. Instead, I spent most of my time on the bench.'

'You have any lingering effects?'

'From the injury? No.'

This was true. She could run and jump without any worries about her ankle.

'You're lucky,' he said.

'I don't feel lucky.'

'About the injury,' he said. 'That it doesn't cause you problems.'

He explained that he'd played college basketball for UNLV, and he was constantly sidelined with injuries. Surgery. Recovery. Re-injury. That was the cycle of his career.

'I was never that good,' he said. 'I mean, not good enough to go pro. But I loved the game. I played through a lot of pain. Nobody ever talks about what a beating your body takes in basketball. What effect it has on you long term. I was fine for a while, but by the time I made it to fifty, my poor knees ached all the time.

'Then, a few years ago,' he added, 'I was heading into the Venetian as a guy comes running out with a bag of money in one hand and a pistol in the other. I was on duty. I took off after him. Have you been to the Venetian? There are canals like you're in Venice. He jumped across one of them to get away. It was a hell of a jump. I thought I was still twenty years old and tried to go after him. When I landed, my knee exploded. I fell into the drink. The perp got away. They caught him later, but not because of me. I was in the hospital. Surgery. Rehab. All that good stuff. Again.'

'Why are you telling me this?'

'It's easy to get hooked on painkillers,' he said. 'Drug addicts aren't just junkies lying around on dirty mattresses in trap houses. Most of them are ordinary people who need a little help getting through the day.'

'So what are you saying?' Caitlin asked. 'You need ten grand to stock up on oxy?'

'No,' he said. 'Oxy, Percocet, Vicodin – those stopped working for me a while ago. At least not the amounts a doctor would prescribe. I need a *little* taste' – he used his thumb and forefinger to emphasize just how little – 'of something stronger.'

Caitlin stared at him.

'It's amazing how quickly you get hooked,' he said. 'I'm a functioning addict at the moment. One bump in the morning to get me through the day. One in the evening to sleep.'

He was talking about heroin, she realized. No wonder he seemed so calm – he was high.

'The amount I use isn't going to cut it forever,' he said. 'And I try to use only the cleanest stuff I can get my hands on, but who knows what it's cut with. Cornstarch, powdered milk, flour – that's OK. But laundry detergent, meth, rat poison? There's no telling what kind of shit I'm putting into my body. I'm terrified of getting some IMF-laced shit.'

She knew what IMF was – illicitly manufactured fentanyl.

'More and more is cut with it. It's a selling point for some people, if you can believe that. "*Fifty times stronger*,"' he said, imitating a voiceover in a commercial. '"*A hundred times more likely to put you in a coffin.*"'

She'd been a cop long enough to know drug addiction wasn't only for the weak-willed. Anyone recovering from an injury could slip down the same slope Levi Grayson had.

'I've got no room for error,' Grayson said. 'If I OD – even if I live – my career is over. But I've got a plan. I need ten grand to pay for a residential rehab facility I've got my eye on in Palm Springs. It's twenty thousand for one month, but I've managed to save ten. I've got a month of vacation time coming up. I'm going to get clean, come back to work, finish out my years till retirement. Never touch another ounce of heroin or oxy or even alcohol for the rest of my life.'

'What about your knees?' she asked. 'The pain?'

He tapped his temple. 'The pain's really in here.'

Caitlin wasn't sure what to say.

'I wouldn't expect you to pay unless my information proves beneficial,' he said.

'I'll get the ten grand for you,' she said, '*if* I find what I'm looking for.'

'Thank you,' Grayson said, and he seemed genuinely grateful.

'So,' Caitlin asked, leaning forward, 'what else can you tell me?'

'I know who's responsible for trying to fix the NBA Finals.'

49

Grayson took a deep breath, ready to deliver what he clearly believed was groundbreaking information.

'A gangster named Alexei Maxim,' he said.

Caitlin tried not to show her disappointment that this was information she already had.

'Ah,' Grayson said, 'you've heard of him?'

Guess she didn't have such a good poker face after all.

'Just the name,' she said. 'Not much else.'

'Back in the old days, the Italian mafia ran Las Vegas,' Grayson said, another non sequitur. 'La Cosa Nostra. You've seen *The Godfather*? *Casino*?'

'Of course.'

'Forget all that. The mafia doesn't run jack shit around here anymore. What we have now is street gangs. Asian gangs doing credit card fraud and identity theft. The Mexican mafia – gang-bangers from Southern California – into burglary and armed robbery. Murder for hire. We've got an Albanian gang into extortion and money laundering. But the guys you gotta fear, the ones really committed to capitalizing off the sin in Sin City, are the Russians.'

Caitlin didn't interrupt him. She figured he'd get to his point about Alexei Maxim eventually.

'In addition to drugs, prostitution, human trafficking, he also takes bets on legitimate sports too. Boxing. MMA. Football. Baseball. Basketball. If you want to place big bets – and I mean *big* bets – you go to Alexei Maxim.'

'How do you know it's him?' she asked. 'I heard another name. Silas Bennett.'

Grayson frowned and shook his head. 'Silas Bennett owns a legitimate brothel in Green Lawn. He's a dirtbag, and I don't doubt he's involved in some illegal shit here and there. But I can't imagine he'd do something on this scale. Or something as risky. No, I'm sure it's Maxim.'

'How?'

'Because,' he said, 'that's who I get my H from.'

'So you don't *know* it's him. You just know him well enough to suspect him.'

'I don't know Alexei Maxim at all,' he said. 'I've never met him. I get my stuff from one of his girls.'

'Girls?'

'They make house calls for two types of clients,' he said. 'Those who want sex and those who want drugs.' He shrugged, a little embarrassed. 'I used to be the former. Now I'm the latter. My delivery girl started asking me the other day about the Finals. She knows what I do, of course. This isn't some street hustler. Her clients are like me. People who need the utmost discretion. She *never* asks me about my job. But the other day she floated it out there, like it was small talk, if I was watching the games and if I'd heard anything about bets going down. There was definitely a subtext. Like, if anyone was talking, Alexei would want to know.'

'And you didn't tell her anything?'

'It never occurred to me anything was going on until I got a call from you.'

She took a chance and pulled out her phone.

'Have you ever seen this guy before?' she asked, showing him the picture of Mr Mustache from the game. 'I think that's a wig.'

'How can you tell?'

'Doesn't it look like one?' she said, trying to pretend it was her police intuition that made her recognize a wig when she saw one.

He studied the image.

'No,' he said. 'Never seen him. Why?'

She didn't answer.

'He doesn't look Russian,' Grayson said. 'Looks kind of like Burt Reynolds. But I'm sure Alexei's got regular old Americans working for him, too. My girl's not Russian.'

Caitlin looked down at the food she hadn't touched. The goo dripping down the bagel was starting to congeal.

'Thanks,' she said. 'This has been helpful.'

She was lying. Grayson really hadn't told her anything she didn't already know. And she didn't trust him. She wanted to get out of this restaurant and never see him again.

'OK, so you already had his name,' Grayson said, 'But I bet you don't have this.'

He reached under the table and picked up a canvas messenger bag, old and fraying at the seams. He stuck his hand inside and, for a moment, Caitlin thought he was going to pull a gun on her. Instead, he brought out a manila file folder, stuffed with papers, about the width of a *Sports Illustrated*.

'This,' Grayson said, 'is everything we know about Alexei Maxim.'

'Who's "we"?' Caitlin asked. 'The Nevada Gaming Control Board?'

Grayson chuckled. 'Every law enforcement agency with so much as a sliver of jurisdiction in Las Vegas.'

He slid the file across the table, but she was hesitant to take it. Could she really trust this guy?

Grayson took a deep breath. He seemed to sense her reticence.

'I've told you about my addiction, so I might as well tell you everything,' he said, the expression on his face changing.

During his confession of heroin addiction, he hadn't looked uncomfortable. Now he did.

'There was a girl I used to see. Her name was Anya. She was Russian. Back before Alexei, these girls could buy their freedom. Get out of the life. We used to talk about her getting out. Then Maxim came to town. Took over. One day Anya calls and says she can't come over anymore. She belongs to the new guy. I tell her I love her, want to buy her freedom. I don't have the money, but I'll find it. She says it's no good. She's crying, says I need to forget about her. Two months go by. I tried some other girls, but none of them filled the hole. Then one day I get word the Clark County Sheriff's Office found a girl's body out at Red Rock Canyon.'

He pursed his lips in an attempt to speak without crying.

'Strangled,' he said, his voice cracking. 'That's the rumor about Maxim – he likes to kill with his bare hands. Wants to be close to see the light go out of your eyes.'

'I'm sorry,' Caitlin said softly.

Grayson blinked, cleared his throat, and said, 'To my eternal shame, I give that evil motherfucker money every week to feed my weakness.'

He leaned forward and gestured to the file in front of Caitlin.

'Yeah, I want the money for rehab,' he said, 'that's true. But my real motivation is simple. Revenge.'

50

Back in her room, Caitlin sat down and started going through the file, which was cobbled together from different agencies: Las Vegas Police Department, Clark County Sheriff's Office, Nevada Division of Investigation, Nevada Gaming Control Board Investigation Division, and the FBI. Each report was formatted differently – and different from her own department – but she was able to navigate the organization easily enough. Some of the reports didn't mention Alexei Maxim specifically, but rather described the actions of the Russian mob in Las Vegas. The FBI file was the most comprehensive. There was a brief biography of Maxim, who was born Alexei Maximov in Novosibirsk, apparently to aristocrats. He spent part of his youth in a private school in London, but when his parents fell out of favor with the Russian government, they disappeared and Maximov was deported back home, an orphan. He became involved with organized crime as a teenager and – it was assumed because he had a more cosmopolitan background than most of the other criminals – left to work abroad. He ran gangs in Copenhagen, Helsinki, and Iceland in his twenties and thirties, proving so effective at these assignments he was given a major promotion: Las Vegas. While the Russian mob had a foothold in the gambling capital of the world, Maxim – dropping the OV from his surname at some point – apparently expanded the Russians' power to the point that they were now considered the most formidable organized-crime operation in Nevada.

One thing Caitlin figured out pretty quickly from the file was that – even though the cops knew more than the general public – there was little they could actually pin on Maxim. Witnesses who gave the police statements seemed to disappear. He was a bit of a ghost. A boogeyman.

There were, however, pictures of him. The photocopies weren't the best reproductions of what she assumed were better images stored in police databases, but the pictures were helpful. She'd recognize him if she saw him. He had an oval face, high cheekbones, puffy lips, and a broad forehead leading to a widow's peak of receding hair. One photo showed him at a blackjack table, wearing a short-sleeved shirt, with his exposed arm revealing a tattoo. There was a close-up of it and, although the photocopy wasn't the best, it was easy to tell it was a coffin with a cross on the lid. A hand-written note stated, *Russian mob tattoos are their own language. Coffin means murder. Burying their victims.*

One of the reports estimated his height at five foot ten – an inch shorter than Caitlin – but he had a squat, muscular frame. Silas Bennett had looked like a clown she could knock out with one punch. Alexei Maxim, on the other hand, looked like someone she wouldn't want to mess with if his hands were tied behind his back and she was carrying a baseball bat.

What she wanted most was to know where he lived, where he might have a base of operations – i.e., where he might hold a person he'd kidnapped.

She found one possibility.

The address of a commercial property that authorities once assumed Maxim owned via a shell corporation, followed by a note saying the property was vetted and discounted as a legitimate lead.

She picked up her phone to call Grayson.

'Do you know if the police staked out this commercial property?' she asked. 'The FBI?'

'I doubt it,' he said. 'Maxim pays off the right people. I assume I'm not the only cop in town he's got his hooks into. There have to be others with drug habits, gambling debts, sex addictions. In Vegas, it's easy to get dirt on people with power.'

Caitlin remained quiet as she was thinking.

'What are you going to do?' Grayson asked.

'Reconnaissance.'

51

Garrett was sitting in his cold basement watching film. Instead of considering strategy, though, he studied the faces of players and coaches, anyone who was in the background. Josh, on the sidelines, with a smile on his face like he wasn't worried about a thing. Jamie, eyes wide and focused. Coach Ware scowling.

He heard footsteps coming down and then Summer walked into the room, texting on her phone. When she finished, she exhaled deeply and sat down on the recliner next to him.

'You look tired,' she said, placing the phone on the armrest.

'I am.

'What's up?' he asked when she didn't say anymore.

When they'd first met, he had been captivated by her beauty, but he soon found her to be so much more than what he expected from a model. She read voraciously, like him, although she preferred nonfiction to fiction and was more abreast of world events than he was. She could comfortably chat with anyone on any occasion, whether at a backyard barbecue in Ohio or a runway show in Paris. But what he really loved about her was the simple, non-glamorous things they did together, like walking along the river or playing board games or watching movies down here in his film room – the kind of stuff he could imagine doing as a family when they had kids.

'Where's Caitlin today?' Summer said.

'Glass?'

'How many Caitlins do you know?'

'Sorry,' he said. 'She stayed in Vegas.'

'Why?'

'She wanted a little break,' he said. 'I told her it was no big deal. She could stay there till Game Six.'

She eyed him suspiciously. It didn't make a damn bit of sense that his ex was supposed to be helping him with his basketball game, yet she stayed behind in Las Vegas. Why wouldn't Caitlin go home to her family?

'Did you tell her we were trying to have a baby?' Summer said.

Garrett noticed the use of the word 'were' instead of 'are.' Which
was true – they'd stopped trying as the playoffs became more intense
– but still she made it sound like it was something they'd only done
in the past and wouldn't try again in the future.

'No.'

'Is it really not on your mind at all?'

'I'm trying not to think about it,' he said, and then he realized
how that sounded. 'I told you I don't want any distractions during
the playoffs.'

'When there's a kid running around the house, that will be a
distraction.'

'I know. But that will be different.'

'I'm just surprised it didn't come up.'

'We agreed we didn't want to broadcast it,' he said.

'We've told our friends, though.'

He rolled his eyes. 'Glass and I only talk about basketball.'

She made a *pfft* sound with her lips. 'You're always talking or
texting with her,' she said. 'I've seen you. You're not talking *just*
about basketball. If talking is what you're doing.'

Garrett glared at her.

'I'll tell her now if that will make you feel better.'

'Put yourself in my shoes, Garrett,' she said. 'How would you
feel if, out of the blue, I fired my closest advisor and brought in an
ex-boyfriend to replace him? The one that got away.'

'She wasn't—'

'Bullshit,' Summer said. 'You used those exact words when we
started dating. You said you hadn't felt this way about someone
since your college girlfriend.'

'She was my first love,' he said. 'That doesn't mean she was the
love of my life.'

Caitlin told him not to trust anyone, but he knew Summer wasn't
behind all this. The thought of it was completely ridiculous. The
reason he hadn't told her initially was because he didn't want her
to get involved. And he knew she'd tell him to go to the police. But
this was getting out of hand. He didn't need her distrust on top of
everything else he was dealing with. He opened his mouth to tell
her everything – to come clean – but then he closed it abruptly. His
eyes had drifted to her phone sitting on the armrest.

He hadn't seen this phone before. It was a burner like the ones
he'd been using to talk to Caitlin. Similar to the one the kidnappers

gave him. She covered the phone with her hands. Then she pocketed it, acting nonchalant.

It wasn't out of the question for her to have a burner phone. She used them from time to time – someone with her level of celebrity didn't give her private number to just anyone – but there was something surreptitious about the way she covered it.

'Whatever,' she said, standing up and pocketing the phone. 'I'll let you get back to what you love the most – basketball.'

Although it seemed like she'd come in here looking for a fight, Garrett was relieved to see her going without it getting any more heated.

'Or am I third now behind Caitlin Glass?' she muttered on her way out.

52

Caitlin awoke to the sound of her phone buzzing. She looked around, unsure for a moment why she was crammed behind the wheel of a vehicle, the bright morning light beginning to warm the interior, then realized where she was and why. She'd spent the night staking out the building Alexei Maxim supposedly owned. Sometime around three in the morning she'd been unable to keep her eyes open and gave in to sleep.

She sat up, grabbing the phone.

'Hi, so Debbie gave me your number,' a female voice said. 'You're looking for a guy who came into the Red Rose Ranch.'

It seemed early to call, but maybe this woman was like Debbie – her working hours ended when the sun rose.

'Yes,' Caitlin said.

'So I think I remember the guy you're looking for. She kind of described him and said what day he was there.'

Her voice was soft with a slight rasp to it, like she had a cold, although Caitlin got the impression that was just the way she sounded.

'I've got a pretty good memory for names and faces,' the woman said. 'Clients are always surprised by how well I remember them. I remember what they like, you know, in bed, which comes in handy.'

She let out a husky laugh. Men, Caitlin suspected, probably fell for that rasp every day.

'What was your name again?' Caitlin said, putting the phone on speaker and pulling her laptop from the passenger seat. She'd been able to pick up WiFi from a nearby florist last night, and she tried again.

'Mandy.'

'Is that your – you know – stage name or whatever you call it?'

'Jordana.'

Caitlin went to the Red Rose Ranch site and scrolled through the women's profiles, looking for Jordana.

'So you think you met my friend?'

'Yeah, was his name Jake?'

Caitlin went cold. She'd never mentioned his name to Debbie or the other girls.

'Yes.'

Mandy gave her a description that was generic enough it could have just been what Debbie passed along. But then she mentioned he was tall, not super tall, maybe six foot, which is something Caitlin hadn't mentioned to anyone either.

'He was good looking,' Mandy said. 'Some of the guys who come in here, you're trying hard to keep from throwing up. But he was fun. The kind of guy I'd fuck if I was off the clock.'

Caitlin found Jordana's profile and was flipping through pictures. The voice fit with the woman, who looked to be about thirty, give or take a couple of years, with dark hair and a smile that was a little bit mischievous and that wasn't the least bit diminished by a few crooked teeth. Most of the pictures showed her in cut-off jean shorts and cowboy boots, a Western-style vest that covered only her breasts but not the space between. The link to her weekly schedule showed Mandy, or Jordana, was off now, and the calendar wouldn't let Caitlin scroll back to see if she was working when Jake was in town.

'Is he your boyfriend?' Mandy asked. 'Or husband? Is that why you're looking for him?'

Caitlin didn't answer.

'A lot of guys in relationships come to the Ranch,' Mandy said. 'It's not that they're unhappy at home. When they're in Vegas, they're looking for something different. Some excitement. Don't go too hard on him, OK? I don't want to break up any relationships or anything.'

'It's OK,' Caitlin said. 'I'm not mad at him. I just want to find him.'

'In that case, when you do find him, tell him to come back and see me.' She let out a dry laugh and disconnected the call.

Caitlin stared at her phone, thinking. She had an explanation for the Uber charge. Both Dickie and Mandy confirmed it. Which meant Jake disappeared sometime after he returned to his hotel.

She considered calling Garrett but opted not to. No need to tell the guy a prostitute was the last person to see his brother before he disappeared.

Instead, she called Levi Grayson.

'Can you talk?' she asked.

'Deputy Glass,' he said dreamily – the voice of someone who just had his morning fix. 'What did you find out?'

She explained that the building she was staking out, the one Maxim might run some of his operation out of, was an L-shaped shopping plaza on the corner of a busy intersection, away from the Strip and in the heart of Las Vegas suburbia.

'There are three businesses here,' she said. 'A mattress store. A flower shop. And a veterinary clinic with a dog shelter attached. The kind of place you can leave your dog for a week if you go on vacation. Called Ace Animal Care.'

'You think the vet works for him?' he said. 'Maybe stitches up fighting dogs in exchange for discounted rent?'

'Probably,' she said. 'You'll never guess what the mattress store is called.'

'What?'

'Going to the Mattresses.'

He burst out laughing. 'I guess Russian gangsters love *The Godfather* like everybody else.'

Behind the building, where she was parked now, the streets became residential, populated by houses that looked old – by Las Vegas standards anyway – and a little run-down. While she wouldn't call the area a slum, it was far from where any high rollers would live. The homes were in need of paint jobs. Sidewalks were cracked and disintegrating. Bikes lay abandoned in yards spotted with dead patches.

A large Going to the Mattresses delivery truck was backed up to the loading door, which was closed. There were no other cars in the lot. But, as she spoke to Grayson, a Honda Civic pulled up, and a girl who looked like she might still be in high school unlocked the door to the florist. Soon after, a Toyota Camry arrived, and a balding guy entered the veterinary clinic.

'Got some employees coming to work,' Caitlin said.

'Any sign of Alexei Maxim?' Grayson asked.

'No,' she said.

As she said this, two more vehicles pulled into the back lot: a Chevy Colorado truck and a Lexus sedan. Two big guys exited the truck, one with a mullet, the other with a mohawk, both the size of NFL linemen. The driver's door of the sedan opened, and a shorter guy with his hair pulled back in a ponytail exited. She thought that was all of them, but Mr Ponytail opened the passenger door of the sedan, and a fourth person stepped out.

'Holy shit,' Caitlin said. 'It's him.'

'Maxim?'

'In the flesh.'

She was sure it was him. He held a phone to his ear, giving her a good look at the tattoo on his forearm. Even from this distance, she could easily distinguish the shape of the tapered hexagonal coffin.

The four approached the door to Going to the Mattresses, and one of the big guys, the one with the mohawk, opened it. Maxim was quite a bit shorter than him, but he had a squat, muscular look. He reminded her of a pit bull – not the biggest dog but the scariest.

Maxim went through the door, followed by the other three.

'Now what?' Grayson said.

'I need to go in there,' Caitlin said. 'As soon as possible.'

'You mean like as a customer?' Grayson asked. 'You going to pretend you're in the market for a mattress?'

'No,' she said. She wasn't sure how much she should say, but Grayson had been helpful thus far. 'I need to break in.' Obviously all three businesses would be in full swing during the day, so she added, 'Tonight.'

He hesitated before speaking. 'What are you hoping to accomplish?'

'I can't tell you.' This is where she had to draw the line. 'But I have to get in there.'

'You shouldn't rush this,' he said. 'A few days of surveillance will—'

'Game Five is tonight,' she said. 'I need to do it before the game is over.'

'The game starts at eight,' Grayson said. 'It won't be dark yet.' Caitlin thought. The Uber lead was a dead end. Silas Bennett seemed like a non-suspect. This was all she had to go on. There might be clues that would lead to his location. Or Jake might even be inside. There was at least one more game after tonight, so the argument could be made that she had time. However, that time was contingent upon Garrett being able to deliver what the kidnappers asked for. They'd already promised that if Garrett failed again, Jake would be killed. If there was any chance she could find him tonight, she had to take it.

'I don't have a choice,' Caitlin said. 'I'm going tonight.'

53

Garrett and Elijah sat at their respective lockers. Elijah was reading a Wolverine graphic novel. Garrett had a newish bestseller that he was pretending to read. This was their routine before games, and he was sticking to it. On game day, there was a fair amount of waiting. Some players listened to music on their earbuds or streamed movies on their phones. Some played cards. Garrett and Elijah were known for reading – Garrett books, Elijah comics. It calmed Garrett's mind before a game, took his mind off his own anxiety.

But there was no calming his mind today.

Once again he'd been told to cover the spread. The Sabertooths were favored at home by five and a half.

He needed to win by six goddamn points.

Across the room, Billy Croft and Kevin Mackey were arguing about who was the greatest of all time, Michael Jordan or LeBron James. Billy was saying Jordan. Kevin was making a case for LeBron. They were getting more and more players involved and came over to Elijah and Garrett.

'Come on, guys. Solve this for us,' Billy said. 'Who's the GOAT? Jordan or LeBron?'

Almost the entire team gathered around the two of them, ready to hang on their words.

Garrett looked at Elijah, who winked back.

'Wilt,' Elijah declared, and both Billy and Kevin groaned in disapproval.

'What about you, Garrett?' Kevin asked him. 'Jordan or LeBron?'

Garrett glanced at Elijah, who grinned.

'Kareem,' Garrett said.

Elijah laughed heartily and reached out to fist-bump Garrett.

'Ah, come on,' Billy moaned, and the crowd dispersed around them, waving their arms dismissively.

Everyone was in good spirits – even Garrett had forgotten his troubles for a few seconds – but then the door banged open and Coach Ware came in, followed by Josh and the other assistants. They stood in the center of the room, underneath the snarling Sabertooth on the ceiling.

'Listen up,' he said. 'Is everyone here? OK, good. This won't take long, but it needs to be said.'

Pre-game speeches were usually reserved for game time. This was early.

'We got word from the league,' he said, 'there might be some criminal activity going on in terms of sports betting.'

There were a few raised eyebrows, but otherwise everyone's reaction was neutral. Josh met Garrett's eyes, then looked away. He often gave Garrett extra looks – they were friends – but Garrett wondered if there was something more this time.

'Apparently there was some dodgy betting going on for Game Three,' Coach said. 'I don't know any other details. We were told to keep a look out for anything unusual. I don't think there's anything to it, personally. All I saw was two teams fighting like hell for a win.'

There were several nods in agreement.

'But,' Coach added, 'if I find out any of you were involved in anything like this, I will personally make it my mission to see you kicked out of the league and shamed for the rest of your life as a cheat.'

'Damn straight,' someone muttered.

As the coaching staff left the room, Garrett pretended to go back to reading, but he could feel blood rushing to his head and was afraid to look up for fear he might find the entire team staring at him.

54

Caitlin pulled her rental back into its hiding spot under the shade of a mesquite tree. She was disappointed to see the sedan that brought Maxim this morning was now gone. She'd hoped to catch him leaving so she could try to follow him to another location. But she'd needed badly to pee – not to mention eat and pick up supplies.

There were now several plastic and paper bags in the seat next to her. The first was from In-N-Out Burger, which she couldn't get back in Ohio, and the second was a big plastic sack from Lowe's containing a twenty-volt hand drill, a package of bits, a framing hammer, a pry bar, a flathead screwdriver, a baggie of zip-ties, and a small flashlight barely bigger than a lipstick tube. A third bag contained something that looked like a larger flashlight at first glance but was actually a stun gun. She'd bought new clothes, too, and put them on in the bathroom at Target: a thin black hoodie with no visible labels, a pair of cargo pants with lots of big pockets, and a new pair of black Under Armour running shoes. She'd also purchased thin black leather gloves.

She'd made a trip to the hotel as well, where she'd picked up her pistol, which was still in its hand-held safe, tucked under the passenger seat.

She scarfed her burger down. Even with evening approaching, the temperature had to be close to a hundred degrees outside. Her engine fan was working overtime, and she didn't want the car to overheat, so she risked turning off the engine and rolling down the windows.

Employees of the three businesses left one by one. By the time the sun lowered close to the horizon, the pickup and the delivery truck were the only vehicles left.

She decided she'd wait at least until the second quarter. There would be more cover in the gloom of twilight, and the big body-guards – whom she referred to in her mind as Mr Mullet and Mr Mohawk – might leave as well. She assumed they were still there. They'd arrived in the truck, and the truck hadn't left.

She turned on the app to listen to the pre-game coverage while keeping an eye on Maxim's building. As commentators and former players gave their predictions for the game, Caitlin opened the package holding the stun gun. She'd left her department-issued taser in Ohio. This was different. The taser shot electrodes that attached to clothing and sent electricity through wires. The stun gun was something you had to hold against the person, a hand-held cattle prod. She read the instructions and examined the device to make sure she knew how to use it.

She tucked the stun gun into a pocket of her pants, the zip-ties in another. The screwdriver and flashlight, too. Then she reached under the passenger seat, pulled out the small safe, and entered the combination. She took her SIG Sauer out and loaded it.

'Just in case,' she murmured, and slid the small gun into a pocket of her cargo pants.

As the game was about to start, she sent a quick text to Debbie thanking her for having Mandy call her. Then she called Grayson.

'I don't feel so good,' he said. 'I need to get well and then I'll call you back.'

Get well must be code for shooting up.

'OK,' she said and hung up.

She kept an eye on the building as she listened to Chuck Walla ask Harding Able and Dirk Justice for their thoughts on the game.

'*Which team is facing more pressure tonight?*' Walla asked.

'*Both,*' Harding Able said. '*In the last forty years, when a playoff series is tied two–two, the winner of Game Five has gone on to win the series eighty-four percent of the time. To say this game is pivotal is an understatement.*'

The black sedan pulled back into the lot and slid into the spot next to the pickup. Caitlin slunk down in her seat and muted her phone.

The man with the ponytail climbed out of the passenger seat, and one of the big bodyguards, Mr Mullet, pulled himself out from behind the driver's door. He held the door and waited. Slowly, another man emerged, this one wearing baggy clothes and a ball cap. It definitely wasn't Maxim. This guy was taller, slimmer.

He appeared to be crying, wiping away tears.

Caitlin's eyes narrowed and she leaned forward.

Is that Jake?

She couldn't tell from this distance. The correct color of hair stuck out from under the cap, but she couldn't get a look at his face. He followed Mr Ponytail to the back door of Going to the Mattresses as Mr Mullet followed.

Caitlin breathed deep, trying to slow her heartbeat.

'*And here we are with the tip-off,*' Chuck Walla said. '*Rodrigo Sandoval tips the ball to Garrett Streeter. The Sabertooths have control as Game Five of the NBA Finals begins.*'

55

'Y ou OK?' Josh asked Garrett as he came over to the huddle forming on the sidelines. 'You look like you're struggling out there.'

Garrett glared at him. He was in no mood to talk. Yes, his shot was off. But he was trying, running around out there like the goddamned Tasmanian Devil. His teammates were lethargic. Coach was going over a play they'd practiced a dozen times, one that should result in a bucket for Elijah and – theoretically – give their offense a spark.

They were already down by nine in the first few minutes.

Elijah looked down at the whiteboard with a lax expression, like a kid not paying attention in class. He'd hardly broken a sweat.

'I want to say something,' Garrett said when Coach was finished. He looked around at his teammates. 'This is the goddamn NBA Finals. Play like the game fucking matters.'

His teammates looked stung by his criticism. To their credit, they didn't avert their eyes, but Elijah seemed more irritated than motivated.

'Wake up, man,' Garrett said to him.

'Don't tell me to wake up,' Elijah snapped. 'You haven't exactly been consistent this series. I'm the only one who's brought my A game every night.'

This wasn't how Garrett wanted this to go. Time was running out – they were due back on the court.

'You're not bringing it tonight,' Garrett said. 'Maybe you need to cut down on your extracurriculars before games.'

As soon as he said it, he knew it was a mistake.

'Go fuck yourself, Streeter,' Elijah said. 'You're one to talk. I saw that girl leave your room.'

The players stared back and forth at the two. Garrett, fuming, opened his mouth to argue, but Coach shoved his body between them.

'Get your asses out there before we get a delay of game called on us.'

As they walked away, Coach held onto Garrett's jersey for an extra beat.

'When I tell you to be a leader off the court,' he said, 'pissing off your teammates isn't what I had in mind.'

Garrett shrugged him off and took the ball from the ref at the sideline. He tried to clear his mind. The ref tooted the whistle, and Rodrigo set a pick for Elijah. It worked perfectly, and now all Garrett needed to do was get Elijah the ball. But when he passed it, Jaxon Luca came out of nowhere and snatched it. He bolted down the court. Garrett jogged behind him with no hope of catching him.

Luca leaped from the second hash mark and swung the ball from his waist in a thunderous windmill dunk. The crowd groaned.

Elijah shouted to Garrett, 'You want *me* to wake up?'

56

Caitlin waited as the pale light of dusk grew dimmer and dimmer until she figured it was about as dark as it would get. On the screen, everything was going the Lightning's way. Every shot – no matter who took it – was going in. Meanwhile, for the Sabertooths, even on good looks or easy layups, the ball seemed to roll around the rim and fall to the floor.

'*If they don't stop the bleeding soon,*' Harding Able said, '*no amount of late-game heroics are going to matter.*'

This was bad. Garrett was supposed to lead the Sabertooths to victory and cover the five-and-a-half-point spread. If the kidnappers kept true to their word, Jake could die tonight.

It's time, Caitlin told herself.

She pulled her hair into a tight ponytail then tugged on her gloves. She took the hand drill out of its little suitcase container and fitted it with a cobalt-fortified high-speed bit. Finally, she picked up the pry bar and hammer.

She'd arrested people for breaking and entering.

She'd never done it herself.

There's a first time for everything, she thought, and she stepped out of the car.

She walked quickly across the street and climbed the grassy berm at the edge of the shopping center's lot. She went to the mattress store's door first and gently tried the handle. It was locked. She'd seen the men go in there, but she wasn't sure where they were inside. If she started to force open the door, would they hear?

She looked over toward the vet clinic, then at the florist. She decided to try the florist. Again, the door was locked, but she thought she was far enough away from the other door that people inside might not hear. She was counting on there being some sort of internal corridor connecting the three businesses.

There was a deadbolt, and she placed the drill against the circular face of the outside housing. She pressed hard and squeezed the trigger. The metal bit whined against the metal lock, but it wasn't as loud as she'd feared. She pushed for nearly a full minute, then the circle of metal buckled and she was able to pry it off with the screwdriver. She jammed the screwdriver into the cylinder, flicked her wrist, and slid the bolt to the side.

Now for the doorknob. There was a gap between the door and the jamb, and she could see the latch bolt wasn't hooked by much. She looked around, made sure no one was watching, and jammed the tip of the pry bar into the crack between the door and the jamb. She slammed the hammer into the bar and sunk the flat blade deep into the crack. She pried the door, using her body as leverage. The metal squealed. She readjusted the bar, slammed it again with the hammer, and the door slipped free of its latch. She eased it open, peeking inside, then closed the door behind her.

The room was dimly lit by the emergency exit sign over the door, but Caitlin pulled out the flashlight to see better. She was in a storage area, with a variety of flowers in buckets of water, along with shelves of vases. There was a pleasant aroma to the room and a trace of humidity in the air. A pegboard filled one wall, holding containers of ribbons and scissors and other tools. Plants hung from the ceiling.

She found a trash can, half full with decorative paper, transparent plastic, and discarded flower stems. She reached in, moved some of the contents aside, and hid the electric drill down at the bottom. She didn't think she'd need it again now that she was inside, and she'd been careful to make sure her fingerprints weren't on it.

There were two other doors. She tried a handle, the door opening into a large warehouse of mattresses. She saw no one. She thought about going through but decided to make sure the rooms of the flower shop were clear. She didn't want any surprises. She told herself she wasn't stalling, but she knew she was. She was too nervous to go into the warehouse. She knew this was a bad idea – going in alone, with no way to call for backup – but what choice did she have? Jake could be in there.

She peeked through the other door, seeing the lobby of the florist. Light from the street poured in through the front picture windows, and she clicked off her flashlight. She assumed she was hidden in the shadows of the room well enough no one outside would see her.

More flowers were on display here, hanging from the ceiling or positioned on stands. A shelf behind the counter was labeled *VIP SPECIAL*, and it held several glass vases with small bouquets. None of the arrangements was anything exceptional. The sticker prices ranged widely in increments of ten dollars, although, to her eye, there was no discernible difference between the arrangements. She went back the way she'd come and into the first room she'd entered. She meant to hurry through it and into the mattress store, but she hesitated. She doubled back and went to the display in the lobby.

She examined the tags. Some of the flowers were fifty dollars. Some seventy. Some only twenty. Yet the arrangements all looked the same.

She set the hammer and pry bar down and picked up the nearest vase. She yanked the stems out of the water and tossed them on the counter, then held the vase up to the light. Distorted by the water and the glass, something was floating inside, like a coin-sized black bubble. She dumped the water onto the counter, and the object flopped out into the puddle. It was a small balloon, uninflated but tied off. She had an idea what it was and figured the fifty- and seventy-dollar vases must contain additional balloons.

She looked around for a pair of scissors. She snipped off the balloon's knot and stretched out the opening, trying to shake the contents out. A hard black blob, like a Tootsie roll mushed into a ball, flopped onto the counter.

Black tar heroin.

57

At halftime, Garrett went straight for his locker and found the burner phone.

I can't do it, he typed. It's impossible.

He knew it was futile to ask for mercy, but he didn't have any other choice. They were down by twenty-nine – a bigger deficit than they had been in for their miracle comeback in Game Three. Behind him, the locker room was quiet as his teammates rehydrated or changed into dry jerseys. Elijah, as was his custom at halftime, changed not only his shirt but his shoes and socks.

Garrett stared at the phone, waiting. A text came through:

Do you want your brother to die?

He typed. I'm TRYING!!!

The kidnappers must see Garrett was doing everything within his power. He was leading his team in scoring, assists, steals, and rebounds – the last category hard to believe considering he was the shortest person in the starting lineup.

Garrett waited. The phone showed the little ellipses icon, suggesting the kidnappers were typing. But the next message held no words. Only an image.

A close-up of Jake's face, the gun barrel pressed against his cheekbone with such force he was wincing against the pressure.

Garrett slammed the phone into his locker, and several heads turned. Josh approached. He seemed to have been hovering nearby.

'Everything OK?' he asked. 'Was that Summer?'

'No,' Garrett said. 'Nothing is OK. Didn't you see the goddamn scoreboard?'

He stomped past Josh, knowing he would need to apologize later, but not giving a shit right now. Instead, he went to Elijah, who was sitting on the floor in the corner doing stretches.

'Hey,' Garrett said, kneeling. The two hadn't spoken since their spat in the first quarter. 'I'm sorry about earlier.'

Elijah looked at first like he might hold a grudge, but then his body changed – loosened like a taut rope given slack – and he said, 'It's OK. I'm playing like shit.'

'We all are,' Garrett said. He cleared his throat. 'The girl from my room, she's my old college girlfriend. She played for the women's team at ASU.'

'She's cute,' Elijah said and chuckled.

By his demeanor, you wouldn't think he was down by almost thirty points in an NBA Finals game. This was how Garrett needed him – relaxed, loose.

'It's not like that,' Garrett said. 'She's married and has a kid.'

'Too bad.'

'I brought her in to help me because I'm struggling.'

Elijah frowned at him. 'You're up and down,' he said, 'but I wouldn't say you're struggling. You're carrying us tonight.'

'She's good at giving advice,' Garrett said. 'You know what she'd say if she was here?'

Elijah said nothing.

'Let's hit the reset button and show these motherfuckers what we're made of.'

Elijah grinned, a big, bright smile.

58

Caitlin slipped through the door into the mattress warehouse. She held the hammer high for attacking, the pry bar low for defense. The room was lit by fluorescent lights, and there were mattresses all over the place, wrapped in plastic, leaning against walls, stacked five high on skids. A workbench lined one wall, messy with utility knives and tape rolls.

No people were in sight.

To her left was the back wall, where the large roller door – now closed – led to the loading dock. The door that the two guys from the sedan came through, escorting what could have been Jake, was next to it. On the wall to the right were a series of offices, each with glass windows, the lights off inside. At the far end of the room was another roller door, this one wide open. The lights were off on the other side, but enough illumination came through from this side that she could tell it was the entryway to the showroom. Fully assembled beds were spread out in a spacious display, with thick comforters stretched over them and pillows piled high against the headboards.

She didn't bother going that way. Instead, she headed for a door on the other side of the room, the one she assumed would access the veterinary clinic. When she was about twenty feet from the door, she heard voices on the other side, and the door began to swing open. She made the split-second decision to duck behind a five-foot-high stack of mattresses.

The voices of two men came into the warehouse, and as the door swung shut behind them, she heard the sound of a broadcast on the other side, audible enough to make out Chuck Walla narrating the game.

'I can't watch that shit,' a voice said, thick with an Eastern European accent. 'I feel like I'm going to throw up.'

Their footsteps came into the room, heading in the direction of the mattresses that Caitlin was hiding behind. In about two seconds, they would come around the corner and see her. She tucked the pry bar into a pocket of the cargo pants and made the decision to pull out the stun gun instead of her firearm. The pistol was a last resort. She wanted to subdue these guys quietly – and she sure as hell didn't want to kill anyone if she could help it. She gripped the hammer in her other hand.

As the first man came into view – the one with the mullet – Caitlin launched out of her crouch and jammed the stun gun at him. She squeezed the release and felt her arm fill with vibrations. Mr Mullet grunted as his muscles locked, freezing him in place. Caitlin held the weapon against him for a long second, and then released it. The man tipped over like a felled redwood and crashed – moaning – to the concrete.

As Mr Mullet writhed on the floor, the shorter Mr Ponytail reached into his jacket, and Caitlin glimpsed a handgun coming out. A little revolver. She was off balance and out of reach with the stun gun, so she spun around and brought the hammer down against his forearm. The snap of bone was audible. The gun fell with a clang to the concrete, and Caitlin put her foot on it and slid it away.

The man backed away, his eyes saucers.

'Stop right there,' Caitlin said, taking a step toward him, 'or I'll light you up with fifty thousand volts.'

His eyes darted to his companion, who was on the ground, grunting loudly and flopping like a fish. A wet stain was spreading from Mr Mullet's crotch.

Mr Ponytail raised his unbroken arm in surrender.

'On your stomach,' Caitlin said. 'Don't think about screaming for help.'

The man did as he was asked. She laid the hammer down on the concrete, pocketed the stun gun, and pulled out the bag of zip-ties.

She wasn't gentle as she pulled Mr Ponytail's broken arm behind his back. He hissed in pain but didn't cry out. She zip-tied Mr Ponytail's wrists together, then, as she was tying the big guy's arms behind his back, Mr Ponytail spoke.

'If you leave now,' he said calmly, 'you might survive.'

'Where's Jake?' Caitlin said.

'I don't know any Jake.'

Caitlin wanted to knock them out, but she was afraid she might kill them if she hit them in the head with the hammer. She looked around, saw a roll of Gorilla tape on the workbench, and ran to grab it.

She unspooled a length of it and taped it around Mr Ponytail's head, covering his mouth. Mr Mullet looked delirious, still squirming on the concrete, and she had more difficulty getting the roll around his mouth.

She grabbed Mr Ponytail's leg and dragged him over next to the big guy. She started wrapping the Gorilla tape around their legs, and passing it through the slat of the palette the mattresses sat on, knotting limbs and wood together in a crazy, haphazard tether. If they could use their hands, or if they could drag the palette to the workbench to grab a utility knife, they might be able to untangle the wrapping with some effort. But with their hands pinned behind them – and with both of them injured – she didn't think they'd be going anywhere. She told them to close their eyes and, for good measure, wrapped tape around their heads so they couldn't see.

She unzipped her hoodie and tied it around her waist. Her tank top, also black, was soaked through with perspiration.

'Try to yell or get someone's attention,' she said to the two men, 'I'll come back and break more bones.'

She started toward the door, but something caught her eye. The top mattress she'd hidden behind was slit along the upper seam, running the length of one side. She wedged the hammer into the seam and lifted, opening the mattress like an envelope and revealing a hidden cavity inside. Vacuum-sealed bags of snowy powder filled the interior of the mattress.

Heroin, she assumed.

Maybe cocaine.

Either way, there was a lot of it. Hundreds of kilos. Millions of dollars' worth of drugs.

She closed her eyes, took a deep breath. Tried to calm her nerves. Like she was at the free-throw line and the entire game depended on her making the shots. She let out her breath, telling herself she was ready.

She jogged over to the door that Mr Ponytail and Mr Mullet had come through. She pulled it open, peeked inside to find a corridor of cinderblock walls, the white paint bright from overhead lights. It occurred to her she probably should have grabbed the gun she'd knocked out of the guy's hand and kicked across the floor.

She thought about going back but decided there was no time to waste.

59

Garrett caught the inbound pass and dribbled up the court. He glanced at the scoreboard. Down by twenty-two, they were chipping away at the Lightning's lead.

The crowd was raucous, but Garrett tuned it out. At his best, he could become so focused on the game he lost all awareness there was even a crowd. He'd heard players talk about how they needed the crowd as a motivator – either the home crowd to pump them up or the road crowd to provide a villain they wanted to silence. But to Garrett, when he was on, he forgot there was anything beyond the ninety-four-by-fifty-foot rectangle that made up the court.

Jaxon Luca met him near half court, then backpedaled and kept his distance. As Garrett jogged forward, he had a gut feeling – a lot of basketball was feeling, not thought – and even though he was six or seven feet from the line, he picked up his dribble and launched a three. The ball sailed in a high arc. As it snapped through the net, Luca bumped into him with a hard shoulder.

Garrett ignored him.

Back on defense, Garrett and Billy Croft both teamed up on Jaxon Luca at half court, a tangle of arms and elbows and sweat-slicked fingertips. Luca passed the ball away. The Lightning were off their rhythm, making frantic, clumsy passes. They launched a bad shot as the shot clock approached zero, and it missed the rim completely, falling into Elijah's hands. Garrett sprinted back on offense, and Elijah launched a football pass down the court.

Garrett caught the ball only feet from the rim and went straight up without dribbling. Luca flung himself at Garrett, slapping his arm and smashing his shoulder into Garrett's ribs as the ball left his hands. Garrett crashed to the ground – pain shooting through his skull as the back of his head slapped against the wood.

He heard the whistle for a foul.

He saw Luca standing over him, fists clenched.

'No comeback today, motherfucker,' Luca snarled.

Elijah ran up and helped Garrett to his feet as Luca glared at Garrett.

'Yo, ref,' Elijah shouted, holding an arm up in disbelief. 'How about a technical foul?'

A Lightning player put his hand on Luca's chest to get him to walk away.

'Come on,' Elijah said to the ref. 'If that was anyone else, you would have tee'd him up.'

The ref ignored him and asked Garrett, 'You OK to shoot your free throw?'

Garrett rubbed the back of his head.

'I'm fine,' he said. 'Did I make the shot?'

Elijah answered for the ref. 'Hells yeah!'

60

There were two other doors in the corridor, besides the one Caitlin just walked through. One at the other end of the hall, about fifteen feet away, and one to the right, about halfway down.

Her running shoes squeaked against the concrete as she stopped at the first door. The sound of the game was coming from the other door, but she wanted to check this one first – clear the room. She tried the handle. Unlocked. She eased it open and poked her head inside.

This was the kennel portion of the clinic. The air stunk of dogs and dog shit, and the walls were lined with cage doors built into the cinderblock. Dogs – all pit bulls as far as she could tell – filled the kennels, some pacing, some sleeping. All were quiet, but Caitlin knew as soon as one of them noticed her, the place would erupt into a frenzy of barking and growling. She started to ease the door closed, but stopped.

Inside one of the cages, curled in a fetal ball, was a human. The person was female, lying on the concrete, apparently asleep. Long black hair spread out from her skull onto the concrete floor, like tendrils of oil creeping from a spill. The caged girl had a petite frame, with a body barely covered by a floral-patterned shirt and jean shorts.

Caitlin unglued her eyes from the girl and more thoroughly inspected the cages. There were more girls, several of them. One wall of the kennel contained dogs – that's where Caitlin's eyes went initially – but the other wall held several caged girls. They mostly looked asleep, or drugged, but one was sitting upright, her arms wrapped around her legs.

Jake wasn't among them. Caitlin was sure of that. She thought about what to do. Look for Jake, then come back for the girls?

But if something happened to her, the girls would stay locked up.

She crept into the room, and, as predicted, the dogs barked and snarled, some of them throwing themselves at their cage doors and baring their teeth where their snouts fit through the bars. Their faces and muzzles were crisscrossed with white scar tissue. Their ears – those that still had them – were torn up like old tattered rags.

Caitlin knelt by the cage door of the girl who was awake. It was padlocked.

'Hey!'

The girl glanced at her – eyes in a daze – then looked away.

Caitlin took the hammer and slammed it down against the lock. It held, and Caitlin attacked it with the same fervor the dogs were attacking their cage doors. The girl stirred now, recoiling from the sound and staring at Caitlin with confusion. Caitlin wedged the teeth on the curved end of the pry bar around the lock shank and smashed the bar with the hammer. The lock gave way. Her fingers shaking, she undid the bolt and opened the cage.

The girl slunk to the back of the cage. She looked younger than eighteen.

'Come on,' Caitlin hissed. 'You're free.'

Caitlin attacked the other locks. The sound was loud, but it wasn't much different than the sounds of the dogs throwing themselves against the bars, their doors rattling against the locks. The other girls stirred. One spoke in a language Caitlin didn't understand. She smashed another lock open. Then another. Then the last.

She reached her arm out to a girl inside, but the girl didn't move.

I don't have time for this shit, Caitlin thought, expecting someone to rush into the kennel at any minute to see what the racket was all about.

'Come on,' Caitlin said again, and she stretched her arm into the cell and grabbed the girl's wrist.

She hauled her out, then pulled out two more. Only the one girl who'd been awake came out on her own, but her eyes looked glazed and distant. One girl could hardly stand, and another held her up.

'Do you speak English?' Caitlin asked.

None of them acknowledged the question.

Caitlin led the girls down the corridor, dogs growling and snapping. She pushed out into the hallway and was relieved to see no one was coming. Maybe the dogs made a racket like this all the time. She ushered the girls back to the mattress warehouse, peeked inside to make sure everything was clear. Mr Ponytail and Mr Mullet were still tied up. But no one else.

Caitlin brought the girls to the back door, opened it, and pointed the way out.

'Run,' she said. 'You're free.'

A girl shook her head.

Caitlin reached into her pocket and pulled out a wad of money – the last of Garrett's cash – and shoved it into the girls' hands. Somewhere in the range of four thousand dollars – a grand for each of them.

'Go. Now!'

They stepped into the night air, hesitant at first, then took off through the parking lot and down the street, their bare feet slapping against the pavement.

Caitlin patted her pockets to find her phone. She wanted to check how many minutes remained in the game, then remembered she'd left her phone in the car.

She had to keep going.

Jake might be inside somewhere – the presence of the imprisoned girls made that possibility seem very high.

There couldn't be much time left.

61

Garrett flopped onto the courtside folding chair and threw a towel over his legs. Rivulets of sweat ran down his face as he looked up at the scoreboard. They were down thirteen, with a quarter to go. Maybe they could win this. Although that wasn't enough, he knew.

He had to cover the spread.

'How's your head?' Josh asked, kneeling and handing Garrett a cup of Gatorade.

Somewhere in the distance – buried beneath the adrenaline fueling him – he could feel the dull throb of a headache. Like a storm cloud on the horizon, the pain would be here eventually. Tomorrow maybe. But for now, the sun was shining.

'All good,' Garrett said.

The break was long enough for the TV network to play a few commercials, then Garrett was back on the floor. He caught the ball on the inbound and headed up court. The crowd's roar was nothing more than dull background static. Jaxon Luca met him before half-court, playing him close. Garrett tried to get past him and Luca's sweaty body slammed against his, all sharp angles and unmovable muscle. Garrett stumbled, went down on one knee, kept his dribble. He expected a foul to be called, but there wasn't one. Luca lunged, and Garrett, off balance, tossed the ball to Kevin Mackey, who was attacked by defenders.

Garrett darted forward, calling for the ball. Luca raced after him. Kevin tossed the ball in a high lob that Garrett caught near the free-throw line. Elijah was down in the post, but when Garrett headed toward the basket, the defender left the big guy alone and tried to stop Garrett.

Garrett looked at the basket like he was going to shoot, and as Luca and the Lightning's center moved to block, Garrett swung the ball in a no-look behind-the-back pass. Elijah caught it and slammed it home, hanging on the rim long enough to pull his knees to his chest before dropping down.

The Sabertooths' bench were on their feet screaming.

The Lightning called another timeout.

Garrett gave Elijah a quick high five before heading toward their bench.

He glanced at Jaxon Luca, who was scowling at him from across the court like a schoolyard bully.

62

B ack in the cinderblock corridor, Caitlin put one hand on the doorknob, the other holding the stun gun at the ready. She could hear a commercial playing on the other side of the door. Behind her, the sound of the dogs had died down.

She started to turn the handle but hesitated.

It was time, she realized. Time to stop deluding herself she was going to get through this without her firearm. She pocketed the stun gun and pulled out her SIG Sauer.

Here goes, she thought.

She threw open the door and rushed into a hallway with several open doors on either side. They were examination rooms, all dark. She followed the sound of the television, which grew louder as she snuck down the hallway and past an L-bend. At the other end of the hall, a door was propped open, light on. One person – maybe Jake, she couldn't tell – lay on an examination table, while two other men stood nearby. The man on the table was lying on his side, wearing nothing but boxer shorts as far as Caitlin could tell. Because of the angle, she was looking at his feet, not his head.

One of the men standing was a doctor, or vet, dressed in a white coat, cigarette in his mouth, holding some kind of instrument and leaning over the prone man.

The second person standing was Alexei Maxim – she recognized him from the picture in Grayson's file. His arms were crossed, and his attention was directed to a small TV sitting on a nearby counter.

The game was playing, the volume turned up loud.

'Here you go,' the vet said, standing upright with some kind of red blob in his hand. 'That's a quarter mill in your pocket.'

Chills shot up and down Caitlin's body. Her scalp tingled. She focused her eyes on the object in the doctor's hand.

It was a bean-shaped organ, glistening with blood.

A kidney.

63

G arrett reached half court when he spotted, in a flash, that there was some confusion on defense. The Lightning players weren't sure who was supposed to be where. Garrett darted past the point guard and drove to the basket. Jaxon Luca cut over from the three-point line. Garrett made the quick decision to go for the rim instead of dishing it to Billy open on the wing, and he jumped for a layup.

Luca's big hand, nowhere near the ball, smashed into Garrett's face, exploding bolts of pain from his nose through his skull. Garrett landed on his feet, but the collision sent him staggering toward the baseline. A cameraman was positioned behind the basket, and Garrett stepped on his leg, lost what remained of his balance, and fell to the ground.

Somewhere, a million miles away, he heard the whistle for a foul.

Garrett rolled to his hands and knees. His eyes burned with tears. Through the blur, he saw red droplets on the hardwood. Warm liquid dripped from his nose.

Anger surged inside him. All the pressure bearing down on him day after day – all series – it was too much. He couldn't take it anymore.

This wasn't a game.

This was life and death.

He jumped to his feet and lunged at Luca.

'*Fucking asshole*,' Garrett roared, grabbing Luca's jersey and shoving him.

Luca tumbled backward while Garrett kept one hand on his jersey. Garrett drew his other back into a fist, ready to smash the son of bitch's nose the way he'd smashed Garrett's. But someone grabbed his arm and pulled him back. Luca, his fists tangled in Garrett's jersey, was taller and stronger and seemed to hold Garrett at arm's length with ease.

'You want to fight, motherfucker?' Luca said. 'I'll kick your little bitch ass up and down this court.'

Garrett squirmed his arm free from whoever was holding him and shifted his body to use a lower center of gravity for leverage, wanting to shove Luca back and this time connect the punch he'd meant to throw. But Sabertooth and Lightning jerseys encircled them in a maelstrom of grabbing and pushing and yelling. It was like he was in the middle of a mosh pit, and Garrett was unable to control his own direction, barely able to stay upright.

Elijah's big arm wrapped around Garrett's chest, gripping him tight and steadying him. He lowered his mouth to Garrett's ear.

'Use your head, man,' he said, his voice barely a whisper.

Garrett could feel the blood running down his lips and chin. Somewhere in the scrum, the refs were pushing and shoving players, trying to get them separated. Debris from the raging audience – cups and food wrappers – rained on the court. Security guards joined the fray.

'*Stay in your seats,*' the announcer stated through the roaring crowd. '*Do not go onto the floor.*'

'We need you, man,' Elijah said, his voice somehow calm in the chaos. 'Be cool.'

The words brought Garrett out of the cloud of rage, and he saw the situation as if he was levitating above it. In all of his career – high school, college, pros – he'd never lost it like this.

He let go of Jaxon Luca and held his hands high, like a suspect facing the police. He let Elijah drag him away while his teammates erected a barrier between him and the Lightning.

'That's right, bitch,' Jaxon Luca called after him. 'Walk away.'

64

'No!' Caitlin screamed, running forward, pointing her pistol with both hands.

She stopped short of the doorway. The doctor and

Maxim both turned to look at her, but she only gave them a glance, her eyes focused on the man on the table, blood leaking from a six-inch incision under the ribcage. He had an oxygen mask over his mouth and nose, but Caitlin could see enough to know this wasn't Jake. This guy was older, probably in his forties. His facial features were all wrong and his body wasn't in the kind of shape she would expect Jake to be in. The height might be right, the hair color close, but this wasn't Garrett's brother.

On the TV in the corner, Chuck Walla was saying, '. . . *never seen anything like it in a Finals game . . .*'

Caitlin, her lungs heaving, tore her eyes away from the unconscious man and focused on Maxim, who didn't seem perturbed in the least. He simply regarded her, his arms still crossed, like a woman charging at him with a pistol was an everyday occurrence. The doctor stared, dumbfounded, still holding the dripping kidney in his hands, which were gloved in blood-smeared latex. The ash on his cigarette was an inch long.

'Who are you?' Maxim said. 'What's this all about?'

She expected an eastern European accent, but he sounded British.

'Where's Jake?' she said, ignoring his question.

'Who is Jake?'

She wished she was better at determining when people were lying, but there was no obvious flash of recognition across his face.

'You know who the hell I'm talking about.' Caitlin tipped her chin in the direction of the game, where some kind of chaos was happening on the court. 'Jacob Streeter.'

'Sorry, mate,' Maxim said, apparently not understanding the connection between her question and what was on TV. 'I don't know no Jacob Streeter.'

'Then why the hell are you watching this?' She gestured toward the TV, almost adding, *While you're cutting someone up?* But it seemed implied.

'I've got ten Gs on the Lightning,' he said matter-of-factly.

'Tell me where he is,' she shouted, stepping forward into the room, 'or so help me I'll shoot you through the fucking heart.'

Maxim looked amused.

'I don't think so,' he said, and his eyes flicked to the corner of the room, hidden from Caitlin behind the open door.

Caitlin turned to look behind the door – too late. A mountainous figure rushed out and wrapped his big hand around the hand holding the pistol. It was Maxim's other massive bodyguard, the one with the mohawk. He was at least six-five and built like a bear. He yanked hard and pulled her off her feet, swinging her into the room and slamming her into a cabinet hard enough the door caved in and the contents clattered around inside. Caitlin got her feet under her as the cabinet door fell open. Boxes of cotton swabs and bandage wraps spilled onto the floor. Mr Mohawk adjusted his grip around the barrel of the gun and prepared to jerk again. Caitlin let go at the perfect moment, and the guy flew backward, almost comically, carried by his own strength.

Before he could orient himself, Caitlin threw an elbow at his head, connecting with his temple. The guy's legs buckled, and he went down on one knee among the spilled medical supplies. She threw a left hook into his nose, and his head rocked backward. The gun dangled limply in his hand. He teetered on the verge of falling. She took a step back and lifted a leg to finish him off with a kick to the face, but someone grabbed her ponytail from behind and hauled her off her feet.

She landed painfully on the concrete floor, and Alexei Maxim leaned over her, the ceiling light bright behind him. He drew his fist back and covered the light like an eclipse. Caitlin squirmed, but the fist came down into her face, rocking her skull into the concrete floor. Pain detonated inside her head. Her ears rang. Comet trails of light eddied in her vision.

Maxim raised his fist again.

65

The refs sought to regain control. Security guards shoved people off the court. The crowd of players dispersed. Every person in the arena was on their feet, but the roar of the crowd died down to a low murmur.

Garrett stood on the sidelines, hands on his head. Josh handed him a towel, which he pressed to his face to curb the bleeding. The refs convened at the scorer's table, discussing what to do, while workers came in with dry mops, pushing the detritus away. Garrett waited, knowing what was coming. Down the sideline, Luca stood with his hands on his hips.

The head ref turned his mic on and declared for the audience, *'Flagrant Two on Lightning Number Five, Jaxon Luca, followed by a technical foul. Resulting in ejection.'* The crowd cheered so loudly he had to wait for them to quiet before he could finish the adjudication.

'Double Technical on Sabertooths Number Ten, Garrett Streeter, also resulting in ejection.'

The crowd booed its disapproval.

66

This time, Maxim hit her in the body. She wriggled and fumbled for the stun gun, but he was strong and didn't let up. He hit her again and again. In the ribs, stomach, breasts. Each blow freezing her helplessly so she couldn't defend against the next. She kicked and writhed and could feel the blade of the pry bar digging into her leg. She got enough leverage to sit up. Maxim backhanded her in the mouth, and she crumpled to her side.

A wave of nausea ran through her. She tried to sit up, but the floor tilted beneath her, first in one direction, then the other, like a small boat on a rough sea. Her head was full of growing pressure, so powerful it felt like her skull was going to split open. Maxim loomed over her, a shadowy silhouette backlit by the ceiling light. Mr Mohawk joined him. From far away, as if she was listening from underwater, she thought the TV announcer said something about a double ejection.

'What are you doing?' Maxim barked, and at first Caitlin thought he was talking to her. 'Put that goddamn thing on ice. You've got a dozen more organs to get before we feed him to the dogs.'

Caitlin scooted away, trying to think, but she collided with the corner and there was nowhere else to go.

'Who do you work for?' Maxim asked.

Caitlin was confused why he would ask his own surgeon this, but then realized he was now talking to her. She didn't answer and he asked her again. Caitlin's lungs heaved. If she couldn't fight her way out of this, she was going to end up on the table, cut open and harvested for organs. She met his eyes, trying to direct his gaze, and slid her hand into the stun-gun pocket.

Maxim looked up at the game for a moment, and Caitlin jumped to her feet and lunged at him with the stun gun. There was no strength in her arm, and Maxim grabbed her wrist and swung her around into the examination table. Her hip collided painfully with the metal edge. The impact caused the unconscious man to roll forward and almost fall onto the floor, but the doctor scurried to keep him in place. Caitlin tried to twist her wrist to get the electrodes on Maxim, but he held her arm aloft, with ease.

She threw her other fist into Maxim's throat and, even though she lacked the strength to put much behind the punch, it was a solid connection and the blow sent him back a step. His grip loosened, and she yanked her arm free and scampered around the backside of the examination table. She sidestepped some sort of machine connecting the guy on the table to oxygen, then bumped into the TV on the counter. It tipped over on its small stand, falling to the floor with a crash. The guy with her gun came around the other side of the table to cut her off. The doctor, trapped between them, backed away and bumped into a foam cooler on the floor. Crushed ice tumbled out in a flood, and the kidney came with it, sliding across the tile like a misshapen hockey puck.

The man with the gun was distracted by the sight. Caitlin jumped, somehow finding the energy, and kicked him squarely in the face with the bottom of her shoe. His head whipped back, blood spurting from his nose, and he collapsed onto the floor, the metal gun clattering loudly and sliding out the door. The big guy groaned and held his nose – smashed twice now – and rolled onto his side.

She thought about tasering him, but she didn't want to take the time. Maxim was still on the other side of the examination table, and she could see down the hallway, the exit within sight and her gun even closer.

She stepped forward but slipped on the icy slush. Regaining her footing, she stepped on Mr Mohawk and hopped toward the door. She made it one more step, as far as the threshold of the hallway, and stretched to grab her gun. Just as she got her fingers on it, Maxim tackled her, and they both went crashing into the corridor. She held onto the pistol and twisted underneath him, but he was strong, and her long limbs didn't do her any favors in a close-quarters wrestling match. He seemed to move so much faster than she could. She pointed the gun at his face, but as she tried to squeeze the trigger, he grabbed her wrist and shoved the barrel away. The gun spit fire, and a lightbulb exploded in the ceiling, showering them in glass.

She had the stun gun in her other hand, and she thrust it at his chest. As she was about to squeeze the trigger, he grabbed a handful of her hair with his free hand and smashed the back of her head against the floor, sending fresh fissures of pain through her skull. She lost time for a moment and, when she came to, her hands were empty.

An object pressed against her collar, and she heard a buzzing noise, like someone opening an electronically locked door. She was flooded with the worst pain she'd ever felt. Her body went rigid. As an athlete, she'd experienced her share of muscle cramps, but this felt as if every muscle in her body was locked up. Her fingers turned into arthritic claws. She heard a gargled screaming and was only faintly aware it was coming out of her mouth.

The buzzing noise stopped, and the relief to her pain sensors was extraordinary. She tried to move her limbs, but her muscles were not responding. A burnt ozone smell filled the air.

Maxim tossed aside the stun gun. He still had her pistol, but – after considering it for a moment – he tossed it aside, too. Apparently he wanted to do this with his hands. She tried to squirm away, but he straddled her, wrapping his fingers around her throat.

She was surprised at how quickly the world started to go black, like someone was lowering a dimmer switch on her vision. She tried to break his grip but had no power. She reached for his face, trying to scratch him. She had a longer reach, but her hands were gloved, and she flailed like a declawed cat. What little strength she had left was going quickly.

I can't die, she thought.

My son needs me.

67

Garrett stormed into the locker room with Josh following behind.

'You OK, man?' Josh asked.

Garrett ignored him. Instead, he felt a fresh eruption of anger, and he grabbed the wheeled chair that sat in front of his locker, swung it over his head, and slammed it against the floor with a loud crash. It bounced away, spilling screws and springs and broken bits of plastic.

'Take it easy,' Josh said. 'You don't want to injure yourself.'

Sports was full of stories of idiots who'd gone into the locker room and punched a wall or kicked a chair and ended up on injured reserve with a broken bone. Still, Garrett didn't want to hear it. He glared at Josh, and even though he'd always liked Summer's old friend, now he hated him. Josh was reaching up with a wet towel to wipe the blood off his face, but Garrett swatted his hands away.

'Could you leave me the fuck alone for a few minutes?' He gestured to the massive TV screen on the wall where the game was playing. 'I just want to watch this alone.'

Garrett wasn't known for being this kind of asshole, and Josh looked at him with shock.

'I'll be out in the hall if you need me.'

Josh shuffled out, and Garrett turned to the TV. The Sabertooths looked disjointed and disorganized, out of rhythm without Garrett there to distribute the ball.

He slumped down in a chair in the middle of the empty room. He put his elbows on his knees and his head in his hands. From what seemed like far away, he heard a distant buzz.

He unzipped his duffel bag and reached for the burner phone. There was a new text from the kidnappers.

68

The world was almost completely black. Caitlin was going to pass out any second.

She fumbled her hand into her cargo pants and felt the handle of the screwdriver. She pulled the tool out. She had no time to waste. She thrust the point toward Maxim's face. The tip sunk into something soft. He let go of her, recoiling and putting a hand to his eye. Caitlin took the biggest intake of breath of her life, and the dimmer switch flipped back in the other direction, washing away the darkness with light that seemed way too bright. She coughed and coughed, and tried to crawl away from Maxim.

'*Bitch!*' he growled, squinting with one eye closed, a thin trickle of blood leaking down his cheek.

She backed down the hall on all fours, coughing, trying to get air in her lungs. Maxim, squatting, grabbed her pistol off the tile floor. She'd bought herself only seconds.

He lifted the gun in her direction, then stopped and looked over her head.

'Hey, Alexei,' said a voice from behind her.

It was familiar, somehow, but she didn't know from where.

Then the crack of a gunshot filled the tight corridor and Alexei Maxim's good eye winked closed as blood exploded out the back of his skull.

69

A re you alone? the text said.

Yes, Garrett typed.

A moment later, he received a text with a video attached. His lungs heaved. With trembling fingers, he pressed the *play* arrow.

His brother appeared on the screen. A fresh gash above one eye leaked blood down his face. His lip was busted. His face was filled with red marks that would turn to bruises soon enough. The camera focused on Jake's face, but Garrett could see enough to tell he was being held by other men. Their gloved hands and black-clad shoulders briefly entered the frame. Jake was having difficulty holding his head up, and a big gloved hand came in and grabbed him by the scalp. A gun entered from off camera and pressed against his forehead. Jake squirmed from the barrel, but he couldn't get away.

'No,' Garrett gasped, but what he was watching wasn't live and whoever was on the other side of the screen couldn't hear him. This already happened – there was no way to stop it.

Garrett blinked away tears. The gun retracted but didn't leave the camera shot. The barrel remained leveled on Jake's face. The gloved hand held its finger inside the trigger guard. If the gun went off, the bullet would punch through Jake's face.

'Tell your brother what you want to say,' the voice on the other end of the phone said.

Jake opened his mouth – strings of red saliva stretching between his lips – and said, 'They told me to tell you that you messed up.' His voice was hard to understand, slurred, because his lips were swollen.

'And?' the voice prompted.

Jake started to cry. 'I love you, brother,' he whimpered. 'It's not your fault if they kill me. It's not your fault, OK?'

Garrett's breath caught in his throat.

'That's not what you were supposed to say,' the voice growled.

Jake took a deep breath. 'They're going to give you one more chance,' he said. 'Next game . . .' he trailed off. Then he looked up, off camera at the person holding the phone, and he blurted out, 'They're holding me in a basement. I can hear music and voices, especially at night. The guys holding me are—'

The hand with the pistol rose up and came back down, slamming the butt against Jake's cheek. Garrett let out an involuntary wail. Jake blinked dazedly. He would have fallen if he wasn't being held up.

'Do exactly what we say for Game Six,' the voice said. 'Or the next time we send you a video, whatever your brother says will be the last words he ever speaks.'

The screen went dark.

Garrett's teammates started filing into the locker room, heads down.

The game was over.

They were down three–two.

One game away from losing the NBA Finals.

70

'That was for Anya,' the voice said.

Caitlin craned her neck and stared in shock at the speaker. Levi Grayson stood in the hallway, holding a gun at arm's length.

'You OK?' Grayson asked, helping her to her feet.

She didn't answer. Her limbs felt like warm gelatin. She leaned against the wall, unable to fully stand on her own. Maxim lay on the floor in a growing slick of scarlet.

Grayson left Caitlin and walked down the hall to where Mr Mohawk sat on the floor. He stuck his hands in the air in surrender, his nose gushing blood.

Grayson shot him in the face.

The body collapsed back into the crushed ice on the floor. The surgeon cowered in the corner, cradling the kidney like it was a shield that could stop a bullet.

'Don't,' he said. 'Please.'

Caitlin opened her mouth to object, but her response was too slow. Grayson shot him, too.

The kidney flopped to the floor.

Each report was loud in the tight hallway. Caitlin's ears, plugged ever since the first blow to the head, were filled with a steady tone, like someone holding down one note on a keyboard. She stared in astonishment at all the blood. It was mixing with the ice to form a pinkish slush. Grayson tried not to step in it as he walked back to her, but he failed and brought bloody footprints with him.

'Is this yours?' he said, prying Caitlin's pistol from Maxim's fingers.

'Yes,' she croaked.

There was an unrecognizable hoarseness to her voice, and she wondered if her vocal cords were permanently damaged.

Grayson pocketed her gun, but kept the other in his hand, which she only now realized was the one she'd disarmed from Mr Ponytail.

'Come on,' he said, taking her by the arm and leading her back toward the mattress warehouse.

She couldn't believe what was happening, couldn't think fast enough to keep up.

'What about him?' she said, turning back to the man lying on the examination table. His kidney lay on the floor in the syrupy mush. 'He'll die without help.'

'We'll call the police once we're out of here,' Grayson said.

He pulled her through the door into the mattress room, and somehow her legs followed without failing her. Mr Ponytail and Mr Mullet still lay on the floor, their arms zip-tied, their legs Gorilla-taped, their eyes covered. Grayson went over to them and raised his gun.

'What are you doing?' Caitlin gasped.

She hadn't spoken up in time to stop him earlier. She had to now.

'Witnesses,' he said.

'No,' Caitlin rasped. 'They haven't seen anything.'

'These aren't good people,' he said.

'Stop.'

Grayson hesitated, thinking. Then he lowered the gun. He knelt in front of Mr Ponytail, who couldn't see him because of the tape over his eyes. Mr Mullet appeared to be unconscious.

'What are you going to tell the cops?' Grayson asked them.

'I didn't see anything,' Mr Ponytail said in his Russian accent.

'I can put a hit on you wherever you are,' Grayson said. 'Prison. Jail. On the street. Wherever. I'll hunt you down in fucking Moscow if I have to. Got it?'

'Yes.'

'And that girl, she just saved your fucking life. Say thank you.'

'Thank you,' he said.

He seemed to mean it.

As Grayson turned away, he stopped, and, as she'd done earlier, he took a second look at the mattress. He used the gun to flip up the top and stare into the acres of drug bags inside.

He reached in and grabbed a kilo.

'Sorry,' he said to her. 'I just cut off my supply. I'll need this.'

He led her to the back door, peeked out, then ushered her through. She hesitated, thinking she should somehow find the strength to keep looking for Jake. But she remembered Maxim's face when she asked about him, what he'd said about having money on the game.

Jake wasn't here.

Maxim never had him.

'What are you waiting for?' Grayson said, and she followed him, limping, through the parking lot, her breath wheezing in her throat.

They arrived at Grayson's car, a government-issue sedan parked a few houses down from her rental. He opened the door for her, and as she climbed in, a panel van pulled into the lot and backed into the loading dock at Going to the Mattresses.

Grayson put the car in drive and said, 'Looks like we got out of there in the nick of time.'

71

She writhed in Grayson's passenger seat, clammy with sweat. Her head pounded, and her ears wouldn't stop ringing. Her face throbbed. With every breath, it felt like her ribs would snap. As he drove, Grayson made a call to the police on his burner. Caitlin's head hurt so badly she couldn't follow the conversation entirely, but she got the gist. He was using some kind of anonymous tip line, mentioning drugs and dead bodies, a man bleeding out on the operating table.

'I think I got their attention,' he said. 'Let's listen to the radio and see what happens.'

He had a police radio in his car.

'I'm going to be sick,' Caitlin muttered.

'Here,' Grayson said, reaching into the back seat and grabbing an empty fast-food sack.

She put it to her face, and the smell of hamburger pushed her over the edge. She retched into the bag, the vomit hot as it left her mouth. Each heave felt like her insides were tearing themselves apart. She couldn't stay in the seat. She slithered to the floorboard, keeping her head and arms on the cushion. The sack was wet and Grayson took it from her. He pressed the button to lower his window and tossed it out. He left the window down, trying to clear the smell.

She slipped out of consciousness. She felt like she was in black water, trying to swim toward the surface but sinking deeper and deeper instead. She woke with a start, thinking it was all a nightmare, then remembering it wasn't.

The car was parked. Grayson was gone. She crawled up into the seat and looked out the window. They were at the edge of a lake. The black surface reflected the moonlight. Grayson stood at the lake's edge and heaved something out into the water. She thought it was the gun he'd used to kill Maxim and his men. He reached into his pocket and she recognized her SIG Sauer. He threw it into the water as well.

That sucks, she thought absently. *I loved that little gun.*

Grayson hurried back to the car.

'You awake?' he asked, his voice shaky.

His hands were trembling.

Probably needed a fix.

He picked something off the seat between them, a pair of shoes in a plastic bag. He carried them over to the water. He was wearing only socks. He knelt down, stuffing the shoes with gravel from the beach, and then tossed them out into the water as well.

He came back, this time to her side of the car.

'The stuff you brought, the taser and screwdriver, your fingerprints weren't on them, right?'

'I wore gloves.'

She held up her hands to show him.

'Give them to me,' he said.

She wrestled her gloves off.

'I hate to do this to you,' he said, 'but you've got some blood on your clothes. Better give them to me.'

He went to the trunk and came back with a large windbreaker.

'Put this on,' he said, then he went down to the water to dispose of her gloves.

She struggled out of her tank top and peeled off her cargo pants. He didn't return until she had the jacket on, which was large enough it covered her body down to mid-thigh.

Grayson took the clothes and her shoes down to the water, tried filling them with gravel, then gave them a heave.

'I think we're going to be OK,' he said when he came back. 'Do you think anything's broken? Any bones?'

'Maybe some ribs,' she muttered, leaning against the car door and closing her eyes.

'You're not coughing up blood, so if they're cracked, they didn't puncture your lungs.'

He said this like she should be thankful she'd gotten off lucky.

'That guy on the table, missing his kidney,' Grayson said. 'He's in the hospital. He's going to live, they think.'

Caitlin became aware again of chatter from a police radio. There was lots of activity on the radio, voices back and forth. Her ears were ringing badly.

'I don't think they're going to look too hard for whoever did this,' he said, putting the car in drive. 'A drug deal gone wrong. That's what they'll think.'

The tires crunched over gravel.

'You killed those men,' she said.

'You're damn right I did. Alexei Maxim is in hell where he belongs.'

'I've never seen a person shot before,' Caitlin said.

'The only one I feel bad about is that vet,' Grayson said. 'Probably some poor schmuck with a gambling problem. Got in too deep and couldn't find a way out. Still, he was gonna take that guy's organs and let him die on the table, right? We saved his life. This wasn't the first time they'd done it. They were all killers.'

His hands were shaking as he steered out of the gravel and onto a blacktop lane.

'I need to get home and get well,' Grayson said.

Caitlin closed her eyes.

She felt like she was on an inner tube in a waterpark wave pool, her body somehow bobbing up and down with the breakers. She drifted toward the blackness that had taken her under before, and this time she didn't fight it.

GAME SIX

72

Glass, Garrett typed into his phone, where the hell are you? It was approaching noon, and he'd called and texted a dozen times since last night's game. None were answered. He was standing in the bedroom, looking out over the backyard. Summer told him she was going for a swim, but the pool sat empty, like a big blue block of ice. His nose hurt, his muscles were sore, and he felt tired all over – the kind of exhaustion a whole off-season didn't seem enough to erase.

The TV mounted to the bedroom wall was tuned to ESPN, where the only thing anyone was talking about was last night's game. Not the game itself, but the fracas he'd caused when he charged Jaxon Luca. Everyone was debating whether the league would hand down suspensions today.

'*If this had been an ordinary game,*' former player Desmond Wang was saying, '*no doubt both Luca and Streeter would be suspended for multiple games. But this is the NBA Finals – no one wants to see two of the three best players in the series sitting on the sidelines. The fans wouldn't stand for it.*'

Garrett thought Wang might be right. Especially since neither he nor Luca had any technical or flagrant fouls since the playoffs began. Still, Garrett secretly hoped they would suspend him. The kidnappers couldn't possibly expect him to influence the outcome of the game if he wasn't playing. But if he wasn't on the court, he had no value to the kidnappers. And if the Sabertooths lost the next game, then the series was over. Garrett was sick at the thought of what the kidnappers would do with his brother when they no longer needed him.

On the screen, for the millionth time, they were replaying the fight. Garrett watched himself charge Jaxon, his nose dripping blood, his face so full of anger he didn't recognize who that person was. He muted the TV and grabbed his personal phone.

Maybe Caitlin lost her burner. He thought about what he could say on her personal phone.

Hey, Glass. I could use some advice after last night's game. You available?

It seemed innocent enough if his phone texts were ever examined as evidence. He stared at the words, willing her to text back.

Nothing.

The sound of a splash awoke him from his trance. Out the window, Summer glided through the water with the grace of a seal.

He could see her iPhone sitting on the arm of a chaise lounge, but there was no sign of the burner.

OK, he thought. *Now or never.*

He checked her office, which held a desk she hardly ever used, and then the drawers in the end tables of their living room. She had her own bathroom, with the counters overrun with lotion and makeup, and he riffled through those drawers as quickly as he could. He checked a drawer in the kitchen where they kept their bills, then even looked in the other drawers among the silverware and oven mitts.

Their phones – their main phones – were wide open to each other. He knew her code. She knew his. It was nothing for one of them to pick up the other's phone, enter their code, and check the weather or do an Internet search. When she got a call or message, he would hand her phone and, without a second thought, glance at the notification. She occasionally used burners for business reasons, and those were treated no differently. She never hid them.

Which made the fact that he couldn't find this one even more suspicious. He checked the window and saw she'd completed her swim and was lying in the sun, drying off. It wouldn't be long now. He had one last idea, and, after double-checking to make sure Summer was still lying down, he climbed the stairs and went back to their bedroom.

He opened the drawer of her nightstand. Inside were earbuds, face cream, chap-stick, and a bottle of sleeping pills she used if she was traveling and needed to get a good night's sleep before a shoot. He saw also, with a rising sense of dread, a pay-as-you-go cell phone.

He should have checked here first.

Kneeling by her bedside, he picked up the phone. It required no passcode. The phone calls in the history – both to and from Summer's phone – were from only two numbers. Both were from Cincinnati's 513 area code. He checked the texts and found there were conversation chains with both numbers. One number was simply a series of appointment confirmations, although it was unclear what the meetings were for or if they were in person or remote.

The latest text stated, How was your appointment with Foley Blanchet Garnier? Reply 1 to 5 with 5 being the best.

The name sounded like a lawyer's office, but he and Summer weren't married yet, so he wasn't sure why that would worry him. The other conversation had an extensive history of texts going back and forth.

Whoever she'd corresponded with asked, You haven't told him, have you?

No.

He's acting weird.

That's an F-ing understatement, Summer responded.

Garrett scrolled through the conversation, trying to find something more concrete.

I wish I could tell Garrett, Summer stated. I hate going through this alone.

You're not alone. You've got me.

Garrett pulled his own phone out to Google the three names that sounded like a law firm, but before he could, he heard Summer say, 'What are you doing?'

She was standing at the threshold to the bedroom, in her swimming suit, with a towel draped over her shoulders.

She stared at him, wide-eyed and angry.

He held up the burner.

'What is it you haven't told me?' he said.

She snatched the phone from his hand.

'You have your secrets,' she snapped. 'I have mine.'

He rose to his feet, full of anger, and leaned over her.

'This isn't a fucking joke, Summer.'

'What are you going to do?' she said, trying to sound tough but her voice was quavering. 'You going to attack me like you attacked Jaxon Luca?'

In her eyes he saw something that unsettled him. She was afraid of him.

He took a step back, trying to show he wasn't a threat.

'I can't believe you,' she said. 'Snooping around in my phone. You are losing it, Garrett. First you freak out on the court. Now this? You are coming unglued.'

'Why do you have a burner?'

'Why do you?' she hissed. 'You talk to Caitlin on a burner. And you guard that thing with your goddamn life. I've been tempted to

go snooping. The difference between you and me is I didn't go
through with it.'

He didn't know what to do. Flop down on his knees and apologize?
Or demand an explanation?

'I'll show you mine,' she said, holding up the phone, 'if you
show me yours.'

He took another step back.

'I'm sorry,' he said, defeated.

She stormed past him into the master bathroom.

'I'm taking a shower,' she said. 'And I'm locking the fucking
door!'

When she was gone and he heard the water come on, Garrett
leaned against the wall and slumped down to the floor. He tried to
remember the three-word name that sounded like a law firm so he
could Google it. The words had slipped from his mind.

He put his head in his hands.

He couldn't take any more. He couldn't carry the weight he was
bearing. Still, each day the weight got heavier.

Summer was right – he was losing it.

73

Garrett's phone buzzed with a call from Coach Ware.
'League just handed down its decision,' Coach said.
'And?'

'Big fines,' Coach said. 'No suspensions.'

'OK,' Garrett said without emotion. He was sitting in his cold
basement but hadn't even bothered projecting any game film on the
screen.

'Is your head on straight now?'

'I'm good,' Garrett said.

'I've been asking you for a long time to be a leader to these
guys,' Coach said. 'Not just the floor general dishing the ball. A
model. The guy who does everything right so that when he tells
everybody what to do, they trust that he knows what the hell he's
talking about. And they want to play *for* you, want to do it right so
they don't disappoint you.'

'I get it,' Garrett said.

'The best teams have a coach off the court and another on it.'

'I said I got it.'

Garrett was seething. He could feel Coach thinking about whether to say more.

'OK,' Coach said. 'Refs are going to be scrutinizing everything you do.'

'I know.'

'All right,' Coach said. 'Get some rest.'

He thought about not texting Elijah, but under normal circumstances that's the first thing he'd do – best to keep up the pretense.

Coach called, he typed. No suspensions.

His phone rang immediately.

'Shit.' Elijah laughed. 'I was hoping Jaxon would get suspended but they'd let you off the hook.'

'More likely it would have gone the other way.'

'It's bullshit, though. Guy takes a cheap shot, gives you a bloody nose, and you're just supposed to take it.'

'Part of the game,' Garrett said. 'That time Serge Ibaka broke LeBron's nose, they didn't even call a foul. I've got to keep my head next time.'

'I guess you're lucky you don't have to play with one of those ugly-ass masks on.'

'Thanks, by the way,' Garrett said. 'For stopping me before I made things worse.'

'I'm here for you, man. All the way. You're my ride or die, Streeter.' He laughed heartily.

As he hung up, his other phone buzzed. He hoped it was Caitlin, but it was the kidnapper's phone.

Lightning are favored at home for Game 6. Forget about the spread this time, the text said. Your job is to win.

A few seconds later another text came through.

It's simple.

Win and he lives.

Lose and he dies.

74

Caitlin was trapped in a thick, sluggish sleep she couldn't seem to wake from. She was aware she was on a couch, aware daylight streamed in through the windows, aware of Levi Grayson occasionally checking on her, yet she couldn't quite force herself awake. After what seemed like hours of trying to kick toward the surface, she finally emerged, sitting upright and shaking her head and running her hands across her scalp. Her skull pounded with the worst headache she'd ever experienced.

'How are you feeling?'

Grayson was sitting on a recliner nearby – she hadn't realized he was there – with a laptop open in front of him. He wore a UNLV sweatshirt and sweatpants.

'I feel like I've been hit by a truck,' she said.

This was an expression she'd used before when she didn't get a good night's sleep, but she meant it literally this time. Her face throbbed, and one of her eyes was swollen, nearly shut. Her arm and leg muscles were sore. Her ribs ached. Her neck felt like rocks were jammed down inside her throat, and her head pounded with such ferocity that snakes of pain slithered through her neck, her cheekbones, even her teeth. Her body radiated with fever.

She was wearing baggy sweatpants and a T-shirt way too big for her. When Grayson saw her looking at it, he said, 'You dressed yourself, remember?'

She had the vague memory of being in a bathroom, peeling the sweaty windbreaker off her skin, Grayson on the other side of the door asking if she was OK. He might have killed those guys in cold blood last night, but he'd been a gentleman with her.

A plastic water bottle sat on the coffee table next to a container of Advil. Caitlin reached for the water and fumbled with the cap. Her mouth was sandpaper dry. Something about the way the light slanted through the windows suggested it was late afternoon. She drank, thinking she'd down half the bottle, but it hurt so badly to swallow that she stopped.

'I gave you some ibuprofen this morning,' Grayson said. 'You're probably ready for more. Might be good to eat something first.'

Caitlin eyed the bottle but didn't have the strength yet to reach for it. It took all the effort she had to sit upright.

'I thought about giving you something stronger,' Grayson said. 'Something that will really take the pain away. But I figured you'd say no if you were in any position to consent.'

She remembered him grabbing the kilo of powder from the mattress.

'No,' she said. 'No, thank you.'

'Smart,' he said. 'Don't start if you can help it. You're lucky to be alive, you know.'

She couldn't remember everything that happened, but she recalled enough. She'd subdued a couple of them, but Alexei Maxim managed to get her gun away from her – the exact thing her sheriff warned her about. She'd felt in over her head at least a dozen times since arriving in Las Vegas, but now she wanted to break down and cry at her own naiveté. Grayson was right – she was damn lucky to be alive. She'd almost deprived her son of growing up with a mother.

'What happened?' she asked. 'I tried to call you, but . . .' *I got tired of waiting*, she thought.

'When I called back, there was no answer,' he said. 'I drove over to check things out. I watched for a while, and then these women came running out the back door, hardly wearing anything and looking scared shitless.'

Caitlin closed her eyes, remembering the women trapped in the cages next to the dogs.

'At least they're free,' Caitlin said. 'I did one thing right, I guess.'

'You got a lot right,' Grayson said. 'It's all over the news today. Drug bust. Human trafficking. Organ trafficking. The guy on the table's in stable condition at Sunrise Hospital. The two guys you tied up are in jail. News isn't talking about this yet, but I made some inquiries – police found paperwork about Maxim's operations. They've raided two locations, and they'll be making two more by this time tomorrow. It's going to lead to more arrests. More lives saved. This is a good thing for Las Vegas.'

Caitlin tried to take another drink.

'Who knows how many lives we saved?' Grayson continued. 'Dog lives, too. They'll have to euthanize some of those dogs – ones that were eating human flesh. But others, from there and another location, are being taken to a rehab center called Paws to the Rescue. They're going to be rehabilitated and adopted by families. And who knows what the hell happened to those girls you freed, but they've got to be in a better place than they were.'

Caitlin dumped out four Advil into her palm and took them one at a time. Her throat couldn't handle swallowing all at once.

Grayson explained the reason he'd brought her to his house was that he didn't know what room she was staying in at the Florentine and didn't want any video footage of him dragging her to her room anyway. He'd taken a sick day from work to keep an eye on her.

'Where's my phone?' she said, looking around.

'You didn't have one on you,' he said. 'I hope you left them in your car and they're not in some evidence bag, picked up off the warehouse floor.'

'Yeah. I left them in my car.' She had a thought. 'You don't think the cops will look at it.'

'Nah,' he said. 'There were lots of cars parked on that street. Residential neighborhood and all. We'll run out and get them for you.' He checked his watch. 'Later though. First I need to show you something.'

He opened his laptop back up and rose to sit next to her.

'What is it?' she asked.

'It's about your boy, Garrett Streeter.'

75

He sat down next to her on the couch. Grayson had a touch of body odor – he either needed to take a shower or change out of those sweats – and it made her feel nauseated. She really didn't want to do this now, whatever it was. She wanted to call her son and hear his voice. Then pass out again.

'OK,' Grayson said, aiming the screen of the laptop her way. 'I've been doing some research while you've been sleeping.'

The web browser was opened to multiple tabs. Some were YouTube videos, but others appeared to be other kinds of video archives.

'So this is the end of the game when Garrett Streeter led ASU to the Final Four. This was in Las Vegas. Remember?'

'I was at that game,' she said. 'The only time I'd ever been here before this trip.'

'Well, let me refresh your memory about the game.'

He pressed *play*, and a video of the closing two minutes began. ASU was down by eighteen to Duke, and it was a foregone conclusion they were going to lose. Garrett never stopped playing, though. Even as the other team was putting in bench players to give them a few seconds of playing time in an already sealed victory, Garrett ran around like a man possessed. He had two steals and scored eight points and then, a fraction of a second before the buzzer sounded to end the game, he launched a three that sailed through the net.

She remembered watching the game from the stands. Her heart broke for her boyfriend, out there trying so hard, never giving up, even when the game was clearly over. But Garrett pushed his team deeper into the playoffs than anyone expected. Any televised sports program talking about March Madness was talking about Garrett Streeter. In a matter of weeks, he went from a virtual nobody to a projected first-round pick.

'You know what the spread was for that game?' Grayson asked.

'Duke was favored, obviously, but I've never in my life paid attention to betting lines.'

'The spread was seven and a half,' Grayson said. He clicked over to a spreadsheet of some sort that showed an archive of betting information. 'Streeter's burst at the end – and that three-pointer – brought them within the spread.'

'So that means?'

'Anyone who bet on ASU would have won their bet.'

Caitlin remembered Jake sitting beside her the whole game. They'd both been nervous, but the game was never really close. She quickly recognized Garrett was going to lose. But Jake squirmed the whole time. For all she knew, that trip to Vegas could have been what started his gambling addiction.

'Here's another one,' Grayson said.

He played the final minute from a game when Garrett was in Sacramento. A similar scenario: the team was losing in a blowout and yet Garrett didn't give up. He single-handedly closed the gap from sixteen to six in the final few minutes, including, yet again, a buzzer-beater that had no bearing on the outcome of the game.

'Again,' Grayson said, switching over to a different spreadsheet with professional betting lines, 'he got them enough points to cover the spread.'

'Garrett always plays that way,' Caitlin said. 'He believes in the
LeBron James philosophy: It's OK to lose as long as you give it
everything you've got – empty the clip and throw the gun.'

'I've got a lot of examples,' Grayson said, clicking through the
tabs on his screen.

He'd found multiple videos and apparently cross-referenced them
with archives of betting lines. It must have taken hours, but of course
she'd been sleeping all day.

'If you're going to cheat at sports betting,' Grayson said, 'conven-
tional wisdom says you're going to shave points. But what if you
weren't favored to win, and you believed you actually could. You
could bet on yourself and then give it your all on the court. If you're
wrong and you lose, you still win the bet, as long as you get close.'

'I've seen enough,' Caitlin said before Grayson could start a new
video.

'Wait. There is one more you should see.'

He pulled up a Sabertooths game. This was from only a few
months ago. The Sabertooths were cruising toward a playoff berth
and had a contentious game against the cross-state-rival Cavaliers.
Caitlin remembered the game. Lots of fouls. Lots of jawing back
and forth between teams. Eventually, there'd been pushing and
shoving, and several players were ejected. Garrett remained, but he
was fired up, yelling at the other team just like his teammates were.
Caitlin was glad she watched the game without Alex because it was
a shining example of poor sportsmanship all around.

Grayson showed the end of the game. The Sabertooths were up
by four with only seconds left. No one was fouling. No one was
trying to stop the clock. The Cavs had given up, conceded defeat.
Yet Garrett drove down the court, practically uncontested, and shot
a three-pointer at the buzzer.

It was a final *fuck you* to a team they'd already beaten.

'The Sabertooths were favored by six and a half,' Grayson said.
'He covered the spread with that shot. Any other player would have
dribbled out the clock.'

He was right. No need to take that final shot if you'd already
won. Unless you wanted to rub it in the face of your opponents.

Or, apparently, make sure a bet was covered.

'What I'm wondering,' Grayson said, 'is if you're in on what
he's doing. Or if he's playing you, too.'

76

'Can we go get my phone now?' Caitlin said, although she really didn't feel up to going anywhere.

She didn't know if she had the strength to walk to the bathroom, let alone leave the house and complete an errand. Grayson checked his watch. He looked twitchy and nervous, the complete opposite of the placid guy she'd met at Atomic Psalm.

'I need to do some self-medicating first,' he said. 'Give me about an hour. How about you eat something?'

She rose from the couch to follow him into the kitchen, but immediately felt light-headed and had to catch her breath. She crumpled into a kitchen chair.

Grayson's house was neat and clean. Probably about the size of her house back in Ohio, but without the telltale mess caused by a kid. He didn't have much taste in how he'd decorated – he was obviously a bachelor – but he took care of what he had and didn't live in squalor. She imagined her own husband would have a sink full of dishes and leave clothes on the floor for weeks if he didn't share a house with a woman.

'Vegetable soup OK?' Grayson said.

'Perfect.'

He walked to a cupboard, and Caitlin noticed for the first time he was limping.

'Are you hurt?'

'My old injury,' he said, looking at shelves that seemed much barer than hers and Owen's. 'That's what starts hurting first. The pain is really in my head, but I feel it in my knee. Then I start to feel sick, like I'm coming down with something. My body gets achy.'

'What happens if you fight it?'

He laughed, like this was ridiculous.

'Imagine the worst case of the flu you've ever had,' he said. 'Then times that by a hundred.'

He opened a can of soup, his hands visibly trembling as he cranked the opener and poured it into a bowl.

'As shitty as you probably feel,' he said, 'if I don't get my fix, I'll feel worse than you within twelve hours.'

As he waited for the soup to cook in the microwave, he opened a cabinet. Sitting among bottles of Advil and Tylenol PM was the kilo of heroin he'd stolen. He reached next to it and withdrew a small cigar box that he carried to the kitchen table. He opened it and set out an extended-reach butane lighter, a twelve-inch length of rubber tubing, and a spoon twisted into a G shape so it could stand upright on the table. He pulled out a small plastic syringe that looked almost like a toy except for the two-inch needle at the end.

There were three plastic baggies inside the box, each containing a small ball of powder no bigger than a marble and sealed off with twist ties. He grabbed one and carefully dumped out the white powder – shiny like sugar – into the spoon. Some spilled onto the table and he reached into the box to retrieve two razors, which he used to scrape up the spilled powder. The table was scuffed here from doing this so much.

He got two glasses of tap water and set one down in front of Caitlin. The other he sat by his drugs. He fetched her soup and gave it to her. Caitlin didn't take a bite yet. It felt too weird with Grayson next to her, preparing a different kind of nourishment for himself.

He took the baggie, empty except for a layer of white film on the inside, and dunked it down into his glass of water. He submerged it with his fingers, and the water turned the slightest bit milky. He pulled the baggie out and let it drip into the water, then wrung it out like a rag and tossed it into the garbage can a few feet away.

She wondered what the hell he was doing.

Inside the cigar box were a handful of small sealed plastic envelope packages, like something you'd buy taco seasoning in. He tore one open and pulled out a plastic strip, similar to something you might use to test for pregnancy or Covid. He dipped one end of the strip into the water, let it soak for several seconds, then pulled it out and laid it on the table.

'Fentanyl testing strips,' he said. 'I do this every time I shoot up.'

She couldn't believe people lived like this.

'That kilo I took from the mattress warehouse,' he said with a nod toward the cabinet. 'I tested it this morning. Full of fentanyl.'

'What are you going to do?' she asked.

'Well, I've got two more doses,' he said, pointing to what was left in the cigar box. 'But my supplier is dead.' He smirked. 'And

I'm guessing I'm not going to get ten grand from you. Not after what I showed you.'

Caitlin didn't say anything. He must have been conflicted as he showed her the video evidence of Garrett's play, knowing he was raising suspicion about the man who was going to be the source of his salvation.

'So either I start using the fentanyl-laced stuff. Or I'm going to have to try to sell the kilo on the street and get something I want. I can probably get at least ten grand. Maybe a lot more. Enough to buy a few weeks' worth of H and have enough for rehab. That's my hope anyway.'

Caitlin didn't like the idea of him selling the brick of heroin he'd stolen, but if she couldn't get the money from Garrett, what else could he do?

'There was black tar in the flower shop,' Caitlin said. 'They hid it in flower arrangements.'

'I wish I'd known that last night,' he said. 'I normally only use the purest stuff.' He pointed to the shiny white powder in the spoon. 'But I'd take black tar over that fentanyl shit.'

Two blue lines appeared across the testing strip, and he exhaled in relief.

'OK,' he said, clapping his hands together. 'Time to launch.'

He grabbed the lighter, squeezed it to ignition, and held the flame under the spoon. The powder bubbled and melted, turning soupy and brownish. A faint vinegary stink wafted to Caitlin's nostrils.

'What's it like?' Caitlin asked.

'Heroin?' he said, not taking his eyes off what he was doing. 'Better than sex. Better than love. If there is such a thing as heaven, it *can't* be better than heroin.'

After all the powder transformed into liquid, he set the lighter aside and picked up the syringe. He dipped the tip of the needle into the liquid and drew back the plunger, slurping it into the tube.

'The euphoria lasts about fifteen minutes,' he said. 'But I'll feel fantastic for a good eight hours. I can walk through the day, my skin glowing, my feet floating six inches off the ground, and no one notices anything different about me. Around mid-afternoon, my feet return to earth, and that's fine too. The symptoms don't really begin until I'm at the end of my shift.'

He picked up a small canister of nose spray from the box. She knew what it was. Naloxone. Used to reverse opioid overdose. She carried one in her car when she was on duty. She'd never had to use it, but she knew deputies who had. Even in rural Ohio, there was plenty of drug use.

He tucked the nasal injector into the breast pocket of his shirt.

'If I OD, which I shouldn't because there's no fentanyl in this, but if I do, stuff this up my nose and squirt.'

He grabbed the rubber tube and carried the syringe into his living room. He sat on the couch where Caitlin had been sleeping. He rolled up the left sleeve of his shirt and wrapped the rubber strap around his arm.

'When I first started doing this,' he said, 'I didn't need the tubing. My veins were healthy. But now they're hard to find and I've got to fatten them up before I can get a needle in.'

He stuck the rubber tube into his teeth to pull it taut.

She watched him from a good fifteen feet away, but she could see his every move clearly. He slapped the ditch of his arm twice where the blood vessel was beginning to bulge, then picked up the syringe. He submerged the point into his bloated vein and squeezed the contents into his bloodstream. Relief washed over his face, and he looked completely different. Unbelievably relaxed.

He opened his mouth, letting the rubber tube fall to the floor. He brought his feet up and stretched out on the couch. Caitlin rose and walked over to him. She stared down at him. His eyes were open, but he wasn't looking at her. His expression seemed ghostlike, as if he was currently inhabiting another plane of existence.

What the fuck am I doing here? she thought, and she ran to the bathroom and dry-heaved into the toilet.

Sitting on the floor, clammy with sweat, she felt moderately better, but the pain in her head still pulsed. She forced herself to rise, and she cupped water to rinse out her mouth and splash her face, which she examined in the mirror. Her skin was bruised and swollen, the engorged flesh around one eye mostly black. The white of her eye was red with inflamed blood vessels. Her neck was purple with visible fingermarks. She lifted her shirt and inspected the damage to her body. More bruises and welts.

She remembered Maxim tightening his fingers around her throat. She remembered the blood spraying out behind him as Grayson shot him.

She put her head in her hands and crumpled to the floor. A dam burst, and she began to cry. All that she'd gone through, and

Garrett might have been lying to her all along. She sobbed loudly, remembering what Grayson said. The euphoria lasted fifteen minutes. She could allow herself to cry for that long.

Then she would have to put her game face back on.

77

'Glass,' Garrett said, sounding relieved. 'What the hell happened? I've been worried sick about you.'

Caitlin sat by the window, looking out over the view of Las Vegas, which she'd come to detest. It was morning. She and Grayson never made it out the door last night. After she'd slept another twelve hours on his couch, he'd finally taken her to her rental car, which was still parked down the road from Alexei Maxim's old building.

She was dying to speak to her son, but there was something she felt she had to do first.

She wanted to get this over as quickly as possible.

'You haven't been forthcoming with me, Street,' she said.

'What are you talking about? Christ, I was afraid you were dead, Glass.'

'I want the truth. All of it.'

There was dead air on the other end of the line.

'Is this about Summer?' he asked.

'No, actually,' she said. 'But if you're withholding something about her, you can spit that out, too.'

'We're trying to have a baby,' he said. 'We're having trouble. Going to fertility doctors. At least we were before Jake disappeared. Now, I don't even know if . . .'

He trailed off.

'I'm not talking about your fucking plans for the future,' Caitlin snapped, harsher than she intended. 'I'm talking about you and Jake. You fixing games for him. All that bullshit about not calling the FBI because they might suspect some impropriety. That's because there *was* impropriety, wasn't there, Street?'

More dead air on the other side of the line. But this time it felt different. She could sense his anger like it was an invisible gas coming through the phone.

'What the hell are you talking about, Glass?'

'I've looked back at your old games,' she said. 'All the way back to the NCAA tournament. The way you kept playing so hard even when the game was lost. You covered the spread with that last-second three, Street.'

'I can't believe this,' he said. 'You wasted time looking into *me*? You know I've always played that way, Glass. Leave it all on the floor. It's the competitor in me.'

That's what she'd always thought.

'But Garrett . . .'

'I bet if you go back through any player's catalog of film, you could cherry-pick examples of when they played better than normal, or worse, and try to line it up with betting lines. I thought you of all people, Glass, would trust me. I've always been honest with you. I failed to mention our intention to have a baby – I don't know why – but I've never lied to you.'

She wanted to believe him. Her hand was shaking holding the phone.

'You say you've never lied to me?'

'Never.'

'What about the night I got hurt?'

'What about it?'

'Did I make the shot?'

'What shot?'

'The goddamn three-pointer to win the game. The night I landed on Jake's foot and twisted my ankle.'

'Jesus Christ, Glass. My brother's been kidnapped, and you're worried about a pickup game ten years ago.'

'I want to know, Street.'

'Yes, you made the stupid shot. You scored every point in that game. Is that what you want to hear? I never lied then and I'm not lying now.'

'I want to believe you,' she said. 'But here's the truth, Street. This job is too big for me. I can't do it. Either you're lying to me and there's something you're not telling me. Or I'm in over my head. Either way, I can't do this anymore.'

She wanted to tell him everything. That she'd seen three people killed. That she'd gotten the shit kicked out of her. How close she'd come to dying.

I'm beaten, she wanted to say to him. *I give up.*

I want to see my son.

She'd come here – at least in part – to prove to herself she could be a detective.

She'd failed.

'Stay in Vegas until I get there,' Garrett said. 'We'll talk as soon as I get into town.'

Caitlin had already looked at airplane prices. The problem was, if she quit now, she was on the hook for her hotel and plane tickets. She'd already spent way more than she could afford. And she had none of Garrett's money left. She'd given it all to the women locked in the cages. The only ticket she could remotely afford wasn't until tomorrow anyway.

'Promise me, Glass. You won't leave until I get there and we can talk.'

'OK,' she said. 'But I'm done, Street. I can't do it anymore.'

She hung up and stared out at the city, the sidewalks clogged with pedestrians who didn't know – or didn't care – about the criminality going on around them.

Fucking Las Vegas.

She dialed her phone. Owen didn't bother to speak. He handed the phone to Alex.

'Mommy, when are you coming home?'

'Soon,' she said.

'Daddy said maybe we need to get used to you not being around.'

The words were a knife to her heart.

God, she thought. *He thinks I'm having an affair with Garrett.*

When she arrived home, she planned to tell Owen everything. She couldn't hide the bruises on her face and neck anyway.

It was time to come clean and hope he'd forgive her for lying.

She missed him. Not just from the trip. She missed the strength of their love before life got so hard. They could get it back, couldn't they? It wasn't too late?

'As soon as I get home,' she said, 'you're never getting rid of me.'

'I miss you.'

'I've never wanted anything more in my life than to see you and Daddy,' she said, glad they weren't on FaceTime so her son couldn't see – in addition to her bruises – the tears streaking down her cheeks.

78

The next day, she was beginning to feel better. Marginally. Her ribs screamed every time she breathed deeply, and her headache never went away entirely. But she wasn't nauseous anymore. Just really sore.

Her flight was scheduled for tonight, smack dab in the middle of Game Six. She didn't know what time Garrett would get to town, and she was dreading seeing him, but she had nothing to do but wait.

She flipped through the channels trying to find anything remotely distracting that *wasn't* ESPN. There was a knock at the door. She turned the TV off and took a deep breath. Better get this over with.

She opened the door slowly, fully expecting it to be Garrett. Instead, Yazmina and her wife stood there. Yaz let out a little squeal of delight and rushed forward to wrap Caitlin in a hug. Brooklyn, towering like a goddess behind them, was beaming too.

'I told you we'd come,' Yaz said.

Caitlin, who'd felt so alone for so long, couldn't believe how good it felt to be in her arms. Yaz, an inch taller than her and built with long wiry muscles, gave her an extra squeeze and Caitlin winced from the pain in her ribs.

'Garrett gave me your room number since you haven't been returning my texts,' Yaz said, her voice hinting at annoyance, then she added in a friendly voice, 'it's so good to see you, bestie.'

'Good to see you.'

They broke their embrace and Yaz's expression clouded over.

'Jesus Christ,' she said, grabbing Caitlin by the cheek and inspecting her face. 'What happened to you?'

The swelling around her eye had gone down, but, if anything, her bruises looked worse than they did when they were fresh, yellowing sickly at the edges and taking on a cadaverous purple color.

'It's nothing,' Caitlin said. 'I had a little accident, that's all.'

Yaz tilted Caitlin's chin up forcefully to examine the bruises on her neck, easily distinguishable as fingermarks. She gestured for her wife to see, and Brooklyn hissed sympathetically.

'Don't lie to me, Cait,' Yaz said. 'This was no accident.' Her eyes widened. 'Did Garrett do this? That fucker. I'll kill him.'

'No,' Caitlin said, turning away. 'He didn't do anything.'

Yaz and Brooklyn followed her into the room. Both were wearing Sabertooths jerseys and looking like a million bucks. Yaz's beautiful braids were pulled into an updo, and she had long silver earrings shaped like seashells. Brooklyn was sporting a short frizzy natural afro. Her wrists were adorned with a half-dozen bracelets, matching as many necklaces hanging from her neck. Both wore high heels, making them even taller, and Caitlin had the thought that both would be intimidating as hell in their professions. Patients must shit bricks when six-three Brooklyn walked into an examination room. And she could picture Yaz strutting into a courtroom, turning every head, including the opposing attorneys whom she would no doubt eviscerate in front of a jury.

These were amazing, unstoppable women, and Caitlin felt unworthy in their presence. The Caitlin these girls knew was no quitter.

'Can I take a look at you?' Brooklyn said.

Caitlin assented, and no one mentioned what caused the wounds as Brooklyn examined her. She felt Caitlin's throat, looked at her eyes, and – when Caitlin lifted her shirt – prodded gently at the bruises until Caitlin squirmed away.

'You should get X-rays,' Brooklyn said. 'You might have a cracked rib or two.'

'Unless they're poking into my lungs or sticking out of my skin, there's nothing the doctors would do for broken ribs anyway, is there?'

'Ice and limited activity, that's what you need,' Brooklyn conceded. 'But you should get checked out. Your head, too. You might have a minor concussion.'

Caitlin sat upright on the bed, wedging a pillow behind her back and stretching out her legs. No sense hiding how badly she was hurting.

'Are you going to the game?' Yaz asked.

'I'm going home,' Caitlin said. 'My flight will be taking off around halftime.'

Yaz stared at her sympathetically, no doubt wanting to ask more questions but hoping instead that Caitlin would be forthcoming on her own.

'Donnie and Danny Blakesly are in town too,' she said.

'The whole gang's here, huh?' Caitlin said.

'We're meeting up for dinner before the game,' Yaz said. 'Jake's here, isn't he? We should invite him.'

'I can't go,' Caitlin said. 'I'm going home to see my son.'

'We can't help you unless you tell us what happened.'

Caitlin closed her eyes. She wanted to tell her. Yaz was the best friend she'd ever had, apart from Garrett. And Owen, of course. But she didn't feel right violating her promise to Garrett, even if he was somehow involved. Cops had to carry their burdens.

She opened her eyes.

'Please trust me, all right? I'm going to be OK.'

She felt guilty as she said this. Regardless of whatever Garrett hadn't told her, she'd seen the videos of Jake being assaulted, the pictures of the gun in his face.

She might be OK, but Jake wasn't going to be.

79

When Garrett knocked, Yazmina and Brooklyn were still there. Brooklyn answered, and he stepped into the room dressed in a silver suit and Gucci shoes that probably cost more than Caitlin's monthly house payment. He would have to catch the team bus to the arena soon – players were required to dress nicely for the cameras. Despite the clothes he was wearing, though, he looked haggard. He hadn't shaved, and the crescents under his eyes were almost as dark as the bruises under Caitlin's.

He gave Yaz a quick, awkward hug. There was tension in the air. But when Garrett approached Caitlin on the bed and saw her face, his eyes went wide with shock. Yaz and Brooklyn could see Garrett was as surprised by her appearance as they were, and the pressure in the room deflated, replaced by a sense of sadness and helplessness.

Garrett knelt next to her. He didn't say anything – not in front of Yaz and Brooklyn – but *now* he understood why she was quitting.

'Yaz,' Caitlin said. 'Can you and Brooklyn let me talk to Garrett alone?'

They agreed and each leaned down to give Caitlin a hug. Yaz told her what restaurant they'd be at and what time.

'It's downstairs,' she said. 'The sports bar next to the sports book. Donnie and Danny will be there. Come say hi before your flight, OK?'

Caitlin said she'd try.

'And Garrett,' Yaz said, shifting her focus to Caitlin's ex.

'Yeah?' He looked sheepish, ready for a telling off.

'Give 'em hell tonight, OK?'

'Will do,' he said, and offered her an indulgent smile.

When they were gone, Garrett sat down next to Caitlin on the edge of the bed, staring at her. She hated him looking at her like that. Like she was fragile.

'What happened?' he said. 'Who did this?'

'It's probably best if you don't know everything,' she said, 'but there was a criminal in town, a bad guy, and I thought maybe it was him. I went to check him out, and . . .' The rest of the story was written on her face.

'Was it him?' he asked. 'Does he have Jake?'

'No. I'm sorry. I was wrong.'

He exhaled.

'I'm sorry I got you into this,' he said. 'I never should have asked you. You're right. You should go home.'

Whatever anger he expressed on the phone yesterday had been replaced with pity. And she hated being pitied.

'Street,' she said, 'are you saying that because you don't want me to get hurt worse than I already have? Or because I figured out you have something to do with this and you don't want me digging deeper?'

He glowered at her. The anger was back. The pity gone.

'Fuck you, Glass.' He stood up and paced away before turning back to her. Behind him, the city and the vast desert beyond were visible out the window. 'I'm sorry about what happened to you. I never should have shown up at your door. But don't – *don't!* – suggest I had anything to do with my brother's kidnapping.'

He glared at her, imploring her with his eyes to believe him.

She did.

She'd been convinced otherwise when Levi Grayson presented her with the evidence. But she knew Garrett. He was a good man. He wasn't perfect. He loved basketball way too much – loved it the way she did – to corrupt the game like that.

'I'm sorry,' she said. 'I had to ask.'

He was still angry, but he didn't say anything else.

'And I'm sorry I couldn't find Jake.'

'I don't want to get anyone else hurt,' he said. 'I'm gonna do what the kidnappers ask and hope for the best.'

He knelt next to her bed.

'Go home,' he said. 'Be with your family. Forget I ever contacted you.'

Tears blurred her vision.

'I hope Jake comes home,' she said. 'I hope you have a long life with that beautiful girlfriend of yours. You're a good man, Street. You deserve all good things.'

'So do you,' he said, and he leaned forward and kissed her forehead.

As he was leaving, she couldn't say anything in return because she was trying too hard not to cry.

80

Garrett was the last one on the bus. The others were sprawled in their seats, listening to headphones or sending text messages, all dressed in designer clothes. Elijah sat in the back reading a comic book. Garrett's usual spot was open next to him. He collapsed onto the cushion as Elijah looked up from the comic.

'Where's your book?' Elijah asked.

'No book today,' Garrett said. 'Just thinking.'

Elijah looked worried. He liked routine.

The bus's air brakes exhaled, and the driver pulled out into the Las Vegas traffic. Elijah went back to his comic.

Garrett's phone buzzed. One of the burners. A text from the kidnappers.

We've been lenient in the past, it said. But if you lose tonight, there's no next game to make up for it.

The Sabertooths were down three–two. If they lost tonight, the series was over.

A second text came through.

If you lose tonight, your brother dies.

Period.

Garrett closed his eyes and breathed deeply. When he opened them, he looked around to make sure no one noticed his anxiety. Halfway down the bus, on the left side, Josh seemed to be watching him. Then he looked quickly away.

Caitlin said it could be somebody close to him.

Garrett pulled out the burner phone and tried to call back whoever texted him. As the phone rang, he looked back at Josh, who was faced away from him now. The assistant coach didn't move. But from somewhere else, the right side of the bus instead of the left, there was a faint ringing.

Jamie, his backup point guard, shifted in his seat, pulled his phone from his pocket, and looked at the number. He had a puzzled expression on his face. He lifted it and answered.

Or pretended to.

Garrett leaped up so quickly that Elijah flinched in the seat next to him. Garrett bounded down to Jamie's seat and snatched the phone from his hand before he even knew Garrett was there. Garrett held the phone to his ear and listened.

A woman, old by the sound of her voice, was going on about a trip to the doctor, oblivious that Jamie wasn't listening anymore.

'Hey, man,' Jamie said, standing up. 'What the fuck!'

'Sorry,' Garrett said, holding the phone out.

Jamie snatched it back.

'That's my grandma!'

'Sorry,' Garrett said again, backing away. 'I got a prank call and thought . . . Sorry.'

As he retreated to the back of the bus, practically every eye was staring at him. Josh had started up out of his seat to intervene but stopped. Coach Ware looked concerned but said nothing.

Garrett headed back to his seat.

Elijah raised his eyebrows.

'Pressure getting to you?' he said.

'Maybe a little,' Garrett said, slumping back in his seat.

Elijah let out a hearty laugh. 'Not me,' he said. 'I'm getting forty tonight. Win or lose, I'll hold my head high.'

'Forty?' Garrett asked.

He grinned. 'Make it forty-five. I don't care if they have to carry me off the court – I'm getting it.' Something in his eyes made him look different – focused, determined. 'What about you, Streeter? Can you promise me twenty?'

Garrett hesitated a beat, then said, 'Thirty.'

Elijah leaned over and gave Garrett a fist bump.

'Then we ain't got nothing to worry about,' Elijah said, settling back to reading his comic.

Out the window, Bolt Arena loomed like the Roman coliseum. Sports, Garrett thought, were long ago played for life or death.

He only wished it was his life on the line, not his brother's.

81

C aitlin rolled her luggage behind her as she walked down the hall to the elevator. As she waited, she pulled out her phone to check to see if Owen had called. She'd texted him to let him know she'd be home late tonight. There was no response.

Before pocketing her phone, she checked a message the sheriff left the day she was at Grayson's. She read the transcription. He said he was checking in to see when she was coming back and wanted to express how excited he was for her to start in the new public relations position. She hated the idea of taking the job, but if this trip taught her anything, it was that she wasn't cut out to be a detective.

As she rode the elevator down, she glanced at the burner and noticed there was a missed call from Debbie about an hour ago – must have been while she was in the shower – followed by a text. The message said simply, Please disregard my call. Pressed the wrong number. Meant to call someone else.

There was a voicemail message, but the burner didn't have transcription capabilities. Her thumb hovered over the *play* icon, but the elevator came to the bottom. She didn't listen and instead pocketed the phone as she stepped off the elevator. She could listen to it later, if she bothered.

The sports bar was on the way to the parking garage, so she decided to stop by and say hello to Donnie and Danny and goodbye to Yaz and Brooklyn. She didn't have time to stay and eat. She had a plane to catch.

It was easy to spot her four friends in the restaurant. In a sea of Lightning blue and black, they were just about the only people in the room wearing Sabertooths colors. Plus, none of them was shorter than six feet.

Yaz spotted her and lit up. She gave Caitlin a gentle hug, and Danny and Donnie did the same. Danny had grown a beard. Donnie's hair was beginning to thin. The brothers, who'd rotated the power forward position back when Garrett played with them, had put on weight over the years. A big frame can hold a lot of weight, and Caitlin guessed they might have gained as much as forty or fifty pounds each.

'It's great to see you guys,' she said, and she meant it.

A few weeks ago, such a reunion would have warmed her heart. Now it broke her heart to see all these old friends. The way they looked at her bruised face but didn't comment on it told her Yaz and Brooklyn had already filled them in on what little they knew.

Donnie reached for a chair at a nearby table to bring to theirs, and Caitlin stopped him.

'I've got to go to the airport,' she explained, and, to her relief, no one asked why she wasn't staying for the game or what had happened to bring her to Vegas. 'I just wanted to stop and say hi.'

The various TVs around the sports bar were tuned to the pre-game discussions.

'I love you, girl,' Yaz said, wrapping her again in a big hug. 'If there's anything I can do for you – anything – you just call. I don't care if it's the middle of the night. I'll get on a plane and be there, wherever you are. You hear me?'

Caitlin couldn't speak for fear she might start crying. She closed her eyes.

'You're the baddest bitch I ever balled with,' Yaz said, and Caitlin let out a choked laugh. 'I'm serious. There's no one I'd rather have holding the ball with a game on the line.'

Caitlin eased up on her hug and opened her eyes. Over Yaz's shoulder, she saw a person she recognized pass by the entrance to the sports bar.

It was Richie – the cowboy John Lennon she'd talked to her first night in Vegas – accompanied by one of the sycophants he'd been hanging out with before. Richie wore the same hat, same round-lensed glasses.

It occurred to her the information he'd given her that first night proved spot on. Despite all of Levi Grayson's efforts to help, he'd actually led her down the wrong path. Richie's intel was solid – particularly his warning that Alexei Maxim was not to be messed with.

She checked the time on her phone. She really did need to get going. The airport wasn't far away, but traffic might be bad. Returning the rental would take time. And, besides, she'd made up her mind to quit her investigation.

Hadn't she?

What could it hurt to ask one quick question?

'Can you watch my bag for a minute?' she said to Yaz. 'Be right back.'

82

Caitlin hurried out into the casino and looked around. She spotted Richie and his buddy walking into a men's restroom over by a bank of slot machines. She headed that direction and didn't hesitate at the corridor to the men's room. She walked in. Richie and his pal were standing at urinals a few feet apart.

'Cowboy John Lennon,' she said. 'I've got a question for you.'

The few remaining men in the room scurried toward the door. Richie's friend whirled around, his expression pinched, but he waited for instruction from Richie about what to do. Richie turned around nice and slow, zipping up his fly, his face relaxed. When he saw Caitlin, a sly smile graced his lips.

'When I saw that stuff about Alexei Maxim on the news,' he said, 'I wondered if you had something to do with it. Now there's a void the size of a black hole in the crime in this city. I can't wait to see what fills it.'

Richie was wearing a shirt that said, *I AM A RAY OF FUCKING SUNSHINE.*

'I don't have any money to bribe you, and I don't want to put up with any bullshit,' Caitlin said. 'I've got one question, and I want you to answer it.'

Richie's relaxed façade cracked a little. When Caitlin first arrived in Vegas, he'd managed to manipulate her into forking over way more money than she should have. But the woman before him was different now. She wasn't someone to mess with.

Caitlin pulled out her phone, found the picture of Mr Mustache – the guy she'd followed from the basketball game – and held the phone out.

'You said you were good with faces. Do you know who this is?'

Richie studied the image.

'May I?' he said, taking the phone and using his fingers to zoom in on the picture.

Caitlin said, 'He might be—'

'Wearing a wig,' Richie finished for her.

Her scalp tingled.

Richie held the phone out for his friend to look at. 'Who does this look like?'

The friend frowned.

'Does that look like Ezra Jewell to you? Look at the eyes.'

Now the friend saw it. Recognition came over his face.

'I'll be damned.'

Richie handed Caitlin's phone back.

'That's Ezra Jewell.'

'Who the hell is Ezra Jewell?'

'He's Silas Bennett's right-hand man. Handles a bunch of Bennett's shady operations. Including Bennett's sports book.' He pointed to the image on the phone. 'That's not his real hair. Or a real mustache. It's a disguise. He's got short hair. Buzzed. Bleached.'

Caitlin stared at the picture. She focused on the eyes. They did look familiar.

'Wait,' she said, and she pulled up her Internet browser and did an image search for Silas Bennett.

She scrolled until she found the picture she was looking for. It was one of the photos of Bennett she'd seen when she'd done her initial Google searches about him. Bennett and another guy were licking whipped cream from the cleavage of a buxom woman in a plunging tank top. The guy had bleached hair, shaved close to his scalp. She'd only glanced at him before, but now she studied his eyes. He had a cool intensity that was unsettling. Silas Bennett was laughing in the picture, having a great time, but this guy seemed creepily focused.

'Is this him?' she asked, holding her phone out to Richie and his pal.

Richie nodded.

'I told you,' he said, unable to keep himself from grinning. 'I don't know what the hell you're actually looking for, but I told you if it was illegal betting, it was either Alexei Maxim or Silas Bennett.'

Caitlin studied the picture. Now she remembered seeing someone with short bleached hair at the Red Rose Ranch walking with Dickie. Caitlin experienced a sudden, panicked thought. She pressed play on Debbie's voicemail and brought the burner to her ear, ignoring Richie and his pal.

Debbie, her voice panicked, said, *'Silas and Dickie are at my fucking door. That never happens, and I mean* never. *What the hell did you get me into?'*

Caitlin lowered the phone.

'My money's on Bennett to fill the void left by Maxim,' Richie said. 'He'll be the new boss in Las Vegas.'

Caitlin looked up at him.

'Not if I have anything to fucking say about it,' she said.

She ran from the bathroom to the sports bar, where Yaz and her friends were throwing cash on the table for the bill. Caitlin grabbed her suitcase and took off running through the casino.

'Cait,' Yaz called to her. 'You OK?'

Caitlin didn't answer.

83

Rodrigo Sandoval won the tip-off and launched the ball into Garrett's hands. He dribbled quickly up the court as the other nine players all jockeyed for position around the basket. The crowd was thunderous. The whole arena felt like it was going to shake itself apart. Garrett could tell during warmups that all his teammates were on edge – his freak-out on the bus couldn't have helped – and he knew they needed a quick, easy score.

Elijah – the only one who didn't seem worried – called for the ball in the low post.

He said he'd get forty-five, Garrett thought. *Might as well get started.*

He lobbed a high pass that landed in Elijah's outstretched hands. The big man put it down, one bounce, and pivoted toward the basket. Jaxon Luca peeled off the guy he was covering to help with the double-team. When Elijah jumped, both defenders crashed into him, but Elijah, still airborne, held strong to the ball and – as a whistle sounded for the foul – banked it off the glass and into the net.

Garrett pumped his fist. He stood back as Elijah, already coated in a layer of sweat, went to the line. He dribbled five times, spun the ball in his hand – his free-throw ritual – and let the shot fly.

Swish.

This was exactly what they needed to settle the team's nerves.

Garrett set up on defense as Jaxon Luca brought the ball up the court, waving off their point guard who normally would do it. Billy Croft was defending him, and Luca hit him with a crossover that left Billy tripping over his own feet. Luca launched a three, and Garrett had a moment to feel thankful that he didn't drive into the lane for a better shot.

But then the ball snapped through the net.

As Luca jogged back down the court, Garrett heard him say, 'We ain't going back to Cincinnati.'

Garrett caught the inbound pass and jogged forward. Elijah made eye contact with him clear across the court, and Garrett heaved a long pass. Elijah leaped into the air, dwarfing his defender, and caught the alleyoop a foot from the rim. He slammed it home, and the Vegas crowd's fervor flattened in an instant.

Jaxon Luca started barking complaints at his teammates. Elijah ran up court and, as he passed Garrett, they reached out and slapped hands.

'Five down,' Elijah said with a wink. 'Only forty to go.'

84

Caitlin wanted to jam the gas pedal to the floor, but she refrained. She set cruise control for fourteen miles an hour over the speed limit and forced herself not to deviate from it. Getting pulled over wouldn't help her.

If Silas Bennett and his partner had Jake, there was no telling where they might have him stashed. But there was one building on the campus of the Red Rose Ranch that Caitlin didn't get to see on her little tour with Debbie: the large storage garage out back. She strained her memory and thought she recalled low windows at the ground level, suggesting there was a basement underneath. What she did remember, she was sure of it, was that the big security guard, Dickie, was carrying a Styrofoam food container and walking toward the building with a blond guy. She'd assumed the guys were on a lunch break, but now she thought the food wasn't for them.

Dickie and the newly identified Ezra Jewell were taking lunch to their prisoner.

In the distance, thunder clouds loomed, glowing purple and red from the setting sun. A snake of lightning appeared soundlessly on the horizon. Sheets of rain were visible, coming down from the clouds like blurred lines from the stroke of a paintbrush. That was the direction she was headed – into the storm.

She turned on the radio and raced through the static and noise until she found a broadcast for the game. It was the first quarter of a back-and-forth contest with several lead changes already.

She wished she had a gun. Levi Grayson had thrown her SIG Sauer into Lake Mead. When she packed her bag back in Ohio, she hadn't dreamed she might need to bring two.

She pulled out her phone and called Grayson. He'd saved her ass last time. Maybe he'd help this time.

There was no answer.

She tried to remember how many baggies of heroin he had left, and tried to calculate how many times he would have shot up since she saw him. Was he now dipping into the fentanyl-laced kilo he'd stolen from the mattress warehouse? She pictured him lying on his couch, foam gurgling out of his mouth as his heart and lungs arrested. She thought for a moment that she should stop the car and go check on him.

She didn't.

If the Sabertooths lost tonight, it was over. Jake was dead. She had to save him. She hated that she'd given up and squandered the last few days of her investigation.

Please, she thought, pressing down on the accelerator. *Let him be there*.

She tried Levi again, and when the call clicked over to voicemail a second time, she tossed her phone onto the passenger seat.

She was on her own.

Tonight, there would be no one coming to save her.

85

Garrett squirted Gatorade into his mouth and tossed the bottle back to one of the trainers. The Sabertooths had called a timeout, and they were on the sidelines, listening as Coach Ware drew up a play.

Garrett and Elijah were playing some of the best basketball of their lives. With only three minutes left before halftime, they were halfway to the point totals they'd promised each other. And it wasn't as if the rest of the team was slacking off. Rodrigo stepped it up on defense and was protecting the rim like he was Dikembe Mutombo. Billy Croft and Kevin Mackey both hit clutch three-pointers as the shot clock was winding down. Jamie Vaughn did his part by knocking in two long jumpers during his stint off the bench when Coach pulled Garrett for a brief rest.

The Sabertooths were putting on a clinic on how to play basketball.

The problem was that Jaxon Luca was playing some of the best basketball of his life, too. He had thirty points already, making baskets from everywhere on the floor: driving through the lane and finding a way through Rodrigo's defense, hitting long threes in transition, and raining in step-back mid-range jumpers no one could defend against. Garrett kept hoping he'd wear himself out, but he'd shown no signs of slowing down.

The lead went back and forth, two or three points for the Sabertooths, three or four for the Lightning. Neither were able to hold onto their lead for long.

'Let's silence this goddamn crowd,' Coach said, practically shouting to be heard, and the five starters all headed back to the court.

Garrett went to the sideline to throw the ball in. Kevin cut toward him, as planned, and Garrett put the ball right into his hands. Garrett ran toward the basket, where Elijah was setting an off-ball screen for him. Garrett's defender got tangled up with Elijah, and Elijah's defender didn't switch fast enough. Garrett darted into the paint, and Kevin lasered the ball to him as Luca came running over. Garrett

caught the ball and went up with it. Luca leaped. A strong hand
slapped Garrett's arm. An elbow collided with the ridge of bone
above his eye. A whistle sounded as Garrett hit the floor, sliding on
his butt. He was able to see his shot swirling around the rim like
it was in a toilet bowl. It almost spun out, balancing for a moment
on the metal, then dropped through the net.

Two points.

Plus the foul.

Luca stood over him, trying to intimidate him – get him to lose
his temper again – but Garrett ignored him. Elijah brushed past him
and helped Garrett up. Garrett wiped his sweaty palms on his shorts
and headed for the free-throw line.

Not today, Jaxon, Garrett thought. *Not today.*

86

The first drops of rain peppered her windshield as Caitlin
arrived in Green Lawn. She didn't take Brothel Boulevard
directly to the Red Rose Ranch. Instead, she turned one street
over – Battle Born Boulevard – and found that it ended in a residential cul-de-sac. Past one row of houses was an expanse of desert
brush, probably no more than a hundred yards, and on the other
side the Ranch compound was visible. There was a wooden fence
encircling it, providing some measure of privacy for those inside,
but she was sure of what she was looking at – she recognized the
red rooftops. The building she was interested in was the closest one.
And if she remembered what she saw in the security room accurately,
there were no cameras on this side of the property.

The rain came down harder, fat droplets that hammered against
the roof of the rental like the rattle of machine-gun fire. The rain
was probably good for her cover. No one in their right mind was
out in this shit. She turned up the radio to hear the final seconds of
the first half. She thought about what to do.

She had no zip-ties. No pry bar. No stun gun. No hammer.

No pistol.

The other thing she didn't have – time.

The game was tied – exactly fifty to fifty. The outcome could go either way. Jake's life depended on a coin toss, already in the air and coming down. It would land with his sentence – life or death – when the game ended.

She had to go now.

When she stepped out, she was drenched instantly, and she hurried up the walk of one of the houses like she intended to knock on the door. Instead, she curved around the house, hopped a short chain-link fence, and headed through their xeriscaped yard. Through the back window, she could see inside. A family – four people all decked out in Lightning jerseys and shirts – sat around a TV watching. Caitlin walked gingerly over the gravel, hopped the back fence, and headed into the desert without turning around.

All of the pain from her injuries – her aching skull, her tender ribs, her sore muscles – hadn't gone away entirely, but they'd taken a backseat to her adrenaline. It was like playing through pain, and she knew from experience the furlough she was experiencing wouldn't last forever. The bill for delaying her recovery would eventually come due.

But she had no choice.

She jogged, maneuvering around clumps of sagebrush. The ground was muddy, sluicing with runoff, and she had to be careful of her footing. The sky was dark, but a red ember burned on the western horizon. The moon had risen over distant hills, where the storm hadn't reached, and illuminated strings of rain in bluish light.

The fence was tall, at least seven feet. She grabbed the top, the sharp edge of the wood cutting into her palms, and pulled herself up. She got one leg over, then strained to drop over the other side, splatting in the mud. She leaned against the fence in a squatting position, surprised how hard she was breathing from what shouldn't have been much effort. She held her hand over her forehead like the bill of a hat, trying to keep the water out of her eyes. The ranch was lit up with external lighting, red bulbs accenting the buildings and strips of yellow bulbs lining the various walkways. Classic rock played over outdoor speakers, muffled by the rain but not entirely drowned out. She heard a woman's cackling laughter from somewhere in the compound.

The external building – a garage or storage building, or both – was only about twenty yards away. There were several windows, and all of them emanated light leaking from the edges of drawn blinds, including – as she remembered – several low windows indicative of a basement.

This is it, she thought, rising to her feet. *Game time.*

87

Garrett dropped onto his seat in the visitors' locker room and toweled sweat off his face. Next to him, Elijah stripped his jersey off and his compression shirt and tossed them on the floor. He started toweling himself off before he put on clean shirts.

Garrett checked his phone for texts or messages and found none from the kidnappers.

So far, so good.

In the center of the room was a large dry-erase board on wheels where the coach drew up several plays before the game. Now Coach walked over to it and said, 'Listen up.' He grabbed the eraser and wiped the board clean.

All eyes turned to Coach, expecting him to start drawing up new plays. Instead, he gestured to the empty board and said, 'If you don't know this stuff by now, what are we doing here?' He looked around the room. 'Go kick their fucking asses.'

He walked out of the room to whoops and applause.

88

Caitlin arrived at the backside of the building. There were no doors here, and she curved around the front, past two large bay doors, both closed. Two limousines were parked outside rather than in. She continued to curve around.

This side of the building faced the rest of the Ranch, and she could see the women's dorms and, behind them, the brothel and restaurant. One girl was hurrying along the boardwalk running from the dorms with an umbrella over her head and impossibly high heels on her feet. Once she disappeared inside, there was no one in sight.

Caitlin peeked in a crack at the edge of the blinds but couldn't see much. No people. The rain hindered her ability to hear anything. Up ahead was the side door. She tried the handle and, when it turned, she eased the door open. If she had a gun, she'd go in fast, checking out every corner. But she didn't, so she stepped in slowly, quietly, and eased the door closed behind her. Water dripped from her and puddled around her feet. Overhead, the rain hammered the corrugated roof.

It was a big room, with a workbench lining one wall and various tools and supplies hanging from hooks on the other: shovels and ladders and coiled extension cords. Next to the door were two cans of gasoline and a wheelbarrow. Metal braces ran the length of the room, spaced every ten feet or so, stretching from the concrete floor up into the rafters.

That's all she could take in before she noticed three things in quick succession.

First, there was a pallet of drugs positioned where a truck could back in through a bay door. There seemed to be as many, if not more, kilos than she'd seen at Maxim's warehouse, tossed into the rough approximation of a pyramid, and she had enough time to think, *Jesus, how much drugs can one town use?*

Next, her ears caught up to her sight, and the sound of the game being broadcast filtered through the noise of the rain. She turned her head that way and saw an open door into a corridor of some sort. Someone – or multiple people – were through that doorway listening to Game Six of the NBA Finals.

That's when she noticed the third thing.

Two people sat on the floor, leaning back-to-back against the support beam closest to the corridor. Their arms were twisted behind their backs, locked together with two sets of handcuffs. Gray rectangles of tape covered their mouths. They were both women.

She'd never met one of them, although she recognized from her picture that it was Mandy, the girl who'd said she'd been with Jake. The other she recognized immediately, with her purple-streaked hair. Debbie.

She stared at Caitlin with pleading eyes that could only mean one thing.

Help!

89

Elijah started the third quarter like he did the first, positioning himself in the low post and calling for the ball. Garrett lobbed a pass to him, and Elijah caught it, put it on the floor, and began backing his defender toward the basket. Luca came over to help, but Elijah sidestepped his opponent and leaped for the basket. Another collision of bodies – Elijah was taking a beating this game – but he managed to set the ball on the rim, where it lingered for a moment before dropping in.

The crowd let out a groan and then quieted.

When Elijah took his free throw, the ball clanged off the back of the rim and came straight back. Elijah took one step, leaped into the air through a gauntlet of other players and grabbed his own rebound. He dunked the ball so hard the backboard shook.

Luca put his hands on his hips and shook his head. He looked like he wanted to kill Elijah.

Elijah gave Garrett another hand slap as he ran down the court, saying as he passed, 'We're not losing this fucking game.'

90

Caitlin hurried over to the women, her wet shoes squeaking loudly against the polished concrete. She hated to be so noisy, but she hoped the rain and the TV would cover her. Voices came from the corridor, muffled and indiscernible.

Caitlin put a finger to her mouth in a *shh* gesture. Then she snatched the tape off Debbie's face.

'They're going to kill us,' Debbie hissed. The other woman nodded vigorously. 'If the series ends tonight, your friend is dead too. But either way, they're going to kill me and Mandy. You've got to get us—'

Caitlin made the *shh* gesture again, this time emphatically. Debbie clamped her lips shut. Caitlin examined the handcuffs. One pair was covered in fur, like the kind she'd seen inside the brothel, but both seemed to be sturdy, legitimate handcuffs – not just playthings.

'Over there,' Debbie whispered.

On the workbench, a few feet from a large red toolbox, sat an overturned cardboard box spilling handcuffs onto the wooden counter. Some of the cuffs were colorful, some fur-covered, some simple steel like the pair Caitlin carried on a daily basis. She ran to the workbench, snatched a pair of keys, and headed back to the women.

She unlocked Debbie's wrists first, but as she went to unlock Mandy's, the door she'd come through opened again. Dickie, the big guard who'd claimed to drive Jake back to his hotel, stepped out of the rain with a pizza box in one hand and a six-pack of beer in the other. He took two steps and spotted her.

Caitlin sprinted toward him, but she was too late.

'Hey!' he roared. 'She's here!'

9 1

'Don't let up now,' Coach Ware said during a Lightning timeout. 'We've got our fingers on their throats. Don't give them any room to breathe.'

Elijah, his face framed by his sweat-soaked braids, nodded. He'd carried the team on his back this far, but he wasn't finished.

As they walked back on the court, Garrett craned his head to look at the scoreboard above the court. The Sabertooths' lead was seven, and it felt like the momentum was shifting their way. Elijah was making good on his promise and already had forty-three points. The third quarter wasn't over yet. At the rate he was going, he might get sixty.

The players got into position, and the crowd made a half-hearted attempt to pump their team up. The Las Vegas fans could feel their hopes of winning in six slipping away.

Garrett hung back from Luca, pretending to guard someone else, but when the ball came toward him, Garrett darted forward and tapped it out of the air. He chased it to the other end of the court, with Jaxon – fast as a cheetah – in pursuit. Garrett picked up his dribble and stopped running. Luca swarmed him, but Elijah ran by, arms raised for the pass. Garrett lobbed it to him, and Elijah, all alone under the basket, caught it easily. He bent his legs, preparing to launch himself for another monstrous dunk.

But something happened.

His leg gave out underneath him, and instead of leaping into the air, he crumpled toward the floor, tossing up a shot before his knees hit. The ball plopped through the net, but Elijah curled up on the hardwood in obvious pain.

The Lightning inbounded the ball quickly and scored on the other end, all while Elijah lay on the floor, holding his knee. Coach Ware yelled for a timeout, and he and the medical staff rushed in. Garrett glanced up at the box scores. Elijah said he was getting forty-five, he didn't care if he had to be carried off the court to do it.

It looked like the statement was prophetic.

92

Caitlin ran at Dickie and kicked the pizza box he was holding. It flew into his face. As he swatted it out of his way, Caitlin swung her forearm up and into his jaw. His head whipped to the side and his knees wobbled. The beer hit the floor, bottles bursting and spraying foam.

She told herself she couldn't mess around. She'd almost gotten herself killed in Alexei Maxim's building. She had to be unmerciful.

Dickie looked like a boxer out on his feet, but Caitlin threw a hard left into his mouth, then a right into his jaw again, the exact same place she'd struck before. He dropped like a trapdoor opened beneath him. A broken tooth was stuck to his lip like a piece of popcorn.

'What the fuck?' a voice said, and Caitlin whirled toward the corridor entrance.

Another guy, as big as Dickie, came barreling toward her.

She ducked down and aimed a hard kick at his kneecap. She missed and hit the meaty part of his thigh. But it was enough to hyperextend his leg, and he fell like a charging horse with its legs slashed from under it. The guy, on his hands and knees, hissed in pain, but he was attempting to get up.

Caitlin stomped on his hand, and she heard – and felt – bones breaking beneath her heel. The guy howled in pain. Then she brought her elbow up high, ready to slam it down on the back of his skull.

'Stop!'

Three more men stood at the mouth of the corridor.

One was Silas Bennett, his pinched face much more hostile than any she'd seen in her Google searches. Another was Jacob Streeter, his hands cuffed behind his back and his face puffy and scabbed with injury.

And the third was Mr Mustache, Ezra Jewell, his cold facial expression recognizable even though his fake wig and mustache were gone and his hair was bleach blond and short.

He held a gun in his hand, pointed at Jake's head.

93

I t took Josh and two members of the medical staff to help Elijah off the court. He couldn't put any weight on his left leg. The knee was swelling already.

Garrett looked around at his teammates. They looked dejected. Defeated.

'Come on,' he said to Rodrigo and Billy, who were watching with horrified expressions as their best player left the court. 'We've got the lead. We need to hang on.'

94

C aitlin stared at Ezra Jewell, her lungs heaving. Her eyes shifted to Jake. The poor guy looked like hell, his eyes wild with fear, his skin bruised from the beatings his captors handed out. The gun aimed at his head was the snub-nosed revolver from the pictures.

The two big guys were still on the floor. Dickie groaned incoherently. The other guy cradled the hand she'd stomped. Silas Bennett was smirking. The egotistical son of a bitch had been worried for a minute there, but now he saw everything was under control, going his way.

'Shoot her,' Bennett said.

'Nah,' Ezra Jewell said. 'If the Sabertooths manage to win this game, we'll have more leverage for Game Seven.'

Caitlin wished she had her Glock in her hand. Or her SIG Sauer. Anything.

She spotted Debbie subtly folding the blade out of her ring.

Don't, Caitlin wanted to say.

Debbie lunged at Bennett, slashing at his face. He backed up, flailing protectively with his arms. Jewell was within reach, though, and he lashed out and smacked her in the face with the butt of the pistol.

Caitlin darted forward, but the gun was back to Jake's temple in a flash.

'Hold it,' Jewell said.

Caitlin stopped, still a few feet from him.

Debbie sat on the floor, holding her forehead, which was trickling blood from a gash. Silas Bennett looked worse. A long slash ran down his cheek, with a sheet of red pouring down his face and neck.

'You fucking bitch,' he roared, and he started kicking Debbie.

Caitlin thought about rushing Jewell. They were dead anyway. All of them. Maybe not tonight but once the series was over.

But, she told herself, if she could buy herself some time, there might be a chance. The handcuff keys had been locked in her fist the whole time she'd been punching Dickie. Now she tucked them into her back pocket.

'Hey, tough guy,' she called to Bennett. 'You like to hit girls? Why don't you try me?'

Bennett stopped kicking Debbie and glared at Caitlin. Ezra Jewell smirked, like he'd enjoy seeing Bennett try it.

'Cuff them,' Ezra Jewell said to Silas Bennett.

The brothel owner did as he was told and walked over to the workbench where the cuffs were strewn. Richie described Ezra Jewell as Silas Bennett's right-hand man, but it seemed like it might be the other way around. Or maybe they were equal partners – Bennett the face of the operation, Jewell the one who got his hands dirty.

Bennett cuffed Debbie first, pulling her arms around the pole where Mandy was cuffed, then tore the ring from her finger and held it up to her face.

'I'm going to use this on you, you whore.'

'Cuff the other one,' Jewell commanded. 'You can torture Amethyst all you want after the game's over.'

Caitlin put her hands behind her back and allowed Bennett to cuff them tight.

Jake's knees seemed to go weak at the sight.

'I'm so sorry, Caitlin.'

Tears chased each other down his cheeks.

'It's OK,' she said. 'The FBI knows where we are. They'll be here any minute.' She shifted her eyes to Ezra Jewell. 'Right now, the charge is only kidnapping. You don't want to add four counts of murder.'

Bennett laughed and said, 'We know you're lying.'

He grabbed her by her wrist and yanked her toward the corridor.

'Hey, boss,' the big guy on the floor said. 'I'm gonna need to go to the doctor. My hand's fucked. And Dickie.' He looked at the man sprawled on the concrete, conscious but practically catatonic with pain. 'His jaw is broken for sure.'

Bennett huffed, annoyed.

'Get his ass up and take him over to the main building. Get what's-her-name to patch you up. Tell her I'll be over later. I'll need some fucking stitches.'

Debbie, still handcuffed to the pole, saw there was no hope and screamed, 'Help! Help!'

The rainfall wasn't making quite the same racket on the roof, but still Caitlin doubted anyone over at the brothel would hear.

Or care.

'Shut that bitch up,' Bennett said, this time giving an order that Jewell followed.

He smacked the butt of the gun into her head again and she let out a pained groan, listing sideways. She wasn't unconscious, but she didn't seem very lucid.

Bennett shoved Caitlin toward the corridor, where a concrete staircase descended underneath the building.

'Come on,' he said. 'We've got a game to watch.'

95

Billy inbounded the ball to Garrett, who jogged up court. Still five minutes left and their lead was down to one.

As soon as the game resumed after Elijah's accident, Luca drained a three, stole the ball on the other end, then drained another.

I can't let this happen, Garrett thought. *I can't let us lose.*

If the series ended tonight, Jake would be of no use to them anymore. The only way to keep him alive was to tie the series up at three games apiece and ensure a Game Seven.

I won't let you die, Jake.

He dribbled to the top of the key, looking for anywhere to pass the ball in the swarming defense. Rodrigo positioned himself by the basket and called for the ball. He was trying to replace Elijah, but his post game wasn't nearly as good.

Garrett took a gamble and lobbed the ball to him. He caught it and put it on the floor, backing his defender down. But his head was turned, and he didn't see Luca sneaking in from the side.

Garrett opened his mouth to warn him, but it was too late. Luca slapped the ball away and took off dribbling down the court. Garrett raced toward him and as the two were crossing half court, Garrett reached in to get the ball but smacked Luca's arm.

The ref whistled the foul.

The Sabertooths were in the penalty, which meant Luca would get two free throws. The first would tie the game.

The second would give the Lightning the lead.

96

The four of them – Caitlin, Jake, Ezra Jewell, and Silas Bennett – watched the final minutes of the game. Jake, who looked as bad as Caitlin felt two days earlier, sat in a recliner, while the others stood. Caitlin stood off to the side, trying to keep her back from Bennett and Jewell. Bennett held a once-white towel – now red – to his bleeding face.

They were in a small studio apartment in the basement. There wasn't much to it, just the recliner, the TV, a twin mattress in the corner, and a door to a bathroom no bigger than a small closet. Caitlin had the feeling, a hunch, that Bennett and Jewell used this as a place to keep immigrants before they could put them to work as prostitutes. It was a step up from the dog cage used by Alexei Maxim, but not too far.

'Let me guess,' Caitlin said. 'When Dickie told you I'd been asking around about Jake, you asked Mandy to call me and claim she'd slept with Jake. But you tied her and Debbie up because they knew too much.'

'Pretty much,' Jewell said, not taking his eyes off the TV.

The Lightning had taken the lead, while the announcers bemoaned that the Sabertooths had little hope without Elijah Carter. Both Jewell and Bennett watched with intensity. She wondered how much they had riding on the game.

'So what really happened?' Caitlin asked.

Bennett looked over at Jake, who sat slumped in the chair.

'You want to tell her?'

'It was my fault,' Jake said, speaking up for the first time since his apology. 'Back when I used to gamble a lot, I never wanted to place my own bets on Garrett's games. I asked a prostitute to do it. She propositioned me in a casino before the Final Four, and I told her I'd give her a cut if she made a bet for me. Every time I was in town, I called the same girl.'

'Mandy?' Caitlin asked.

'Yeah,' Jake said, looking at Caitlin with apologetic eyes. 'But I quit. I hadn't gambled in months. Then I came into town for the Western Conference Finals, and I fell off the wagon. I bet on the Vegas–Utah game. Then, unable to stop myself, I called Mandy and asked her to place a bet on the Sabertooths' closeout game.'

'And she told these guys about you?'

'She sent me a text saying I had to come out here to collect from her. I took an Uber and she walked me out to this garage. Next thing I knew there was a gun in my face.'

It was that simple: Word had gotten to the wrong people that Jake was betting on his brother's games.

'Bennett,' Caitlin said, 'I don't think you've really thought this through. It's one thing to kidnap a guy, but if you kill us – even one of us – they will find you.'

'Please shut your mouth or I'll have Ezra knock your teeth out.'

Caitlin quieted. She had a million questions, but none of them really mattered. What mattered was finding a way out of here.

On the screen, Jaxon Luca hit a short-range jumper, giving the Lightning a seven-point lead – a fourteen-point swing since Elijah went down. Luca and Garrett had been scoring back and forth, but for every shot Garrett scored, Luca scored twice. Or hit a three. Or made a two-pointer plus a foul. Garrett already had thirty-one points for the game. Even on top of Carter's forty-five, it didn't seem like it was going to be enough.

'*You can feel the Sabertooths' chances slipping away*,' Dirk Justice said. '*There's only so much they can do without their superstar.*'

The Sabertooths called for a timeout, and the camera shifted to NBA officials wheeling a cart with the Larry O'Brien Trophy down the tunnel. On the sidelines, officials were stringing ropes between the court and the seats, preparing to keep fans off the court for the trophy presentation.

'*They're getting ready for the celebration,*' Dirk Justice said.

'Fuck,' Silas Bennett muttered.

Fuck is right, Caitlin thought. *If the series ends, we're all dead.*

The timeout ended, and Garrett ran the ball up the court. Jaxon Luca defended him, but Garrett hit him with a crossover that sent Luca off balance. Garrett stepped back past the three-point line and shot.

Swish!

Caitlin focused on the replay, where, in slow motion, Garrett shifted from side to side so quickly that Luca couldn't stay in front of him.

It gave her an idea.

She kept her eye on Bennett and Jewell as she eased her hand into her back pocket and fingered the handcuff keys.

97

'Get these fucking ropes out of here,' Coach Ware shouted. 'The game's not over yet.'

The guy who was stringing the orange cord in front of the courtside seats looked abashed.

'That's some bullshit,' Kevin muttered, gesturing to the tunnel where workers wheeled the two-foot-tall trophy in.

'Come on,' Garrett said. 'Focus.'

Billy positioned himself to throw the ball in, and Garrett stood nearby, with Luca making himself a barricade between the two.

Garrett darted away from Luca and snatched the bounce pass. He ran down court. Rodrigo stepped out to set a pick, and Garrett raced past him to the basket. He leaped into the air, kissed the ball off the glass and into the basket.

The Lightning called a timeout.

The Sabertooths were down by two with twelve seconds to go.

98

With her hands behind her back, Caitlin struggled to get the key into the keyhole. Her body was wet from the rain, but she could feel fresh beads of sweat building on her forehead.

On the TV, the Sabertooths were only down by two, although the Lightning would get the ball after the timeout.

'That's what the Sabertooths need,' Harding Able said. *'They need Garrett Streeter to play like he's got nothing to lose.'*

He has everything to lose, Caitlin thought.

And I have to play the same way.

Caitlin got the key into the cuff. She felt one of the wristbands free up. She couldn't bother with the other one – she'd have to let the handcuff dangle.

'Christ,' Bennett said, the blood on his cheek drying into a rust-colored mask. 'He might do it.'

He and Jewell were standing on the other side of the recliner to her. The gun hung limply in Jewell's hand. Both of their eyes were glued to the screen.

It was time for Caitlin to make her move.

99

J axon Luca caught the inbound pass and dribbled, trying to run out the clock. Garrett ran after him, and Luca jogged away, fully expecting Garrett to foul him to stop the clock. Instead, Garrett snaked his hand past Luca and whapped the ball.

It went bouncing down the court. Both he and Luca scrambled after it.

100

C aitlin darted in front of Jake and the TV. Both Jewell and Bennett flinched, surprised by the movement. Caitlin was almost to them when Jewell jerked the pistol up. Caitlin juked sideways, like Garrett had with his crossover dribble. The gun went off – earsplitting in the tight concrete chamber – and Caitlin felt the breath of the bullet as it sailed inches from her cheek.

But that was the only shot Jewell had time for.

Caitlin finished her crossover by slamming her elbow into his face, rocking his head backward. She grabbed the gun, first with one hand then both, the open cuff bouncing around her wrist. Jewell tried to pull the gun away, but she held firm, thrusting the barrel toward the ceiling. She drove her knee into his groin; when he grunted in pain, she jerked the gun downward and ripped it out of his hands.

Silas Bennett grabbed her from behind, wrapping an arm around her neck. She grabbed his arm with one hand and prepared to duck her body to flip him over her. But Ezra Jewell recovered enough that he was able to get his hands around Caitlin's wrist.

The two men pulled her in opposite directions, Jewell trying to get the gun back, Bennett choking her with a headlock.

101

Garrett got his hands on the ball and ran toward the three-point line. Luca was right behind him. The game clock raced toward zero.

Garrett jumped. He let the ball go. Luca crashed into him and the two tumbled toward the floor.

The horn sounded.

From their tangled pile on the floor, Garrett and Luca watched – along with twenty thousand people in the arena and another twenty million around the world – as the ball sailed toward the basket.

It hit the backboard, came down against the front of the rim, slapped against the backboard again, bounced twice more on the rim.

Then dropped through the net.

102

Silas Bennett squeezed Caitlin's neck, and she tried to claw at his arm with her free hand. She couldn't get any leverage with Jewell in front of her, yanking on the gun. He pried Caitlin's index finger out of the trigger guard and twisted it backward. The pain was excruciating, but she held onto the gun. Her vision darkened. Then a blur came from her periphery.

It was Jake.

He lowered his shoulder and rammed his whole body into Ezra Jewell. The two went sprawling. No one was tugging on Caitlin's gun anymore. She had it all to herself.

She smacked the metal barrel over her shoulder and felt it collide with Bennett's skull. He loosened his grip, and she managed to lean forward, lifting him off the ground and flipping him onto the floor in front of her. He started to get up. Caitlin whacked him – even harder – on the top of the head again. His legs turned to noodles and he collapsed, conscious but barely.

Jewell was getting up. One hand gripped Jake's collar, and the other was pulled back in a fist, poised for a punch.

Caitlin pressed the barrel against the back of his head.

'Stop,' she said. 'I'll kill you where you stand.'

He let go of Jake's shirt and lowered his fist. He was gasping for breath.

'It's over,' Caitlin said, and his body relaxed in understanding.

Caitlin glanced at the TV to see what had happened in the game. But the screen was black, with a bullet hole dead in the center.

103

Jake waited until Silas Bennett and Ezra Jewell were handcuffed around the pole Mandy and Debbie had been fastened to before he wrapped his arms around Caitlin in a hug.

'Thank you,' he said, sobbing.

She patted his back, but she didn't want to take much time for a reunion. She had things to do.

'What now?' Mandy said. She and Debbie, free of shackles, stared at Caitlin. 'They'll come after us. All of us.'

'You're going to have to kill them,' Debbie added.

Caitlin thought about what to do.

If Jewell or Bennett had tried to continue fighting, she wouldn't have hesitated to shoot them dead. But she had no intention of killing anyone in cold blood – not the way Levi Grayson shot Maxim's guys. Still, she didn't want to lead any authorities to Garrett. The apartment downstairs would have Jake's DNA all over the place.

'Where's the phone you used to call Garrett?' she asked Silas.

Resigned, his face pinched in pain, he gestured toward his pocket, and Caitlin retrieved the phone. She opened it and found the pictures and videos that had been sent to Garrett, along with others they hadn't shared.

'Go,' Bennett said. 'We won't come after you.' He looked at the girls. 'Any of you.'

'Bullshit,' Debbie said.

'Sorry,' Caitlin said to Bennett. 'You're not getting away with this. Come on, Jake. Help me out.'

She walked over to the palette heaping with drugs. She grabbed the palette jack, which was positioned nearby, and swung the forks into the space between boards. She jacked up the handle, and the skid lifted off the floor.

'Open the door,' she said, and Jake found the button to raise one of the bay doors.

Caitlin hauled the palette of drugs out into the driveway next to the limos, a good ten yards from the building. The rain had stopped, but the whole landscape was wet, bringing the fragrance of the sagebrush to life. She went back into the garage and, one at a time, undid Bennett and Jewell's handcuffs and marched them out to the palette. She cuffed their wrists to the triangle-shaped handle of the jack and used extra cuffs to pin their ankles to the skid itself, underneath the mound of drugs.

'What the hell are you doing?' Jewell asked, but Caitlin didn't answer.

Instead, she went back into the garage and grabbed the two gas cans by the door. One was full, the other about half empty. She lugged them down the stairs to the basement. She tipped the full one over, and the gas glugged out. The chemical smell burned her nostrils. She tossed Bennett's cell phone into the puddle. Then Jewell's pistol. She used the other can to make a trail of gas up the steps, through the garage, and out the building.

'Anyone got a light?' she asked Mandy and Debbie.

They shook their heads.

She checked Bennett and Jewell's pockets and found a Zippo with an engraving of the rose from the brothel's logo.

'You're making a huge mistake,' Bennett said. 'No charges will stick. I'll be out in twenty-four hours. Then—'

'Then what?' Caitlin said, shaking the gas can. 'There's a little bit left. How about I dump it on you?'

He didn't answer.

'You listen to me, you sack of shit,' Caitlin said, squatting in front of him. 'You will forget we ever existed. You will tell the cops nothing of what happened. You will never bother Garrett Streeter or his brother again. You will never bother me again. Or these ladies. I've been merciful this time, but if you ever get out of jail and I get the sense that you're coming after any of us, I will take a hammer and smash your balls like they're grapes. Got it?'

She figured threatening his manhood might be effective against a guy who'd made his life all about sex. It seemed to work – he shut his mouth.

It was the best she could do, short of killing them. She'd crossed a lot of lines to rescue Jake, but killing someone was a line she wouldn't step over unless she absolutely had to.

She asked Debbie and Mandy to do her a favor.

'Go into the brothel,' she said. 'Pull the fire alarm.'

'OK,' Debbie said. 'Then I'm getting the hell out of here.'

'I'm sorry I got you into this,' Caitlin said.

'I'm just glad you got me out of it.'

Mandy apologized to Jake for setting him up and to Caitlin for lying, but Jake seemed like he just wanted to get out of there and Caitlin was so exhausted she barely acknowledged the apology.

As the two women hurried toward the brothel, Caitlin brought a tongue of flame to the lighter and lowered it to the gasoline. It ignited with a whoosh, and she jerked her hand back from the heat. A trail of blue and red flame raced into the garage.

As they walked through the desert back to Caitlin's rented SUV, they heard the fire alarm in the brothel go off. The glow of the burning building grew brighter and brighter, casting long flickering shadows across the desert.

Jake started crying again, and Caitlin put her arm around his shoulder as they walked. She checked her phones and saw Levi Grayson had not called her back.

'I'm going to take you to Garrett,' she said. 'I need to make a quick stop first.'

104

Caitlin stomped on the brake pedal, and the SUV came to a rocking halt in front of Levi Grayson's house.

'I'll be back,' she told Jake, but he had fallen asleep on the drive.

Caitlin ran up the steps and pounded on the door. No answer. She tried the handle. It wouldn't turn. She shook the door, trying to get a sense of whether the deadbolt had been thrown or just the knob locked. She couldn't be sure. She shuffled back, looked around the neighborhood to make sure no one was watching. Then she took two steps forward and brought her foot up in a hard kick. The door banged open.

Levi Grayson was lying on the couch. His left sleeve was rolled up like before. His drug paraphernalia was spread out on the coffee table, including the massive kilo he'd taken from the warehouse.

'Levi!' she said, shaking him.

He wasn't dead – yet – but he wasn't responding. A stream of drool ran down his chin. She looked around for the nasal inhalant he'd shown her.

She couldn't find it.

'Shit,' she said, then she remembered something he'd said and checked his breast pocket. It was there. She jammed the projector into his nostril. As she was about to squeeze it, Grayson's eyes opened and he sat up, scooting away from her.

'What are you doing?' he said dreamily

'Thank God,' Caitlin said. 'I thought you OD'd.'

'I'm OK.' He wiped the drool from his chin.

'Did you take that shit?' She pointed to the fentanyl-laced kilo.

'Yeah, but I'm OK,' he said. 'Guess I have a pretty good tolerance to opioids by now.'

'I'm going to get you your money,' she said. 'It might take a day or two, OK? Don't die in the meantime.'

'Did you, uh, figure out what was going on?'

He still had no idea who or what she'd really been looking for.

'I did,' she said. 'It was Silas Bennett. Watch the news tomorrow. I bet there will be something about it.'

Grayson looked mildly surprised, although how stoned he was clearly affected his response.

'And,' she said, 'I wanted to tell you that you were wrong about Garrett Streeter.'

It felt good to say the words. She hated that she'd ever doubted him.

Grayson nodded dreamily.

'Thanks again for saving my life,' she said.

He chuckled. 'Thanks for trying to save mine.'

105

G arrett stood at the window, looking out over the glowing nebula of Las Vegas. The game was a blur in his memory. He'd been on edge ever since. He hadn't heard from the kidnappers.

There was a firm knock at the door.

They're coming to kill me, he thought.

'Who is it?' he called.

'Glass,' he heard Caitlin say.

He thought she'd be in Ohio by now.

'I've got something to show you,' she said.

He swung the door open. Jake jumped forward and threw his arms around Garrett with such force that they lost balance and tumbled to the floor, hugging.

'I'm so sorry,' Jake cried. 'I'll never gamble again.'

Garrett was in shock, unable to believe what was happening. But his brother wouldn't let go. Garrett squeezed him tighter, as if fearing he might disappear from his arms like a dream.

'I love you, brother.'

'I love you, too.'

Caitlin stepped into the room, closed the door behind her, and watched the reunion. From the floor, Garrett looked up at Caitlin's bruised face.

Thank you, he mouthed.

106

An hour later, Jake and Garrett were in the master bedroom. Garrett said he'd lie beside his brother until he fell asleep. Caitlin, sitting on the couch, picked up the remote and turned on the TV. She was exhausted – more tired than she could ever remember being – and all her aches from before were coming back with fresh new pains. She'd just booked a flight for her and Jake to return to Ohio in the morning, and there was nothing else she needed to do tonight. But she wanted to talk to Garrett before she crashed, so she turned to ESPN to try to stay awake, keeping the volume low.

'*In the history of the NBA Finals, there has never been a game where three players – three! – scored at least forty points each,*' Dirk Justice was saying in an interview. '*We've had two a handful of times – Jordan and Barkley, Shaq and Allen Iverson. LeBron and Kyrie on the same team. But three! Two on the winning team and an opposing player! With his buzzer beater, Garrett Streeter had exactly forty. Elijah Carter had forty-five before he left the game. And Jaxon Luca – forty-nine points in a losing effort.*'

The coverage cut to after-game interviews, where the Lightning's coach was saying something similar.

'*Honestly,*' he said, '*we expected it from Elijah Carter. Early on, it felt like one of those big games with two superstars fighting back and forth. But then Garrett Streeter stepped up. He's really established himself as an elite player this series. It's hard to fight a one–two punch like that.*'

Caitlin remembered a conversation she once had with Garrett about his basketball dreams. More than having his number retired or making the hall of fame, he wanted one game – just one – where he really stepped up when it mattered. Like Magic Johnson in his first Finals appearance when Kareem went down with an injury. Or Isaiah Thomas scoring twenty-four points in one quarter on a broken ankle. Or a young LeBron's famous one-man victory against the Pistons.

Garrett said he knew he'd never be on the Mount Rushmore of the NBA – he'd be lucky to make it to the pros – but if he could be the best in the world for one night, one game that really mattered, his basketball career would be complete.

Garrett walked out of the bedroom and collapsed onto the couch next to Caitlin. He looked as tired as she felt. She muted the TV.

'He's out like a light,' Garrett said. 'I can't believe what they did to him.'

'You sure you don't want me to call Yaz and get Brooklyn to take a look at him?'

She'd suggested this earlier. Jake needed a doctor – and Yaz's wife was an ER doc – but the two brothers talked her out of it. No need to get anyone else involved. And Jake insisted he would be OK until they got back to Ohio.

'You know what's really messed up?' Garrett said.

'What?'

'Some of the beatings they gave him were for no reason. Game Three. They told me to cover the spread. But Jake says they didn't make a bet on the spread. They made a money line bet – all I needed to do was win. But they told me to cover the spread to give themselves a little cushion. Try to make sure I didn't cut things too close. And if I came up short, we'd still win and they'd still win.'

Caitlin remembered Jake in the video saying, 'But he *won!*' Jake's surprise made sense now. Jake knew what bet they'd made and knew Garrett had delivered.

'But they beat him anyway to make me think I messed up,' Garrett said. 'To fuck with my head, I guess. Keep me afraid.'

'So out of all the games,' Caitlin said, 'you actually delivered what they wanted on all but one. You only actually failed on the game you got kicked out of.'

'And,' Garrett said, 'Jake got the impression they bet less on that game – another money line – so they didn't lose *that* much. What they were really mad about was us going down three games to two. Jake said they made a big futures bet at the beginning that the series would go seven games. They wanted us up three–two for a bit of breathing room. They didn't want to be in a win-or-go-home situation.'

It was impressive, Caitlin thought. With Garrett's help, they'd successfully rigged four out of five. Actually, if you counted tonight, Garrett delivered five out of six times. Doubtless they would have told him not to cover the spread for Game Seven – or just straight up lose – as an easy way to guarantee a final windfall in the last game.

Caitlin thought of Jake, taking those beatings just so the kidnappers could keep the pressure on Garrett. She thought about how she'd let them live.

Those sick assholes got off easy.

'Jake's going to need more than a medical doctor, you know,' Caitlin said. 'He'll need a therapist.' The physical damage he'd suffered was probably secondary to what he suffered psychologically. 'He's already been going to gambling counseling, so maybe his therapist will be of some help.'

Garrett nodded in agreement then let his eyes drift to the TV. 'What are they saying?'

'One for the history books,' she said.

He let out a forced chuckle. 'If I've realized anything over the past couple of weeks, it's how much basketball doesn't matter. I was playing for my brother's life tonight. Playing for a championship seems so unimportant by comparison.'

Caitlin said nothing.

'It's over anyway,' Garrett said. 'Elijah texted me from the hospital. He's got a fractured kneecap. No way we beat the Lightning without him. It's a relief, honestly.'

'You have to give it your all,' Caitlin said.

'I'll go through the motions,' he said. 'That's about all I can muster.'

Caitlin leaned forward.

'You owe it to your teammates,' she said. 'Your fans.'

He rolled his eyes.

'I'm serious, Street. You owe it to your brother. You owe it to a little boy in Hill Haven, Ohio, who wants to see his basketball hero play his heart out.'

'I'm no hero,' he said. '*You* should be your son's hero.'

'Well, then,' she said, 'you need to give it your all for me. If you don't owe anyone else, you do owe me, don't you?'

'I'll do my best,' he said. 'Don't expect any miracles.'

'There are a few other things I want you to do, OK?'

'Name it,' he said. 'If it's in my power to give, it's yours.'

'Three things,' she said, and held up her index finger. 'First, I need ten thousand dollars. Not for me. For a friend who helped me.'

'Glass, I'd give you ten million dollars. No matter what happens in the last game, Cincinnati is going to give me a max contract now.'

She shook her head. 'I didn't do this for money, but someone helped me and he needs it.'

'OK.'

'Second, I'd like you to make a couple of charitable donations. First to Paws to the Rescue in Las Vegas. It helps rehabilitate pit bulls that have been used as fighting dogs. You can decide the amount, but I want you to help them out.'

He frowned, knowing there was a story behind the request but resisting the urge to ask.

'Also,' she said. 'Human Justice International. They help victims of human trafficking. Make a donation to them as well.'

'No problem,' he said. 'And the third thing?'

She smiled. 'I want three tickets to Game Seven. For me, my husband, and my son.'

'Done. Done. And done.'

'I'm sorry I almost gave up,' Caitlin said.

He waved his hand dismissively. 'You did it. That's all that matters.'

Caitlin knew she'd better get some sleep before the flight. But Garrett seemed to want to talk.

'I bet you'll be glad to get back to your family.'

'You have no idea,' she said. 'I've never been away from my son this long.'

'So you like it?' he said. 'Having a kid?'

'It's the best,' she said. 'You always wanted to be a dad, didn't you?'

He nodded solemnly. 'More than I want an NBA championship.'

She remembered he'd said he and Summer were having fertility issues.

'I hope you get the chance, Street. I really do.'

He opened his mouth to say more, but there was a knock on the door. Caitlin sprang to her feet, worried some of Silas Bennett's men might have tracked them down.

'Who is it?' she called through the door.

'It's Summer.'

She sounded pissed.

107

Caitlin and Garrett looked at each other. She nodded, answering his unspoken question, then swung the door open. Summer did a double-take, noticing the bruises on Caitlin's face. Caitlin knew what was going through her mind – why was Garrett's ex-girlfriend in his room at one o'clock in the morning? And why did her face look like she'd gone ten rounds with Mike Tyson?

'What the hell is going on?' Summer said. 'I want some fucking answers, you two.'

'Come here,' Garrett said. 'Let me show you something.'

She followed him into the room where Jake was sleeping. He pointed to Jake and asked her to take a close look at his face. She gasped.

Caitlin could hear them talking in whispers. She went back over to the TV, but could hardly focus she was so tired. A few minutes later, Summer came out and stood before her with her arms crossed.

'It's my fault Garrett didn't tell you what was going on,' Caitlin said. 'I didn't know who we could trust until Jake was back safe.'

'Get up,' Summer said.

Caitlin had no energy, but she complied. She half expected to get slapped, but instead Summer threw her arms around Caitlin's shoulders. Caitlin lifted her limp arms and embraced Summer. She'd been holding herself together all night, but – she didn't know why – this was the moment she broke down.

She sobbed into Summer Morgan's neck, pouring tears into her hair.

108

Caitlin pulled Owen's old Toyota truck up in front of her house. As she closed the truck door, Alex appeared at the front step.

'Mommy!'

He sprinted to her, and she fell to her knees in the grass to embrace him. She squeezed him, breathed in his scent. She felt his small body in her arms, how delicate he was. She could feel how much he needed her from his hug.

'I'm never leaving you again,' she said.

When they relinquished their embrace, Owen was approaching.

'Mommy,' Alex said, 'what happened to your face?'

'Oh nothing,' she said. 'I was playing basketball with Garrett and I tripped. Clumsy Mommy.'

Owen stared at her. She could tell he was angry, but the bruises on her face also made him concerned. He didn't know what to think. Like Summer just hours ago, he wanted some goddamn answers.

'I want to hear about everything you've been doing,' Caitlin said to Alex, 'but why don't you play basketball for a few minutes while Daddy and I talk.'

It didn't take any more persuasion. Alex ran to the garage and grabbed his ball. Caitlin took Owen's hand and led him inside. They stood in the front living room where they could see Alex out the window. She took a deep breath.

This was a good man. All he ever wanted was for Caitlin to be happy, and she knew – on that front – she'd been impossible to satisfy.

'Garrett's brother was kidnapped,' she said. 'They were using him as leverage for Garrett to fix games. I found Jake. I got him back. It wasn't easy, but it was the right thing to do. They were going to kill him. I'm sure of it. But I should have told you. You and Alex are the most important things in the world to me. I'm sorry I wasn't honest with you. I'll never lie to you again.'

She stopped there. She could go on – she thought about offering to go to couple's therapy – but she figured she'd probably made her case about as well as she was going to.

His eyes were wide in shock. She expected him to say, *So you're not having an affair?* Or: *Seriously? Kidnapping?*

Instead, he took her face gently in his hands and said, 'Are you OK?'

She thought his concern for her was a good sign. They'd have a lot to talk about in the coming hours and days, but at least his first question was about her well-being.

She took his hands in hers and held them to her chest.

'I am now.'

GAME SEVEN

109

The Sabertooths' arena was filling with fans. Garrett's teammates were doing their warmups. He dribbled two balls, one with each hand, as he always did in his warmup routine. He felt like he was moving in slow motion. One ball hit his foot and bounced away and, as he lunged to get it, he lost control of the other. He stood, hands on his hips, breathing heavily. Josh, standing nearby, gave him a look of concern.

Shit, I'm tired, Garrett thought.

His whole body felt sore, his mind a fog. It was like he had a terrible case of jet lag. He'd slept so hard the last couple of days, the relief of having Jake back catching up with him, and he'd skipped all the treatment his trainers advised – ice baths, acupuncture, muscle massages. He just wanted the season to be over.

Yet he had to somehow get through one more game.

Elijah, decked out in a sharp Sabertooths-orange suit, came onto the court with crutches under his arms. His leg was in a black cast, and he leaned over the crutches severely as he swung himself forward. They'd probably gotten the biggest crutches they could find, and still they weren't long enough.

'You ready?' Elijah said.

'As I'll ever be,' Garrett grumbled.

'Remember that interview you did with the *Cincinnati Enquirer* when you first came to town?'

'You read my interviews?' Garrett asked.

'Of course,' Elijah said. 'Don't you read mine?'

Garrett laughed.

'Remember what you said about playing in high school?'

Garrett knew what he was referring to. When he was a freshman and sophomore, he'd been the highest scorer on the team. But the team lost a lot of games. Before his junior year, his coach took him aside and asked him *not* to shoot.

'I need you to make your teammates better,' the coach said. 'And at your height, if you have any chance of going far in this sport, it's as a point guard. Pass first, shoot second – I promise it will pay off. For your team. And for you.'

All through Garrett's junior year, he – and the team – went through growing pains. But Garrett got better as a point guard, and every other player around him improved in their positions. The team went undefeated his senior year, winning the state championship and securing Garrett a scholarship to ASU.

'This game,' Elijah said now, looking more serious than usual, 'it's time for you to go back to shooting. This ain't a pass-first, shoot-second kind of game, you feel me?'

Garrett nodded.

'One game,' Elijah said. 'On our home court. You got this, Streeter. Tonight's your night.'

110

Caitlin and Jake made their way down the steps toward their seats amidst the bustling crowd of Sabertooths fans. These seats, a few rows behind the Sabertooths' bench, were even better than what she'd had in Las Vegas. Summer was already there and gave them both hugs.

Owen and Alex were on their way. They'd driven separately because Caitlin spent the day with Jake in Cincinnati, taking him to doctors' appointments – it turned out he had a fracture in his cheekbone and a cracked rib. Her own injuries had healed well. Her bruises hadn't gone away, but most of her pain had. A soreness lingered in her ribs, but at least her headache was gone.

She'd been following the news from Las Vegas. Silas Bennett and Ezra Jewell were both in jail. There'd been enough evidence in Bennett's office at the ranch – not to mention the seven hundred pounds of heroin – to charge them with a long list of crimes. Once they were behind bars, several witnesses came forward with corroboration.

It was Sunday night, and she had to return to work tomorrow. She hadn't made up her mind about the PR job. She'd proven to herself she could be a detective, but, of course, no one in law enforcement would ever know what she'd done.

Caitlin could see Garrett talking to Elijah down on the floor. Garrett didn't look nervous or particularly relaxed – more like a guy who wanted to be somewhere else.

On the other end, Jaxon Luca appeared calm and resolute. He usually seemed so intense but, at the moment, he simply looked confident. Why wouldn't he? Without Elijah Carter – who led the Sabertooths in points, rebounds, and blocked shots – how much threat could the Sabertooths be?

'You know,' Summer said to her, 'I hope he has fun tonight, gets to remember why he loves basketball.'

'Me too,' Caitlin said.

It wasn't the worst tragedy that happened as a result of Silas Bennett and Ezra Jewell kidnapping his brother, but Garrett's disillusionment with a game that had once meant the world to him – not caring whether he won tonight or lost – was an unfortunate side effect.

She looked over her shoulder, trying to spot Owen and Alex. They should be here by now.

She'd spent every minute she could with Alex over the last two days, and Owen seemed to forgive her for lying and embarking on a secret investigation. This morning he'd come back from his bike ride with a bouquet of yellow roses and orange lilies bursting with color. She'd never much cared about those kinds of gestures, but today she'd been moved almost to tears. She hugged him tightly and gave him a long firm kiss.

As the players left the court, and the lights dimmed, Caitlin pulled out her phone.

Where are you? she texted Owen. You're going to miss tip-off.

Traffic is a fucking nightmare, he typed back. Exit ramp is backed up.

Owen almost never swore, so he must be really frustrated. He also never texted while he drove, so he must be sitting in gridlock.

Game's about to start, she wrote. Hopefully you won't miss much.

He didn't text back. As player introductions began, Caitlin felt a cold sense of fear sitting in her stomach like a brick.

She told herself she was being paranoid.

111

Garrett took the ball up the court slowly. It was hard looking for offensive options without Elijah on the court. Garrett was the floor general, but offensive plays hinged around Elijah. Whether he got the ball on a play or not, the other team had to focus so hard on stopping him that he dictated how the defense was played.

Not tonight.

Garrett's limbs felt heavy, his mouth dry. Game Sevens in the NBA Finals were usually a bit sloppy, with both teams exhausted. A war of attrition. Whoever could hold on and give it their all until the final horn had a good chance of pulling out the victory.

But Garrett felt like he had nothing left.

The shot clock was ticking toward zero, and Garrett made a pass to Billy Croft, who made a quick pass to Rodrigo down low. But Rodrigo fumbled the ball and nearly had it stripped. He lobbed it back to Garrett.

With the shot clock down to one second, Garrett jumped for a long three. The horn sounded before the ball left his hand.

Shot clock violation.

'Shit,' Garrett muttered, walking back down the court.

The game had barely begun and already he wanted it over.

112

'Where the hell is my husband?' Caitlin muttered, checking her phone.

No messages.

The first quarter just ended, and still Owen and Alex weren't here. The Sabertooths were playing like shit. They were only down by eight, but that was largely due to Garrett's teammates playing decent defense. They were stagnant on offense. Garrett had exactly zero points and zero assists.

If anyone in law enforcement had any reason to be suspicious about his performance in the Finals, this game would stand out more than any others. He really didn't look like himself. The emotional turmoil of the past two weeks had taken its toll, not to mention the simple fact that this game didn't matter in the same way the last six had.

Come on, Garrett, she thought.

She tried to call Owen. No answer. She looked up into the stands, wondering if maybe they were lost. No luck.

Her phone buzzed with a text.

In line at the entrance, it said. Be there soon.

This update should have quelled her worries, but it didn't help. Her imagination was running riot. She told herself the recent events – everything that happened in Vegas – had rattled her, and there was nothing to worry about.

Can't wait to see you, she typed.

113

Coach Ware was squatting before Garrett and his seated teammates, drawing up a play. Elijah, with his crutches, stood outside the huddle, looking more intently than Garrett was. Garrett wiped a towel across his forehead, but it was out of habit – he was hardly sweating. He was hardly trying.

'Don't let them get too far ahead,' Coach said. 'If we can keep it close, we can put ourselves in a position to win.'

Garrett rose to walk back on the court. He glanced up at Summer, sitting with Jake and Caitlin. They all looked anxious.

Come the fuck on, he told himself. *Don't let them down.*

He took the inbound pass, jogged up the court, then darted forward when Rodrigo set a screen for him. He put his head down and charged toward the basket. Jumped. A smack on his arm and the ball popped free.

Whistle.

Foul.

He went to the line, tried to clear his head. He told himself to forget about the game. Focus on making one shot. He dribbled, bent his knees, stayed low for nearly a second, then stood straight, extended his arms.

Release.

Swish!

OK, he thought. *That's a start.*

114

C aitlin watched, her stomach clenched with anxiety, her heart aflutter with hope, as Garrett began to play better. He made two free throws, then a layup, then made a nice no-look pass that resulted in a Rodrigo dunk. He took a long three and, while the ball sailed in the air, Caitlin thought, *Please go in*, and when it did, she and Summer high-fived.

Watching Garrett come alive on the court was a beautiful thing, and it helped to take Caitlin's mind off her irrational fears.

Garrett got the ball with only two seconds left on the clock before halftime. He took two quick dribbles and lobbed the ball from beyond half court. It clanged off the rim, and the crowd let out an 'Awe!' But the Sabertooths were only down by five, which she thought was fortunate. The Lightning would come out with everything they had in the third quarter, and if the Sabertooths could withstand the barrage, they might have a chance.

Caitlin leaned back in her seat and watched Garrett and his teammates leave the floor.

Where the hell are Owen and Alex? she thought.

She reached into her pocket to check her phone. There was a text message from Owen. No words. Just a photo.

A gun – the same battlefield green Glock used in some of the pictures of Jake – was now pointed at a different target.

Alex.

Caitlin's eyes went wide, and fear scratched icy fingernails along her spine.

In the background of the photo, she recognized her own living room, the couch and pictures on the wall easily identifiable. Alex was trying to be brave, but it was clear he was terrified. That was her son – *her child* – in his own home, with a gun aimed at his head.

Her phone began to ring. It was Owen's number, but Caitlin knew it wouldn't be Owen on the other end – just as it wasn't him sending the misleading texts about traffic being the reason they were late. With trembling fingers, she brought the phone to her ear.

'I assume you got my picture,' said a hoarse, familiar voice.

115

'**I**f you hurt him,' she started to say, but the voice cut her off. 'Save your threats,' Levi Grayson said. 'I'm in charge.'

Caitlin's whole body felt numb. A strange tunnel vision overcame her, and everything around her – an arena of twenty thousand people all talking and making noise with music playing and lights flashing – seemed to disappear.

'I waited until halftime because I knew there was no way you could get home before the game is over,' Grayson said. 'So here's what's going to happen. Are you ready?'

'Are they OK?' Caitlin asked. 'Tell me that. Are they hurt?'

'They're both alive. I had to rough up your husband a bit – he's tough for a skinny fucker – but I haven't hurt him any worse than what you went through recently.'

Some kind of noisy halftime show was beginning, and Caitlin turned the volume up on her phone and put a finger in her other ear to hear better. Her hands were shaking badly. Her heart pounded with such force it felt like it might explode. She was distantly aware of Summer and Jake looking at her.

'The Lightning are favored by three and a half, thanks to Elijah Carter's injury,' Grayson said. 'But I placed my bet before it was revealed his injury was season-ending. The Sabertooths were favored by three and a half the other way. Those odds are fixed in place for my bet. I bet on the Lightning.'

'What does all that mean?' Caitlin said.

'It means your boy can try to win the game if he wants, but he better not win by more than three,' Grayson said. 'Without Carter, they don't have much of a chance anyway. But if by some miracle the Sabertooths are winning – I don't know, maybe Jaxon Luca goes down with a broken ankle or something – you tell Streeter to shave points. If, somehow, the Sabertooths win by more than three, you'll find your son and your husband's brains splattered on the walls of your home. Got it?'

She imagined what he described, and she felt chills up and down her body, from her toes to her scalp.

'Why are you doing this?' she said. 'I told you I'd get you the money.'

'Pfft,' he said. 'I never wanted your ten thousand. I don't want to sit in some rehab facility, sweating bullets and dreaming of a needle and spoon. I want to sit on a beach and take heroin every day for the rest of my life. Silas and I had a nice plan worked out. You came in and fucked everything up.'

No wonder he'd pushed her in the direction of Alexei Maxim. He'd been working with Silas Bennett all along.

'Please,' she said, hating the pleading sound of her voice. 'Garrett will give you whatever you want. Five million. Ten.'

'As long as the Sabertooths don't win by more than three,' Grayson said, 'I stand to make a lot more than that. My pile of chips has been growing each game.'

'Haven't you made enough then?'

'You really don't know anything about gambling, do you? Or breaking the law? There's no such thing as enough. Now when the teams come back on the court, you get word to Streeter about what he has to do.'

'I can't exactly talk to—'

'Get the message to him. I don't care how. And if he comes through, I'll walk away and leave your family behind. You can come home, cut the tape off their mouths, and forget I ever existed.'

Caitlin's mind was reeling.

'And, Caitlin, don't even think about calling your friends in the sheriff's office. If I hear a siren in the distance or so much as a twig snap outside, I'll kill your family and take as many goddamn cops as I can on my way out. I'm not going to prison. I'm a cop with a heroin addiction, understand? I've got nothing to fucking lose.'

With that, he hung up on her.

Summer and Jake were both staring at her, knowing something was wrong. Her whole body was trembling. She wanted to put her head in her hands and curl into a fetal position and hide away from the world.

Get it together.

Your family needs you.

She grabbed Summer by the arm and spoke loud enough for both her and Jake to hear.

'I need your help.'

·116

Garrett stepped back on the court to warm up. He leaned down to tear his athletic pants off when he heard Summer screaming for him. He jerked up his head and saw her, Jake, and Caitlin – all of them looking terrified – waving for him. They'd made their way down to a group of courtside seats that were unoccupied at the moment.

'We need to talk to you,' Summer shouted.

He could tell something was wrong. Really wrong. Entering the stands wasn't allowed, but the first row was a blurred line where players sometimes hugged or interacted with fans. He jogged over, and Caitlin, Summer, and Jake threw their arms around Garrett's shoulders, and the four of them stood in a huddle.

'They've got my son,' Caitlin said, her voice thick with fear.

He remembered the little boy running to embrace him. He wanted to ask a million questions, but he asked the only one that would matter to Caitlin.

'What do you need me to do?'

'He says you can't win by more than three.'

'OK.' Easy enough. It would take a miracle to win at all. 'We're going to lose anyway.'

'But what *I* want you to do is slow the game down,' she said. 'Give me time to get there.'

'Your house is almost two hours away, Glass. You'll never make it.'

'Slow the game down. Use all your timeouts. Get your teammates to commit fouls. Whatever you can do to stop that fucking clock. And,' she added, 'I need to borrow your car.'

Grayson had waited until halftime knowing Caitlin couldn't drive there in time to stop him – but she might be able to make it if she was in a sports car. Jake, who had a key to Garrett's Mercedes, would take her down to the players' garage. Summer would stay here and communicate with Garrett if need be. Caitlin would call or text to let her know her status.

'It's too complicated, Glass. We need to call the police.'

He stared at her, their faces only inches away. Before, he'd insisted she not call in law enforcement. Now it was her who was adamant they didn't.

'He's in my home,' she said. 'I know the cops who will be responding. I don't want to put the lives of my family in their hands. Please, Street, this is the only way.'

'OK,' he said. 'I'll slow the game down. And I'll make sure we lose, just in case you don't make it. If we start fouling like crazy, they'll pull ahead anyway.'

'No, Street. You have to keep the game close.'

'Why?'

'Because I need you to extend the game as long as you possibly can. Understand?'

'Oh, shit,' he said, recognizing what she was saying.

And he thought the kidnappers had asked for the impossible.

117

Garrett waved for his teammates to huddle up. Coach Ware and Elijah both gave pep talks at halftime, but now it was Garrett's turn.

'Listen up. Here's what I want you to do. I want you to foul them. Got it? Foul like you've never fouled before.' Coach Ware looked at him skeptically, but he didn't interrupt. 'Foul when they shoot. Foul before they shoot. Foul people who don't have the ball. We're going to slow this game down. We're going to throw them off. That's our strategy.'

Most of the players didn't seem to understand the severity of what he was asking. They seemed to think he just wanted a little extra aggressiveness on defense.

'Coach,' he said to Ware, 'get ready to sub players in and out. All you bench guys are getting minutes.'

Coach looked skeptical; he'd been wanting Garrett to speak up more – become a de facto assistant coach – but this might be going too far.

'If we're in the penalty,' Rodrigo said, 'we're giving them free points.'

Garrett shook his head.

'They have to make their free throws,' he said.

'Jaxon's a ninety percent free-throw shooter,' Josh said skeptically.

Elijah pointed out that both the center and the power forward for the Lightning were terrible free-throw shooters.

'That's true,' Josh said. 'Barely fifty percent.'

'Foul them,' Garrett said. 'If Jaxon's got the ball, foul away from the ball. Or foul him before he shoots. We don't want any three- or four-point plays.'

They all stared at him, dumbfounded.

'I'm serious,' he said. 'I want the goddamn NBA record for the most fouls in a half. I expect at least half of you to end the game in the locker room.'

'But if we're all fouling out,' Rodrigo said, indignant, 'who's going to score points?'

'I am,' Garrett said. 'I'll score.'

All eyes stared at him. Garrett knew they were teetering, and he didn't know which way they were going to fall. Coach Ware cleared his throat, no doubt to put the kibosh on this crazy strategy, but then Elijah spoke up before he could.

'You heard the man,' Elijah said, his voice booming. 'Garrett's going to have zero fouls and fifty fucking points and all you other guys are going to have five or six fouls. That's our strategy. Get it done.'

Coach Ware closed his mouth.

Elijah grinned. 'Now, go get me my ring.'

118

Caitlin adjusted the seat as Jake told her what she needed to know to drive Garrett's car. There was apparently a *Comfort* setting and a *Sport* setting on the Mercedes, and Jake put it on *Sport*.

'This is basically a racecar now,' he said. 'Twin turbo V8s. Five hundred and seventy horsepower. Zero to sixty in about three seconds.'

'Jesus.'

Her cruiser did it in about eight seconds, which felt fast as hell when you were behind the wheel with your foot on the gas.

'There's electric rear-wheel steering,' Jake said, 'which means if you're going over seventy, the rear wheels will turn with the front. Makes passing easier. And the tires are wide as hell. They'll grip the road like you're glued to it. But be careful. This thing will top out around two hundred. You won't be doing anyone any good if you're dead in a ditch.'

'OK,' Caitlin said. 'Got it.'

'Why don't you let me drive? I drive this car as much as Garrett does.'

'You've been through enough,' she said. 'You sit this one out.'

The truth was she didn't want anyone else involved. She could trust Garrett to do his best on the court, but she couldn't possibly sit in the passenger seat while someone else drove her to rescue her son and husband.

She was in a hurry, but there was something she needed to know first. She did a search on her phone for the Nevada Gaming Commission's law enforcement branch and found the picture of Levi Grayson she'd first looked at when she thought he looked like Huey Lewis.

'Was he one of the guys?'

Jake nodded.

'They didn't have any qualms about letting me see their faces,' he said. 'That's how I knew they were going to kill me when it was all over. He wasn't around as much as the others, but he was there. He seemed to know how things worked – the betting stuff. He was mad as hell after one of the games. I guess they made some in-game bets that alerted a watchdog group or something. But he wasn't in charge. I got the impression he was kind of like a technical advisor.'

It made sense now that she thought about it. Who would know how to place bets on sporting events without alerting anyone? Without cluing in the casinos and changing the spread? And without raising any red flags among law enforcement?

Answer: the law enforcement officer actually in charge of sports betting.

She remembered the dispassionate way Levi Grayson had shot Alexei Maxim and his men. He wouldn't hesitate to kill Owen and Alex.

'And did they talk about me?' Caitlin asked. 'Did they know I was looking for you?'

'Yeah, but I didn't hear everything,' he said. 'I only heard a little, and I couldn't always pay attention.' His voice started to crack. 'They beat me up. I was in and out, hard to tell if I was dreaming sometimes.'

Caitlin needed to go.

'But they did say there was a girl working for Garrett. I didn't know it was you until I looked out the window of the basement and saw you talking with one of the hookers. I started yelling, but they really beat the shit out of me that time.'

Caitlin was sickened, knowing she'd been so close. How much hardship she could have saved herself if she'd heard him that day.

'I gotta hurry,' she said. 'You're safe now, Jake.'

He swallowed.

'Go get 'em, Glass.'

Caitlin reversed hard out of the parking spot, then she stomped the accelerator and squeaked the tires on her way up the garage ramp.

119

The streets close to the arena were clogged, and there wasn't much she could do, but once she merged off the entrance ramp for I-75, she pressed the gas down and raced around the other cars like they were standing still. The Mercedes had more torque than anything she'd ever driven, but she liked the way it handled. Jake was right – the tires gripped the road like Velcro.

Every nerve in her body seemed to be revolting. Her hands were shaking, her shoulders were bunched with tension, and the contents of her stomach boiled, ready to erupt up her esophagus. But driving helped – it gave her a task to focus on – and she felt a calmness begin to replace her panic.

Fear turned to anger.

She'd trusted Grayson, and now he was holding a gun to the most important thing in her life. She'd never felt such fury.

Once she got away from the city, she pushed the car to a hundred and forty and made herself stop there. For now. The highway wasn't clear enough to go faster. She held tight to the wheel and her stomach clenched every time she blew past another vehicle. Besides losing control of a car she wasn't familiar with, she was also afraid of passing a highway patrol cruiser.

Every mile was a gamble.

Jake had tuned the radio to the game so she could listen, and so far it sounded like Garrett was carrying through on slowing the game down. His teammates kept committing fouls and within minutes they were in the penalty. That was a good thing. The clock would stop every time the Lightning took free throws. On offense, Garrett wasn't messing around. The shot clock was twenty-four seconds, and he was barely waiting half that time. He was trying to put the ball back in the hands of the Lightning, so his teammates could foul again and stop the game clock.

The announcers picked up on the strategy, and all of them questioned its efficacy.

'*It seems to be throwing off the Lightning a little bit,*' Harding Able said, '*but as long as they're making their free throws, it's not doing the Sabertooths much good.*'

'*They're desperate,*' said Dirk Justice. '*That's what it is. They're doing everything they can to get the Lightning out of their rhythm.*'

'*Can you blame them?*' Chuck Walla asked. '*In the history of the NBA, can you name a single NBA team that prevailed in the Finals when its star player was injured?*'

'*Magic Johnson,*' Justice said. '*When Kareem went down in 1980. Magic's rookie year.*'

'*Yeah,*' Harding Able said, '*but Garrett Streeter is no Magic Johnson.*'

What they didn't know, of course, was Garrett's true strategy – extend the game.

So far, it was working.

amie Vaughn picked up four fouls in a matter of minutes, and Garrett gave him a high five while the Lightning's center was walking to the free-throw line.

'Next time they call a foul on you,' Garrett said to Jamie, 'argue it. Make a big fucking deal. Let them T you up. Take your time being escorted off the court.'

Jamie had bought into the strategy wholeheartedly and gave Garrett a fist bump.

The center missed the first free throw, bouncing it off the back of the rim, but then clanked the second in off the glass. Jamie inbounded the ball to Garrett, who sprinted the length of the court. Luca stayed on him. Kevin Mackey was calling for the ball on the wing, and Garrett faked a pass to him. Luca bought the fake and flinched in that direction, then Garrett jumped for a long two-pointer that bounced in off the glass.

Luca called for the ball – he'd figured out they were mostly fouling everyone but him – and as soon as he got it, Jamie ran in and slapped his arm while bumping him chest to chest. Luca stumbled away, almost losing his feet, as the refs called the foul. Jamie threw his arms up like this was the most ridiculous call in the history of the NBA.

'Yo, ref,' he yelled. He seemed to be enjoying himself. 'You need some fucking glasses.'

The ref made the gesture for a technical foul and blew his whistle hard. He signaled Jamie was out of the game. The crowd booed halfheartedly. They wanted to support their player, but they didn't seem to know what was going on. Why was their team fouling on practically every defensive possession?

Josh and another staff member came onto the court to get Jamie to leave, but Jamie was stomping around, jawing at every Lightning player he could find. Coach Ware stood on the sideline stone-faced. He was taking a risk on Garrett's strategy.

Garrett's chest heaved with each breath. He didn't know how much longer he could keep this up. He wished Caitlin had just let him throw the game, but, of course, she didn't trust that the kidnappers would let her family go any more than he had. But what she'd asked, extending the clock *and* keeping the game close, was counterintuitive – there was a reason teams didn't use this strategy.

As security approached, Jamie headed toward the tunnel, taking his time and complaining the whole way. Down by the visitors' bench, the Lightning coach shook his head in disgust. Jaxon Luca looked even more irritated than usual. Garrett could hear him complaining to a teammate, 'This isn't fucking basketball.'

No, Garrett thought. *It's life or death.*

121

C aitlin slalomed around a pickup truck in one lane and a Camaro in another, passing them like they were cones. On the radio, Harding Able was complaining that the clock was stopping so frequently the quarter seemed to be taking forever.

'*I'll be darned if it isn't working, though,*' Chuck Walla said. '*The Lightning seem to be completely thrown off, and they haven't been able to extend their lead.*'

'*There's no way this would work,*' Dirk Justice added, '*if it weren't for the fact that Garrett Streeter is on absolute fire. Every time the Lightning put points on the board, Streeter scores, too. Win or lose, Garrett Streeter is putting his stamp on NBA Finals history.*'

Caitlin focused on her driving. She'd driven her cruiser over a hundred plenty of times, and this car was built for speed like no other. But driving it wasn't like relaxing on cruise control. Both hands on the wheel. A nervous energy in her stomach. Her hands had stopped shaking, though. Adrenaline had focused her.

Up ahead, a car was cruising in the center lane, and she was on top of it before she saw the light bar on the roof and the State Highway Patrol logo on the door.

'Shit,' she muttered as the Mercedes blew past the cruiser.

In her rearview, the car's blue and red lights came to life. Caitlin pressed the accelerator down, and the cruiser faded from sight, the lights hardly a blip in the distance.

It would never catch her.

Even if it could match her speed, she was too far ahead for it to ever close the gap. But what it could do – what the driver was probably doing this second – was radio ahead. Every highway patrol vehicle within twenty miles was probably getting ready for a yellow Mercedes sports car to come flying into their territory.

122

G arrett launched a long three that clanged off the rim. Rodrigo jumped for the rebound and put the ball back up and into the basket.

It was one of the rare times this half that any Sabertooth scored except for Garrett. As he jogged back down the court, the ball went straight to Jaxon Luca. Rodrigo, God bless him, body-slammed him with his seven-foot frame and knocked Luca out of bounds and into the front row of seats.

The ref blew a flagrant foul on Rodrigo. Luca ran back on the court, throwing his arms up and screaming. His teammates got to him before he could make a mistake that would earn him a technical. Everyone from the Lightning to the refs to the fans in the closest rows looked absolutely frustrated. This game was getting out of hand.

'You're embarrassing yourselves,' Luca spat as he walked to the free-throw line. 'Lose with fucking dignity, why don't you?'

123

U p ahead, Caitlin could see flashing blue and red lights. She was gaining ground on its source, but not as fast as she should be. That told her the trooper was probably cruising along, a hundred miles an hour or so, waiting for her to get close so it could match her speed without falling behind.

The next exit would put her in her own county, still a long way from home, but she knew her way around those backroads. Those roads were her home court. She took her foot off the gas, and the digital speedometer dropped fast. Fifty yards ahead, the cruiser passed the exit ramp and headed toward the corresponding underpass. Caitlin eased her foot onto the brake and pulled the wheel. Rubber squealed as she crossed all three lanes and slid through gravel to barely make it onto the ramp.

The cruiser up ahead tapped its brakes, but it couldn't exactly make a U-turn at a hundred miles an hour on the interstate.

Caitlin zoomed up the ramp, blasted through a flashing yellow light, and barreled down an empty rural road in the direction of her house.

124

Coach Ware called a timeout, and Garrett headed over to the sideline with his teammates. He didn't bother to sit. He'd never cared less about the outcome of a game but never played so well.

Five minutes to go.

Three points down.

Garrett looked up at Summer in the stands. He tried to ask with his eyes, *Any news?*

She shook her head and put up her hands in an *I don't know* gesture.

'It's working,' Coach declared to the team, as if the strategy had been his idea. Three players had fouled out. 'We've thrown them off their rhythm. Now, let's settle in and play solid basketball. I want good defensive stops and I—'

'No,' Garrett said, practically bellowing. 'Same strategy. Foul. Foul. Foul.'

'Garrett,' Ware said, 'we can't keep . . .'

He trailed off, aware of the players all staring at him. This was Garrett's team now. If they had to choose between Garrett and Coach Ware, they were going to choose Garrett.

'OK,' Ware said. 'You've led us this far, Garrett. Carry us home.'

125

Caitlin roared around a curve, the fat tires hugging the road. Cornfields blurred by. She'd passed two cops, but, in both cases, she'd known their hiding spots and slowed down to the speed limit before crawling by. Once out of their sight, she was back on the gas.

She zoomed by the county water storage buildings – approaching the spot she'd been parked more than two weeks ago when she watched Game One. There was a good chance a patrol car was camped out there, and as she approached the familiar copse of poplars, she tapped the brakes. She decelerated to forty-five, which, in this car, felt like fifteen.

As she guessed, a cruiser was sitting there, eying the roadway. She maintained her slow speed, checking the rearview mirror. When the curvy road led her out of sight, she punched the gas.

The radio declared there was less than a minute left in the game.

'Goddamnit!' she yelled, smacking the wheel.

She wasn't going to make it.

126

Twenty-two seconds left.

Two points down.

Billy Croft tossed the ball Garrett's way and he let it bounce. The clock wouldn't start until he touched it. When it was about to cross half court, Garrett grabbed it and walked forward in a slow dribble. He risked a glance at Summer, who shook her head.

Still no word.

As Garrett approached the three-point line, Luca stepped out to meet him.

No open shots – no matter how far away Garrett was.

Garrett backed off and dribbled. It would be smart to take a quick shot. If he missed, they could get the rebound. And if the Lightning got the ball, they could foul and hope they missed at least one.

The seconds ticked down.

Fourteen.

Thirteen.

Twelve.

That's not what Garrett was doing. He wasn't putting the ball in anyone else's hands.

He was going to take the last shot.

At the last second.

127

C aitlin zoomed into the residential area where her house was located. She thundered past the park where she and Garrett had talked, and then she raced onto her road.

'*Five seconds on the clock,*' Chuck Walla said on the radio. '*It all comes down to this.*'

128

G arrett burst forward. Luca played perfect defense, staying tight but not fouling. The clock hit one second, and Garrett lowered his shoulder, stepped forward, planted his foot on the three-point line, and jumped.

He let the shot go a fraction of a second before the horn sounded. The ball banged the back of the rim at a downward angle and bounced through the net.

Twenty thousand people cheered in celebration.

The Sabertooths had won.

Or so they thought.

Garrett didn't bother to celebrate. He walked toward the bench. The refs were waving their arms, trying to get everyone's attention and quell the boisterous crowd. Above the court, the replay zoomed in on Garrett's feet. His toe was half an inch onto the line.

It was a two-pointer, not a three.

The game was tied.

Overtime.

I bought you more time, Glass. I hope it's enough.

129

Caitlin was about to slam on the brakes in front of her house when the announcers declared the game was going to overtime. Instead, she let the car cruise down her street.

'*Unbelievable*,' Chuck Walla was saying on the radio. '*If his toe was an inch back, the Sabertooths would be champions right now.*'

She eyed her house as she rolled by. Nothing looked out of the ordinary. She took a right at the end of the street, turned one block over, and parked in front of the residence her own lot backed up against. Just like when she'd rescued Jake from the Red Rose Ranch – she was going in the back way.

'*In the heat of the moment*,' Dirk Justice said, '*sometimes you can't be sure if your foot is behind the line or over it. Garrett Streeter just knew he had to make a shot.*'

Caitlin had no doubt Garrett knew exactly where his foot was. He could have won the game. But he tied it.

For her.

She picked up her phone and texted Summer. I'm here.

130

There was only a one-hundred-thirty-second break between the end of regulation and overtime, and Garrett stood with his teammates, listening to Coach. Summer waved at him from the stands. He stepped out of the huddle and walked over to the sideline, as Summer climbed down the seats in front of her.

The cameras were probably on them, the announcers likely commenting on what this might be about.

He leaned in and she whispered in his ear.

'She made it.'

He cupped his hand and spoke into her ear.

'Are they safe?'

'I don't know.'

'Should I throw the game?' he said, speaking directly in her ear and making sure his hand covered his mouth so no one could read his lips.

'You can win, remember?' she said into his ear, her hand shielding her mouth. 'As long as you don't win by more than three.'

She kissed his check, and he stepped back with the group. Jaxon Luca was eying him from across the court, hands on his hips.

'Anything you want to say?' Coach Ware said to Garrett.

'No more fouls,' Garrett said. 'Let's play ball.'

131

Caitlin closed the car door quietly, looking around the neighborhood to make sure no one was watching. She walked along the side of the house and through the yard. There was a five-foot-high privacy fence separating this yard from her own, and Caitlin scurried over it, dropping to the other side.

The curtains of her sliding-glass door had been pulled, but they were thin and she could make out the shape of someone sitting on the couch, staring at the glow of the TV. A smaller shape, Alex, was slumped next to him. She stared hard, hoping Alex wasn't already dead.

There was the second sliding-glass door into the master bedroom – the one Owen always forgot to lock – and Caitlin jogged over to it. She prayed it was unlatched and felt overwhelming relief when she found it was. She slid it open as soundlessly as possible and stepped into her own bedroom. Down the hall, she could hear the TV.

'*Both teams are tired.*' She heard Harding Able's voice. '*You can tell by all these missed shots.*'

Caitlin knelt next to her bed and slid the safe out with her Glock. She punched the numbers, cringed at the soft beep as the lock disengaged, and picked up the gun. She slid the magazine into place, hoping Grayson couldn't hear the noise.

'*Jaxon Luca has the right idea, taking it to the basket. When your jump shot's gone, you have to go to the rim.*'

Holding the gun, she crept over to the closet. From there, she could see down the hall into the living room, but only the corner of the couch. She couldn't see anyone.

Caitlin eased open the closet door, quietly lifted her other gun safe off the stop shelf, and stepped back over by the bed. She punched in the code and withdrew Owen's grandfather's Walther PPK. She loaded it, then tucked it into the back of her jeans. She took her Glock in both hands and crept down the hall.

Her heart was a jackhammer. She always remained calm in important moments, both on the basketball court and wearing a police badge, but this was different.

This was her family.

This was Alex.

'I can hear you, Caitlin,' Grayson's voice called from around the corner. 'I've got a gun on your son's head, so step out real slow.'

132

Jaxon Luca hit Garrett with a crossover, then he stepped back with a long two-point jump shot.

Swish!

Luca jogged backward down the court, staring at Garrett. The Lightning were up by four again. Overtime was only five minutes, and they were already two minutes into it.

Coach Ware called a timeout, and Garrett headed for the sideline. Caitlin's family's fate was now in her hands, not his. Whatever he did on the court now was just a backup plan. The easy move would be to simply throw the game, let the Lightning take it. But they could still win by three. He didn't think there was any chance of winning by more than that. This game would go down to the wire.

As he walked over, shoulders slumped, he looked around at his teammates, wide-eyed and anxious. A win might not mean much to him now, but it did to them. And to the twenty thousand people in the stands. To millions of people throughout the Cincinnati Tri-State Area.

You've got three minutes left, Garrett told himself. *Leave it all on the floor.*

133

Caitlin stepped out, her gun up.

Levi Grayson sat on the couch, with Alex's small fifty-pound body held in front of him like a shield. Alex was limp but looked alive. Grayson's gun was pressed against her little boy's cheek. Grayson's own head was ducked behind Alex's mop of hair. Owen lay on the floor, his mouth taped shut and his hands secured behind his back. The tape was overkill – he was unconscious anyway. A trickle of blood ran out from his hairline down his slack face, staining the carpet.

'With all those goddamn fouls,' Grayson said, 'I knew you were up to something.'

She could make out one of Grayson's eyes peeking from behind Alex, and the crown of his head: the receding hairline and the small birthmark that looked like Ohio.

'Alex isn't moving,' Caitlin said. 'What did you do to my little boy?'

'Just gave him a little painkiller.'

'You gave my son heroin?' Caitlin said, unable to hide the panic in her voice.

'I only gave him a little,' Grayson said. 'Rubbed a dusting on my finger and stuck it in his mouth.'

'That fentanyl-laced shit?'

She could see Alex's chest moving. He *was* breathing. But for how long?

'He's OK. Don't worry. Game's almost over, and I'll be on my way.'

'Let him go *now.*'

'No,' Grayson said, his voice jumpy. He must need a fix of his own. 'In fact, you put that gun down. *Now.*'

'Fuck you.'

'You're not going to shoot,' Grayson said. 'Not at the risk of hitting your boy.'

Caitlin stared. She was a good shot, but she'd never shot a person, and she didn't have any room for error. It would be like taking a three-point shot, only instead of losing the game, if you missed, you'd kill the thing you loved most in the world.

'I'll count to three,' Grayson said.

'Fine,' Caitlin said, not waiting.

She lowered the Glock, then tossed it gently forward to the corner of the couch. Grayson relaxed.

'How did you find where I live?' Caitlin asked, wanting to keep him talking. Biding her time until she could do something.

'Your buddy, Detective Pete Ryle,' Grayson said, letting his eyes dart to the TV to see the score, then back to her. 'I popped down to the station and said I was an old acquaintance, wanted to say hi. This big-bellied detective coming out the door was more than happy to help out. Gave me your address and told me step by step how to get here. Practically drew me a map with his hand gestures.'

He glanced at the TV again, and she thought she might be able to make a move if he kept looking away like that.

She needed to keep him talking.

'So I figured almost everything out on the drive,' she said. 'You said a prostitute brought you your heroin. Alexei Maxim wasn't the supplier, though. Silas Bennett was. Your delivery girl was Mandy, right? By fluke luck she was the one Jake also used. She mentioned to you that some basketball star's brother was asking her to make bets, and a lightbulb went off in your brain. You hatched the plan for Bennett.'

'Honestly,' he said in response, 'the fact that it was Streeter is what gave me the idea. I'd seen him play in that Final Four game. I'd followed his career. He was good – not the star of either team but good enough to affect the outcome. I told Silas this was someone who could add or subtract points however we wanted, make sure the series went seven games so we could maximize profits. Big bets on the spread in the games where he shaved. Smaller money line bets on the games we needed him to win. Throw in some prop bets and some over-unders based on how we knew he was going to play. Even if he fucked up once or twice, as long as he came through most of the games and pushed the series to seven, I knew we'd make a fortune.' Grayson nodded toward the TV without taking his eyes off Caitlin. 'Look at him. Playing as well as anyone has ever played the game. He should be thanking me.'

'You hubristic psychopath,' Caitlin said.

His hold on Alex was slipping. She could see slightly more of Grayson's face.

'How long were you in his pocket? How long have you been corrupt?'

'Silas was my college roommate,' Grayson said from behind the shield of her son. 'I used to shave points for him back when I was playing for UNLV. We were kids then. I blew all my winnings on prostitutes. Silas was smart. He got hookers to work for him. Used the money I made him to start his empire. The Red Rose Ranch wouldn't exist without what I did. We lost touch for a while, but when I started using H, I knew who I could trust to get it for me.'

'You probably couldn't believe your luck when I called asking for your help,' Caitlin said.

Grayson let out a hearty chuckle. 'The one person helping Streeter and you landed in my lap like a fucking Christmas present.'

'What about the story of Anya? Was any of that true?'

'Mostly,' he said. 'Only it wasn't Alexei who strangled her to death. It was me. I killed her when she wouldn't run away with me. Chose her pimp over me. That's when my heroin use got bad. It wasn't the injury. Or wasn't *just* the injury.'

Caitlin gaped in disbelief.

'You bought my whole athlete-hooked-on-painkillers story, though, didn't you?' Grayson said. 'So gullible.'

Alex's skin was losing its color. His lips were purple. She was running out of time. She stared at the roughly quarter of Grayson's face that she could see from behind Alex. Was it enough? She wished she hadn't dropped her Glock, but she still had the PPK tucked into the back of her jeans.

Could she make the shot?

134

Garrett dribbled up the court, his eyes on the shot clock.

Down by four.

Forty seconds to go in the game.

Nineteen on the shot clock.

Play had gotten sloppy, with both he and Luca missing their last shots. He'd played the best basketball of his life – he and Luca already surpassed forty points again – but it wouldn't be enough.

Everyone said at the beginning of the series that the Lightning might have the best player in the world, but the Sabertooths had the better team.

Garrett still believed that. Even without Elijah.

I need help, he thought.

He'd taken nearly every shot in the fourth quarter and overtime – just like Luca – and every player on the court would expect nothing different.

He put his head down and charged forward. Luca stayed on him, and the Lightning center left Rodrigo to help out. Garrett faked a shot, and as both defenders jumped, Garrett lasered a bounce pass to Rodrigo. The seven-footer bobbled the pass – as surprised as everyone else that he was getting it – then he wrapped his big hands around the ball and jumped into the air, slamming it through the rim.

The Lightning coach called for a timeout.

Sabertooths were down by two with twenty-nine seconds left.

135

'Y ou played me,' Caitlin said, taking a step to the left, trying to give herself a better angle. 'You sent me after Alexei Maxim. I bet Silas had his eyes on Maxim's organization for a long time. You figured, best-case scenario, that I'd inadvertently help you bring down Maxim, or, worst-case scenario, Maxim would kill me and you wouldn't have to worry about me anymore.'

'Exactly,' Grayson said proudly. 'It worked brilliantly, I might add.'

'I should have seen it,' she said. 'Not you. I don't know how I would have guessed that the cop who cracks down on sports betting was the criminal behind it. But there were things I should have seen.'

On the screen, the announcers were effusive in their praise of how brilliantly both teams were playing, how it was a shame either team had to lose.

'When the news reports talked about Maxim's death,' Caitlin went on, 'they mentioned organ trafficking, dog fighting, and drugs – but they never mentioned the *amount* of drugs. What was hidden in that mattress would have been a dream for any PR flack in law enforcement. But the reports about Maxim never mentioned a huge cache of heroin stuffed in a mattress. Because by the time the police got there, the heroin was gone, wasn't it? The heroin in the garage at the Red Rose Ranch was the same heroin we saw in Going to the Mattresses, wasn't it?'

'Ezra and Dickie pulled up in the van as you and I were leaving,' he said. 'They went in and took it. *Then* I called the cops. I figured that poor bastard on the operating table would be dead by the time they got there, but it was his lucky day.'

Richie – the cowboy John Lennon – had told Caitlin that the death of Alexei Maxim would leave a power vacuum in the criminal underworld of Las Vegas. Caitlin hadn't realized she was being used as a tool – or a weapon – to create that vacuum.

She thought about how close she might have come to accidentally figuring it out. The night she rescued Jake, she'd even driven to Grayson's house. Jake had been asleep in the car. If he'd been awake and come in with her, he would have recognized Grayson immediately.

'One thing I don't understand,' Caitlin said, 'is why you didn't kill me instead of saving my life. You could have shot me and left me in the warehouse. Or dumped me in Lake Mead with the gun. Or just not go in to save me.'

'I guess I was hedging my bets,' he said. 'I wasn't sure if Silas Bennett could pull the scam off and I thought maybe you would be a good insurance policy. Turns out I was right.'

'And you'll walk away?' she said. 'Leave me and my family alone?'

'Of course,' he said, but she could tell he was lying – she'd gotten better at reading people over the past week.

She'd played into his hands, she realized. She was here, which meant he could kill all three of them and leave no witnesses behind. As soon as this game was over, they were all dead.

Alex looked dead already.

She couldn't tell if he was breathing.

'The thing is, Caitlin,' Grayson said, 'you might have come rushing in here like the fucking cavalry, but you don't have it in you to take me down. You couldn't take down Alexei Maxim without me. You didn't kill Silas or Ezra, even though you should have. And I heard from your pal, Detective Pete Ryle, you couldn't pull the trigger even when a scumbag meth head was beating the shit out of you. You're no killer, Caitlin Glass. You don't have it in you. I should know. Because I am.'

These fucking men, Caitlin thought. *Always underestimating me.*

On the TV, the Lightning's timeout came to an end.

'*Here we go*,' Chuck Walla said. '*No timeouts remaining for either team. A five-second differential between the game clock and the shot clock. This is what it all comes down to.*'

'Everything you're saying about me might be true,' Caitlin said, watching Grayson's eye peek from behind Alex. 'But you're forgetting one thing.'

136

Luca walked the ball down the court, taking his time. He was running the shot clock down. The Sabertooths had to keep the Lightning from scoring. And keep them from getting the rebound.

Twenty seconds.

Nineteen.

Eighteen.

Luca made his move, charging forward, trying to fake out Garrett with a crossover, but he stayed in front of him, and Luca backed up, running more of the clock out.

Thirteen.

Twelve.

Luca lurched forward again, and Garrett stayed on him, hand held high. Luca pump-faked, and Garrett didn't fall for it.

Then Luca jumped and so did Garrett, springing with all his strength and reaching for the ball as it left Luca's hand.

137

Grayson's eyes bored into Caitlin, challenging her. It was a look that said, *You're no match for me and never were.*
'What did I forget?' Grayson sneered.

138

Garrett's fingertips brushed the bottom of the ball and it spun straight up into the air. Luca's big hand got to it first but, before he could control it, Garrett slapped it away and it bounced down the court.

He took off after it, with Luca close behind.

139

From the TV, Chuck Walla was practically shouting with excitement. Grayson got tired of waiting for Caitlin's answer, and his eyes drifted from her to see what was happening on the screen.

140

Garrett caught up to the ball, dribbled it past the half-court line, keeping his body positioned so Luca, right behind him, couldn't reach in for the steal. He thought for a split second – drive to the basket or shoot a three-pointer?

Go for the tie?
Or go for the win?

141

'You're forgetting,' Caitlin said, throwing her right arm
behind her back and snagging the subcompact pistol from
her jeans, 'none of those assholes held a gun to my son's
head.'

142

One second.
Garrett positioned his foot – firmly behind the three-
point line – and jumped into the air, leaping sideways with
an off-balance shot to avoid Luca's outstretched arm.
The ball sailed through the air in a high arc.

143

Caitlin brought the gun up, put her left hand under her right
to stabilize her aim, and leveled the sight directly on
Grayson's birthmark, only about two inches from the hair
of her son's head.

Grayson's eyes shifted back from the TV in surprise, and Caitlin
squeezed the trigger.

144

S wish!

145

Caitlin dropped the gun and ran forward, flinging Grayson's limp meaty arms off her son. She ignored the blood splattered against the wall behind the couch. She pulled Alex into her arms and then laid him out on the carpet. She ran her fingers through his hair to make sure the bullet hadn't grazed him. She searched for his pulse, couldn't find it, and pressed her fingers deeper into the flesh of his neck until she finally felt it, as faint as a whisper. His breathing was almost nonexistent. She pried open his eyelids and found his pupils to be tiny black pinpricks. His skin was colder than any living human's should be.

'No,' she wailed. 'Please. *No!*'

She rushed over to Grayson, with his head tilted back like he was taking a nap, blood seeping from a hole in the upper right quarter of his skull. She felt the breast pocket of his shirt. The inhalant was in there. She tugged it out, tore it from its package, and shoved the nasal tube into her son's tiny nostril.

She squeezed, and Alex came awake with a start.

'Oh, thank God,' Caitlin said, grabbing him into her arms.

His chest heaved with panicked breaths. She gathered him up, held him with one arm, and shook Owen. Her husband's eyes came dreamily awake. She tore the tape off his mouth, which woke him more.

'Are you OK?'

'Yeah,' he breathed. His face was bruised and beginning to swell, but he seemed cognizant. 'Is Alex . . .?'

'He's OK,' she said. 'Don't give the police any kind of statement until you talk to our lawyer, OK?'

There might be a way to get out of this without Garrett being connected, but she needed her husband to remain quiet.

Owen nodded.

In her arms, Alex gripped her tightly, his face buried in her neck. She turned from Owen and rushed out of the room, hoping her boy wouldn't catch a glimpse of the carnage. On the way through the kitchen, she spotted Owen's phone on the table and grabbed it. She pushed through the front door, held Alex with one arm and called 911 with the other. She quickly told the dispatcher who she was, where she lived, and how many ambulances to send. She hung up, pocketed the phone, then grabbed her own from her front pocket. She could feel Owen's phone buzzing from the dispatcher calling her back. She ignored it.

Instead, she texted Summer.

We're OK.

Holding Alex in one arm, standing in the grass, she dialed Yazmina.

'Can you believe that game?' Yaz shrieked.

'Are you still licensed to practice law in Ohio?' Caitlin asked.

'Yeah,' Yaz said. 'Why?'

'Get on the next flight you can,' Caitlin said. 'I need you.'

Then she hung up, put both arms around her son, and waited at the curb with Alex's head resting on her shoulder for the police to arrive.

146

Confetti rained from the rafters. Fans jumped up and down. Celebratory cannons exploded paper streamers that drifted through the air like jellyfish tentacles. 'We Are the Champions' by Queen played over the loudspeakers. Garrett walked around in a daze. Players chest bumped him and hugged him, but he hardly responded. He walked through the bedlam – reporters and camera operators swarming the floor – and found Summer and Jake coming down from their seats.

Summer threw her arms around his neck and said, 'She's OK. They're OK.'

He hugged her, and a dam broke inside him. He sobbed into her neck. Plenty of players cried when they won the championship, but that wasn't it for Garrett. It was the relief. It was over. He let go of Summer and embraced his brother, who was crying, too.

The snowfall of confetti began to slow.

Elijah Carter came swinging through the crowd on his crutches, his cheeks streaked with tears. Garrett wiped his own eyes with the back of his hand.

'You did it,' Elijah said to Garrett, wrapping his big arms around him and lifting him into the air, balanced on only one leg.

'*We* did it,' Garrett said.

Security guards struggled to keep fans off the floor. Camera operators crowded around Garrett and Elijah. A reporter from ABC loitered next to them, microphone in hand, but they both ignored her. Nearby, the Lightning's coach came over to congratulate Coach Ware. Josh was bouncing around the court, highfiving any player he could find. Jamie and the others who fouled out were returning to the court, tackling Rodrigo in celebration.

Garrett spotted Jaxon Luca walking toward him and Elijah. He looked like he was grieving, but he offered his hand to Garrett. As Garrett shook it, his rival for the past two and a half weeks pulled him into a hug.

'Respect,' Luca said into Garrett's ear.

'Thank you.'

Garrett didn't know what else to say.

Then Luca looked back and forth between him and Elijah, and he smiled – he almost never smiled, but he did now – and said, 'Let's do this again. Same time next year?'

Elijah bellowed with laughter. Garrett, dazed, could only offer a half-smile. As Luca walked off, someone shoved an *NBA Champions* ball cap down over Garrett's head. He took the hat off and stared at it, thinking surely it must be a mistake that this belonged to him. He'd accomplished what he'd wanted ever since he was a little boy, playing on the sun-cracked Phoenix courts.

Jake ran off to congratulate other players. And while the hovering reporter wanted to interview Garrett, Elijah stepped in and grabbed the microphone, giving Garrett a moment alone with Summer.

'I know all your secrets,' she said. 'Now do you want to know mine?'

He nodded.

'I'm pregnant,' she said.

Her eyes darted back and forth between his, gauging his reaction.

'Why didn't you tell me?'

'You said you didn't want any distractions,' she said. 'And things had gotten so tense between us. I didn't know about Jake. I didn't know why the hell you were acting the way you were.'

Understanding suddenly dawned on him.

'The message on your phone,' he said. 'The appointment that sounded like a law firm. That's the doctor's office?'

She nodded. 'High-risk pregnancy specialists. Since we've had so much trouble.'

'And those texts?'

'Josh,' she said. 'I had to talk to someone.'

Of course, the Sabertooths' assistant coach who had introduced them. Summer's old friend.

'I figured he might have some inkling of what was going on with you,' Summer said, shrugging. 'He said I should tell you, but you were in such a state, I didn't know what kind of reaction I'd get. Are you happy?'

He looked all around, fans crying in the stands, the last of the confetti drifting down. He held his arms up, gesturing to all of it.

'Let me put it this way,' he said. 'Winning the NBA championship is just about the least important thing to happen to me this week.'

POST-GAME

147

Caitlin shuffled her legs, arms raised. She was playing defense. Or *pretending* to. Her opponent was, after all, her son Alex, who'd recently turned eight. He dribbled once between his legs – God, he was getting good – and darted around her to shoot a layup. The ball clanged off the rim, and Caitlin feigned a lunge for it. Alex got to it first and threw up another shot.

This time it went in.

'And the crowd goes wild,' Owen said from the sidelines, applauding.

Alex beamed and ran over to highfive his dad.

'Can we play again, Mom?'

Before she could answer, Garrett's yellow Mercedes pulled up to the curb.

'They're here,' Alex yelled, and ran toward the street.

Summer – her belly beginning to bulge – climbed out of the passenger side, and Garrett came around to help her. She somehow made jeans and a Sabertooths T-shirt look glamorous. And Garrett, of course, was decked out in Nike athletic pants and shirt, a bottle of wine in his hands.

The leaves were changing, but it was unusually warm for October. Garrett's season was about to start, and it had been Owen's idea to invite them over for dinner before the newly minted NBA Finals MVP's schedule became crazy for the next seven to nine months. Crazier still because the baby was due around the All-Star Break in February.

Owen said inviting Garrett to see the house was the least they could do, since Garrett had given them the down payment for it. Neither Owen nor Caitlin wanted to move back into their old house, not with the memory of Levi Grayson's brains dripping down the living-room wall. When she'd asked Garrett for a loan, he'd offered to buy the house outright. Caitlin insisted she only wanted a down payment *on loan*, but Garrett stood firm – he'd give them the money for the down payment, but only if it was a gift. Caitlin only relented because Owen talked her into it.

'You did a lot for him,' he said, 'and you suffered – we all suffered – because of it. Accept the gift. For me. For Alex.'

Alex claimed to remember nothing of Levi Grayson, to Caitlin's relief. She was grateful Alex had not been conscious to see his mom shoot someone. Instead of being traumatized for life, his memory had been wiped clean by the drug.

As for Caitlin, she woke up at least once a week from nightmares, reliving her showdown with Levi Grayson. In her dreams, she wasn't fast enough. Or she missed.

Or hit Alex.

She would lie awake, heart pounding, staring into the darkness, reminding herself what actually happened. And that Alex was safe.

One thing she never felt was guilt.

No one was allowed to do that to her son – it was that simple.

As Alex continued shooting baskets, Caitlin and Owen gave Garrett and Summer a tour of the house, which was a good thousand square feet larger than the previous house. The yard was considerably bigger as well, almost two acres, with a vast expanse of grass and big maples in the backyard, which abutted a small wood. Caitlin didn't see how Garrett and Summer could be impressed – having seen their house – but they at least acted interested as Owen pointed out what kind of work they wanted to do to it: a new kitchen counter, shelves in the bedroom, eventually a new bay in the garage for Owen to work on his bikes.

'So far,' he said, 'the only thing we've done is put up the basket-ball hoop.'

'Don't forget the jungle gym in the backyard,' Caitlin added.

They'd been spoiling Alex lately – they couldn't help it.

Out on the back deck, which overlooked a lush green lawn behind the house – including the new wooden jungle gym with an A-frame treehouse attached – Caitlin asked how Jake was doing.

'Well, I think,' Garrett said, taking a sip of lemonade. 'He's traveling. Busy.'

The younger Streeter had started a new job with a sports agency, representing professional athletes. It was an entry-level position, but he liked the work so far.

'How's the new job?' Garrett asked, referring to the PR position she'd started back in July.

'It's OK. Educational actually. I'm learning a lot about the department and the community.'

When the police arrived the night of Game Seven, with Pete Ryle looking as bewildered as she thought he'd be, Caitlin refused to give an account of what happened until her lawyer arrived. In the early hours of the morning, her husband and son both safely under care at the hospital, Caitlin and Yaz sat down with Pete, the sheriff, and the undersheriff. Yaz did most of the talking, explaining that while Caitlin was on vacation in Las Vegas for the NBA Finals, she happened to meet an agent with the Nevada Gaming Control Board while eating lunch one day. The guy apparently became infatuated with her, flying all the way across the country to threaten her family. Here is where Yazmina pointed out that Pete Ryle had given this madman Caitlin's home address – an obvious breach of professional protocol. As the sheriff and his colleagues were beginning to squirm in their seats, envisioning a lawsuit and a lot of bad press for the department, Caitlin had spoken up, as she and Yaz had rehearsed, and said she didn't want to create any embarrassing publicity for the department.

Everyone left the meeting agreeing the investigation seemed clear cut and would be wrapped up quickly. Caitlin didn't want anyone scrutinizing Levi Grayson's past too carefully, and it turned out Pete Ryle was just the man for the job. In fact, the sheriff was so impressed with Caitlin's willingness to be a team player – and perhaps the fact that she was now the only person in the department who'd ever shot someone – he stated the next time a detective position opened up, her name would be at the top of the list.

Instead, she asked if the PR job was still hers if she wanted it.

'Are you going to tell them the rest?' Owen asked.

'What?' Garrett said.

'Well, I've been thinking,' Caitlin explained. 'The sheriff is retiring in two years. He's pegged the undersheriff to replace him. But . . .' She shrugged.

'She's going to run for sheriff,' Owen finished for her.

Garrett's eyes widened.

'This new job makes me the face of the department,' she said. 'I'm there at every county commission meeting, ribbon cutting, and photo op. I think I've got a decent chance of being elected. If I don't like the way these good old boys do things, maybe I need to take over and do it myself.'

Garrett grinned, clearly proud.

'And if I lose,' Caitlin said, 'maybe I'll become a private investigator. Be my own boss.'

Summer tapped her finger against her lips in fake contemplation.

'I might be able to think of someone who'd be willing to make a sizeable donation to your campaign,' she said.

'No, no, no,' Caitlin said, waving her hand in objection, but Garrett and Owen and Summer all nodded and laughed about the idea.

When Summer tapped her finger against her lips, Caitlin noticed something. She took it as an opportunity to change the subject.

'I see you've got a ring on your finger,' she said.

Summer smiled big and bright.

'With a baby on the way, we decided to make it official.'

She held out her hand to show Caitlin the lovely silver engagement ring adorning her finger. The round-shaped diamond was beautiful, the facets making a brilliant prism from the light, but Caitlin was pleased to see the ring wasn't nearly as big and ostentatious as Garrett could certainly afford.

After Caitlin and Owen showered them with congratulations, Summer asked Alex to show her his new jungle gym, and Owen went inside to finish up the lasagna he was preparing. For a few minutes, Caitlin and Garrett were alone – or at least out of earshot.

'I saw you got your max contract,' Caitlin said. 'Local news was all over it. The sports columnist for the *Enquirer* says it's money well spent for the Sabertooths.'

He'd be making more than forty million dollars a year for the next seven years, which would probably take him to retirement.

'And I read endorsements have been pouring in.'

He'd long been sponsored by Nike, but now he was getting his own shoe line. His first commercial was set to air during this year's season opener. She also noted, though didn't mention it, that Vegas sports books were listing the Sabertooths as the favorites to win the championship again next year.

'It's weird, to be honest,' he said. 'I'm suddenly considered one of the best players in the world, and I can't imagine what it's going to be like stepping back on a court. I thought about retiring instead of taking the contract, but I hope I can rediscover a love for the game again. Where playing doesn't feel like someone's life is on the line.'

Owen came out the back door, saw they were talking, and headed down the deck steps to where Alex was showing Summer how high he could swing. As she watched them, Caitlin's heart swelled with love. She couldn't believe how close she'd come to losing both Owen and Alex. She felt thankful for every second with them, no matter how tired she was or how annoyed she was at her job.

She was lost in thought for a minute, but now she tuned back into Garrett, who was explaining he and Summer were starting a charitable foundation. So even if he couldn't ever play like he did in the Finals – if he never loved basketball the way he used to – he could do some good with his salary.

'You get to play basketball for a living,' Caitlin said. 'You have more money than you can spend. You have an amazing wife and a baby on the way. Enjoy it.'

He smiled sheepishly.

'You went through hell, my friend,' she said, 'I think you're due for a little happiness.'

'You were in hell with me,' he said. 'I wish you'd let me do more for you.'

She waved off his suggestion.

She looked down at Alex swinging on the jungle gym, smiling unabashedly as he kicked his feet up toward the sky. Summer, resting one hand on her bulging belly, was smiling and saying something to Owen, who was cheering Alex on and laughing.

'I've got everything I need right here,' Caitlin said.

It was true. For the first time in a long time, she didn't envy Garrett's life.

She couldn't imagine any life but her own.

Acknowledgments

Thank you to Amy Tannenbaum and everyone at the Jane Rotrosen Agency; Berni Vann and her team at Creative Artists Agency; Rachel Slatter and Severn House; Michael Olah and Dreamscape Media; my early readers, Aeryn Rudel and Maura Yzmore; my first reader (always), my wife Tiffany; and my children, Ben and Aubrey, who aren't old enough to have read anything I've written but who are always my biggest champions.